Hungry Shoes

Lynn and Lynda Miller Southwest Fiction Series
Lynn C. Miller and Lynda Miller, SERIES EDITORS

This series showcases novels, novellas, and story collections that focus on the Southwestern experience. Often underrepresented in American literature, Southwestern voices provide unique and diverse perspectives to readers exploring the region's varied landscapes and communities. Works in the series range from traditional to experimental, with an emphasis on how the landscapes and cultures of this distinct region shape stories and situations and influence the ways in which they are told.

Also available in the Lynn and Lynda Miller Southwest Fiction Series:

The Half-White Album by Cynthia J. Sylvester
Girl Flees Circus: A Novel by C. W. Smith

HUNGRY SHOES

a novel

Sue Boggio and Mare Pearl

University of New Mexico Press | Albuquerque

ISBN 978-0-8263-6534-7 (paper)
ISBN 978-0-8263-6535-4 (electronic)

Library of Congress Cataloging-in-Publication data is on file with the Library of Congress

Founded in 1889, the University of New Mexico sits on the traditional homelands of the Pueblo of Sandia. The original peoples of New Mexico—Pueblo, Navajo, and Apache—since time immemorial have deep connections to the land and have made significant contributions to the broader community statewide. We honor the land itself and those who remain stewards of this land throughout the generations and also acknowledge our committed relationship to Indigenous peoples. We gratefully recognize our history.

Cover illustration by Felicia Cedillos
Designed by Felicia Cedillos
Composed in Adobe Garamond

We dedicate *Hungry Shoes* to Sue's daughter, Holly Glazebook-Gonzales, who has devoted her life to educating children with special needs. And to everyone who needs help and support with mental health concerns, may you find the kind of compassionate expertise shown in these pages.

———

Call 988 for Suicide & Crisis Lifeline. The 988 Suicide & Crisis Lifeline is a national network of local crisis centers that provides free and confidential emotional support to people in suicidal crisis or emotional distress twenty-four hours a day, seven days a week in the United States. We're committed to improving crisis services and advancing suicide prevention by empowering individuals, advancing professional best practices, and building awareness.

PROLOGUE

Dr. Mary Swenson

The touch of a velvet paw wakes her as it does every morning, tapping gently on her forehead. Her eyes open in the half light to see her calico cat, her self-appointed alarm clock, inches from her nose. "Good morning, Myrtle."

She shifts in the heap of the three large dogs who share her bed. Heads lifting, bleary-eyed yawns, tags clinking as they maneuver themselves to the floor. After supervising her morning detour into the bathroom, they escort her to the kitchen.

While cans are opened and dumped into a line of food bowls for her impatient gathering of rescued cats and dogs, she again considers retiring from her position at a children's and adolescents' inpatient psychiatric center. After thirty-five years in the trenches, the option tempts her. But with rumors of budget cuts and new administrators mandating changes that threaten to undermine the therapeutic milieu, she can't abandon her post just yet. As one of the old-timers, she pushes back against these ego-driven upstarts jostling to assert their power and leave their mark like dogs desperate to pee on every fire hydrant. She's outlived their type before and she will do it again.

Once the indoor animals are fed and watered, she steps into her mud-caked wellies, ties the belt on her robe, and heads out the back door. The sun has just cleared the Manzano Mountains, illuminating her acreage in bright early-summer light. Her Nubian goats greet her with wild bleating as they rush the corral fence. Her sixty-year-old shoulders complain as she spears alfalfa into their troughs. She pauses to stroke some noses, including the downy one of Jasper, the three-legged burro she saved from a neighbor's shotgun after the young animal's right hind leg became entangled in barbwire. One expensive amputation surgery later, Jasper gets along fine.

Chickens stream from their freshly opened coop. She tosses handfuls of scratch that rain down to their excited clucking. Her resident wild peacocks swoop in from their overnight roost in the cottonwood tree. Festus, her male turkey, puffs out his feathers, spreads his tale, and drags his wings, strutting his stuff for the female who is more interested in feeding than in his courtship display. His head purples with excitement. "Tough luck, dude. She's just not that into you," Dr. Swenson tells him.

Retirement would mean she wouldn't have to rush to shower and dress in professional clothes and drive the thirty minutes into Albuquerque every day of the work week. She could lavish her attention and energies on her animals instead of abused and neglected children and teens.

She chose this work after growing up in a family who loved puzzles of all kinds. Her dad was a happy car mechanic who viewed every broken-down car as a puzzle to solve based on clues their owners provided. Various rattles, pings, leaks, and shimmies were analyzed until the mystery was solved and he could describe his successes around the dinner table while her brothers hung on his every word.

Her mother voraciously consumed paperback mysteries. When she got sick and died, she left her only daughter her prized possessions: a collection of vintage Japanese wooden puzzle boxes passed down in her family. To solve a puzzle box, one or more sliding parts in one end are moved, allowing the other end to be moved. This unlocks a side panel, which allows other pieces to be moved. These, in turn, partially unlock the top or bottom. This method is continued, moving around the box, until the top panel can slide, opening the box to reveal the mystery inside. Japanese boxes have a variety of difficulties, ranging from less than ten to over a hundred moves to perform in the proper sequence before the box will open.

"People are like puzzle boxes, Mary," she told her thirteen-year-old daughter the week before she died. "Their true selves are hidden. Sometimes even from them. But with patience and persistence, you can get past their barriers. It can't be forced, and each one is different. Only after dis-covering the right moves will they open up for you."

Mary spent the year after her mother's death learning how to open each of the nine boxes, finding notes of congratulations and encouragement from her mother tucked inside the secret compartments. That's when she decided to become a child psychiatrist.

After one more lingering gaze around her acreage, Dr. Swenson turns back to her old adobe house to get ready for another day of cracking the code of her wounded kids' behaviors to discover the truth beneath their pain. Because her life's work is not about her at all. It's about them. It's all about the kids and learning the stories that brought them to her.

Only then can the healing begin.

CHAPTER 1

Maddie

First the ambulance rushes Maddie to the ER, where they suture the self-inflicted knife slash on her neck and give her a shot of something that makes her woozy but doesn't prevent her from fighting anyone who tries to get near. Trapped by restraints and her horrifying flashbacks, she feels helpless in an all too familiar way. Then the ER doctor says something about an emergency admission "up the hill," which turns out to be a loony bin for kids.

An ambulance takes her the short trip up that hill. The fresh stitches in Maddie's neck pull and burn as she writhes against the straps securing her to the gurney that's wheeling her into the children's and adolescents' psychiatric center.

The paramedics roll her down a hallway where kids gawk at her through the windows in their closed doors. She gives them the finger as she passes them. They unstrap her and help her stand in the large, open space they call the dayroom. The paramedics leave, taking their gurney with them.

A large Black man stands near enough to catch her if she falls or grab her if she tries anything funny. He motions for her to enter the kitchen that adjoins the dayroom, visible through a wall of safety glass.

"Get them away from me!" Maddie says as her dad and her stepmother, Lesley, follow her into the kitchen, where a woman stands before a line of tables pushed together, a stack of papers in front of her. The woman is short and round, and her rumpled brown suit looks as if it needs to be sent to the cleaners. The woman waves her parents away with a flick of her wrist and the man escorts them out. What universe is this?

"Hello, Maddie, I'm Dr. Mary Swenson. I'd like to ask you some questions."

Maddie agrees with a nod of her head. If this lady is a doctor, then she must be the one to decide her fate.

"Can I get you some juice or something?" Dr. Swenson asks as soon as Maddie sits at the table.

Maddie shakes her head no. The kitchen smells like scorched tomato sauce. The odor, along with the shot they gave her, makes her nauseous. Dr. Swenson clomps to the refrigerator in her sensible brown pumps, pours some milk into her coffee, and sits back down. As she sips, she studies Maddie, letting some silence hang in the air, which is fine. It gives Maddie time to force her demons into hiding. Maybe neither one of them will say anything. Maddie sucks gently on the split and swollen lip she got when the cops took her down at the airport.

"Maddie, I've read the police report and the detailed written description from your stepmother about what happened. To me that's just hearsay." Dr. Swenson says. "You're the only one who knows what's really going on. I want to help you. You must be so angry and hurt."

Maddie begins to cry. She feels her face crumple like a squeezed soda can. She's never heard anyone say those words to her before.

Dr. Swenson points to the wound on Maddie's neck with her lips, the way Maddie has seen her Navajo friend Hector do a hundred times. "Did you plan or have you ever planned to kill yourself? It's on the admission form, see?" Dr. Swenson says holding it up.

Plan to kill herself? All she can do is cry. She hates herself for slipping up after all her careful planning. With her face hidden in her hands, Maddie goes from tears to laughter. "I only planned to go to fucking France. If I'd paid cash, I'd be almost there by now." Her laugh feels like machine-gun fire.

"Why France?"

"It's a long story." Maddie wipes the hot tears from her face.

"Do you think it's safe for a teen girl, a minor, to travel to France by herself?"

"Safer than staying with them."

"I see." Her face reflects what Maddie guesses is compassion.

"Look, I don't belong here. I'm not crazy. I just need to get to France and everything will be fine. Maybe you could help me get a ticket on another flight—I'll pay you back. That's how you can help me."

"I don't think you're crazy," Dr. Swenson says. "Except for asking me to get you another ticket. I want to help you, Maddie, but not like that. Since you've just turned seventeen, you can sign yourself into the hospital for a short stay. Give us the chance to help you learn how to change your life for the better."

"I'm not putting myself in a psycho hospital. I'm outta here." Maddie stands up. The man just outside the door comes back in. She sits back down. She will run from here the first chance she gets. He seems to sense that and leans against the doorway, casually reading the university's student newspaper.

"Jackson, would you mind calling the nurse to bring Maddie's parents back?" asks Dr. Swenson.

"I don't want them. Don't bring them back here." The doctor is betraying her. Her head begins reeling, spinning like the Wheel of Fortune heading to Bankrupt.

Jackson speaks into a walkie-talkie. In a surprisingly short time, her parents come back, escorted by a nurse in lime-green sneakers.

Maddie can't look at her parents. She knows this is a test. They expect her to go berserk—they're all in on it. But she holds it together, the effort sending waves of pain through her chest. The pounding arteries in her neck make her wound throb.

"What is it, Doctor? Is it bipolar disorder?" asks wicked stepmother Lesley.

"I don't know anything about Maddie's biological mother's family history. This could run in her family," says her father. "We'll approve whatever treatments you think will help."

Dr. Swenson holds up her hand for them to stop. "Mr. Stuart, legally, Maddie's old enough to make these decisions for herself. She and I were discussing her options." Dr. Swenson meets Maddie's eyes. "You know,

Maddie, if you aren't admitted, you'll go back home with your parents. Or I'll write a physician's hold and then a judge will decide what happens to you. You sign yourself in and you take the control."

Maddie considers her words, a tear escaping. She can't look at her dad. She curses the tear that exposes her heartbreak.

"Do you ever feel like hurting yourself or others?" Dr. Swenson once more reads from the paperwork.

Maddie meets Dr. Swenson's gaze and sees something warm and beckoning, like the benevolence of a full moon over her Old Town balcony. "I'd rather be dead than go back with them," Maddie says. "Where do I sign?"

Grace

It was the chairs. The chairs clattering to the floor, their sound echoing through the gym and into the adjacent boys' locker room, alerted the janitor, whom they're calling a hero.

He had run to Grace and, standing on a chair, slung her limp body over his shoulder and loosened her poorly tied ropes, thereby opening her briefly occluded jugular veins and preventing her brain from basically exploding from the pent-up pressure of blood.

"Most people think you die from hanging by cutting off the air supply, which helps, but more often than not, it's brain edema that leads to respiratory arrest, followed by cardiac arrest maybe fifteen minutes later. Or if you do it right, you snap the C2 neck vertebra and spinal cord—that's a lot quicker. Luckily you didn't do it right. You didn't even have time for your face to break out in petechiae—red pinpoint marks left by burst capillaries—before the janitor disrupted your plans." The doctor speaks in a soft southern gentleman cadence, holding his gaze steadily into hers. "The whites of your eyes are bloodshot, so there wasn't too much time to spare. But aside from some colossal bruising, abrasions on your neck, and a little soft-tissue swelling, your physical damage is minimal. Your neurological exam was normal, indicating little or no brain damage from the two or three minutes of anoxia you suffered. The concerning thing is why you did this and how to make sure you don't try anything like it again. But you'll need other doctors to figure that one out. I am curious, though, can you tell me why you tried to die?"

Grace attempts to give his question some thought. She might not have measurable brain damage, but she feels as if her brain has been thoroughly wrung out like a dank sponge. "I didn't want to go to Disney World," she says in her hoarse, whispery voice. It's the short answer.

His blue eyes widen in a way that tells Grace he's ready to give her over to the other doctors he mentioned.

A nurse tells her they will be monitoring her overnight and other arrangements will be made the next day. They discontinue her oxygen but leave an IV drip in her arm, and the monitor beeps her heart rate. Grace notices she is devoid of any feeling and is not at all curious about these other arrangements. She eats orange Jell-O. She pees in the pan when they ask her to. The gown she wears is as soft as gossamer and when her teeth begin to chatter, they cover her in blankets from a warmer, making her feel like she's being wrapped in a steaming tortilla.

The next morning, a doctor appears who refers to himself as Dr. Murray, a fellow in child psychiatry. He interviews Grace for forty-seven minutes, according to the wall clock. She answers what she can and shrugs if she's stumped. He seems petite for a man; his white coat hangs on him as if he's playing dress-up.

"You haven't asked about your father," Dr. Murray says.

Grace shrugs, again noting her own lack of curiosity.

"He was here when you were in the emergency room, right after you were brought in by ambulance. He was disruptive, probably under the influence, and security had to escort him out. He came back during the night and left a bag of your belongings and a letter to give to you. Would you like me to read it to you?"

"Okay," she says since he seems eager to read it.

"Grace, how could you do this to me after what your mama done? They wouldn't let me see you so this is all I got. Jill and I decided to go ahead with our plans since you made it plain you didn't want any part of it. Don't worry. I'll set everything up down there and you can join us when they are done with you if you want to. I hope you do but Jill is right, you are at an age to decide for yourself. I hope they can help you so you don't end up like your mom. Wish you just would of come with us instead of all this. I brought you some of your stuff and there's still a few days on the rent if they let you go and you want anything we left behind. Good luck and I'll look you up after we get settled. You're still my daughter. Mitch."

Grace could hear Mitch's voice in place of the doctor's. Mitch is gone. She can feel herself thin the way a thick San Francisco fog does just before it gives way.

"Grace, how do you feel about what he said?"

She's too amorphous to respond, her essence diffusing through the room in diaphanous wisps. Not a girl in a bed anymore, just her patchy spirit, drifting nearby.

Maddie is taken from the kitchen to her room by the lime-green-sneakers nurse. She focuses on those shoes as they walk down the hallway to a room near the door she entered on the gurney.

"I'm Sharon, the cottage nurse. I need to check through your clothes and do a body map of you." She hands Maddie a white cotton hospital blanket to wrap around her and asks her to strip down to her underwear.

The body mapping consists of Sharon looking at every scar, scrape, bruise, smudge, or bump on Maddie's body and drawing it onto a paper body outline, front and back.

"I'll just show you what you want to know." Maddie turns around and drops her blanket to expose her bare back. She knows the burns Jeffrey inflicted still show in pink, glistening scars. "That's what the son of a bitch did to me. Wax, cigarettes, and tools he'd heat up with a lighter. They didn't believe me, but he left his mark, as good as his signature." Maddie feels Sharon touch and trace each one lightly.

"I'm sorry you've been so terribly hurt." It's the empathy in Sharon's eyes and the tone of her voice that resonates. This woman channels a radiance that Maddie can only guess is mother energy. It shocks her to have her private pain validated by another human being.

Sharon runs her hand tenderly down Maddie's hair and pushes some out of her eyes. "In the morning, you'll see Dr. Brock, our pediatrician. She's going to examine you. We can document what you've gone through. It's evidence."

"Good," Maddie says.

HRP. High-risk precautions. Every fifteen minutes, checks by staff. The doctor's orders could have been worse—they could have designated a constant line of sight by staff. Then they'd have to follow her into the bathroom. At least she has fifteen-minute snippets of privacy. They gave her a journal and a crayon, but little else. Things like glass, anything breakable, alcohol-based hygiene stuff, pencils, and pens are forbidden. The empty other side of the double room is set up exactly as hers, with a twin bed, a desk and chair, and a tall wardrobe. The backs and fronts of the desk chairs have been carved by past patients, with various gangs' graffiti and "fuck you" messages.

She has been here twenty-four hours. She lies on a threadbare sheet on a plastic mattress. "Ninety-nine bottles of beer on the wall, ninety-nine bottles of beer . . ." she sings while trying to balance and roll a paper cup on her feet like a Chinese acrobat. Maddie shifts, the plastic noisily buckling under her. If only she could jump on her horse, Moonshine, and ride along the Rio Grande, or watch her France videos and figure out a new plan to get to her mother.

She sits up and sips the sweet early-summer afternoon air from the narrow opening she's allowed to have in her exterior safety window, hoping it will ease her headache and nausea. She catches the scent of teasing rain in a burst of cool breeze. A sudden thought of her father is a sword slashing through her. The same sword he used to slay her dragons in a fairy tale once upon a time.

A light knock on the door brings in Dr. Swenson, followed by a blank-eyed girl probably Maddie's age and not any bigger. She's kind of scraggly, with a bandage around her neck too. Her eyes have big, red broken vessels webbing through them. She isn't looking at Maddie, but more through her, as if she's a wounded hologram from a future apocalyptic war.

"Maddie, this is Grace. She'll be your roommate," Dr. Swenson says.

"Hi." At least this girl is someone to rot with, a distraction.

Grace moves her hand up and down in a slow wave back.

Dr. Swenson reminds Maddie of that actress in *Fried Green Tomatoes*, the Towanda one, except now playing the part of a psychiatrist. "I'll leave you two to get acquainted."

Grace is napping on her bed when Maddie says her name a couple of times. When she finally opens her eyes, Maddie tells her, "They want us to go to the dayroom for some kind of meeting."

She sits up and tries to clear the grogginess from her mind. She was in a deep, dreamless sleep. When she rubs her face, she can feel striped dents left by the ribbed institutional bedspread. She rakes her fingers through her hair where it's plastered against her cheek with dried drool.

"You were out for like two hours," Maddie says. "Must be nice. I never sleep that well."

A rap at the door and Jackson's voice. "Come on, girls. You're the guests of honor."

Grace and Maddie look at each other. Grace has the sudden feeling that the two of them are in this together. Whatever this place is, she has someone to share it with. Her dad might be over a thousand miles away, but she isn't completely alone; she sees something in this fellow traveler, something she recognizes.

The dayroom is the center of Brazos Cottage—what the staff call the unit that houses thirteen- to seventeen-year-olds in need of inpatient psychiatric care. When Grace was admitted, Jackson told her there were six units called cottages, holding various age groups, plus a school and a few other buildings used for assorted therapies, activities, and administrative offices spread over eleven acres of manicured lawns and playgrounds.

Grace follows Maddie down the east hall into the dayroom, which is drenched in late-afternoon sun. The staff desk and back office creates the perimeter to the south. The kitchen is visible through safety glass to the north, and another hallway with more patient bedrooms, a bathroom, and a laundry room is on the west, opposite Maddie and Grace's hall.

Grace stops when Maddie does, surveying the curved sectional sofa holding five other kids, who are apparently responsible for the various shouts, cries, and bursts of laughter Grace has heard from her room since she arrived.

"Take a seat, girls, so we can get started," Jackson says. He holds a clipboard in his large hands.

"We won't bite," says a guy. At least, Grace thinks it's a guy, but as he shifts in his seat, he seems to have breasts moving under his large T-shirt. "Actually, Aaron's a biter, but he only has a taste for staff."

"I haven't bitten a staff member in over three weeks and two days, so your information is inaccurate or, at the very least, out of date," a younger boy, apparently Aaron, says, a green velvet yarmulke perched atop his dark wavy hair.

Maddie sits on the end of the half circle, leaving just enough room for Grace to squeeze in next to her. The nurse, Sharon, meets Grace's eye and smiles, her lime-green-sneakered foot jiggling.

"Let's get started," Jackson says. "Maddie, Grace, welcome to Brazos Cottage. We're going to go around the circle and make introductions. Name, age, and why you are here. I'm Jackson. I used to play pro ball for the Denver Broncos. When I got injured, I decided to go back to school and find a career where I could help young people, so I got a degree in counseling. I'm the program manager of this cottage, so I head up the team of staff. I'm thirty-six."

A Native American boy sits next to him, examining the plants suspended from a long skylight high over their heads. He seems oblivious to everyone's expectant stares. Finally, Jackson gives him a gentle nudge with his beefy elbow. "Percy, you're next."

"Earth to Percy," Aaron says.

"Aaron, are you earning your relationship points right now?" Jackson says.

Aaron scowls, crosses his arms over his chest, and sinks down in his seat.

The Native American boy speaks softly. "I'm Percy, uh, sixteen, from Zuni Pueblo. I'm here because my teachers think I spend too much time in the spirit world."

"You're a spook, all right," a Hispanic kid says with a wide grin.

"Abdias," Jackson admonishes and checks off something on his clipboard.

"Don't be taking points from me, man. It was a joke. *Spook* ain't that bad. Shit!" Abdias says, sudden anger flashing across his handsome face.

"Language," the other kids say in unison.

"Take your turn, Abdias," Jackson says.

"I'm fifteen and I'm here for evaluation and treatment before they send me to Springer to do my stint for accidentally shooting a little kid when I was getting ranked into my gang. I was supposed to shoot his big brother, but shit went down all wrong. Oh, and I did a lot of drugs that, like, messed me up." Abdias rattles this off as if it's the weather report.

Grace looks sideways to see Maddie's expression just as Maddie glances her way. Their eyes meet only briefly, but it's enough to convince Grace that Maddie's as freaked out as she is.

"Thank you, Abdias. Gabe?" Jackson says.

It's the boy who has breasts. "I'm Gabe. I'm sixteen. I'm transgender, or trans, meaning I was born a male into a female's body, so I live as a male and I'm saving up to go to Trinidad, Colorado, for my corrective surgery. It's hard to live like this because people can be such assholes, so I got anger problems and I cut on myself when it gets really bad, but I'm learning not to do that anymore."

"I guess I'm next," Sharon says. She smiles again at Grace, who decides Sharon smiles more than anyone she's ever seen. But it seems natural as it spreads across her wide face because her brown eyes smile too. "I'm Sharon, I'm thirty-one and the cottage nurse. I've been here about eight years and I love it. You guys inspire me and I love working with you."

"Yeah, you love shooting us in the ass with needles," Abdias says.

"If you're out of control and are a danger to yourself or others and all other attempts to help you haven't worked, then, yes, I will help you by giving you medicine to calm down, and if you aren't able to take it as a pill, I have to inject it. But that's the extreme situation and you get a lot of choices before I have to make the choice for you. Not my favorite part of the job, but keeping you safe is my top priority." Sharon smiles again, and Grace notices Abdias and the others seemed to relax under her gaze.

"You're next, Lucas my man," Jackson says and stifles a yawn. Grace wonders if he ever leaves this place.

"Hi, I'm Lucas. I'm thirteen," he says with a Texas twang. He's dressed as a cowboy from the waist down, complete with red cowboy boots, and as a soldier from the waist up. Some sort of stuffed animal—a bird of some kind—is peeking out of the top of his camouflage shirt. "I'm here because I got bad memories of the war—left me with that post-traumatic deal."

There's a general outburst from his peers, but his strident voice rises over it. "I was in Nam for two tours, and it weren't pretty neither."

"How do you explain the undisputed fact the Vietnam War ended decades ago and you're only thirteen? Are you some kind of idiot? Do the math," Aaron says.

Grace figures Aaron is one of those guys who lives for math and all things logical and precise. Lucas's infraction against the space-time continuum seems more than Aaron can handle.

"Wars don't always end when they say they do, and I ain't no idiot. Typical lack of respect for the Vietnam veteran. Oh, and this is my war buddy Sam—we were stationed together. Say hi, Sam." Lucas makes the stuffed eagle in his shirt nod a hello.

Aaron slaps his own forehead in frustration, nearly tossing his yarmulke.

"Aaron, focus on telling us about yourself," Sharon says. "It's your turn."

"I'm Aaron, fourteen. I'm from Israel originally. They've labeled me with Asperger's syndrome, which is their way of admitting I'm far too smart to function cohesively with others. I don't suffer fools gladly, and for that sin I am locked up in a psychiatric hospital."

"Way to take responsibility." Gabe rolls his eyes.

"Shut it, *girlfriend*," Aaron says, his pale face flushing crimson.

Gabe jumps from his seat, a fist drawn back and ready. For a huge man, Jackson leaps between them remarkably quickly. "You want to put that fist away before I see it, and sit back down, Gabe?" Gabe complies, looking as if it takes every ounce of his self-control not to pummel Aaron into hamburger meat. Grace estimates Gabe has about forty pounds on Aaron, and his tattooed, bulging biceps indicates long hours of pumping iron.

"Aaron, you may either apologize to Gabe or head to your room." Jackson says it calmly, but his well-over-six-foot height and linebacker physique loom over Aaron in a way that makes Grace think no one in their right mind would try a third option.

But this is not a place for those in their right minds. Aaron jumps at Jackson, head-butting him in his generous gut. Jackson grabs Aaron by his shoulders and begins to walk him away from the group.

"Unhand me, you dickless Christian!" Aaron screams. "You philistine!"

Abdias begins to laugh. Sharon gives him a stern look, and Abdias pulls up his T-shirt to cover his mouth while he fights to control himself, his shoulders rising and falling with silent snickers.

Aaron begins some generic yelling, muffled now as Jackson gets him into his room. The low rumble of Jackson's voice provides the bass notes to Aaron's high-pitched tirade.

Sharon turns to Grace and Maddie. "While Jackson is helping Aaron, which one of you girls would like to go first and tell us a little about yourself?"

Grace looks at Maddie, who shrugs and looks down at her hands.

"She's got some wicked hickeys on her neck," Abdias says, making Grace wish Sharon hadn't removed her bandage to "let it breathe." Maddie's hand reaches to cover her own neck wound.

"I hung myself," Grace says, her voice still hoarse and whispery.

"What was that?" Lucas asks, leaning forward.

"She hung herself," Abdias repeats. "Did you die and come back 'cause my homey Joker—he was shot this one time and he went to this place with bright lights and all this crazy shit, but then God made him come back— or it could have been the meth he was doing and me standing over him with a flashlight."

"Somebody must have found you and cut you down," Gabe says. "Are you sorry you didn't die or are you relieved?"

"I don't know yet."

Gabe nods. "Too soon to tell. I feel you." He extends his arms to show her the old silvery scars over both wrists.

"Maddie?" Sharon says. "Why don't you finish this up for us and then we'll set up for dinner."

Maddie looks at Grace, distress in her eyes. Grace can feel Maddie's tension like heat emanating from her body. "It's complicated," Maddie says.

"We told you ours, so you have to tell us yours or you don't earn your participation points," Lucas says.

"Mine's way more personal," Maddie says.

"You have a cut on your neck—did you try to kill yourself too?" Gabe asks.

"I was just trying to get my father to back off," Maddie says, blinking back tears. "I was telling him how my stepbrother hurt me, and my own father wouldn't believe me."

"Did your stepbrother hurt you sexually?" Gabe asks.

Maddie gives a quick nod, her head bending forward, hiding behind her hair.

"Fucking prick!" Gabe says.

No one says "language," not even Sharon.

Grace puts her hand on Maddie's hot back. She lightly circles her fingertips to try to comfort her.

"Good job, ladies. It's nice to have some girls in the cottage to balance out all this boy energy. So that was task group. We sit down together a few times a day to work out issues, problem solve, check in with each other. Lucas, you have kitchen setup for dinner. Percy, you can help him since Aaron is busy. Everyone else, wash up."

Maddie stands and Grace follows her to their room. Each sits on her bed, facing the other. Maddie hugs her bed pillow to her stomach. "I can't believe the son of a bitch won't believe me," Maddie says, tears streaming down her face. "For years I kept the secret to keep his ass safe and now he fucking won't even believe me."

"My dad took off to Florida with some skank when I was still unconscious in the emergency room," Grace says. As much as she has sometimes wished to be rid of Mitch, now that it actually happened, it's like part of her is missing. She's never been away from him, as far back as she can remember, and it's nearly impossible to wrap her brain around it.

"Do you have a mom?" Maddie asks.

"She died when I was little."

"Mine's in France. I was on my way to find her when I was captured and brought to this hellhole."

"I don't mind it here," Grace says. "I don't have anywhere else to be. Better than being hungry, living on the streets. Air conditioning, a bed, food . . . a roommate that doesn't seem any crazier than I am . . . I'm good."

"What about those guys out there? They're seriously nuts," Maddie says, a smile twitching at her lips.

"Except Gabe. He has potential. But then, he started out as a girl, so that gives him a distinct advantage. But yeah, the other guys are about what you'd expect in a psych unit."

"Dickless Christian!" Maddie gives in to a grin, the tears still wet on her cheeks.

"Dickless Christian!" Grace repeats and gives her a thumbs-up.

Grace, Age 7

Tucson, Arizona

Grace stood in front of the torn screen door on the small stoop. María's mother spoke in Spanish to María on the other side of it and then opened the door for Grace to enter. María was in her first-grade class at school. The kitchen smelled like the pot of beans on the stove. There was always a pot of beans on the stove. Nothing was ever on Grace's stove.

"Where is your papá?" María's mother said. She always asked and Grace never had an answer for her.

Grace shrugged. "Maybe at work?" María's mother threw her hands up in the air and began to talk to herself in Spanish; it sounded like she was scolding someone who wasn't there.

Grace felt her stomach growl like the scary black dog that circled the neighborhood looking for little kids like her to eat. Tomás, María's older brother who was ten, told her, so it was true. Grace just turned seven, so it took two hands to show her age. Five plus two.

María grabbed her hand and pulled her through the tiny one-bedroom duplex apartment that looked exactly like where Grace and her dad lived on the other side of the wall, except Grace's apartment was not as clean and nice. María and her mama and Tomás all slept in one big bed. At least Grace had her own bed, even if it was a small mattress on the floor. Her dad slept on the sofa in the living room that smelled like onions and some kind of animal.

María handed her a half-naked Barbie doll with a blond ponytail and red panties. Grace's hair was too short to make a ponytail since her dad took the scissors to it, and it wasn't all shiny like Barbie's, but María told her that her hair was yellow too, so that's why she got that Barbie to use. María's Barbie had black hair like María and she wore a silver princess dress.

"Where's her top?" Grace didn't like the way her Barbie's chest jutted out like two hard beige mountains. One time her dad brought home a woman like that, but when Grace saw her naked chest, it didn't look so hard and pokey.

"You could make one," María said and handed her a tissue from a dented box atop an orange crate that served as a nightstand.

Grace wrapped the tissue around the doll's chest, but it fell off. María grabbed it and the Barbie. "Not like that. Like this, see? Now it's a poncho."

Grace examined it. María had made a little rip in the center of the tissue and stuck Barbie's head through it, and now it fluttered nicely around her, covering her nakedness. Poncho. Grace smiled. María had lots of good ideas. She also had long, shiny black hair in two braids and pretty brown skin.

"So, your mom is in heaven," María said. "Did your mom have yellow hair like this Barbie? With her white poncho she could be your mom in heaven, like an angel. Make her fly."

Grace looked at the Barbie in her hand. She tried to remember her mother, who died when Grace was five. Her dad said they didn't have any pictures of her. She thought her mother had yellow hair, but everything was fuzzy from back then, like a dream she couldn't remember. She perched on her knees on the bed and made the doll fly over their heads, which seemed to satisfy María. Her black-haired Barbie was jumping on the bed, nearly as high as Grace's dead-mom Barbie was flying. "I don't know about heaven," Grace said.

María sighed the way she did when Grace was dumb about something, which wasn't really fair since Grace was a lot smarter than María at school. She could read and write sentences and do numbers, while María still had trouble writing her own name. "You go to heaven when you die, but you have to believe in Jesus. Did your mom believe in Jesus?"

Grace didn't want to admit more dumbness. She knew her dad said "Jesus Fucking Christ" a lot. Was that the same as believing? "What's heaven like?"

"It's all white and golden and everyone is happy because there's no problems there, only goodness, and you fly around like angels and sit on clouds. My grandmother is there. She believed in Jesus. See, that's her Bible right there and her rosary." María scooted over to the orange crate and picked up the Bible. "Look, there are pictures of Jesus."

The black book was as soft as skin. Grace opened it and the pages were thin and slippery and packed with tons of tiny words. She could pick out some words she knew and began to read. She loved books and used to have three of them, but the last time her dad moved them to a new city, she lost them all. She hoped they were done moving. She liked it in Tucson, going to school and living next to María.

"No, skip to the pictures in the middle," María said, tugging on the Bible, but Grace didn't let go. "I could do it," she told María. She flipped through and found the pictures that were on thicker paper and very colorful. A man with wavy, long brown hair and pretty blue eyes looked back at her.

"So he's born on Christmas in a manger, and then they killed him on Good Friday and he came back from the dead on Easter, and if you believe it, you go to heaven, where he and God are watching to make sure you're being good and not doing sins like lying and stealing and that you are saying your prayers and brushing your teeth."

"I know about the baby in the manger," Grace said. He must have grown up. If her mom was in heaven, she should try to get there. Her dad lied a lot and stole from stores because he needed stuff to sell for money or sometimes for food. He called it taking care of her. Sometimes he took her with him and made her wear a baggy coat so he could stick stuff under it. But she really wasn't the one stealing, so she should be okay. He wasn't going to heaven, but she still wanted to go if she could be with her mom. "How do you say your prayers?" Grace asked, since she had the part about brushing her teeth down. Her dad had taught her one thing right.

María smiled and Grace had to wonder about María's teeth-brushing skills; it seemed her teeth wore a scummy coat over them. "I'll teach you the one you say at bedtime. Do this." María slid off the bed onto the floor. She kneeled against the side and made her hands into a little tent. Grace slid down next to her. "Close your eyes or it doesn't work."

Grace scrunched her eyes closed but had to peek a little so she wouldn't miss anything María was doing. "Now I lay me down to sleep, I pray the Lord my soul to keep, and if I die before I wake, I pray the Lord my soul to take. Now do it with me."

Grace mumbled along and by the time they said it twice she knew it by heart.

María looked at her intently. "Your soul is the part of you that's not your body. So if you're good and believe and say your prayers, God takes your soul when you die to be with your mamá and you live forever."

The thought made Grace's insides flutter like birds were caught there. "You are my best friend, María."

"I know."

María's mother stood in the doorway. Grace liked how big and soft she was and imagined what it must be like to crawl up into her lap and nestle like a baby animal. "Dinner is ready. Wash your hands."

They scrambled from the bed, leaving María's mother to smooth the covers they had disturbed. The Barbies got dumped into a cardboard box in the corner that held a few other toys. Grace looked back to see María's mother kiss the black book before placing it on the orange crate.

Tomás sat at the table, his sneakered foot banging against the chrome leg of his chair. He looked all sweaty and breathed hard like he had raced home. Grace sat down next to him in what had become her chair. Luckily there was no father, so the fourth chair was always open.

They sat in silence while María's mother thanked God and Jesus for their food and they crossed themselves and opened their eyes. Grace paid more attention to the prayer this time, since she knew about heaven and wanted to go there to see her mom. She didn't know if she was allowed to cross herself, so she didn't. She'd have to ask María about it.

The beans had been reheated so many times they were like gloppy glue, but Grace's growly stomach didn't mind. The tortillas were soft and steaming hot under the towel. Tonight they had Mexican rice too, dotted with peppers, carrots, and celery. It was a little spicy, but Grace liked how it warmed her mouth. She watched as Tomás spread the beans like peanut butter onto his tortilla, then spooned his rice over the top, and then dumped hot sauce over it and rolled it up.

Grace liked to keep everything separate because it seemed like more food that way. She ate as slowly as she could, tasting with every corner of her mouth, rolling every bite over her tongue until it disappeared.

"How was school?" María's mother asked.

"Grace is in the smart kids' reading group," María said. "Miss Molly had her read in front of the whole class. She reads chapter books that Miss Molly gets from the school library."

"Bueno," María's mother said and smiled. Grace saw she was missing a front tooth just like her and María. "Maybe Grace can help you two do better."

Tomás was picking up the rice that fell out of his tortilla with his fingers and sticking it into his mouth. "Can I have seconds?"

"You've had enough. This has to last us all week," María's mother said.

"We'd have more if we didn't have to feed her all the time," he said. "Her dad should give you money for babysitting her too."

"Shush now, Tomás. Grace is our guest. Neighbors take care of each other."

Grace had a little rice left and a strip of tortilla. She wanted it, but Tomás was right and, besides, he was bigger and needed more food. "You could have this, Tomás, if you want it."

Tomás took her plate and put it on top of his empty, licked-clean one. Grace watched him take every bite and found herself chewing along on nothing, her teeth hitting each other, her tongue searching for little grains of rice that were hiding in her cheeks.

A loud pounding on the door made them all jump. María's mother got up and answered it. "Hello, Mitch," she said to Grace's dad.

"Grace, come on now, we got to go," he said.

Something in his tone rooted Grace in place. "I want to stay here."

"I said now, girl. Move your behind." He had the look, all right. Eyes darting around, biting his lip. His brown hair half out of the leather tie he pulled it back with.

When he reached up to stick some hair back behind his ear, Grace saw that his knuckles were bloody. She felt her insides cave in on themselves and she got so cold that a big shiver shook her in her seat. When she didn't move, he grabbed her by her arm and pulled her toward the door. Grace broke free and ran to María's mother, clinging to her softness, who said into her ear, "I can't keep you, mi'ja. You belong to your papá."

María was hanging on to her waist from behind, seeming to sense this was it. This was the end.

"Where will you go?" María's mother asked as Mitch pulled Grace up like a rag doll onto his big, muscled shoulder.

"If anyone comes asking, tell them we went to Denver," Mitch said, and as he walked out, Grace stared over his shoulder, her arms still reaching. They looked back at her, even Tomás, with such sadness that she knew they didn't want her to go and it tore her heart. She prayed to God and Jesus, as the screen door slammed shut, that she would always remember their faces.

CHAPTER 2

"DO YOU STILL FEEL like dying?" Dr. Swenson asks Grace. They're sitting in Dr. Swenson's office for their first individual therapy session.

Grace looks around the large room containing Dr. Swenson's cluttered, paper-stacked desk and extra chairs. The walls are covered in kid art curling at the edges and faded from the sun that pours in from the large window overlooking the grounds, which are so green the scene seems to vibrate, like a virtual world. Their water bill must be insane.

"It wasn't about dying," Grace says.

"What was it about?"

Grace stares out the window and the outdoor scene dissolves into the image of her walk into the abandoned gym. "I just couldn't do it anymore."

"Do what?"

"I couldn't . . ." Grace's chest fills with pain, her mind whirls with all the things she couldn't do anymore.

"I read the letter your dad left you at the hospital—I hope you don't mind. Maybe we can talk about that."

Grace grips the seat of her chair as if she might spin off her axis and be flung through the glass window. "Did he call? Does he even know where I am?"

"We haven't heard from him yet. I've talked to patient information services at the main hospital and asked that any calls regarding you be transferred here. We're in the same system, so that'll work."

Grace nods, not meeting her eyes. The silence hangs between them for a few long moments while Grace wonders if Mitch and Jill made it to Orlando or died in a drunken crash somewhere along the way, and, really, how would she ever know?

"Here's the deal, Grace," Dr. Swenson finally says. "You're here because you tried to kill yourself. It's my job to help you, but we do it together. I have no magic dust. I'm not your fairy godmother. We have to do the hard work of talking about it. We have to start somewhere, so you pick a topic, anything at all. I'm not real choosy at this point as long as I hear words coming out of your mouth. If you want some choices, I'll throw out your dad, your mom, your life leading up to what brought you here, first memories, last memories, or anything in between. I'm easy that way."

Grace thinks of all the times she would have loved to have someone to talk to, how alone she has been for most of her life. Now the opportunity is on a silver platter in front of her and she doesn't know how to take it.

"When I was a kid, growing up in Iowa," Dr. Swenson says, "it'd be so hot and muggy. One day I was old enough to go to the swimming hole with my big brothers. They'd swing off a rope tied to a tree branch and drop into that cold, delicious water. I stood there, not knowing how to swim, dizzy from the heat, wanting to follow them, but frozen with fear. Finally my oldest brother said, 'I got you!' and gripped me around my waist and took off on that rope and dropped us both into the water. I went under, held my breath from the shock, and came back up, my brother still gripping me tight. I got you, Grace."

Grace looks at her then. Smiling gray eyes, lips set in a determined line, the tilt of her chin when she meets Grace's gaze. Her plump arms folded over her ill-fitting blue jacket. "I don't remember my mother," Grace says, plunging from a great height. "There's something wrong with me. I should remember something. I was five."

"You were five?"

"When she died," Grace says.

"I see," Dr. Swenson says. "You think there must be something wrong with you that you can't remember her."

"I don't remember my life until I was like seven in Tucson with

Mitch—my dad. He told me about her and how she was with me like every second of my life and then she died but it's all a blank. That's not normal."

"I can see it troubles you. Memory is a tricky thing. It's different with everyone, so it's hard to say what 'normal' is. But it's something we can work on together, see if we can't fill in a few missing pieces. If it's important to you, it's important to me. No guarantees, no magic dust. But we'll try. Maybe you could start with something you do remember. See, I'm at a disadvantage since I don't get to interview your dad to get your basic history. I need you to fill in those blanks for me."

"He'd just give you some bullshit story anyway," Grace says, with more fatigue than anger. "He's a liar and a con artist, but he sucks at it."

"Well, it's good I've got you then."

Once Grace begins to speak, the words come tumbling out of her like coins from a winning slot machine. She recounts every stupid, lousy thing Mitch ever did and all the heartbreak she suffered through the last ten years with at least that many moves.

Dr. Swenson doesn't say much or take any notes. She just listens intently. Finally, when Grace describes climbing aboard the tower of chairs in the gym, Dr. Swenson says, "You just couldn't do it anymore. You built a life with your own two hands and it was demolished. You lost everything."

"It was the first time I had that much to lose," Grace says. "It was a gamble. I knew it was, putting all my chips on a loser like Mitch. I just had to try; I wanted it all so much, I got stupid." She leans back in her chair, spent. Truth is exhausting.

"I think you deserve more credit than that. Taking over when Mitch was incapacitated, building that life, having close friends, Mitch doing well for what, almost a year? You have guts. You have determination. You had goals and you fought for them. The risks you took were for the right reasons. Those qualities are inside of you and you still have them. So here's what I propose. You spend some time here healing, getting your legs back. We can work on your concerns about your memory of your early life and the loss of your mother and of course all the daddy stuff. When you're ready, we'll work on how you can make a life for yourself outside of here. You'll be eighteen in less than six months, am I right?"

"Yes. In November." How desperate she's been to reach that day. "What if Mitch doesn't come back?"

"Whether he comes back or not, I think it's time to separate your future plans from his. If he comes back and you want to have a relationship with him, we can work on how to do that with some safe boundaries in place. But I don't think your life should ever depend on how he's living his ever again. Am I being too pushy? I can do that sometimes, so speak up if we're not on the same page regarding Mitch."

"We're on the same page."

"If you're ready to be out of here before you turn eighteen, we can discharge you to a transitional place that is designed to help teens become ready to live autonomously. But you'll be in the loop on that decision. Meantime, does what I've described sound like something you can do? When you put the rope around your neck, you say it was because you couldn't do it anymore. So I'm asking, does this sound doable to you? Are you willing to stick around for it?"

Grace feels a jolt of conviction. "Absolutely."

Dr. Swenson smiles with her entire face and Grace catches a glimpse of the girl she once was, swinging from a rope in the arms of her brother, brave and terrified.

"Then I'll tell Jackson you're no longer a risk to yourself or others, take you off high-risk precautions, and advance you to level one, where you'll have a tiny bit more freedom. He'll go over the particulars. Good job, Grace. I'm looking forward to working with you."

Maddie has a hard time sleeping the night before her first family therapy session. She told Dr. Swenson that she doesn't want to see her dad or Lesley ever again, but Dr. Swenson pointed out that refusing to see them would hinder her healing process and delay her from moving on in her life. Maddie has no choice but to trust Dr. Swenson. At least Dr. Swenson believes her.

It's hard enough to sleep with a staff member coming down the hall every fifteen minutes and shining a flashlight on her. She finally gets up and asks for something to help knock her out, which comes in the form of an antihistamine pill.

After what felt like a short nap, she drags herself to the kitchen, where the others are already eating breakfast. She feels a little hungover, but it's her dread of family therapy making her slippers feel like they're lined with lead. Cereal boxes on the table form a mini-skyline as kids nab them like the gargantuan Japanese monsters in the old movies she watched with her dad. Her dad. She shakes off the thought of him as she takes her seat next to Grace.

Day staffer Judy is dishing out food. She's also the educational assistant in the classroom, and older than all the other staff. Soft wrinkles make her face look like a slept-in sheet. Her British accent makes it sound as if she's running a posh boarding school.

Maddie sits by Aaron, who's cutting his food into obsessive little stacks on his plate. With all his genius, he can't reason away his craziness.

"Ugh. Plated kosher crap cooked to disintegration in the hospital cafeteria. At least it was blessed," Aaron says. Abdias throws a piece of bacon at him and Aaron raises his arms and cowers like an abused laboratory assistant, his embroidered skullcap with the gold star falling backward onto the floor. Maddie cringes at Abdias's meanness as an image of her stepbrother, Jeffrey, appears in her bowl of cereal. She stabs at the wilting flakes with her spoon.

Next to Aaron, Lucas is coaxing Sam, his stuffed eagle, to eat a Cocoa Puff, and Percy stares at the green melon balls as if they're eyeballs staring back. Maddie turns to meet Grace's eyes, which reflect her own thought: even with their bandaged throats and misery, they are perhaps the rational ones.

After the silverware is counted and everyone excused, Maddie has just enough time to brush her teeth before Dr. Swenson arrives at her room. "Ready?" Dr. Swenson puts her hand on Maddie's shoulder. "I'm proud of you, going through with this."

"Just another walk to the guillotine." Maddie shuffles alongside Dr. Swenson on the way to her office, especially as they ascend the stairs to the second floor of the administration building, where she knows her dad and Lesley wait. Maddie entertains a fantasy that when the office door opens, her dad and Lesley will fall to their knees, beg her forgiveness, and promise to take her to France because they feel so horrible about their betrayal. Moonshine is outside, ready for her to mount and ride away, and they will hire a psychopathic hit man to give Jeffrey the slow and torturous death he deserves.

Instead, her father stands as she enters. Maddie can tell he wants to hug her, but she backs away to hide behind Dr. Swenson. He looks hurt and she's glad. He also looks as if he's been put through his rock tumbler.

"I just want to start out by saying we're willing to do whatever it takes to get Maddie better," her father says. "We love you, Maddie."

"I'm relieved to hear you say that, Mr. Stuart. Maddie will need all your support to get through this." Her dad smiles as if everything's going to be okay. Who's the sucker for happy endings now? They all take seats in a small circle of chairs.

"We just want you to get well and come home," Lesley says. "You need to take whatever medicine the doctors give you so you can get back to normal. Moonshine misses you terribly."

"What is normal?" Dr. Swenson asks Lesley.

"You know, riding her horse, reading in her room. She's always in her room. I suppose that's typical for a seventeen-year-old girl, though," Lesley says.

"I don't know, I have a seventeen-year-old niece who's always out with her friends," says Dr. Swenson.

"Are you saying Maddie's been sick longer than we thought?" her dad asks.

"I tried to get her involved in school activities, but she'd have no part of it. She could have friends if she wanted," Lesley says. "But she's a loner."

"It sounds to me as if you did notice something was not quite right with her," Dr. Swenson points out.

"We figured she just needed to adjust to our marriage and the combined family," her dad says. "I'd never had a teenager before. What did I know about bad moods and girl stuff, like getting her periods? I see now she was maybe depressed or something and I missed it."

"Didn't you marry five years ago? What if that wasn't the cause of Maddie's depression? What if it was something else?" asks Dr. Swenson. Lesley's foot starts to jiggle as she pulls at her long blond braid. "We can't dismiss what Maddie divulged to you before she cut her own throat." Dr. Swenson takes a healthy chug out of her coffee cup while Lesley sits there as if Dr. Swenson just farted and Lesley is left to smell it. Her dad's hands are cupped over his knees as he looks down at his feet. Maddie waits and holds her breath.

"But isn't that why she's here? Because she made such awful accusations about her stepbrother? If you knew Jeffrey, you would know how irrational these lies are," Lesley says. "I think she's always been jealous of him, so they never got along. Couldn't it be schizophrenia that is making her paranoid enough to say such a thing? I mean, that's what medicine is for, right? To stop her delusions?"

Maddie holds herself back from swirling into another black rage. Not in front of them. She must appear reasonable, since Lesley called her a schizomaniac.

"What about you, Mr. Stuart? You've known your daughter her whole life. What does your gut tell you?" Dr. Swenson asks.

Her dad shakes his head. "It's hard to think that Jeffrey would ever . . ."

Lesley's face crumples and she begins to cry. "I can't do this. He's my son. I can't sit here while you give this insanity your credence."

Dad looks nervous and begins to fidget. "I don't know what to think. On one hand, I want to support my wife, and on the other, I need to be here for my daughter." Maddie wants to tell him that he always forfeits her for Lesley. Instead, she pulls chunks of her bangs with two fingers, harder with each yank. Lesley looks everywhere except at Maddie. Her dad holds Lesley's hand.

Dr. Swenson calls the administrative assistant to her office. "Maddie, can you wait out in the hall with Dorthea while I talk with your parents for a bit?"

Maddie follows Dorthea into the hallway and they sit in reception chairs. Maddie wishes she could hear what they're saying, but Dorthea tries to keep Maddie distracted with small talk. She feels her heart race and thump against her chest. What if Dad and Lesley are able to persuade Dr. Swenson to their side? Then she'll have no one.

Finally the door opens and Dr. Swenson waves Maddie back inside. Lesley will not look at Maddie, her face is red and puffy, and she has clumps of crumpled white tissues in her lap. Her dad rubs and squeezes his knees, as if this is giving him an arthritic attack.

"Maddie, your parents and I have decided that for now Lesley won't be participating in family therapy. Later on we can bring her back, but for now it will just be you and your dad," says Dr. Swenson.

Lesley's lips are rippling and her eyes are still tearing. Maddie doesn't feel sorry for her in the least. Lesley gave birth to and raised a monster. Deep down somewhere, she must know it.

"Fine," Maddie says. Getting rid of Lesley seems like a victory.

"I'll wait outside." Lesley gathers her purse and snot rags.

"We won't be much longer," Dr. Swenson says.

Lesley gives a quick peck on Maddie's dad's cheek, but still doesn't look at Maddie as she turns to leave.

"So we'll meet again on Thursday, same time?" Dr. Swenson asks.

"I'll be here," her dad says. "I love you, honey." His eyes look trapped beneath his rutted brow.

Without Lesley at her dad's side, Maddie can begin to see remnants of how he used to be, once upon a time, when he would do anything for her. A pinhole of hope pierces her. "She's out of the room, so you can tell me you believe me now. You believe me, right?" Maddie's voice is high and pleading, the voice of a little girl begging her daddy.

Her dad looks as if she dropped a dead fish in his lap. "I don't think this is the time to get into it. Right, Dr. Swenson?" Before Dr. Swenson has a chance to answer, he stands and pulls the car keys from his pocket. "Lesley's waiting."

Dr. Swenson walks Maddie back to Brazos Cottage. Patients from other cottages are outside playing games with their staff, little kids on tricycles zoom past, Percy spins on the red metal wheel they call the Vomitron, and chains of the swings squeal like something in pain. Gabe waves from the volleyball court, but Maddie's unable to move her arm to wave back. She's completely numb. She has coiled back into that place where she can't feel or think.

He doesn't believe her. Those words chide her now with every step, her anger building like a rolling snowball growing big enough to crush a house by the time they enter Brazos Cottage. Dr. Swenson has Maddie sit on the couch in the dayroom while she ushers Jackson to the small-windowed office behind the desk to debrief.

But Maddie can't sit. She gets up to pace. She wraps her arms around herself to try to keep from shattering. She lets out a furious scream as her foot connects with the metal trash can. Orange peels, apple cores, and graham cracker wrappers fly across the dayroom. Jackson comes running, but Maddie's already heading to her room.

She hears Jackson ask if she's okay as she clenches her fist. She anticipates the pain of the punch before her knuckles connect to the hallway wall. The physical agony of her perhaps now broken hand can't approach what she's feeling inside. She's about to land another blow to the wall when Jackson's arms engulf her from behind.

She squirms hard for that second punch, but with her arms crossed over her chest and one elbow tucked under the other, she can't move them. She kicks with all her might and screams herself hoarse. Jackson calmly backs up against the wall and slides them both to the floor. He lets her scream and rage until she's out of breath and her limbs are spent. Her hand throbs and finally she breaks down crying. Jackson's arms loosen into a gentle, protective embrace, a foreign gesture to Maddie, reminding her how alone she has been. For that, she cries all the more.

Maddie, Age 7

Old Town, Albuquerque, New Mexico

"Wake up, sleepyhead," Daddy called from the kitchen.

Maddie turned and pulled her covers over her head, desperate to remain in her dream. She was with her mother in a faraway place from one of her mother's rare postcards. They danced on brick streets, against the backdrop of tall golden buildings with roofs shaped like ice-cream cones. Fountains sprayed colored glitter instead of water.

"Rise and shine, birthday girl, or you'll miss turning seven." Daddy stood in her doorway, holding a spatula. "I'm making your favorite breakfast."

Her birthday! The church bells from San Felipe church accompanied her as she straightened the quilt on her bed and stepped into her *Beauty and the Beast* slippers. Beast was really nice and not as scary as he looked. And she loved Belle for loving Beast from the inside out. Daddy said that was the way it should be.

"Happy birthday, princess," Daddy said, planting a kiss on her cheek as she sat at the table. "Eggs and apple cinnamon pancakes coming up." He danced his way back to the stove.

She had prayed the night before for her mother to return for her birthday. She'd often lie in bed and imagine her mother flitting through her open bedroom window and whisking her into the night to her far-off gypsy camp, where they would dance and feast around a big open fire. Maddie would be crowned princess of the gypsies and everyone would rejoice, then she would return to Old Town because that was her home.

Old Town shops, galleries, and restaurants were brown adobe, but splashes of color decorated the adobe walls and brick walkways. The bright-blue doors, the painted benches, the designs painted on walls made her happy. Flower pots overflowed with purple pansies, pink snapdragons, and deep-blue lobelia. This was her kingdom.

When she was really little, she believed that Cinco de Mayo celebrated her birthday, since it happened outside her window every year on her birthday. It wasn't until her teacher told her what the holiday meant in Mexico that she finally figured it out. Her birthday on May 5 just happened to fall on the anniversary of Mexico's victory over France, which was confusing because her mother came from France. Daddy told her to enjoy her birthday and Cinco de Mayo, and it would be all right with Mommy.

She opened her presents on the balcony with the fiesta unfolding below her. "This one is from Otilia," her daddy said, handing her a box wrapped in gold paper. She tore open the box to find a handmade fiesta dress, the prettiest she'd ever seen, turquoise blue with white trim and pink rosebuds and ribbons. Her neighbor and babysitter, Otilia, had been like a grandmother to Maddie her whole life. "She wants you to wear it today," Daddy said.

"I will! It'll be the prettiest dress on the plaza." Maddie holds it up to herself.

Cinco de Mayo made the plaza look like the three-ring circus Daddy took her to last year. A troop of Mexican folk dancers performed on the gazebo stage, their hair pulled back real tight, wearing colorful skirts with ribbons that they held up, shook around, and twirled without ever showing their underpants. A mariachi band wearing silver-studded jackets, sombreros, pants, and boots, popped up below her as if they had sprung out of a windup music box. Families started spreading blankets on the plaza grass with picnic lunches. Cinco de Mayo was a day for people to celebrate. Daddy said it was about freedom and democracy for Mexican people, but he said her birthday was more important to him than that. Kids ran around their parents as if they'd been let out of cages. She was the birthday princess on her balcony overlooking her people. "Be merry and rejoice!" she declared.

Daddy held her hand as they walked around the crowded plaza. Maddie noticed women taking second looks at him and she was proud he was so handsome. He let her stop to look as long as she wanted at the Native American jewelry displayed on blankets, her long dark hair falling in her face every time she bent over to look. Their friend Hector gave her a silver and turquoise bracelet for her birthday. He was a big Navajo man who wore his hair in a ponytail, bundled up like a papoose in pretty woven material. He felt as big as Beast when he hugged her. She wore her bracelet proudly with her new fiesta dress as she skipped along with Daddy.

"Let's give Toes a visit," he said, leading her to her favorite cove of shops on San Felipe Street. They found the blond six-toed cat, which was owned by the Ye Olde Town Cat Shop lady, sleeping in a large pot of spring flowers. He gave a drowsy purr as she scratched him from his head to his overstuffed belly, his six toes on each paw opening and stretching. The cat shop lady said Toes got in as much trouble as a toddler because he had thumbs and could open cabinets and doors.

"Bonjour! Bon anniversaire, ma petite. Bonjour, Michel. Comment ça va?" called Mimi, their friend from the French restaurant Le Crepe Michel. It still seemed funny that she called Daddy Michel like in her restaurant's name, even though Maddie learned it was the French way to say his name. Mimi was a tall, thin woman, older than Daddy. Mommy had been working for Mimi when she met Daddy. She guessed her mommy had felt at home in this little corner of France in Old Town. Mimi was her mommy's closest friend and wanted to see her again too.

Daddy gave Mimi a big, long hug. Tears were in their eyes when they finally let go of each other. Mimi led them past the crowd waiting to be seated in the small restaurant, to her favorite table on the enclosed patio next to the tree that grew right up out of the brick floor and through the roof. Since the ceiling was see-through, she could see the branches arching overhead with their new green leaves fluttering in the breeze. The whole room was green with plants and she felt like Maid Marían in Sherwood Forest. In the middle of the table on the white cloth was a vase of red roses opening under the afternoon sun. The helium balloons anchored with ribbons kept bonking their colorful heads together.

"They're beautiful, Daddy." She hugged the roses to her, the petals soft like she imagined her mother's cheek to be. She nuzzled in their scent.

Daddy ordered some lavender honey goat cheese that came with crackers. Maddie took her white cloth napkin and placed it carefully over her lap to protect her new dress. Her cracker broke when she tried spreading the goat cheese.

"Do you mind if I have a glass of wine?" he asked. She never minded, but he always asked. She saw from her balcony how some kids were treated by their parents. Pushed, pulled, smacked, and yelled at. Daddy really did treat her like a princess and she knew she was lucky. He was her faithful knight. They had had a real ceremony and everything, except she had to use an umbrella instead of a sword to dub him.

Mimi pulled up a chair and sat backward on it with her legs apart. She had a pencil and a pen sticking out of a loose bun on the top of her head. When Mimi sat that way, Daddy said she looked like one of those French cabaret singers from a movie. She leaned over and gave Maddie a kiss on each cheek. "Bon anniversaire, ma petite. I cannot help but be back seven years and remember your mama struggling to give birth to you," she said.

"The happiest day of my life. These hands were the first to ever hold you" Daddy said, taking Mimi's hands and kissing them.

"Your mother was so strong and brave," Mimi told her. "She labored for twenty hours and barely a peep out of her. She couldn't wait to hold you."

"We took turns holding her hand. I think I still have the marks where she dug her nails in from the pain," Daddy said, looking at his right palm. Maddie craned to see.

"You were the most beautiful baby I'd ever seen," said Mimi. "You took your first breath eagerly, as if you wanted to get a big taste of the world."

"They put you on your mother's chest and she cried because she was so happy," Daddy added. He had tears in his eyes too and so did Maddie. She wished she could remember being held and loved by her mother. Of all the kids in the world, why did her mommy have to be a gypsy queen?

"Madeleine. Renée always knew you'd be a girl so she had you named from the beginning," Daddy said. "I started calling you Maddie when you'd get cranky."

Mimi laughed. "Your mother would sing you a song to get you to hush. Ma pere m'donne un mari mon dieu, qelle homme que petit homme," she sang. "After she left, I sang it to you too." There was something familiar about it, just out of Maddie's reach. Mimi excused herself when the waitress whispered something in her ear. "Tout mon amour toujours," she said, blowing a kiss.

"How come we never know where Mommy is?" Maddie asked.

"Unfortunately, a gypsy queen has to keep moving. But I bet you she's thinking about you today, wherever she is, and sharing the same memories of your birth that we have." He squeezed her hand. "She knows where we are, baby. That's what's important."

"Because we're her lighthouse, so she can always find her way back home?" Maddie chewed her buttery crepe epinard. *Epinard* was French for *spinach*, which Maddie loved when mixed with the cream and seasonings and wrapped up in the soft, chewy crepe. The melted swiss cheese on top pulled like taffy on her fork. She even loved the buttered skinny carrots and green beans that came with it.

"Who in their right mind would stay away from you forever?" said Daddy.

Maddie often wondered about that. "Can't she make someone else queen?"

"She's from a long line of not any old gypsies but magical gypsies. That's why she's royalty. It's something she was born into. Can't get out of that."

Maddie's eyes widened. "Why didn't she take me with her? That makes me a magical gypsy too."

"We both knew her life was no life for a baby. Besides, I would have missed you too much and cried for the rest of my life. But don't doubt that she loves you. She'll always love you." He leaned over the table with his napkin and dabbed off a piece of cheese dangling from her lip. In Daddy's eyes, she saw he still loved Mommy. His smile reassured her. "And when she does decide to come home, we'll be here waiting."

"With roses and balloons?" Maddie asked.

"Roses, balloons, and fireworks!"

But waiting was the hard part.

That night Maddie snuck out of bed and onto the balcony while Daddy slept. Under a fat, bright moon, the quiet plaza became a fairyland. How could her heart feel so full and so empty at the same time? If Mommy loved her as much as Daddy said, why did she leave? She wrapped herself in her quilt, pleading with the moon to grant the same wish she made when blowing out her candles. She slowly rocked herself. The rhythm began to soothe her. She began to sing Mimi's lullaby. She sang the words she remembered and made up the rest. Her kingdom blurred with the tears she always hid from Daddy. She let them slide down her cheeks as she sang, and did not wipe them away.

"You did quite a number on yourself," Sharon says as she examines Maddie's swollen hand and bloody knuckles, palpating her bones. "Move your fingers for me." Maddie's fingers are hard to move because they're so swollen, but she manages a wiggle. "I don't think anything's broken."

"Everything's broken," Maddie says under her breath as Sharon slathers gooey salve on her knuckles and wraps them in a gauze bandage. Grace sits on her bed pretending to read, but she hasn't turned a page for a while, so Maddie knows she's listening.

Sharon gives Maddie a grieved look. "Keep the ice bag on it." She strokes Maddie's hair. "The Tylenol I gave you should help with the pain. No more run-ins with walls, okay? There are much better ways to deal with your feelings."

Maddie can't imagine what they are.

CHAPTER 3

AFTER SHARON LEAVES, GRACE peeks around her wardrobe, which is positioned as a room divider between her side of the room and Maddie's. Maddie lies on her back in bed, examining her freshly bandaged hand.

Grace feels shaken, her pulse pounding in her ears. Just being in the presence of Maddie's rage caused her to feel as if it had penetrated her own body and mind, and if Grace was experiencing only the secondhand portion, what must Maddie be suffering?

"Come on over," Maddie says to Grace's lurking.

Grace pulls Maddie's desk chair over next to her bed and sits down. She doesn't know what to say.

"Lesley took herself out of family therapy because she doesn't want to hear the truth," Maddie says, still sounding as if she could punch a wall. "So it'll just be me and Dad, who still won't believe me because it would upset Lesley. He's choosing her over me. Again."

"Maybe without Lesley, your dad will figure things out."

"He still goes home to that bitch and her lies. She'll still brainwash him on a daily basis." Maddie's chest heaves as she cries. "It is so fucking unfair."

Grace suddenly knows what to say. "What I think is unfair is how you hurt yourself. Your dad hurts you and you come back here and about break your fist punching through a wall and make Jackson have to hold you like some kind of wild animal—you gave him no choice. When are you going to stop paying the price? Haven't you suffered enough already?"

Maddie glares at her and shakes her head. "You just don't get it. You haven't been hurt like I have."

"I've been hurt enough to hang myself. But see, that's my wake-up call. I almost died. I'm through paying the price for how fucked up Mitch is. Screw that. I'm worth more than that and so are you."

"But Jeffrey's off having some great life. And here I am, all fucked up because of him, in a psych hospital—so I am paying the price."

Grace struggles to get Maddie to understand. "I'm just saying, it's not about Jeffrey anymore, it's not about Lesley, and it's not even about your dad. It's finally about you. You're what matters now. You were a victim, but you're more than that. And if you don't start treating yourself better, what kind of life are you going to have? We're going on eighteen, this place— Dr. Swenson—can help us."

Maddie's face twists in an angry smirk. "This place can't help me."

"If that's what you decide, you'll be right. If you decide to stay the victim, then that's all you'll ever be. But I think you can be more than that. You can't let the past fuck up your future, or the bastards win."

"News flash! The bastards won. Game over."

"We've both been hurt and been helpless—because we were children. But now our lives are up to us—even in a psych hospital. We have to take the power back from them and claim it for ourselves. Or you can punch walls and pitch fits and stay the victim," Grace says, shaking with anger. Was it Maddie she was trying to save, or herself? "I'm done with that shit. I want you to be done with it. I don't want to see you like that ever again!"

Maddie retreats into silence and examines her bandaged fist like it's something precious. It makes Grace nauseous to realize Maddie treasures her wounds as if they are testaments to what she has been subjected to, comforting her in a perverse way. How can Grace compete with the insidious power of that?

She gets up and places the chair back under Maddie's desk. Maddie doesn't seem to notice. Grace goes over to her own side of the room. She opens her wardrobe door to look at her neck in the scratched, dull safety mirror. In the week she has been here, the abrasions have dried and the thin layer of scabbing is yielding to fresh pink skin. The angry redness has receded to the edges of the healing wound. She hopes that in another week, there will be no more trace, no more residue of Mitch's stain on her life. She will never let herself believe, ever again, that anyone has more power in her life than she does. The look she sees in her eyes, even in the foggy reflection, is fierce and unyielding.

Grace, Age 11

San Francisco

Grace woke after a fitful night. A deep ache radiated through her low abdomen and into her back. It had provoked a dream about a rat gnawing into her flesh, burrowing into her. It had seemed so real she had to turn on the light and shake out the covers. She'd had close encounters with rats before, but this time it was confined to a nightmare.

Despite her discomfort, she smiled, remembering it was Saturday. Not that she minded school—sixth grade was pretty cool—but she didn't feel like jumping up, getting ready, and running for the bus. Maybe her stomachache was something she ate. But living with Twyla, she ate better than she ever had. Twyla was obsessed with natural and healthy foods, and she loved to cook. She wasn't rich but she had a funky, converted Victorian house. Grace had her own attic room there, and Twyla and Mitch shared the big bedroom right underneath her, where she often heard them having loud sex. At least she heard Twyla, who was pretty loud even when she wasn't having sex.

They had lived there four months already, so Grace was getting nervous that Mitch would do something soon to fuck everything up. He always did eventually. She tried not to get attached, but it was hard not to like Twyla, who smoked a lot of pot and danced to music and cooked strange but mostly good food. Twyla also had about million houseplants because they put clean oxygen into the air. Grace enjoyed living in a jungle, even on cool, foggy days.

Twyla didn't work. Grace figured she'd gotten her money from her parents, whom Twyla talked a lot about but were dead now and had left her the house. She lived in the upper level and rented out the lower level. But Twyla did not throw money around the way Mitch did whenever he had any, which wasn't often. Twyla sewed her own clothes from items she found at thrift stores, ripping things apart and putting them back together again, only better. Grace thought that was what she was trying to do with Mitch. He was one of her projects. She was trying to turn him into someone who matched the guy in her head, a guy she was already in love with.

She had him working instead of mooching off her like he tried to do in the beginning. He worked on a fishing boat, which according to him was hard, dirty work. He did come home stinking until Twyla washed him in her big claw-foot bathtub and did his laundry in the machines they shared with the downstairs renters. Twyla was older than Mitch and maybe that's what he needed. Plus the pot seemed to help keep him mellow, a change of pace from him being an angry drunk looking for trouble and always finding it.

Since Grace wasn't stupid, she avoided having hope. But maybe, with Twyla in charge and Mitch hooked by a nice place to live, the great food, the loud sex, and all the pot, just maybe things could last like this for a while.

Grace liked roaming their neighborhood, Haight-Ashbury, and the nearby Castro District. When Mitch was gone, sometimes a few days at a time, she and Twyla would rummage through vintage junk shops, bookstores, and the food co-op. Everyone seemed to know Twyla, especially gay guys who told her their troubles and cried on her shoulder. They were mostly nice to Grace too, except for Alvin, who had a mean poodle and blamed Grace when it bit her and she wasn't even doing anything.

Grace could hear Twyla turn on the music and could smell her morning hit of pot waft up the attic stairs. When she sat up in bed, she felt a warm gush between her legs. She reached down and her fingers came up bloody. After the initial wave of panic, Grace remembered about periods from the films they watched in school last year in San Jose. Mitch had never talked to her about anything to do with sex. He was more of a show than a tell kind of guy. And she had seen plenty.

She wadded the skirt of her nightie up into a ball and pressed it between her legs to catch the blood. Good, nothing on the sheets. She stood there a moment considering her options. She could duckwalk down the steep attic stairs all the way to the bathroom with her hand wedged into her crotch, or she could yell for Twyla. Another wave of cramps hit. "Twyla!"

After a few louder shouts, she heard the clomp of Twyla's Birkenstocks coming up the stairs, and the door flung open. "Good god, Grace, what is it?"

"I started my period," Grace said. "I didn't get anything on the sheets."

Twyla looked at her, a small smile spreading across her lips and her eyes getting misty. "Is this your first period ever?"

"Yeah, so I don't have any whatever you call it, supplies," Grace said.

"Oh, baby girl. I feel so privileged to be the one who is with you when you become a woman." Twyla gathered her into a hug, ignoring the fact that Grace still had her hand caught between her legs. "We're going to have a very special day. We'll go to the goddess shop and get some books and hematite stones you can put on your stomach for cramps. Oh, and I'll make you my special tea from chamomile, raspberry leaf, and pine tree bark. You can even bathe in it, doesn't that sound soothing?"

"Sure, but do you have, like, pads or something?" Grace said when Twyla released her.

"Normally I would just have tampons, which at your age, you wouldn't want to use. How old are you?"

"Eleven. I'll be twelve next month. I don't want tampons."

"No, you don't need to be sticking anything up there yet. I think I have some pads left from when I took care of Wendy after her abortion. You can't use tampons after an abortion either. You can get infected."

"Good to know," Grace said.

After drinking two cups of Twyla's tea and soaking in a hot tub full of it, Grace had to admit she felt better. Twyla found adhesive-backed maxi pads in the antique buffet that held plants in her bathroom. Twyla also recommended walking, so they struck out with their canvas shopping bags.

Twyla was tall and walked fast. As she rushed along trying to keep up, Grace tried to ignore the thick pad and just hoped it was doing its job as she felt her insides squeezing little gushes out of her. Twyla had her take a spare pad in her purse, and now Grace worried one might not be enough if they were making a day of it.

The goddess shop was narrow but deep and filled with spiritual books, tarot cards, healing gemstones, herbs, natural remedies, and women shoppers of every description—and one who looked like she may have been a man in the not-too-distant past. Twyla was on a first-name basis with the owner, Ginny. Ginny had thick, long gray hair, wire-rim glasses, and a body that reminded Grace of Mrs. Santa Claus. Ginny referred to herself as a crone.

Twyla took Grace's hand and presented her to Ginny. "This young woman has just started her very first period."

Ginny beamed and hugged Grace, who caught a whiff of some combination of essential oils. "I have a wonderful menarche section. Follow me. Oh, and Madam Claudia is doing readings in the back. Twyla, you should treat Grace to a reading on such an auspicious day."

After loading up on books about such things as the moon and menstruating, and shiny gray hematite stones to lay on her uterus to decrease cramping by opening up the blood flow and also helping her build new red blood cells, Twyla insisted Grace meet with Madam Claudia.

Ginny led Grace to an area in the back partitioned with yards of blue moon-and-star fabric. Madam Claudia beckoned her into the semidarkness. Fat candles flickered on every available surface. Jasmine incense sent a thin line of gray smoke undulating around the small space. Ginny made introductions, handed Madam Claudia Twyla's twenty-dollar bill, and left them.

"Sit, my dear," Madam Claudia said, indicating the folding chair opposite her position behind the velvet-draped table.

Grace sat on the pillow Madam Claudia had thoughtfully placed on the metal chair. Her eyes adjusted to the dim light and she found her heart beating faster in anticipation. She'd never seen a real psychic before. Madam Claudia didn't look like a fortune teller from the movies. She just looked like a regular middle-aged woman with dyed-red hair.

"Grace. What I do is very simple. I will hold your hand and go into a light trance to communicate with your spirit guides. Then I will tell you their message. I find cards and coins, things like that, just get in the way. Are you ready?"

"What do I do?" Grace asked, giving Madam Claudia her hand.

"Oh, just relax and open your heart and mind to the unseen. You can close your eyes or keep them open, however you are most comfortable. Shall we begin?"

"Okay," Grace said, and decided to close her eyes. Her hand was sandwiched between Madam Claudia's warm smooth hands.

While Madam Claudia went into her trance and listened to spirits, Grace breathed in the spicy scent and listened to the slight hiss from the candles as a draft seemed to pass.

After a moment, Madam Claudia began to speak. "They want you to know you are stronger than you think. You have chosen a difficult path in this lifetime, but you are not alone. You are a sensitive girl and if you open up to them, your spirit guides can help you."

Grace thought the part about a difficult path was true enough, but she never remembered choosing it.

"You've had a great loss and suffer from it still. You were young. Was it your mother?"

"Yes," Grace said. She wanted to jerk her hand away and leave right then, but her hand seemed to want to stay where it was. Everyone seemed to know about her dead mother, as if it were tattooed on her forehead.

"Your mother loved you very much and loves you still. She wishes she could be with you today to teach you about womanhood. She hopes you can forgive her."

"For what?" Grace said.

"For leaving you the way she did. Because of that, your path is hard, with many obstacles. I get the image of the thorny brambles and briars that the prince must fight through to reach Sleeping Beauty. And like the prince, your struggle will be rewarded. Your mother named you Grace for a reason. You will emerge from these trials embodying the kindness, mercifulness, and benevolence that will be shown to you at critical times along the way. Do you understand?"

"Sort of . . ."

"Let me put it more clearly. I believe what they are saying is that your mother's death has made your journey very difficult at times. But there are angels in the form of humans who will enter your life to help you. So even though your mom can't be with you, these other people you will encounter will step in and be there for you when you need them most. Twyla is one. Maybe there have been teachers who have encouraged you or others you can remember who were there for you. The important thing is to realize that despite this very big loss you've had, you are not alone. Seek the help you need and it will be there for you. And never give up. They want me to stress that you should never give up."

Grace nodded even as she thought of all the times she had wanted to give up. How hard it was with Mitch. How every time they got on their feet somewhere, he found a way to ruin it and she had to leave behind people and things she'd come to want. Tears began to spill out of the sad place she carried inside of her, a place that somehow seemed even bigger than she was. And yet what Madam Claudia said was true. She'd had angels too, but they just became more people to miss when they were gone. When she was gone. Because she was always the one leaving.

"Tears are good. Never be afraid of your tears or shamed into thinking they are wrong. Sadness is a part of earth life, but remember, you are stronger than your sadness. And the next angel is just around the corner. Try to trust in that," Madam Claudia said, and handed her a tissue. "Do you have any last questions for me?"

Grace wished she could think of a good question, but she was overwhelmed. She had so many questions and it was rare she had the chance to ask someone so wise. "No, thank you."

"All right then. We'll end with a blessing. Mother Father God, please bless our Grace. Help her to remember her strength, even as it is tested. Surround her with angels and help her to recognize them. We give thanks to our spirit guides for their generous offerings and we go in peace." Madame Claudia gave her hand a squeeze and then released it to her.

Grace opened her eyes, which were still a little wet. "Thank you."

Madam Claudia stood, so Grace stood and was surprised that this all-knowing and powerful woman was as tiny as she was, not even five feet tall. Angels come in all sizes, Grace decided.

Mitch had been home several days in a row. He said he was just taking some vacation days, but Grace knew he must have lost another job and was hiding it from Twyla. So even though it was her birthday, she was on edge.

"How's it feel to be twelve? Christ, it blows my mind," Mitch said as they sat at Twyla's table after her birthday dinner of vegetarian lasagna. Twyla was in the kitchen frosting her homemade carrot cake.

"I know you lost your job," Grace whispered.

"I quit it, smarty-pants. I got better things to do than busting my ass almost getting killed out on that fishing boat. What would you do then, huh?"

Live happily ever after, she thought, but then felt a little guilty. "What're you going to do?"

"I'll find something—now shut up about it before Twyla hears you."

"Like she won't figure it out? Don't mess this up with Twyla. I mean it, Mitch," she said. "I'm happy for once. I have a good school. If you mess this up, I'm telling you right now, I'm staying here."

"There you go with your Princess Grace routine. You go where I go."

"Happy birthday to you," Twyla sang, carrying the cake with about a hundred candles blazing.

"Shit, she's only twelve," Mitch said over her singing. He scowled and folded his arms over his flat stomach.

Twyla finished the birthday song and then said, "You can't have too much light in your life, right, Grace?" She sat the cake in front of her.

Grace filled her lungs with as much air as they would hold and then blew with all her might. Row after row of candles was extinguished with her powerful breath. But she ran out before she could get all of them. So she took another quick breath and finished them off.

"That's cheating. Now your wish won't come true," Mitch said.

"Shush," Twyla said. "Her wish will come true because she has a pure heart."

Mitch got up and nearly knocked his chair over as he strode off to the kitchen.

Twyla eyes followed him, but then she smiled at Grace and began to cut a big square of cake for her.

Mitch returned with a beer in each hand.

"Where did that come from? I told you I don't want alcohol in this house," Twyla said.

"It's my baby girl's birthday, I have a right to celebrate. 'Sides, you're high on pot half the time, so you don't have a say," Mitch said.

Grace put down her fork. The rich, moist cake turned to sawdust in her mouth.

She wished she hadn't said anything to him about wanting to stay. Now he was going to show her. She would lose everything, and it would be her own fault.

Twyla seemed to gather herself and instead of getting sucked into the fight, she smiled. "You know, I'd like to hear the story of Grace's birth on her birth anniversary."

"This ain't her birth anniversary, it's her fucking birthday, Twyla. Get a grip on reality for a change." Mitch set down the beer bottle he'd emptied and reached for the next.

"I want to hear it too," Grace said quickly. She met Twyla's eyes and silently pleaded with her to be her angel.

Mitch downed half the second beer in one big chug and belched loudly. This seemed to reestablish his dominance over them. "Your mom, Karen, and I were living on South Padre Island, Texas, in a sweet little trailer in the park at the beach. She bartended part time and sold her paintings to the tourists, while I worked the shrimp boats for local restaurants. We were an hour away from the nearest hospital over on the mainland in Harlingen, and Karen was so nervous she wouldn't get there in time that we made like three different trips for false alarms.

"Then one night her water broke, so it was the real deal. Off we went, and wouldn't you know, it was raining like a son of a bitch—I mean, you couldn't see your hand in front of your face—so I had to creep along, and it took like an extra hour to get there. Karen crying the whole way, thinking you was going to pop out in the middle of nowhere. So we got to the hospital and it still took her like ten hours to get you out. Karen was small like you, only taller, but with your narrow hips, not really made for childbearing. But finally, out you came—"

"You were there?" Grace said. "You saw me?"

"Hell, yes, I was your daddy, wasn't I? The nurse and the doctor were all saying how beautiful you were and Karen was crying out of happiness for once, but all I could think about when I saw you was a skinned squirrel. My daddy used to take me squirrel hunting when I was boy. It was all we had to live on sometimes. I was skinning squirrels by the time was eight."

"Did you wish I was a boy?" Grace asked.

"Naw. I didn't want to be outnumbered and have to keep the toilet seat down, but Karen wanted a girl, so I was okay with it," Mitch said. The second beer bottle was empty but before he could get up for more, Twyla handed him a slice of carrot cake and the small pot pipe she kept handy. He took a hit off the pipe and began to eat the cake. "Damn, this is good."

Grace felt herself begin to relax. She could taste her cake again.

Mitch found work bartending, which was like letting the rooster into the henhouse. He took up drinking again and lost his taste for pot.

Instead of loud sex beneath her room, Grace heard loud fights. It was Christmas vacation from school, over a month since her birthday and they were still there. Twyla, her angel, was looking exhausted and pale. She was seeing Madam Claudia frequently.

When Mitch was at work or doing god knew what, Grace found Twyla crying as she watered her plants, which were looking limp and a little brown around the edges. Grace figured it was all the bad vibes in the house or maybe that Twyla had no positive energy for them.

Grace went to her and led her by the hand to the sofa, where Twyla bent forward and cried loudly into her hands. Her brown hair flopped over her face and Grace realized there were little strands of gray hidden in there.

"I don't know what to do, Grace. I've tried everything. Mitch is just lost to me. He doesn't love me anymore. I think he's seeing other women. I can't live like this. I talked to my social worker friend about trying to keep you, but he said Mitch would have to agree to it and we both know he never would. I don't want to lose you. You are like my very own daughter, Grace. I love you that much." The pain in Twyla's face was almost more than Grace could bear.

"I love you too," Grace said, and put her arm around Twyla while she cried some more.

Then Grace realized the hardest truth she had ever known. It was her turn to be the angel. She had to stop hanging on to Twyla to save Twyla from Mitch. She heard this strange, strong voice come out of her. "You're too good for him, Twyla. Mitch was the best I've ever seen him with you. But he always goes back to being this Mitch. You have to let him go."

"But what about you? I'd lose you too. What will happen to you? Oh, Grace, this is so awful," Twyla said.

"I'll be okay. Mitch will never let me go until I'm old enough to be on my own. I had over six good months here and that's some kind of record, but this is what always happens. He thinks you won't throw him out because of me, so you have to do it anyway. He'll end up leaving as soon as he has a plan anyway. So be strong, Twyla. You have to tell him to leave. Please, I can't stand watching him hurt you like this." Grace swallowed her tears as fast as they tried to come.

"You'll write to me? I have to know you're okay. Maybe when you're older you could come back to me," Twyla said, hugging her tightly. "I'll always be right here."

Grace hugged her back and tried to imagine some future reunion with Twyla, but the fantasy evaporated like San Francisco fog in sunshine. Once people were lost to you, they were gone forever.

"Who do you live with?" Grace asks Gabe as Jackson walks them to the greenhouse. Turns out, on level one, she's allowed to go outside with staff. Jackson picked the two of them to accompany him to the greenhouse so he could check on a sick plant he brought from home to recuperate. Grace knows he chose them as a reward for their leadership in task group. The rest of the kids are doing homework during quiet time after school.

"I live with my mom. She always wanted a girl, so I'm a major disappointment, but she's pretty cool now. Things have gotten better between us once she gave up trying to talk me out of being a boy. I mean, I get it. She wanted a girl so she could take her shopping and paint her nails and curl her hair. I don't hold it against her. She's mostly over it."

The grounds are pretty amazing. Playgrounds, fountains, flowers, and all that green grass. A baseball diamond and field take up the northwest corner. A full basketball court is adjacent to the main walkway. Six cottages that look more like single-family homes, with the typical flat Albuquerque roofs, are in two clusters: the younger kids, starting around age three up to age ten, are in the south cluster of three cottages, and the older kids are housed in the three cottages at the north end, where her cottage, Brazos, sits. Kids are riding tricycles on the walkway that slopes to the south and have shade ramadas overhead in the middle section, with a low wall and bancos built into them.

Kids climb jungle gyms and play tag with ever-present staff. Tall cottonwoods provide crucial shade. Listening to the squeals and laughter, Grace can imagine she's attending some elite camp or expensive private school. Even the wall that surrounds the perimeter looks more ornamental than functional—it isn't any taller than Grace. The unobstructed view to the west is of the ancient, jagged volcanoes on the West Mesa. It looks like the earth falls away after that. The sky is pale and overbearing. The sun burns her scalp as they walk.

"I used to live with my dad, but that won't be happening anymore," Grace says. "I'll be eighteen in the fall. Then I can be on my own."

"Wish I could be on my own. Two more years until I'm eighteen, and then I can have my surgery," Gabe says. "Whenever I have it, I'm going to make that my new birthday."

They reach the greenhouse. With its pitched glass roof, Grace feels as if she's entering a temple. She deeply inhales the musky smell of fertile earth and the humid mist in the air. A dizzying perfusion of green erupts in all directions. The tiny, delicate, white flowers of baby's breath crowd around the stepping stones and in among other plants as if seeking shelter. Towering treelike plants heavy with pink blossoms larger than her head bob against the glass slant of the ceiling. Palms, banana trees, and various flowering vines claw their way toward the open panes of glass that allow sparrows to dart back and forth between contrasting climate zones. Fans circulate the tropical air and keep the temperature bearable.

Scattered droplets of moisture hang like jewels from leaf tips, and rust transforms a water spigot into an object of art. Water drips and taps out snatches of songs she can't quite place. Four long, waist-high wooden tables hold mounds of potting soil, terra-cotta pots, and potted plants in various stages of convalescence.

Jackson bends over a large Boston fern whose tips are brown and curled. "Grace, Gabe, meet Betsy. Betsy here has belonged to my mama for as long as I can remember. When Betsy started to die, my mama asked me to save her. I tried to ask her where did she see a green thumb on these black hands, but she had her mind made up. She said if I could help kids get better, I would do all right by Betsy."

He tenderly pinches off the dead pieces. "Lord, Mama, the faith you place in me can be a burden."

Gabe begins to play around in the dirt, using a hand rake, making zen-garden wavy lines and spirals. Grace thrusts her fingers into the black peat moss and kneads it like biscuit dough. She lifts her eyes to the rustle of the sparrows overhead and remembers the bird that had thought it was trapped in the abandoned gym, fluttering against the closed windows along the high ceiling. She'd watched that bird as she tied the rope around her neck. She almost died. As she watches the birds now, darting in and out, pausing to perch on green leaves and vines, she feels a surge of gratitude that she's still alive to breathe this pungent air, hear the chirping birds, and caress the earth between her fingers. She looks at Gabe and smiles, tears blurring her vision. He nods, as if he somehow knows what she's thinking, and smiles back. He asked her in that first task group if she was relieved or disappointed to have survived. She didn't know then. She knows now.

Jackson begins to hum a tune, and then with a deep and velvet tone, he sings, "Amazing grace, how sweet the sound . . ."

CHAPTER 4

AFTER THEY GET BACK to the cottage, Grace and Gabe get to hang out in the dayroom, and they decide to play Crazy Eights. Grace is shuffling a worn deck of cards and Jackson is sitting at the desk doing paperwork when the phone rings.

Jackson meets Grace's observing gaze while he speaks. "He's got some of her belongings? Who's this guy again?"

Realizing the call has to do with her, Grace abandons the cards and Gabe to join Jackson at the staff desk. She leans over the counter, the ledge above the long desk, the demarcation between the kids' space and out-of-bounds staff space. "Is my dad here?" she asks.

Jackson shakes his head no. "Do you know a Rudy Maestas?" he asks.

"That's my old neighbor. He's my friend."

"Would you like to see him? He's up in administration," Jackson says.

"Yes!" Grace can't believe it. Her sort-of adopted grandfather has tracked her down.

"Tell him we'll be right up." Jackson waves to the oncoming evening staff planning their shift in the kitchen to come out and cover the desk. The halls are quiet; half of the kids are probably asleep instead of doing their homework. Gabe deals himself a hand of solitaire.

Grace fidgets while Jackson unlocks the cottage door. Once outside, Jackson asks, "So this man was your neighbor?"

"Rudy lived next door to me and my dad. He's a retired firefighter and really nice. He used to wait outside in his lawn chair for me to get home from work at night. He's more like my grandpa. He has some of my stuff?"

"I guess he took a box of your stuff to the main hospital—your dad had told him you were there before he left. Patient information services sent him over here."

The administration building houses the public entrance to the place, where visitors have to check in and be cleared and escorted if they are going beyond that point. Dr. Swenson's office is upstairs, along with group therapy rooms and other therapist's offices. On the main floor are conference rooms, the staff lounge, medical records, and the front lobby, which is where Grace and Jackson meet up with Rudy. He stands with his back to Grace, examining some of the framed Southwest-themed paintings on the walls.

"Rudy!" Grace puts her arms out for a hug. He turns and grins in what looks like relief and gives her a big hug.

"Mi'ja, it's so good to see you," he says, holding her out to look her over. Rudy is not much taller than Grace.

"I'm Jackson, Mr. Maestas. I work with Grace here. I understand you're a friend of hers." Jackson towers over him. "Why don't we have a seat?" He motions to the sofa and chairs that are arranged as if they are in someone's living room. Tall potted plants and the artwork complete the homey vibe the staff seem to be attempting.

Grace sits next to Rudy on the sofa and sees he has brought a box, and leaning against the box is her art portfolio. Her stomach lurches.

"How did you get my stuff?" Grace asks.

Rudy begins with a huge sigh. "That last day of school, the cops came looking for your dad. I thought he was maybe in some kind of trouble, you know, but they came to tell him you'd been taken to the hospital. So off he went. When he got back, it was during the ten o'clock news, he banged on my door and told me he and that woman were leaving for Florida and to take whatever I wanted from the apartment. He gave me the key to give to the landlord. I asked him what about his deposit and he said the landlord would probably keep it since he wasn't cleaning the place. I said, 'But what about Grace?' And he goes, 'She doesn't want to come, so she's on her own now.' I could tell he was very drunk." Rudy shakes his head.

"Sounds like Mitch." Grace feels every muscle clench. She feels Jackson's eyes on her, gauging her reaction. She blows out a breath and tries to calm herself.

"Mi'ja, he told me what you did. I was so sad to know how hopeless you must have felt. I wish you could have come to me. I've been kicking myself that when I saw things falling apart, I didn't reach out to you."

"No, Rudy, don't blame yourself. It was a lot of things, but I'm not thinking like that anymore. I don't care about Mitch leaving—I'm glad to be rid of him. I'm in a good place and I'm going to be fine." Grace tries to look strong even as tears prickle behind her eyes.

"I went over to your place the next day after they left and what a mess! I was cleaning up and then I called my son and we loaded up the furniture and kitchen stuff and sold what we could at the flea market that next Saturday and donated the rest. We made one hundred eighty-five dollars, so I wanted to give you that money along with the things I brought from your room," Rudy says, digging for his wallet.

"No, no, you keep the money, Rudy, for all your trouble. I don't need any money here. But I'm glad you saved my stuff. Mitch only brought me some dirty clothes in a garbage bag."

"I could never toss out your beautiful paintings, and I knew you'd want your art supplies and those pictures of your friends. I'm just glad I was able to find you and that you're okay. It's a huge load off my mind. I've been so worried about you. Can't I give you some spending money at least?"

"She's right that she doesn't need any money while she's here. But, sir, if you'd like, I could see about getting you on the visitor list, since Grace doesn't have any family here," Jackson says. "And if you have a phone number, I could keep that for Grace when she has phone privileges."

"I would like to stay in touch, but that's up to Grace. Maybe she doesn't want some viejito coming around." Rudy smiles.

"Of course I do," Grace says. "Can you give him the Brazos phone number too?"

After exchanging phone numbers with Rudy, Jackson turns to Grace. "We need to get you back to the cottage for dinner, so you and Rudy can say good-bye for now."

This time Rudy initiates the hug and Grace holds on tight. What is it about the contact of a caring human body that feels so necessary, so essential? It's been so long it's hard for Grace to let go.

Jackson shakes Rudy's hand. "Thank you for coming, Mr. Maestas. I'll be in touch."

Grace watches him leave through the double doors that separate the real world from this place. She's happy to be on this side of them.

Grace, Age 15

Phoenix, Arizona

For the last few years, Grace had lived in Oakland—Mitch's flight from Twyla took them only over the bridge. Then three moves within that sprawling place with new schools each time—and then San Diego, where Mitch worked on the docks and she had four months of stability in a good school. A fistfight ended that job and Mitch moved them to Chula Vista, where he hung on to a bartending job for half the year while Grace was pestered by Hispanic kids who took issue with a blond girl invading their school.

After Mitch was caught pocketing some "tip" money from the cash register at the bar, they landed in Phoenix, where she completed the eighth grade while Mitch worked in a Mexican restaurant. When Mitch fell behind on the rent of their crap efficiency, a guy at his work said they could move in with him and his old lady.

Felix was a schemer like Mitch—Grace knew it as soon as she met him at the restaurant and he wouldn't make eye contact. His weasel eyes darted around just like Mitch's did when he was trying to pull one over on her.

Mitch had picked up a few tattoos along the way, but Felix had made a religion out of it. She'd seen guys like this before and had decided there was a mathematical correlation between the number of tattoos guys had and how messed up they were—but then, if that were true, Mitch should be covered in ink, so maybe she shouldn't judge Felix on that assumption. But she could judge him on his fake niceness and weasel eyes. She stood in front of his door with all of her worldly possessions in a garbage bag, feeling doomed that she would be at the mercy of this joker.

"Now don't expect nothing fancy," Felix said. "I got three kids, and you know what that does to a place. And Loretta, she gets these awful bad headaches that keep her in bed a lot."

"Grace and I are just grateful to have a roof over our heads. She can help out around the house—she's good at that stuff—and now with school being out, she can help watch the kids, too," Mitch said.

Grace shot him a death glare, which he ignored. She knew before they got to the decrepit building that it was going to be bad, but this was the worst she'd ever seen. It was four flights up with no working elevator. The sounds (yelling and loud music) and smells (urine and burning onions) along the dark corridor assaulted her. As Felix strode ahead to apartment 417 to "warn the old lady," Grace kicked the back of Mitch's calf to get his attention.

"Let's go somewhere else," Grace said.

"It's just for a little while till I figure out something better. Don't be ungrateful." Mitch strode even faster so that Grace had to scamper to keep up, the slippery garbage bag heavy and sweaty in her arms, but she didn't dare set it down. At least she'd gotten her hepatitis shots at school this year, but she knew from health class that a myriad of other diseases had to be flourishing along this bare cement hallway. Profane pictures and unintelligible graffiti adorned the walls. "Once we get inside the apartment, it'll be better," Mitch said, sounding about as confident as she was.

Felix stood by his open door, in full weasel. "Come in. Mi casa es su casa."

Mitch led the way, his own garbage bag catching on the doorjamb on the way inside.

"We only got the two bedrooms, so Mitch you can have the couch, and Grace, you can bunk with the kids," Felix said. "Loretta says welcome, but she's suffering with her head."

The kitchen and living room were combined into one chaotic heap. Stacked dishes and crusted pots and pans obliterated the sink and countertops and spilled out onto every available surface. Well-fed cockroaches brazenly held their ground in broad daylight. A television with a rolling picture yammered in the far corner. Mitch's couch held the three kids, who looked in their direction with curiosity.

"My big girl is Juanita—she's five already. She'll be in kindergarten next fall. Then comes my boy, Oscar, who's three, and our baby, Tina, for Cristina, who's nearly two," Felix said.

Grace's every instinct told her to run, just to turn around and run like hell out of there. Within thirty seconds, she knew what she was in for. The piles of liquor bottles told her Loretta was a drunk, not suffering from some other malady of the head. The filth and the half-naked, runny-nosed, tangled-haired kids told her told her the rest of the story. And she was supposed to help? It would take a team of social workers and medical experts to sort this mess out. And one of those cleaning companies that specialized in crime scenes with hazmat suits and industrial chemicals.

"Well, hi there," Mitch was saying, his game face on.

Felix dropped his plastic bag full of cartons of scavenged restaurant food onto the couch and the children dove for it like dogs. "Save some for our guests! Don't be so greedy!" Felix smiled watching them.

"My shift starts pretty soon, Grace, so get yourself settled in, and I'll be back later," Mitch said, dropping his garbage bag near the end of his couch. To Felix, he said, "Tell Loretta thanks and hope she feels better."

Grace watched Mitch make a break for it and felt a whole new layer of hatred form in her heart.

"Grace, the bedroom is just through there; bathroom on the right," Felix said. "I'm going in to tend to Loretta. Get some food before those little rats get it all."

The food cartons were being eviscerated by a blur of scooping hands, refried beans and shredded lettuce coating their fingers, the plastic-wrapped utensils cast aside. Any hunger she might have felt was soundly squelched. If the figurative rats didn't eat it all, she had no doubt that literal rats would finish it off later.

The bedroom was exactly what she expected. A full-size mattress on the floor, topped with soiled sheets, took up most of the space. A plastic wastebasket overflowing with dirty diapers lodged in the corner. Some broken toys and tattered paper obliterated the floor. The stench from the diapers was thick. Large black flies buzzed over them in a territorial display.

The closet floor was strewn with clothes, and some bare metal hangers hung on the rod. She'd start there. She hung up her clothes and stacked the rest on the top shelf above the rod, where the kids couldn't reach. Grace could take a lot, but she couldn't take filth. She stripped the bed and pillows and gathered up the kids' soiled clothing from the floor and put it into her garbage bag. She had a pocket of quarters from Mitch's tips. She'd seen a sign for a laundry room on the bottom floor.

She went to Felix and Loretta's shut door. "Hello?"

Felix came to the door, the scent of marijuana wafting through the small slit he'd opened. "Huh?"

"I'm cleaning up. Where do I put the dirty diapers? Do you have trash bags?"

"Try under the sink," he said and shut the door.

Grace felt her anger give her a full head of steam. She found a few garbage bags under the sink and filled them with the diapers and other trash. She found a glorious can of Lysol and sprayed every surface. "Juanita, take Oscar and go pick up your toys—now!"

"What are you doing?" Juanita asked.

"It's cleanup time. Do you ever see houses look like this on TV?" Grace asked her, madly dumping an armful of dishes onto the already full table with a satisfying crash.

"No," Juanita said, and grabbed Oscar by the hand and led him to their room. Baby Tina sucked her fist.

Four hours later, Grace had done four loads of laundry, including the towels she found on the bathroom floor. Gagging uncontrollably, she had scrubbed the toilet, tub, and sink with bleach she found easily accessible to the children on the kitchen floor. The kids' meager clothes, frayed and faded but at least now clean, were sorted and stacked into the drawers of the broken-down dresser in their room. The mattress was made up with fresh sheets. She'd washed piles of dishes but had barely made a dent. At least the rest could now be stacked next to the sink for tomorrow. The living room was cleared out. She'd taken countless trips to the dumpster outside. The refrigerator was cleared of rotting food and washed with hot, sudsy water. Miraculously, a jug of unexpired milk was there to make Tina her bottle. Grace figured Tina was old enough to drink it cold. She changed her diaper, noting Tina's blistered diaper rash as she wiped her as well as she could with toilet paper and then applied some Vaseline she had in her makeup bag. Tina whimpered softly when Grace dabbed at her raw, open flesh. She added baby wipes to the grocery list she was making for Mitch. And rubber gloves for her own cracked and bleeding knuckles.

That night she brushed her teeth with her own toothpaste and settled onto the mattress, where the three kids were already in a heap. Her legs ached from all of those trips up and down the stairs. Her back throbbed from all the bending and lifting. The fight was out of her. All she could think about was how happy she was that the air conditioning worked, especially as three warm bodies gravitated to her in the dark.

Grace soon realized she was the only one who was trying to keep up the apartment. She tried to enlist the others by stating a few commonsense rules like, if you get something out, put it back. If it's trash, it goes in the trash bag. If it's a dirty dish, rinse it and put it in the sink. Mitch took her aside and said she was being a bitch and to knock it off, that they weren't paying rent and she shouldn't mind a little housekeeping. So it was a constant and exhausting battle to keep the place livable, let alone tend to the children that the adults seemed to think required less care than potted plants.

Loretta made a few appearances over the following days, usually on her way to the kitchen for a cold beer. She was skinny and moved like a spider. Long dark hair obscured most of her angular face. The kids would mob her and she would coo to them, kiss their heads, and then peel them off her before returning to her sanctuary. They never tried to go with her.

Grace felt sorry enough for them that she willingly gave them her attention. Chatting endlessly while coloring with Juanita (with the same five broken crayons), stacking blocks so that Oscar could knock them down. Rocking Tina in her arms and blowing raspberries onto her tummy when she changed her diapers. She put the dirty diapers into plastic bags and took them downstairs to the trash bin at least twice a day to control the odor. She was caught up with the dishes and had thoroughly bleached the kitchen. Loretta seemed oblivious. Felix thanked her, at least, even as he eyed her with suspicion. When she realized Mitch took it as a sign she was on board with the arrangement, she pulled him into her room.

"Get me out of here," she said. "I am not these people's maid and nanny."

"You're being real good about it, Grace, I give you that. It won't be long. But see, here's the deal. Felix has an inside connection with a trainer at the dog tracks. And, well, without going into details, we're supplying this guy with this stuff that makes the dogs run faster, see, and then he'll rig a few races and we'll all make out big-time."

"You're into dog doping? That's illegal."

"This stuff is so space age, they can't even test for it. This EPO stuff, all it does is help the dogs make more red blood cells—so, see, it helps the dogs—it don't hurt them. Those dogs love to run, they're made for it. So we have a big payday coming like next month and all we have to do is sit tight and cash in. Easy-peasy."

"I can't do this for a month," Grace said. "Loretta is some kind of drunk or drug addict and she neglects those kids. You and Felix are never here. I have to do everything. Those kids wouldn't eat or get bathed without me! Let alone get any attention. You saw how this place was when we got here."

"Look, Grace. I wouldn't ask you if it wasn't a sure thing. We're going to end up with thousands of dollars out of this deal and I'll take you wherever you want to go. Just think about what an important thing you're doing for those kids. Don't that make you feel good?"

"It'll all go to hell again once we're gone, so what's the point?" Grace tried to search his dark eyes for the conscience she hoped was in there somewhere.

"Maybe it won't. Felix will get thousands too, and he said it's all to give his family a fresh start. He said Loretta is depressed and he knows if he can bring home major cash, she'll snap out of it and they'll move out of this dump and give the kids the life they deserve."

"Felix said that." Grace watched for Mitch's tell, the sign he was lying.

When he lied, his right eyebrow always twitched until he rubbed it with his thumb. His right eyebrow nearly jumped off his forehead until he smoothed it down. "Trust me, Grace. This whole deal is for those sweet babies. He's a good friend to cut me in on it."

"Okay," she said. "Here are my conditions. You and Felix buy me anything I need to take care of this place and the kids, and that includes real food. And most important—you have to give me one week's notice before this payday is going down and we leave as soon as you get your money. Deal?"

When the one-week warning came, Grace felt guilty. For her plan to work she had to stop doing everything. She feigned a right-arm injury, tying her forearm up in a makeshift sling. She let dirty dishes sit where they were abandoned. The diapers piled up and the flies returned. Dirty laundry stayed strewn on the floor. Food rotted on the kitchen counter. Within the week, the place was nearly as bad as when they first arrived.

It broke her heart when Juanita asked, "Why aren't you taking care of us anymore?"

"My arm won't work, so I can't," Grace said, feeling her own eyebrow twitch. "But I can still read you a story. Get one of the library books and I'll read to you guys." She had taken them on the bus to a nearby library a few times, and she could tell Juanita was really bright and could do well if she had half a chance. And that was what Grace was trying to give her before she left, but she couldn't tell Juanita that.

No one else seemed to notice or care that they were living in squalor once more, and they all bought her story of the strained elbow and that she needed to rest it for it to get well. But she didn't let the kids go hungry and she tended Tina's bottom to ward off any more diaper rash now that she had finally healed. She sang to them and loved them as well as she could. Even Oscar was hugging her and had started to talk a little. He loved books about farmers and tractors.

The timing of her plan was the part she worried about.

"So today's the day," Mitch said, his face flushed from excitement and a slight beer buzz. "Felix and I go place our bets and—bingo! Big wins on fifty-to-one odds."

"You're sure . . . nothing can go wrong? And we leave tonight?"

"Whatever you say, Grace. I was thinking Denver—somewhere not so damn hot."

"All right. Get your stuff ready, Mitch, I mean it. We're leaving tonight, no matter what happens at the track."

She made the call from a pay phone on the corner and spoke with three different people from the Arizona Department of Child Safety. She described the conditions, gave all the names and ages, and the address, and ended up crying. "You have to promise me you'll get those kids out of there! I'm the only one feeding and changing them and taking care of them and I have to leave! So they'll have no one! You have to come quick! And don't believe anything the parents tell you—they just drink and do drugs and hole up in their bedroom, leaving those kids to rot!"

By the time she'd gone through it again with some manager, she got her promise that they'd keep the siblings together and would swoop in to get them that night.

When Mitch and Felix returned from the track around dinnertime, Grace was shaking with nerves.

"What the fuck happened?" Mitch kept asking Felix.

"How do I know? We gave him the shit—the dogs were supposed to be doped and ready. I'll call him and see what's up," Felix said.

"What's up is we lost! We put it all on those dogs and they crapped out!" Mitch paced across the garbage-strewn floor, kicking at trash with his boot, his ponytail bouncing against his brawny back. Grace had never seen him get violent, but he looked close now and she was sure he could snap Felix like a twig if he had a mind to. Felix seemed to come to the same conclusion, and disappeared into his room.

Grace placed herself in front of Mitch. "I need to talk to you."

"Not now, Grace," Mitch said.

She grabbed his wrist and said, "Now! Unless you want to get arrested."

Mitch stopped. Tina was crying and hugging her leg. Juanita and Oscar were wrestling on the floor in their food-caked clothes. Loretta and Felix were ensconced in their room, the fog of marijuana smoke rolling out from under the ill-fitting door. Grace whispered, "I called child services on them and they're coming tonight. We have to leave right now."

"You did what?" Mitch looked uncomprehending.

"They don't deserve these kids! I'm getting them busted and the kids will go to a foster family. Anywhere has got to be better for them than this. You promised, Mitch. So we have to go now." Grace lifted Tina and kissed her teary, snotty cheeks. She gave Juanita and Oscar a hug and told them not to be afraid, that everything was going to be all right. They stopped their wrestling and watched her with grave expressions. She grabbed her garbage bag of belongings. Mitch finally snapped out of it and grabbed his garbage bag.

"What am I supposed to tell Felix?" Mitch said as they reached the door.

"Nothing! It's over. We're done here." Grace flung open the door, trying to ignore Tina's fresh wailing.

Mitch hurried to catch her as she all but sprinted down the corridor to the stairs. "I bet you didn't even really hurt your arm."

"You think?" At least that was a bet he could have won.

Midway down the second flight, they passed them. Two cops and three women in suits. They looked tough but kind. She had to stop herself from telling them Tina liked to be rocked and sung to and that Oscar really could talk, it just took him a while to warm up, and that Juanita was the smartest little five-year-old there was. Instead, she kept her head down and muttered hi when they said hi, and hoped they took her and Mitch for tenants taking out their trash.

They passed a squad car with lights still strobing, parked in the tow-away zone. A DCS van, with three car seats in the back, was parked next to it. When Mitch and Grace reached their truck, they sat in it, watching.

Before long, the women emerged with the kids. Juanita was holding the hand of one of them and Oscar and Tina were being carried. Grace saw they weren't crying. Each was holding a new stuffed teddy bear. She smiled even as tears filled her own eyes.

"Felix loves those kids, they both do," Mitch said.

"It didn't look like love to me." Grace watched the van pull out and head up the street toward something better.

After a few more minutes, the cops escorted Felix and Loretta, both in handcuffs, to the squad car, Loretta's first time outdoors in who knew how long. Their expressions were resigned.

"I bet they know who made the call," Mitch said.

"I hope so," Grace said.

"What if somebody had called about you? Huh? Turned me in for being a bad father?"

What if? She imagined the possibilities all the way to Denver.

Maddie laces her shoes for PE, and even though it's been three days since she punched the wall, her hand still hurts like hell. She was stupid for using her dominant one. She'll be embarrassed for Coach Pacheco, the PE teacher, to see what she did to herself. Once he sees the taped injury on her hand, he'll have her walking the track during class. He's a handsome Hispanic man with no body fat and no chest, arm, or leg hair. He's kind of a hard ass, having previously worked at Springer, the juvenile prison where Abdias would be going.

Maddie's ashamed for losing it and hurting herself, but it's still easier to blame Jeffrey or Lesley or her dad. Sharon has been working with her on other ways to express her anger. Hurting herself is not the answer, but neither is keeping everything stuffed inside. Her feelings are sacred, Sharon says, but her behavior is a choice. And Grace is right—Maddie has been continuing Jeffrey's victimization of her, and being his accomplice is the last thing she wants. Will she ever be free of him? Will it always be this hard to stay in control? When Sharon suggested she punch a pillow next time, Maddie had to face the fact that she chose the wall precisely for the damage it would inflict.

Coach marches the group outside. Judy and their teacher, Mr. Zamora, take up the rear to sit under the trees next to the huge orange thermos of water they pull in a wagon.

Tough kids always talk about how easy it would be to jump the wall around the grounds, but like staff say, this place is not a prison. Maddie knows that now. She knew imprisonment, and has never felt more emancipated than she does here. Kids who want help stay and work the program. Sharon says everyone's on a path and all staff can do is try their hardest to reach them, but if kids won't accept their help, all the staff can do is let them continue on their chosen path. Those kids jump the wall.

Abdias, Lucas, and Aaron run to the stacked baseball bats and start swinging them wildly, as Gabe, Grace, and Maddie try to stay out of their way. Percy stops to study a squirrel who studies him. Coach redirects them, which in his case includes some yelling.

Judy taps Maddie on the shoulder. "Dr. Swenson wants you for therapy. She's up on the basketball court. I'll watch you go from here."

"Lucky," Grace says. Maddie strides up the shallow hill to the basketball court.

"There's someone here I'd like you to meet," says Dr. Swenson.

When they enter Dr. Swenson's office, a tall Black woman stands. "This is Detective Davis. She works for the Crimes Against Children unit of the police department."

"How do you do, Maddie?" the woman says. "I've been assigned to your case."

"Already?"

"I told you I called the Children, Youth and Families Department after your disclosure. Since you're safe in the hospital and your offender is in Massachusetts, you're not a high priority right now, so I called in a favor and got Detective Davis to take your case right away."

"I'm going to do everything I can to bring your offender to justice," Detective Davis says. There's a look in her eyes that conveys a motivation beyond Maddie's own revenge. Perhaps she's another former mistreated and broken child. "And you can call me Lucille." Her smile is warm and bright, with white teeth like on toothpaste commercials. She wears a black suit over a white T-shirt with a gold badge clipped to her belt.

Even the *possibility* that Jeffrey will have to pay for what he did to her is thrilling.

"We'll set up a time when I can interview you, fill out the paperwork, and explain the process. You had your interview with S.A.F.E. House?"

"Yes." S.A.F.E. House is a place where kids' disclosures are filmed and often used later in court, sparing them from having to testify in person and face their abusers. Her filmed testimony against Jeffrey stretched over an hour.

"Your case might take a while," Lucille says. "There're some obstacles to get past—but I was a pole vaulter in college." She smiles but the look in her eye is fierce. "I never give up."

Maddie hopes to see that mama lioness look in her own mother's eyes someday. "Get him."

Maddie, Age 11

Old Town, Albuquerque, New Mexico

Maddie tried to decorate their Christmas tree as pretty as the trees in the shop windows in Old Town, even if nobody else saw it but her dad, Otilia, Mimi, and Hector. At eleven, she knew there wasn't a Santa Claus, even though her presents under the tree were signed from him. Dad didn't want to admit she was growing up. Funny, because in her eyes, she took care of him now as much as he took care of her. She didn't know what he would do without her.

Now that she was eleven, Dad let her help more in the gallery, assisting customers, and in his jewelry studio, where he taught her basic techniques working with certain metals. She wasn't allowed to use the blowtorch yet, but with her hair tied back and her safety glasses on, she was allowed to watch while he worked. He let her design a special ornament to hang on the tree, even letting her pick which gemstone to put on it. She loved holding a handful of stones, imagining she could feel the unique vibrations in each one. It was kind of like believing in God: you had to trust something was there. She chose a green topaz. Green because it was Christmas and topaz because Dad said it helps bring peace and forgiveness. It now graced a punched tin star she crafted herself. She placed it at the top of the tree.

Christmas Eve and the sun was setting. Old Town was crowded with people shopping, eating, and enjoying the luminarias lit and lining streets and sidewalks. Amazing that a candle glowing inside of a paper bag could look so magical. At San Felipe church, luminarias lined the bancos, ledges, walls, and roof. White twinkling Christmas lights wound around every-thing in the plaza. Maddie still found it breathtaking.

From her balcony she could see the large Jewish star and the cross formed by luminarias on the plaza. On the sidewalk underneath her, someone was selling tamales. The smell of them made her wish her dad would get home from running errands so they could eat. She left the posole simmering on the stove. Otilia had helped her make it, demonstrating how to grind the red chiles that were so hot they burned her eyes and made her cough.

Maddie watched as a man proposed to his girlfriend, down on one knee, in front of the Old Town Christmas tree. He placed the ring on her finger. The woman hung onto his neck and kicked wildly, a fairy tale unfolding in front of her eyes.

She didn't think about boys much yet. No eleven-year-old boy in her class looked like Prince Charming. Most of the other girls thought about boys all the time and were wearing makeup and clothes they must have thought were sexy. She thought they were nuts. Dad said using the words *sexy* and *eleven-year-old* in the same sentence was sick. He didn't want her to have those girls as friends, so she didn't really have any friends except for him, her teddy bear, and her Old Town family. But that was enough. It has always been just the two of them.

Even after she came inside, she could smell the piñon smoke from the fireplaces in the neighborhood. Maddie stacked a few piñon logs in their kiva fireplace and lit them using bunched-up newspapers. People traveled from all over to experience this enchanting night in Old Town. As royalty, of course, she had box seats.

She heard the jingle of her dad's keys outside the door and flung herself across the room to open it. "Joyeux Noël!"

"Oh my god, Maddie. The place looks great," he said. With the radiant tree, roaring fireplace, about fifty lit candles, and the glow from the plaza streaming through their windows, she was able to switch off all the lamps.

She took his coat and hung it on the rack, along with the wool scarf she knitted him last Christmas. It was red and white striped, like something a Dr. Seuss character would wear, because he was always so silly. He didn't seem to have any last-minute presents with him—maybe in his pocket?

"Sorry I'm late. It was crazy trying to get home through the traffic and crowds," he said, walking to the windows at the balcony. "Mmm, smells good."

"I made posole. It's hot as in spicy hot. Not sure you're man enough," she said.

He laughed, but more in a nervous way. Maybe he was still recovering from the crowds. He stood quietly for a while, his arms crossed, staring out the window. He hadn't even wished her a "Joyeux Noël" back.

They both ate buttered tortillas and honey with the posole to help thwart the fire in their mouths. Afterward he brought some chilled white wine to the table with two glasses. He poured himself a glass and just a taste for her.

"Before we toast, we need to talk," he said.

She swirled the light pee-colored wine in her glass, giving it a sniff. "Sure." Probably one of his end-of-the-year speeches about feeling grateful for all they had and the life they shared.

"You're going to be twelve in the new year, almost a teenager. Your life will start to change. You'll make friends, have new interests. . . . what I'm trying to say is you won't need your old dad around as much." He uncharacteristically chugged his wine.

She couldn't imagine where this was going. Of course she would always need him. They were a team in perfect sync with each other. Besides, he'd be lost without her. Couldn't they just bask in the spirit of Christmas Eve? "Okay . . ."

"Maddie, I'm just going to say it. I've met someone."

It felt like a kick to her stomach. "Met someone? Who? Have you asked her out? How did you meet her?"

"We're getting engaged next week on New Year's Eve. I know this is sudden, but I wanted to be sure she'd say yes before I told you."

"How . . . wait a minute, what?" Her heart squeezed tight. She thought about the newly engaged woman hanging on her boyfriend, legs kicking. But this was no fairy tale.

"Her name is Lesley. She's a widow and she's a real good person. She has a ranch in Corrales with horses and a big house. You'll love it there."

"Move from here? What about Mom? This is where she knows to come find us. And Otilia? Mimi? Hector? We can't leave them."

"Maddie, honey, your mother isn't coming back. Remember, she and I were never married. For all we know, she could be happily married in France somewhere. We haven't even gotten a postcard in years. I've held vigil long enough. I'll always love her for giving me you, but I'm forty and deserve to move on. And it's not like you'll never see Otilia or Mimi or Hector again. We'll still have the gallery. You can visit anytime. Corrales is just ten or twelve miles up the road."

"I can't believe this. You're ruining my life." Her eyes stung with tears as hot as the posole.

"I can give you a better life this way. You'll have a bigger room, and your own horse. Imagine taking riding lessons. This could be a dream come true if you only let it. You'll like Lesley, I promise. We'll come to Old Town all the time, you'll see. It'll be the best of both worlds. Lesley is so excited to have a daughter."

Maddie didn't want to be anyone else's daughter. She felt her lip curl. She had a mother somewhere and would not give up that dream, even if her dad had. She looked around at the perfection of her world and what this meant. No more Christmas Eves on the balcony. No more French lessons with Mimi. Or eating Otilia's cooking. She had never shared her dad with anyone. All his evening "appointments" the past few months, getting later and later, now made sense. She'd been sharing him all along.

"I want you to meet her. I told her we'd come out tomorrow for Christmas dinner. I love you, Maddie. Nothing will change that. But I love Lesley too. Please give this a chance. It would be the best Christmas present you could ever give me."

Maddie thought the new pocketknife would be the best present ever. But she loved him and wanted him to be happy, even if she wasn't. He had made her years on earth happy when he wasn't. Deep down she knew that. She was old enough now to let go of her childish selfishness. Even though that child went kicking and screaming. She picked up her wine glass for their last Christmas Eve toast in her kingdom. She had been dethroned. Quick as the blade of a French guillotine, her life changed. She wanted to down her wine in one shot for courage. Normally they would raise a glass to her mother, wherever she was, and wish her back into their lives. But they didn't share that dream anymore and it was breaking her heart. The outdoor lights and festive crowd offended her now. Still, she forced a smile for him. "To our new life."

"C'mon, Maddie. Wake up, we have to get going," her dad said, startling her awake. She had been up most of the night, bundled up on the balcony and finishing off what was left in the wine bottle after he had gone to bed. Oh god. It was coming back to her. Lesley. She put the pillow over her face to smother herself.

She was not in the mood to dress to impress. Even though she had a closet full of great clothes, she put on her raggedy jeans with the holes at the knees, her dad's Grateful Dead Lithuania basketball team T-shirt that ended up too small for him, and the Native-print wool Pendleton coat Hector's son outgrew.

Her dad was perky around the breakfast table, humming and making coffee in his new espresso machine, which he'd said a client had given him. At the time, she had thought it was awfully expensive to be a gift from a client. But he looked so happy, and even younger somehow, like an eager kid on Christmas morning. This Lesley person had better treat him right. Espresso machines didn't impress her one bit.

"Isn't it beautiful out here? More space and everything's spread out, and look at that view of the mountains. Not like cramped, closed-in Old Town, huh?" Dad said, driving up Rio Grande through the North Valley. "Maybe the bison will be out at that ranch up ahead."

"Maybe they'll be wearing Santa hats," she said, looking out the window. The cottonwood trees were bare, the grasses dead; what was so beautiful about this place? So what if the houses were big and spaced far apart, with white rail fences dividing their pastures.

They turned right off of Alameda onto Corrales Road. They passed a winery, and a handmade furniture shop tucked in among all the natural landscape. The road opened up to a little more activity: a quick mart, a post office and a gas station. Dad stopped there to make a call to Lesley to announce they were a few minutes away. Maddie fished around in her bag for enough change to buy a Coke to settle her stomach. The wine had been a bad idea. She wanted to get the whole thing over with as quickly as possible. It wasn't as if they were getting married any time soon; maybe it wouldn't even happen.

Lesley's driveway was long and winding, so Maddie couldn't see the house from the main road. When the property finally came into view, she had to admit it was awesome, but she was not going to let Dad know that. A big barn and corral with four grazing horses came into view. Which one would be hers? If she had a choice, she wanted the white one. He'd be perfect with wings. She could fly him away from there.

They parked next to a shiny new Range Rover in front of a big hacienda, the kind movie stars had. She didn't realize Lesley was that kind of rich. A peacock honked and glided down from a tall cottonwood to land right in front of them, spreading its tail feathers like on NBC.

Dad started up the walkway, Maddie taking her time behind him. She thought of Anne Boleyn and her final steps, each one taking her closer to the guillotine.

"Michael! And this must be Maddie," a woman said, bounding out to meet them. She was tall and lanky. Not how Maddie imagined her. She looked older than Dad by a few years, or maybe it was from being out in the sun riding her horses. She had on jeans and riding boots. A long, thick blond braid hung over one shoulder. Her tan face smiled. "I'm so happy to meet you, Maddie," she said, extending her hand. "I'm Lesley. Welcome. Merry Christmas."

Lesley's handshake was firm and confident. Dad gave Lesley a kiss on the cheek and nervously bounced in place holding the presents he had brought.

"Merry Christmas," Maddie said, managing to smile. Lesley didn't seem too bad.

In the distance Maddie heard what sounded like a motorcycle. It was getting closer. She could see a cloud of dust like the Tasmanian Devil coming up the long drive. It was a quad ATV. When was this maniac going to slow down? It skidded to a stop sideways, spewing gravel on them.

The maniac took off his helmet. He was only a teenager.

"Jeffrey! I'm going to take the damn thing away from you! Apologize," Lesley told him.

Maddie gave her dad a nasty look for not telling her there was a Jeffrey involved. Obviously, this was Lesley's son.

"Sorry about that. I just got it for Christmas and I'm not used to it yet." He shook his dark-blond hair and it landed in the same style Leonardo DiCaprio wore in *Titanic*. "Hi, Michael," he said, shaking Dad's hand.

"Jeffrey, this is my daughter, Maddie. Maddie, this is Jeffrey," Dad said.

So Jeffrey knew Dad, and Maddie had been the only one kept in the dark. She waved an embarrassed hello.

"Cool T-shirt," he said.

"Thanks." She supposed the girls at school would call this guy a hunk. She would not go that far, but he caused her to be at a loss for words when she met his castle-gray eyes.

"Jeffrey attends the Academy and is an honor student. A perfect GPA." Lesley beamed at her son.

"Maddie gets good grades too. She's above grade level in everything," Dad said.

"What are you, like, in fifth or sixth grade?" Jeffrey said, with an amused sniff. "High school is when it gets real."

"Yeah, well don't break your arm patting yourself on the back," she blurted before she had time to think. Damn, she was always doing that. He gave her a sneer.

As they headed into the house, Maddie wasn't positive, but she thought Jeffrey tripped her on purpose. She stumbled and heard him mumble, "Klutz."

Maddie reluctantly agrees with Dr. Swenson to be patient with her dad. Telling him about the detective's visit and the investigation will be enough for now, and it will show him that complete strangers believe her. Dr. Swenson says her dad needs time to face such hard truths and their consequences. Her father's weakness makes her doubt he will ever be there for her. He chose Lesley, and how can family therapy change that?

In their very first encounter, Dr. Swenson told Maddie she believed her. Dr. Swenson's validation feels as soothing as the salve Sharon puts on her torn knuckles. Maddie sees her own anguish reflected in Dr. Swenson's eyes when she tells her the details of Jeffrey's abuse in individual therapy. The power of Dr. Swenson's compassion, the effect it has on her, is staggering.

"Mr. Stuart, I know that you've raised Maddie as a single parent since she was six weeks old, but can we talk about the circumstances that led up to that situation?" asks Dr. Swenson.

"You can call me Michael. Maddie's mother and I met and I fell in love. She loved me, in her way, but she told me right off that she had a gypsy spirit and travels all over the world and has never stayed in one place very long. She told me to live in the moment with her and not think about the future. So I did, because that was the only way I could be with her. Then she found out she was pregnant. I convinced her to carry the baby to term, which wasn't easy for her because it meant staying longer than she wanted. I got Renée to agree that after the baby was born, she would help care for her the first six weeks and then leave if she still wanted to. I thought she'd change her mind once she held Maddie in her arms, but she didn't. She couldn't wait to leave."

"That must have been devastating for you," says Dr. Swenson.

"I had Maddie. My world became about her. Believe me, she didn't give me time to feel sorry for myself."

Maddie is taken aback. She never considered her dad's feelings or what he went through.

"What did you tell Maddie about her mother?"

He blushes and shrugs. "I told her that her mother was a gypsy queen off on one adventure or another. That helped explain the sporadic postcards from Renée that came from all over the world. I thought about hiding them from her. Maddie was too young to understand. She was into princesses, fairy tales, and magical kingdoms. It was easier that way. She loved the thought of her mother being a gypsy queen."

"I thought Old Town Plaza was my court and all of Old Town my kingdom. I had my own balcony that overlooked my land," Maddie says. "It was real to me."

"Maddie was my princess, and I her loyal servant," her dad adds. He catches Maddie looking at him, and she quickly averts her eyes. Judas and Brutus were once loyal servants too.

"So it was just the two of you?" Dr. Swenson asks.

"We had Otilia, our neighbor who helped take care of her. We had other artists from the gallery and Mimi, who owned the café . . . but yeah, most of the time it was just the two of us."

"You didn't date?" Dr. Swenson asks.

"I guess I was still hung up on Renée."

"What about friends her own age for Maddie?"

"I figured she had friends at school. At home, it was just us."

"No parties or sleepovers or friends to play with outside of school? You didn't date or socialize with other adults much. The picture I'm getting is the two of you were rather isolated," Dr. Swenson says. "You comprised each other's entire worlds."

"I had to be both mother and father to her and make a living. We had our Old Town friends. It seemed like enough."

"What do you remember about those early years, Maddie?" Dr. Swenson asks.

Her early memories hurt. She looks into her lap.

"Is it hard to think about that time?" Dr. Swenson asks.

Maddie can only nod her head and hold back tears. Her dad may not have been a perfect parent, but she thought so at the time. She felt loved and safe. "I didn't feel like I was lacking anything but my mom. But she was coming back to us. We were waiting for her."

"You knew she wasn't coming back, though, right, Michael? But you kept telling Maddie she might. At what point did you tell Maddie the truth?"

"As she got older, I let the stories of her mom die off. I thought she'd figure it out on her own."

"I wonder how Maddie felt about the conversations about her mother dying off," says Dr. Swenson, turning to her.

"Like my mom fell off the face of the earth."

"She did," Dad says. "I'm so sorry, Maddie."

"I lost her twice." Maddie looks him in the eye.

"The fact that Maddie was brought up in a world that was mainly just the two of you, hearing stories about a magical mother who would some-day swoop back into her life, didn't prepare her for you to fall in love and marry someone else," Dr. Swenson says. "How did you ease that transition for her?"

"I wanted to make sure we were going to work out before I involved Maddie. I was trying to protect her. I know I messed that up. I should have introduced them a lot sooner, so it wasn't so abrupt. I was so shocked to find love again I didn't handle it right. I forced her into a new family because I wanted it so much."

"You were a good dad before you met Lesley," Maddie says. "I liked that it was just the two of us—I wanted it to stay that way—I was so happy back then. Everything was perfect. And then it all went to hell." Maddie's throat aches from her unshed tears.

"Your father could have better prepared you, he's taking responsibility for that. But Maddie, his falling in love and wanting to marry Lesley is separate from what happened to you after that. No one could have pre-dicted that," Dr. Swenson says.

Maddie breaks down, her tears choking her. "You keep saying you were only trying to protect me. Everything you did was to protect me. But when I needed you to protect me, where were you? Huh? Where were you?" As she sobs, she's aware of Dr. Swenson excusing her dad, his exit from the room, and Dr. Swenson's strong arms around her shoulders.

CHAPTER 5

Maddie, Age 12

Corrales, New Mexico

By the end of May, Maddie had turned twelve and her dad had married Lesley. Maddie cried when she had to move out of Old Town and say good-bye to her friends. They were her family, not Lesley or stupid Jeffrey. Her friends put on a brave face when she said her good-byes, telling her how wonderful it would be for her, and how she deserved this new life. But she saw a tear from Mimi as they said "A bientôt" with mutual kisses on each cheek. Maddie spoke fluent French because of Mimi, and Mimi was Maddie's last link to her mother.

Now that the weather was warming and the earth was greening, she liked Corrales better because she was spending more time outside around the horses. They were friendly and came up for nose rubs when she stood at their corral fence. Her riding lessons would start soon, and she was excited.

Maddie hardly saw Jeffrey because when he wasn't in school, he was playing spring baseball or exchanging saliva with a girl somewhere. He had big muscles and shaved a faint moustache. According to Lesley, he was Mr. Popular at school, but to Maddie, he was an unfamiliar species. Jeffrey had warned her not to go near his room or touch any of his stuff. She had already decided to steer clear of him. Dad said older brothers were like that and to take it as a compliment that he treated her like his annoying little sister so soon. Except, she wanted to say, she hadn't been annoying. More and more, her dad made pronouncements rather than have actual conversations with her.

Lesley fawned over her and loved taking her shopping and to expensive restaurants for lunch on Saturdays. Maddie's dad had always given her everything she ever wanted, but Lesley upped the ante big-time. That part did feel like a fairy tale come true. Maddie went to a new school and had not made too many friends yet, but when she did, she could have them over anytime for a sleepover or a night of movies in the home theater. Lesley bragged about how Jeffrey's friends thought she was the coolest mom. It was fun to think about parties, but Maddie doubted she'd ever have the nerve for any of that. The idea of having a boy-girl party made her feel queasy.

Lesley seemed to have plans to transform her into a social butterfly, one of those kids who ran for student council or tried out for cheerleading. Maddie couldn't picture it and figured she'd end up disappointing her. Lesley had already become involved in her school activities and parent meetings, and Dad seemed happy to take the back seat. He had become more involved at the spa that Lesley owned, becoming a licensed masseur and doing massages for her rich clients, and co-running the business. She couldn't remember the last time he made jewelry, and he only occasionally checked in on his Old Town gallery, which was now being run by their friend Marsha, a talented fiber artist whom Maddie used to think had a crush on him. He did set up a workspace in a spare bedroom. When he offered to take Maddie with him to Old Town, she decided it would be too painful to visit and have to leave all over again, so she avoided the whole ordeal.

"Hey, how you doing, girl?" Maddie said as she rubbed the nose of her favorite horse, Moonshine, the one she spotted on her first visit. Maddie gave her a carrot. Moonshine's nose was pink with big brown freckles and soft like the Velveteen Rabbit. Her nostrils sniffed like small vacuums on Maddie, who kissed between them. They both inhaled the sweet smell of the first cutting of alfalfa coming from the four-acre field. It lay in puffy rows for the baler.

One of Maddie's chores was to feed and water the chickens and gather eggs. They had ten fat laying hens that formed an anxious mob when she came near with the scratch. This animal stuff was new to her, but she loved it. She even liked shoveling out horse dung from the stalls because she knew they couldn't do it for themselves. Mothering did not come naturally to Maddie, but the animals were patiently teaching her. She screamed when she found baby mice in the scratch, and when she saw a bull snake slithering away after scavenging eggs. The two goats sneezed pieces of wet alfalfa in her hair, and there was one particular goose that had it in for her. But even so, she felt their dependence and love. Now that school was ending for summer break, she'd have all the time in the world for them. She tried to forget about her thwarted plans to work in the gallery for the summer. A stack of books under the shade of a huge cottonwood tree, surrounded by animals and the sweet, pungent smells of the farm, would help her get over it.

There were five horse stalls and by the third one her hands and arms ached from shoveling dung into a wheelbarrow. Then the wheelbarrow had to be dumped into the trailer that hooked onto the back of Jeffrey's quad. It was his job to empty it into a compost pile at the end of the acreage. He didn't have many farm chores because his time was spent in important Jeffrey activities. To Lesley, he was golden. With a pang of longing, Maddie remembered how it felt to be adored, and hoped when her father slowed down for five minutes and actually paid attention to her again, she would feel the love that now seemed so distant.

Maddie sat on a hay bale to rest. She had never been athletic. She never tried hard to be physical in PE class, but she could already feel the solid muscles forming in her arms and legs from all the bending, scooping, and dumping of dung. At least it was physical work with a purpose—not something stupid like doing jumping jacks or windmills. Lesley said a person needed to be strong for horseback riding.

Maddie heard a crash outside and peeked out of the barn to see what happened. Jeffrey had knocked over some stacked crates, obviously pissed off about something. With his inflated ego, it wouldn't take much: a lost game, being snubbed by a girl, his hair out of place.

He was heading toward the barn to do his chore. Why hadn't she started earlier? The gabbing gander came to chase him off, but he punted the poor thing like a football. "Get the fuck away from me!" he said. The goose lay crumpled, and she feared he had killed it.

She stormed out of the barn toward him. "Stop it! What would your mom think?"

Jeffrey looked at her with the same venom. Thankfully, the goose got up and hobbled away. "It's just a fucking goose."

"I'm going to tell if I ever see you hurt him again." Maddie shook with anger.

Jeffrey walked closer to her, right up into her face. "You say one word and you'll be sorry." He hacked up a big phlegm ball and spit it near her feet, then hopped on his quad and sped off.

Every night they had to have dinner as a family, except when her dad and Lesley dragged her to one of Jeffrey's baseball games. That night Jeffrey blessed them with his presence. Maddie was still furious; the goose incident kept replaying in her mind. She fidgeted, desperate to tell, terrified to tell.

Jeffrey was all smiles at the table, except for when the adults weren't looking. That's when he'd give Maddie the stink eye. He talked with her dad about current events and sports. Dad was never interested in sports in the past, but he was all ears for Jeffrey's blather. Jeffrey ended the year with his perfect grade point average, Jeffrey couldn't wait to play varsity football in the fall, Jeffrey pitched a no-hitter in his last game. Maddie couldn't wait to get her dad alone so she could talk to him for once.

Lesley brought out a huge cake to celebrate Jeffrey's last day of his freshman year at the Academy. She cut a humongous piece for him and kissed him on his cheek. Jeffrey smiled sweetly. "You're the best, Mom," he said as Lesley ruffled his hair. He quickly groomed it back into place.

"I love you, honey. And I'm so proud of you," Lesley told him, all choked up.

Maddie's last real day of school had been today too, except she had to go a half day on Monday. She didn't see what the big deal was for Jeffrey. So he was going to be a sophomore. So what?

"I'm proud of you too, Son," Dad said, patting Jeffrey on the shoulder.

Jeffrey got up and gave Dad a hug. "Thanks, Michael. That means a lot coming from you. It's great having another guy in the house." Maddie didn't believe he meant one word.

"You've been quiet, Maddie. How are things going for you?" Dad asked as if he had just noticed her sitting there.

Maddie looked up to see Jeffrey's frozen smile taunting her, his vacant eyes pretending to care. She shrugged her shoulders and picked at her cake. "Okay, I guess."

Lesley poured herself more coffee. "You'll be starting riding lessons soon."

"I can't wait," Maddie said, purposely stuffing cake into her mouth so she wouldn't be able to say anything else. She wondered which riding stable she would attend. She had noticed one on Corrales Road that she could walk to; it would be perfect.

"We'll make an equestrian out of you, won't we, Jeffrey?" Lesley added. "Jeffrey, you don't mind teaching Maddie how to ride, do you? How about I pay you for your time, like a real summer job?"

Maddie's cake became a lump of cement she couldn't swallow. She spoke with her mouth partially full. "That's all right. Jeffrey doesn't have to . . ."

"I don't mind, squirt. At least you'll learn from the best. And Mom, I wouldn't think about taking a dime for it. She's family," Jeffrey said. "Time I start acting like a big brother."

"Psst, Dad . . . Dad," Maddie called as he brushed his teeth before bed. She didn't want Lesley to hear because she would butt in. It was impossible to have a private conversation with him now, something she had taken for granted for over eleven years in Old Town. And now she had to resort to stalking him down in his bathroom. "Dad, can you come to my room so we can talk in private?"

He wiped the green foam from his mouth. "Sure thing, sweetheart," he said, following her to her room. Maddie shut the door. "What's up?" he asked, sitting on her chair.

"Today I saw Jeffrey come home super mad about something. He trashed some crates by the barn and kicked the goose, hard. I thought he'd killed it, so I ran out to yell at him. He was awful and even threatened me if I told."

"Yeah, Jeffrey has a temper. Lesley pushes him, gives him high expectations and he's hard on himself, always trying to be perfect. Kicking the goose was mean and wrong, so I'm not making excuses for him, but sometimes right or wrong, that's how guys let off steam. Especially at his age. I'm sure he didn't mean what he said to you. You saw how he was at dinner."

"Yeah, like Jekyll and Hyde," said Maddie.

"I think it's good that he was able to turn his bad mood around and be nice to you again. You're just not used to having a big brother. And remember, he's not used to having a little sister who can squeal on him. Guys like to think they're tough at that age."

"He's like conceited Gaston in *Beauty and the Beast.*"

"Nobody's perfect. And now that we're a real family, we have to adjust for one another to get along. Our family is still new. There's bound to be a little conflict here and there. Try not to take it so seriously." He reached over and brushed some hair out of her face.

What did he mean, now they were a real family? Hadn't she and her dad been a real family? It had felt more real than this. A rap came at the door, followed by Lesley's voice through the door. "You guys all right in there?"

Dad squeezed Maddie's hand. "Better?"

"Yeah, you can go." Maddie felt as if she had given up her space in the sandbox. When he opened the door to leave, she saw Jeffrey had joined Lesley, waiting out in the hallway, peering over his mom's shoulder. After Lesley and her dad left, Jeffrey stood in her doorway. "How do you like sleeping in the haunted room of this old adobe? Our guests have seen ghosts walking out of the walls with hatchets, hanging over the foot of the bed. You can hear their footsteps dragging on the wood floor, sometimes they whisper things," he said, looking around the room. "Shh, I thought I heard something." He held up an index finger and then shut off her light, plunging her into darkness. He closed her door except for a tiny crack, through which he spoke before shutting it. "Sweet dreams, squirt."

Maddie had spent the last two weeks bonding with her white horse before she began tack lessons and actually riding her. She fed and groomed her while learning basic anatomy and a little horse psychology. But today was the day—she would mount Moonshine for the first time. From her bedroom window, she could see Moonshine nibbling hay in the paddock.

Maddie grabbed a bagel for herself and a carrot for Moonshine, and headed to the stalls. She had read books from the library about horses. Jeffrey showed her some things in the beginning, but for the last two weeks, she was pretty much on her own with the bonding, grooming, and her usual mucking and feeding. When Moonshine started to nuzzle Maddie and respond to her commands, she felt honored. Maybe all this upheaval was for a good reason. She felt such connection looking into Moonshine's fudgy-brown eyes. It was a love like no other. "I'm your mom and I will never leave you," Maddie said to her horse.

Jeffrey's horse, Bullet, was feisty and unpredictable like Jeffrey. Bullet was slow to trust anyone, so Maddie made sure he was far from his stall before cleaning it. It seemed everything Jeffrey touched had it in for her. But she had found her soulmate in Moonshine, a power greater than Jeffrey.

When Jeffrey arrived, Maddie stood at the pipe fencing of the paddock, watching Moonshine munch on the sweet new grass in the pasture.

"You're going to have to go catch her and lead her back," he said, showing her how to unbuckle one side of the bridle and slip the halter onto her right arm. "Always have your shit together before approaching a horse." He handed her the lead rope and buckle. He acted as if there were a hundred other things he'd rather be doing. Maddie happened to know Lesley was paying him after all. "Remember to approach her slowly—back off if you lose her. Approach her at the shoulders. Scratch her withers. Introduce the halter, then act like you're going to hug her, slip on the halter and buckle it. Got it?"

Maddie nodded.

"Good luck, squirt. You're so short, you're going need it."

Maddie walked out into the pasture, her new cowboy boots sinking into the moist grass. Her heart pounded in excitement at seeing

Moonshine, who stood like a white jewel against the backdrop of the hazy purple mountains. Maddie called to her and Moonshine perked her ears and looked. Maddie made kissing noises. Moonshine gave a little snort, as if she wanted to run around in the beautiful morning. Who would blame her? Maddie backed up a bit. "Moonshine, sweet girl," she called approaching again. "Good girl." She scratched Moonshine's withers. The horse gave a shudder of delight. "You might have to have to help me with this," Maddie said, trying to reach up and around the horse in a hug while at the same time slipping on the halter.

She felt Jeffrey's eyes on her back, looking for reasons to give up on her. As if Moonshine read her thoughts, she bent her head down for Maddie to easily slip on the halter and buckle the lead rope. They walked shoulder to shoulder all the way back to the paddock, and she tied Moonshine with a quick-release knot that got Jeffrey's attention.

"Nice to see you're not a total idiot," Jeffrey said. Maddie couldn't help but smile. He had never given her a compliment before, however backhanded it was. "Now we have to find a saddle that fits you and Moonshine."

She followed him to the tack room, where there were several saddles on thick wood stands. His riding ribbons covered the walls, along with a collection of trophies. She had to admit Jeffrey knew his stuff when it came to horseback riding. Maybe they were on their way to some kind of mutual respect.

"I know these two fit Moonshine. Now which one is best for you?" Jeffrey patted the seat of a tooled leather saddle with silver conchos. "This one was my grandmother's. She was puny, like you. Hop on." Jeffrey held the pommel while she put her foot in the stirrup and swung on.

"Ear, shoulder, hip to heel—straight line," instructed Jeffrey as she sat in the saddle.

Maddie straightened like she saw in the pictures of her books.

"It's all about balance. Your muscles holding you in the saddle," he said sticking his hands between her thighs. "These are your adductor muscles. Now squeeze. Show me what you've got."

Maddie was shocked at first, but Jeffrey remained calm and

professional, sort of like a doctor with a stethoscope. She squeezed her inner thigh muscles.

"Good," he said as she captured his hands against the saddle seat. "Those are what hold you in the saddle. Tighten them again." Maddie complied, even as his hand reached deeper between her legs. "Yeah, you'd be able to ride about anything with those babies."

Maddie started to hop off.

"Whoa, Nelly," Jeffrey said, stopping her in the saddle. "We're not through. We have to check your seat bones, your pelvic tilt, and the space of saddle between your thighs."

"It all feels fine to me," said Maddie, reaching her hand behind her butt to feel the saddle.

"Nobody does that one-hand rule anymore, dork. You must be reading books from the 1950s. Now just sit straight and let me do my job," he said, running his hand into her pelvic region, which was hot and moist from the heat. His large hand opened up and pushed against her mound. "Checking for pelvic positioning," he explained like a gynecologist who had done this a million times. "Don't freak out."

Whether he was or wasn't checking in earnest, she'd never had a doctor, or anyone, touch her there. She felt her face flush hot, and quickly dismounted, almost taking his hand with her.

"What the hell are you doing, twerp?"

She picked up the saddle that nearly weighted her to the ground. "Only way to really find out if it fits is on a moving horse."

He grabbed the saddle from her, and she followed him out into the light of day, where anyone could see them.

By the end of July, Maddie was a capable rider. Jeffrey's summer schedule had become erratic and he hardly showed up anymore for lessons, which relieved Maddie to no end. Jeffrey creeped Maddie out even more now, and she kept her distance from him as much as possible.

She didn't need more lessons anyway, not with Moonshine, who was already used to riders. Moonshine knew the subtle feet and leg movements better than Maddie. And it was as if Moonshine didn't want Maddie to fail, so the horse tolerated whatever was asked of her. Maddie swore they could read each other's minds.

She found a step stool in the tack room, and with a lot of determination and all her strength, she was able to saddle her horse on her own. That gave her the independence to ride whenever she wanted.

After riding one morning, she led Moonshine into the grooming station on the side of the stables and hooked the crossties. Even though Maddie curried Moonshine every day, it was hard keeping her white since she loved to roll in the dirt. That was a horse's way of taking a bath, but after a brief rain Moonshine had become muddied, especially her tail and mane.

She started the hose pointed at the ground and moved to Moonshines feet and lower legs. After Moonshine had time to adjust to the spraying water, standing on her step stool, Maddie slowly worked her way up the horse and around. "See, you like that. Doesn't that feel good?" She cooed to the horse as she soaped up her tail. She balled up the wet tail and scrubbed, pulled her fingers through, and scrubbed again.

The goose that followed Maddie everywhere happily honked and flapped in the little water tributaries forming. After Moonshine was rinsed, Maddie took a sweat scraper and squeegeed off the excess water. Then with a dry sponge, she wiped her down, absorbing any leftover water, taking special care to dry the fetlock and pastern joints to avoid peeling or fungus. Since New Mexico weather was so hot and dry, Maddie kept a keen eye on Moonshine's hooves for cracking.

She was leading Moonshine back into the stable when she heard Jeffrey's quad approaching in the distance. She put Moonshine back in crossties in the stable to sponge her eyes and wipe her ears. Maybe he'll just pick up the trailer of muck and be gone. Whenever their parents were around, he was all fake smiles and compliments. She had tried a couple of more times to tell her dad about his strange behavior, but her dad made excuses and smoothed over her concerns. Jeffrey was perfect. She finally gave up.

Two weeks ago, Jeffrey thought it would be funny if he locked Maddie in a closet. At first, she wasn't going to give him the satisfaction of freaking out, but after about thirty minutes, she began pounding on the door. But Jeffrey was long gone. The housekeeper finally found her. It made Maddie wonder what Jeffrey did for amusement before he had a little sister to torment. He sure was making up for lost time.

"Easy, girl," Maddie told a spooked Moonshine as the quad skidded up to the stables.

"Hey, squirt, want to go for a ride with me on my quad?" Jeffrey said, coming into the stable. He had on a pair of frayed cutoffs, tennis shoes, and no shirt, no socks. He didn't seem to burn, only tan. With the light shining on his back, his fuzzy body hair formed a golden aura.

"Yeah, right," she said. "And my name is not squirt or twerp or penis wrinkle. It's Maddie."

"What's the matter, squirt, scared?" he said sauntering closer. "Of me or the quad?"

"You on that quad. You'd probably drive me over a cliff and jump off at the last second."

"I'd never do that. I've had so much fun since you've moved in, Maddie." He was so close she heard his dry mouth crackle when he smiled.

She tried to ignore his half-naked body near her as she began to wipe out Moonshine's ears. He peered at her as if she were under glass.

"Have you even started your periods yet? Your tits are way small," he said.

"That's none of your damn business!" Maddie threw her cloth on the ground and climbed down from her stool. Moonshine gave a huff of uneasiness. "Why don't you just leave so I can finish." Now that he knew he had crossed the line and totally antagonized her, maybe he was through with his stupid games.

"I do what I want, when I want," he said, backing her up against a stall with his full-grown body.

Maddie turned her head sideways so as to not be smothered by his chest. "Cut it out, asshole!" She gave him a hard push, but he outweighed her by a lot. He just laughed and pinned her tighter, his hard penis pressing against her abdomen.

"Show me your pussy, and I'll let you go."

"No! I'll scream if you don't let me go."

"That can be easily remedied," he said, putting his cupped hand tight against her mouth. It obstructed her nostrils and she could barely breathe.

"I want to see if you have a little girl's pussy or a woman's pussy," he told her. Maddie screamed as hard as she could against his hand as he unbuckled her belt and unzipped her jeans. "No, you won't scream. And you won't tell," he said, his searching fingers finding her. "Because if you tell, I will make sure you're very, very sorry." Maddie fought him, writhing in disgust. Breathing hard in her ear he said, "You're wet. I'm turning you on, you little slut."

Maddie bit his hand, and he jumped back. She tried to get away, but he caught her and held her tight by her wrist. "You tell anyone and so help me god, you're dead. I know how to kill and get away with it. I do a lot of things and never get caught." He rubbed his bite mark. "Bitch."

"I hate you!" She struggled against his hold, but his fingers gripped her around her forearm. She tried to hit him with her other fist, but he blocked her blows.

"I'm warning you. Don't try me." He finally let her go.

She quickly zipped her jeans and buckled her belt extra tight. "Don't you ever touch me again," Maddie said, fighting tears.

"Oh, I'm just getting started." He turned and started to walk out of the stables.

Shaking with rage and shame, she wanted to kill him. "I'll tell and they'll arrest you and lock you up!"

Her goose was drinking water out of a bucket at the stable entrance. "You will keep your fucking mouth shut or you'll find out what I'm really capable of," he said. He picked up the goose by its neck and gave it a quick yank and a twirl. He threw its lifeless body at her feet.

Maddie somehow managed to get through her first semester of seventh grade. She already had all the pressure she could handle at home and now she had even more pressure from the middle school social scene. Popular kids had become even more popular and powerful, and everyone else was divided into groups according to a caste system. Her school had a Winter Whirl dance, in which Lesley became totally and obnoxiously involved.

Lesley ordered a dress for her from New York City, so Maddie went to the dance even though she would have much rather stayed home escaping into a book. She confided in Moonshine only when she was absolutely sure she was safely alone.

But she never truly felt safe. Not after that attack from Jeffrey in August. Since then, he had stalked and threatened her constantly. Then one time he caught her in the barn and grabbed a painful handful of her hair and forced her to her knees. She hoped it was to lick his boots, because after all she was only twelve, and a young one at that. But after the experience that followed, Maddie knew the vernacular of whores and madmen. For a few months, he had been content with forcing her to suck him and then coming all over her face. She was sure she'd suffocate. She didn't want to die while hearing this demon call her a cunt, slut, whore. And all the while, he described in detail what he would do if she told.

Maddie stopped fighting. His madness got worse if she was biting him or struggling like she did in the beginning. Besides, he either twisted her arm back or got a good chunk of her hair. She tried to escape into one of her fantasy lands, but she had stopped believing in white hats and good guys.

When her dad and Lesley went to Taos for a weekend retreat for spa owners, Maddie wanted to ask a friend to sleep over, but she wasn't close enough to any of the girls for it not to sound weird. And kids already thought she acted weird. She couldn't make eye contact with anyone. What if they found out the terrible things she did to save her life?

She tried to run out of the house to hitch a ride to Old Town, but he bolted the security doors and kept the keys in his pocket. He said he was the official babysitter. She was not allowed to leave the couch while he served popcorn and lemonade and made her watch horrible sex movies where people hurt each other. He masturbated, using her as a target.

Then he grabbed her hair and poured a glass of lemonade down her throat. She choked but he pulled her head back farther until she finished drinking. "Go ahead and choke, you whore. Save me the trouble."

She became woozy and found it hard to move her legs. Her brain couldn't work right and her body was heavy and limp. Jeffrey walked around naked, drinking booze and watching disgusting movies. She could hardly hold her head up. Then she passed out.

After she briefly woke from whatever drugs he had given her, her anus hurt. He kept her drugged over the whole weekend of torture and sex. Just before their parents were due home, he made her shower while he watched. His voice boomed over the glass shower stall, eerily even toned as he spoke. "Now that I'm actually getting pussy out of you, I don't want to have to kill you. So I'd kill your dad. He bugs me anyway. Mr. Nice Guy. What an idiot."

Maddie broke down sobbing into her soapy hands.

"Did you know that only one milligram of castor bean will kill an adult? Jimsonweed is another good one. Actually, one petal of oleander would do the trick. How easy that would be. There are lots of ways to kill your dad and never get caught. You could squeal on me, sure, but your dad would be dead already. Daffodils, azaleas . . ."

"Stop!" Maddie stood naked, clutching her hair, water streaming down her face. She knew he was capable. He was a monster and he owned her.

"I'm glad you understand me." Jeffrey closed the bathroom door behind him.

CHAPTER 6

GRACE SITS ON HER bed, waiting for Jackson to finish rounds with the staff and Dr. Swenson so that she can finally dig into the box of her belongings. It seems stupid to have to be supervised while going through it. Jackson said it's a safety issue, plus he has to document everything brought in to Brazos Cottage. She assured him he wouldn't find any weapons. He reminded her she had hung herself with jump ropes.

She begins to pace. Staff would tell her to name what she's feeling. Impatience, for sure. Frustration that she's being treated like a mental patient who's locked up in a psych unit. Resentment that she doesn't have the power to do what she wanted. Anxiety. She stops her pacing. She looks down at her hands, which are trembling, and notes the butterflies in her stomach that are frantically swirling as if caught in a wind tunnel. Her breathing is rapid and her mouth is dry, even as her palms begin to sweat. Panic attack? Over getting to see her stuff?

The paintings. The thought of them nestled in the cardboard portfolio runs a shiver through her. Okay, so seeing the paintings might bring back some of the panic that accompanied the process of creating them. Seeing them again might poke like a sharp stick into the soft underbelly of her subconscious mind that refuses to yield its secrets. But that's what she wants. She wants to remember her mother. Painting the South Padre Island shoreline where they lived together was the most direct link she has. Why does it unnerve her so much? Why is she afraid?

She glances over at Maddie, who's napping after her rough family therapy session, her back to Grace, curled up against the wall. She looks too small to have endured the horrors she suffered. It was a wonder she could sleep at all. She'd probably give anything to have her memory wiped clean.

Jackson's face appears in the rectangle of glass in the door. She motions him in. He carries the box, and Dr. Swenson follows with Grace's portfolio. Grace sits at one end of her bed. Jackson puts the box down next to her. "Dr. Swenson's going to be with you while you go through your things. I'll come in and catalog everything afterward."

"I'm just nosy that way. I truly am. I love going to garage sales to paw through people's stuff." She smiles her girlish smile and sits down on Grace's desk chair, the portfolio balanced on her lap. Jackson leaves them to it. "Well, where would you like to begin?"

Grace eyes the portfolio. "I told you about how I'd get panic attacks when I first started painting."

"I remember. How are you feeling now?"

"I want to get it over with." Grace smooths her sweaty palms over her jeans.

"You have some anxiety."

"A little. Go ahead and open them up."

"You can do it." Dr. Swenson passes the portfolio over to Grace, who unwinds the string that holds it shut. The loose paintings begin to shift and slide from her lap. She catches them, her eyes scanning the roll of the waves, the shiny, wet sand of the first one. She hands it to Dr. Swenson.

"Man, you're good. I'd never guess a kid did these."

Grace looks at them and passes them in sequence.

Dr. Swenson examines each one in silence and then says, "Describe how you feel, seeing them."

"These paintings are what I can remember, like if I took a picture with a camera. But that's not what I want to see. I want to see who's behind the camera. I want to see my mom."

"What happens if you try to swivel the camera around to get that view? Try to visualize it, you have the camera in your hand and you are looking through the viewfinder and you slowly turn away from the ocean. What do you see?"

Grace closes her eyes and puts herself on the wet sand. She can feel it under her feet, solid but yielding. She turns a quarter turn to her right and can see down the beach, the swath of sand, the edge of the surf as it sweeps in and out, shore birds darting on stick legs, sharp beaks jabbing into the shallows for tender morsels. She turns another quarter turn and the scene dissolves like melting film. "Nothing. Once I look behind me, it goes blank."

"Uh-huh," Dr. Swenson says. "I'm going to start you in art therapy. I have some ideas, and you'll like working with Janice. I notice these last paintings are of New Mexico. What happened to make you stop painting the South Padre scenery?"

"I was painting South Padre to try to remember my mom. I tried to find out what happened to her, but I didn't get anywhere. Finally Mitch told me everything about how she died and none of it jarred anything loose. So I gave up."

"We'll talk more about that later. Let's see what's in this box."

Grace rips off the tape Rudy used to seal the flaps. On top are a few overdue library books, along with *The Naturalist's Guide to Coastal Texas*. Grace smiles. "I'm so glad to have this back. My friend Robin gave it to me before she left. She's the one who gave me these art supplies and started me painting." She pulls out the art kit and brushes that are bound together with a rubber band, and lays them on her bed. She runs her fingertips over the soft, clean tips of the brushes and remembers how Robin always knew just what she needed, even before Grace knew. How Robin selected her and gave her friendship and love when she might have just walked on by the way everyone else did. It was so unexpected and magical.

"You look happy, Grace," Dr. Swenson says. "I'm glad I'm here to see it."

"Robin and Duc were my best friends. They were amazing."

"Why the past tense?" Dr. Swenson asks.

"They moved to New York City after they graduated. They're so talented. They're studying musical theater and they're going to be famous." Grace lets herself feel the joy of her love for them. She hugs the book to her chest.

"So they didn't die together in some tragic, fiery crash. Can't they still be your best friends?"

"But they're not here."

"Have you not heard of letters and emails and visits? Just because they moved doesn't mean they're gone."

Grace feels tears threaten but she wills them away. Instead, she digs into the box and pulls out the photo album Duc gave her. She pages through it, Dr. Swenson craning her neck to see. "Aren't they great?" Grace laughs even as tears begin to stream down her face. She hands the album to Dr. Swenson.

"Yeah, they look great. So do you, Grace. Look how happy you are in these pictures. *This* girl, *this* Grace, doesn't look suicidal, does she?"

"But then they left and I didn't have anyone and Mitch fucked up and everything went to shit—so fast—it all happened so fast."

"I know about that part and we'll be talking more about it. Right now, I want to know more about *this* Grace." Dr. Swenson taps a picture.

"Mitch was sober then and dating our neighbor Jane, who was helping him. I went to school and met Duc and Robin and life was so good—it was the happiest I'd ever been—so it scared me."

"Every time you'd gotten attached to something or someone in the past, you lost them, so you were waiting for it to happen again."

"Well, they were seniors and I was a junior. I knew they'd be graduating and moving away." Grace wipes at the tears that refuse to stop.

"But you took the risk anyway and it paid off, looks to me anyway," Dr. Swenson says, motioning to the album in her lap. "You have their address? I want you to start writing letters to them. They can write to you here. It's time to break the pattern of losing people who are important to you. I can tell they would want to hear from you. Consider it doctor's orders."

"Why can't I stop crying?"

Dr. Swenson grabs the tissue box from Grace's desk and tosses it to her. "You have a deep well of grief inside of you, my dear, starting from before you can remember and then compounded by all the moves and losses. Crying is healthy, so go for it. You're safe here. Holding it inside, becoming a walking zombie, well, that leads to nasty rope burns. Feeling your sadness, your anger, your anything—and dealing with it—that's how you survive."

Grace blows her nose and then reaches inside the cardboard box to pull out the wooden box with the shells inside. "Robin gave me these too. When I hold them, I can almost remember holding shells when I was little."

"Good. Handle them several times a day. Get relaxed and hold them and let your mind be blank, don't force it. Just feel their shape and textures."

"Doctor's orders?" Grace manages a weak smile.

Dr. Swenson stands and rummages through the rest of the box and pulls out a jewelry box that Jane gave her. "Anything interesting in here?"

Grace opens it. Just some thrift store jewelry, a few barrettes, and then, twinkling at the bottom, the yellow topaz pendant necklace Duc gave her. She lifts it out and holds it up. She stopped wearing it after Duc and Robin left.

"Pretty," Dr. Swenson says. "It looks handmade by a jewelry artist, not mass produced."

"From Duc, for my birthday." Grace remembers how it felt to wear it against her heart, her amulet.

"Since your roommate is still on high-risk precautions, we'll have to keep it in your cubby behind the staff desk for now, chain and all. But once Maddie's on level one, I want you to wear it."

Grace puts it back in her jewelry box and hands it over to Dr. Swenson. The only thing left in the box is the hat and scarf Jane knitted her for Christmas. She puts them on. "Jane made these."

"A little warm for June, but I like them on you. What I see here, Grace, is a lot of love. I see people who care about you. And they aren't as gone as you think."

"I never thought I'd see any of this again." Grace wants to hold it all, bury herself in it. "This was the first time I got to keep anything. Whenever Mitch uprooted us, it was usually so sudden I had to leave what little I had behind."

"Thanks to Rudy, you have this tangible evidence that you had a life, one worth living. These objects are connections to people, that's what makes them important," Dr. Swenson says. "Jackson will be in to do his inventory and take anything he doesn't want you to have in here for now, and I better get home to feed the animals or I'll never hear the end of it."

"What kind of animals do you have?" Grace notes the variety of stray hairs on Dr. Swenson's dark clothing.

Dr. Swenson gives a quick laugh. "It'd be easier to tell you what animals I don't have. Good night, Grace."

Grace gets to keep all of her belongings except the scarf and the jewelry box, due to its glass mirror and the topaz necklace with its long chain, until Maddie advances to level one. Having artifacts from her prior life gives her unexpected comfort. She begins to think of Robin and Duc as real people again, not just a happy dream that was taken from her by some malevolent force.

She writes a long letter to them, telling them all that has happened and what she did, and where she is now. When Dr. Swenson reads it, she says, "Good. Telling the truth to your friends, being real, is how to stay connected to them. Maintaining connections is important for you, Grace, since your life has been all about broken connections."

She studies *The Naturalist's Guide to Coastal Texas* and takes it with her—along with her portfolio—to her first art therapy session. Dr. Swenson is right—she likes Janice, a petite woman with a long tumble of brown, wavy hair. Janice has a pleasant face and a soft-spoken demeanor as she welcomes Grace into her large, sunny art room. Janice says she will work with her twice a week individually, using art to help Grace access her early years with her mother. Hearing her state that as their mission gives Grace hope that maybe with a licensed art therapist, her mind will finally open to reveal its secrets.

By the end of her second week at the hospital, Grace is hooked. She loves the staff, especially Jackson and Sharon, but also the young college-aged staff, whose enthusiasm sometimes overreaches their experience when dealing with the continual challenges that Aaron, Abdias, Percy, and Lucas present on a daily basis. Aaron argues with anything with a pulse and usually escalates into verbal tirades and sometimes physical tantrums. Percy finds meaning in the hum of the refrigerator and resists leaving its side. Lucas tells tortured tales of being held in a North Vietnamese prisoner of war camp.

Abdias finally breaks down and cries uncontrollably in a task group about the four-year-old boy he accidentally shot and killed, saying the child had been coming to him in his dreams and telling him he should kill himself. That earns Abdias a return to high-risk precautions and the loss of his belt and shoelaces. Even as he shuffles in his untied shoes and has to hold his pants up with his hand, he admits he feels cared about since staff are keeping him safe.

Gabe and Grace emerge as leaders, earning the most privileges. Before long, Maddie talks more in task group, crying out her pain but controlling herself physically. Grace and Maddie often talk after lights out, laughing about something ridiculous one of their peers has done or said, or marveling at the mystery that is Lucas, with his stuffed bird Sam and his detailed delusions of war. They also begin to share with each other more about their lives. Grace tells Maddie about her brief but happy life in San Francisco with Twyla, and Maddie talks at length about her life in Old Town. Grace decides they tell each other the good times to remind themselves it hasn't all been shit.

At the end of that second week, Grace is advanced to level two and Maddie has earned her level one.

"I'll get my level two by next week, watch," Maddie says as they get ready for bed that night. "I'll catch up to you."

"I hope so. Gabe and I have to wait to go on off-campus outings until a third kid makes level two because there's not enough staff with so many on level one and Abdias on HRP." Grace turns down her bed. She fluffs her damp hair and notices again the relief of having shampoo when you need it, and tampons, and food, and a bed. She begins to wonder what it says about a person that they love being in a psychiatric hospital. But she suspects this is no ordinary facility and then has something else to feel grateful about.

Grace watches as Maddie puts lotion on her arms and legs. Maddie often seems nervous at bedtime, which seems to fuel her talkativeness after lights out. She figures a lot of Maddie's abuse happened during the night, so Grace stays awake to be there for her.

"Hey, did you get the rest of your stuff back? I'm off HRP, so they should give it to you," Maddie says.

"I forgot to ask about it."

A knock and then Sharon's face appears in the doorway. "You ladies about ready for lights out? I heard you both went up on your levels today, way to go."

"Can you get Grace her stuff from her cubby since I'm off HRP?" Maddie asks.

"I can get it in the morning," Grace says. "I don't need the scarf. Just my jewelry box."

"I'll get it," Sharon says. "That way you'll have it in case you want to wear something tomorrow."

Maddie walks over to Grace's side of the room. "I got my level because of you."

"No, you earned it."

"But you made me want to."

Sharon returns with Grace's jewelry box. "Here you go. Five minutes until lights out." She hugs them both and then pauses at the doorway. "Seriously, I'm so proud of you guys."

Grace opens the box. "Mostly cheap stuff, except for this." She pulls out the topaz pendant set in silver.

"Let me see!" Maddie snatches the pendant from Grace's startled grasp. "Where did you get this?"

"Duc gave it to me. Why, what's the matter?" Grace watches as Maddie flips it over to examine it from all angles.

"My father made this," Maddie says. "I can't believe you have it."

Grace digs around in the jewelry box to retrieve the card lodged along the seam at the bottom. She hands it to Maddie.

"Michael Stuart, see? That's my dad. This is his business card." Maddie turns over the card and reads aloud. "'Yellow topaz strengthens faith and optimism. It assists in recognizing your own abilities, instills a drive toward recognition, and attracts helpful people. Bestows charisma and confidence, with pride in abilities.' This is his handwriting." Maddie looks at her in confusion and amazement. "I couldn't be any more freaked out right now."

"Duc bought it in Old Town, and that's where your dad's shop is, right?" Grace says, trying to normalize the bizarre coincidence.

"Do you know how many jewelry stores there are in Old Town? Do you know how many necklaces? Thousands! Your friend Duc walked into my dad's shop and bought this from him—he wrote on the card! When was this?"

"My birthday, it's my birthstone. Last November," Grace says. "I wore it every day until after Duc and Robin left in May, when it made me too sad to look at it."

"And that's when your life went to hell and I was preparing to run away to France," Maddie says. "We were both on track to end up here."

"It's a weird coincidence," Grace says, a little concerned that Maddie is so wound up.

"It's more than that," Maddie says. "It's a sign."

"A sign of what?"

"We were meant to meet. It was destiny. I had a feeling when I first met you and this—this confirms it. Isn't it cool?" Then Maddie smiles. "It almost restores my faith a little. Like maybe, just maybe, the world isn't as totally fucked up as I thought."

Grace relaxes. What Maddie says makes its own crazy sense. Maddie's father's hands, the same hands that cradled her and nurtured her after her mother deserted them both, created the one object Grace treasures most. A connection.

Maddie hands the pendant back to Grace, who tucks it back into her jewelry box.

"Lights out, girls," Sharon's voice from the hall.

Grace switches off their lights and climbs into bed.

"Good night, Grace," Maddie says with a yawn.

"Good night, Maddie." Grace waits for Maddie to start one of her after-lights-out conversations, but all she hears is the soft breathing of sleep.

Maddie, Age 15

Corrales, New Mexico

Maddie sat shoulder to shoulder with fellow classmates in her high school auditorium, listening to an annoying pep rally. For the past two and a half years, she had been a fragile bubble willing herself not to burst. It was especially hard during all this rah-rah shit. She didn't like the closeness of others, and she saved her smiles for when she was in front of her dad and Lesley, because it took so much out of her.

Girls leaned over in the bleachers and asked Maddie where she got that top or those shoes, crap that Lesley kept buying her, but Maddie couldn't have cared less. She put on a show at school to not alert any of the teachers. Without much effort, Maddie could get Bs, so that was what she brought home on her report cards. She put all her energy into not raising any red flags, especially one in front of a raging Jeffrey. She ate only to keep up appearances. Everything she put in her mouth tasted like Jeffrey. He threatened to kill Moonshine if she did anything to displease him. He always got pissed at her about one thing or another. She fought fear like some people fought cancer.

Some jock stood in front of them now, speaking about team spirit. Maddie didn't even know what sport they were cheering for. It was fall, so maybe football. The girls around her swooned over the jock, but he only repulsed her. He reminded her of Jeffrey and she fantasized about shooting a silver bullet through Jeffrey's heart. Or a spike. What killed monsters for good?

She envied and hated the kids around her. Young and happy. No worries. Their smiles natural eruptions of joy. But then they weren't prostituting themselves to keep their loved ones alive. The shame never went away. In the auditorium, each student mirrored what she had lost. She swallowed her fate with nose-pinching disgust, day after day. She was surviving. Jeffrey would graduate in the spring.

Most of Maddie's free time was spent with Moonshine. There were not many things Maddie felt thankful for, but the heated barn was one of them. There, she and Moonshine plotted ways to outsmart Jeffrey. It was a meager piece of power, but it kept her going. Not that she'd actually follow through with any of her ideas. She snuck into her father's studio and took some amulet stones to slip under Jeffrey's mattress: amethyst for transforming negative energy to positive, jade to facilitate inner peace, onyx to smooth out emotions. Around her neck on a long cord she wore stones of her own for protection: sugilite, carnelian, black tourmaline. But her secret weapon was her labradorite. It allowed her to transcend her body when she needed to. In her darkest moments, she thought about taking her own life and setting Jeffrey up for the fall in her suicide note.

One afternoon Maddie came home from school early due to menstrual cramps. She took her literature homework to the barn to hang out with Moonshine.

Maddie heard the crunching of boots outside the barn and froze. Was it Jeffrey? He must have skipped out on his study hall. Sometimes he was disgusted by her periods and did things to her with objects. She held her breath, praying it wasn't him.

Now there were voices outside. It was Dad and Lesley. She was glad to be able to breathe again, even if it was the scent of stall muck. It was obvious they were talking about her.

"She doesn't show any interest in anything," Lesley said. "I wanted her to try out for cheerleading, she wouldn't do that. At least join the pep club, she wouldn't do that. Prom committee, I really wanted to be involved in the prom with her, but she turned her nose up at that too. How is school supposed to be any fun if she won't get involved?"

"She wears the clothes you buy her," Dad said.

"Like a walking mannequin. I'm just really disappointed I don't have one of those high-energy daughters, a girl who's more like Jeffrey."

"She's so serious," her dad said. "Her conversations, if you can call them that, are so superficial. She's never around, always with her horse or reading. Maybe she's just growing up and thinks her old man doesn't understand things anymore. I never thought she'd be like this. I thought we'd always be close."

Had her father forgotten who she was? Had Jeffrey taken her soul completely? What her dad didn't understand was how much she needed him. At night she'd lay awake and send him telepathic messages. She silently begged for him to come to her and say that he suspected what was happening to her and only needed confirmation. He would kill Jeffrey for what he had done—if Jeffrey didn't kill him first. Her dad, her knight in shining armor, had no fucking clue.

Maddie wanted to be brave in that moment. She wanted to jump up and tell them everything. But what would be the point so close to Jeffrey's graduation? Soon he'd be going off to his Ivy League college. She would get her life back. Why ruin her dad's world after she had withstood so much for his ignorance and safety? And she would just look crazy anyway, and they probably wouldn't believe her, and who knew what Jeffrey would do to her or her dad then.

"At least she and Jeffrey aren't at it anymore. School keeps them in separate worlds."

Oh, he's at it, Maddie seethed. Why did they think she walked around like a windup toy, running down and completely collapsing by the end of the day? Or why she scrubbed herself to the bone? Or ate like a chemotherapy patient? She had gaps in her memory as if she had been on some kind of autopilot.

Jeffrey still crept into her bedroom at night. Her only peace was in surrendering. At least he had to be relatively quiet. Maddie had developed a technique where she could zone out during his abuse. It was Jeffrey's touch and his alone she knew. He ordered her to stop hugging or kissing her father. He covered her head with a pillowcase and pretended to be a quieter, gentler rapist as the pillowcase sopped up her tears of shame and her futile desperation for even one ounce of human compassion.

Maddie thought she would soar in her newfound liberation after Jeffrey went off to college, but even as her cage door stood open, she huddled in its corner. She had no energy and preferred to sleep more than anything.

She had nightmares about Jeffrey almost every night. And sometimes even during the day. Like in the middle of government class, where even the untraumatized had a hard time staying focused. She found fingernail cuts in her palms and her jaw ached where her teeth clenched, fighting off her attacker in her mind. Suddenly she'd be back in class again, trying to wrap her head around the Electoral College.

She slogged through her days in tenth grade. It took every ounce of energy she and her healing stones could muster. They hung all over her in the shape of bead necklaces, earrings, bracelets, belt buckles. She would wear a breastplate embedded with gems if they allowed them in school. She walked down the halls like a furtive rodent, obsessively counting her steps to her next class. Kids who managed to notice her at all thought she was dangerously mysterious. Especially the goth ones who lurked like dark shadows, wanting her to let them in. But there was no way in or out of her solitary hell.

Just before the holidays, Maddie plunged into panic, anticipating that Jeffrey would come home for Christmas. Then a visibly disappointed Lesley announced Jeffrey was going with a fraternity brother to his family's estate in Connecticut for the holidays. Sometimes his threats would come back to her so fresh she thought he was right behind her, his hot breath whispering into her ear. Grocery stores, movie theaters—it didn't matter where she was, he'd be there too.

Headphones helped. Blasting music made it easier to ignore everyone around her. Dad and Lesley called it teenage moodiness. Maybe they worried she was on drugs. Maybe she should have been. But what did she need drugs for? She was already numbed out, unable to feel.

It was as if she operated herself with buttons and levers from a faraway control tower. There was a button for a fake smile, one for getting up, getting dressed, eating. Levers worked her arms and legs and propelled her through her day.

She kept to herself at school, ate her sack lunch alone, and spoke only when a teacher called on her. Except for the few times she spaced out, she had the correct answers when asked, and teachers didn't worry about kids who supplied the correct answers. She was well groomed and blended in, hiding the purple circles around her eyes with concealer and eye shadow.

She drank malts to keep weight on. She was getting by on curb appeal, when on the inside she was an abandoned, condemned wreck of a soul.

When kids are admitted during the school year to this place, they attend accredited school in the education building, so no one has to flunk because they have problems. During the summers, they also attend class, but instead of grueling grade-level work, they do some remedial work, art, reading groups, music, and indoor and outdoor structured games, along with their therapy sessions.

Maddie welcomes the distraction, especially in the form of the Brazos Cottage teacher, Mr. Zamora, whom she loves. Judy is his assistant. She usually reads the newspaper at her desk or does crossword puzzles, unless one of the boys is being a PITA (pain in the ass). Then Judy rolls her chair where she's needed to diffuse a situation.

"This week we're going to work on painting retablos." Mr. Z holds up an example. "I won a blue ribbon at the state fair last year with this one. This is San Miguel, my patron saint," he says, also showing the tattoo on his meaty upper arm of the winged, sword-wielding saint with one foot holding down the devil. "If you don't want to do a saint, you can choose any historical figure you admire, it doesn't have to be a religious icon."

Mr. Z is a jolly, round man who wears a little mustache and goatee surrounding his perpetually smiling mouth. He has thinning black hair tied back into a ponytail that looks more like a kitten tail. Today he's dressed in a long, white gauze shirt and white gauze pants. Maddie guesses he buys his elaborate outfits from *International Male* catalog, because he keeps a stack of them on his desk. An Indonesian skullcap with sequined elephants perches on his head.

Mr. Z hands out small blocks of wood as he walks around his classroom. The walls are plastered with cartoon feelings faces that float like yellow balloons. Maddie thought it was for the younger or slower kids at first, until she finds herself studying each expression with its captioned feeling, and realizes she is now able to name feelings she has long denied. Jeffrey's power begins to fade while her power grows. Grace says avoidance or staying stuck is not an option. Maddie has to move through what has been done to her in order to heal. Remaining a victim at this point is a choice.

Percy holds his block of wood to his face, sniffing its greenness, while the rest of them go to the front of the room to pick a saint to draw and paint as Mr. Z tells each saint's story. Most were tortured, Maddie discovers, and still found forgiveness. She knows she's not headed for sainthood anytime soon. She picks Saint Francis because he's the patron saint of animals, in honor of Moonshine. Grace chooses Saint Catherine, the patron saint of artists.

"It's bad to be all artistic, like when me and my homeys tattooed each other with ink we learned how to make out of burned rubber and piss from Eduardo's uncle who's on parole," Abdias says, drawing on his block of wood. He reaches his hand deep into his big, loose pants pocket like he might scratch his crotch. He instead produces a royal-blue finger comb. His slicked-back hair glistens with little waffle prints from the hairnet he sleeps in, as he scrapes his hair back with the teeny, tiny teeth of the comb. He's obsessed with his hair. Maddie has never known a gang kid. He fascinates her with his fragile, inflated ego. She wonders how many gangsters out there are just hurt little boys like Abdias, all from lousy homes. He's wickedly handsome, and Maddie can tell he's used to attracting female attention.

After only three weeks, these fellow patients and staff feel more like family than what she was subjected to in her home in Corrales. The boys have become her pesky little brothers.

Lucas concentrates on his Joan of Arc, his tongue sticking out sideways as he draws her figure. Sam, peeking out of Lucas's shirt as always, looks equally intent with his fish-eyed stare. Maddie feels like Wendy to this lost half cowboy, half soldier. He listens to Maddie and actually looks up to her.

Mr. Z plays the Gipsy Kings and dances around the room, lending his expertise wherever he can and praising everyone's drawings to the highest. When he gets to Aaron, Mr. Z stops. Aaron sits with his chin on his hand, no pencil, his block blank.

"A quandary, Mr. Z. Intellectually, I know that drawing one of your

Catholic saints won't harm me, but I can't in good conscience do it," Aaron says. "The voices of my ancestors will haunt me."

"You too?" Percy asks. With a half-chewed stub of a yellow pencil, he's drawing what he calls Crow Woman.

"How about you draw Moses?" says Mr. Z. "He's a saint in my book."

"I can accept that." Aaron picks up his pencil.

As level twos, Grace and Gabe are allowed to work on the patio. Mr. Z made the small courtyard into an oasis with potted flowers, bird feeders, and a birdbath. Maddie earned back her level one a week after punching her fist into the wall. The plant manager, a man known only by his last name, Decker, came to confront her about the damage she did to "his" wall and made her help him repair it. He scares the bejesus out of her with his rock-hard scowl and grouchy demeanor. Dressed all in black, he's so foreboding even Jackson looks nervous when Decker approaches.

Dr. Swenson says Maddie might earn her level two by next week's rounds, when the team of doctors, therapists, and staff reevaluate everyone based on their behavior and progress in working on their treatment goals. It embarrasses her to be a level one. Maddie vows that by next week, she'll be on the patio with Grace and Gabe.

But until then, she's stuck in the classroom with Abdias, Aaron, Lucas, and Percy. Maddie sometimes wonders if she's psychotic, like she's heard Percy might be. She has not confessed the full extent of her flashbacks. She's afraid of being labeled crazy, like Lesley said. Although her flashbacks have diminished, something will still trigger one and the present reality gives way to her vividly reliving Jeffrey's torture.

Abdias, chewing a piece of neon-green bubble gum because he can't smoke, blows a ginormous bubble. He keeps huffing it bigger and bigger, his eyes widening, until Aaron jabs his pencil through it and it explodes on Abdias's face, coating his hair. The look on his face! But the gum doesn't stick to his hair due to all the Tres Flores oil he has in it.

Maddie feels the jiggle in her stomach before it bursts into full-blown laughter. She laughs so hard she stomps her feet and begs for air. It feels so damn good. When was the last time she truly laughed? Her stomach hurts heaving out so much laughter. With each guffaw, she feels some of her darkness be cast out.

Maddie's still catching her breath when a female staffer from Capitan Cottage arrives to escort her to the girls' Sexual Issues Group. Maddie joins the other girls and follows them to the group room, where Dr. Kaye presides. They form an amoeba-shaped circle with their chairs and settle in before Dr. Kaye goes over the rules of the group. Maddie's anxiety level soars thinking she'll have to talk about her abuse to these strangers. They go around the circle for introductions. It's Maddie and three teenage girls from the other older-kid cottages, Pecos and Capitan.

Dr. Kaye's eyes are cornflower blue, her blond hair soft and natural. "You don't have to say anything you don't feel comfortable talking about right now." Her rose-petal-pink lips part into a warm smile. "But you're expected to try. You're all here for the same reason, in one way or another."

Maddie assesses her fellow abused souls, trying not to stare, but they're doing the same thing. Across from her sits a heavy girl who introduces herself as Desiree. Maddie has seen her during center-wide activities. Rumor has it she has put on thirty pounds since admission, but still squeezes herself into her same old provocative clothes. She's proudly showing as much skin as she can get away with. Aaron told Maddie that Desiree has done so many drugs her brain doesn't hold a charge anymore. Desiree also appears to have cornered the mascara market. Her full, black-lined lips do acrobatics with the blob of gum in her mouth when she speaks. "My name is Desiree, and I'm here because my dad sexually abused me when I was little, and now they say I have a promi . . . promi . . ."

"Promiscuity," Dr. Kaye says quietly, like a person feeding lines from the orchestra pit.

"Yeah, promiscuity with older men, but do they ever stop to think I just like older guys?" Desiree's head bobs like a lowrider displaying its hydraulics.

Next to Desiree is a girl so thin she seems to sway under the air-conditioning vent. She has to be encouraged by Dr. Kaye to say her name to the group. "Kathy," she whispers. She obviously isn't eating, but whatever she has suffered sure is eating her. She shuts down after that, her bony wrists and hands forming a barrier for her to hide behind.

"My name is Nishoni and I'm from Gallup," says a Navajo girl. On her buttered-toast skin, her arms and legs are covered with scars and cuts in different stages of healing. Some look round like cigarette burns, others jagged and purple done with sharp objects, and some still-dark red scabs. She sits in the chair like a guy, knees open. "I'm not ready to talk today, but my mom and aunties want to know if they can come to a group like this too," Nishoni says.

"I'll set something up for them." Dr. Kaye makes herself a note. "When you talk to your mom, find out when she can get back to the trading post for my call."

Maddie's next. By appearances alone, never in million years would she think she has anything in common with these girls. As different as each of them are, they share the same pain—different scenarios, but the same violation. Grace says the words have to be spoken for healing to begin, and for Jeffrey to become an inconsequential piece of crap in her rearview mirror.

With her heart racing, she prepares to speak. In front of Maddie sits hickey-necked Desiree, with drawn-on eyebrows, huge breasts stretching her tight shirt, in dangerous denial. And Kathy, who obviously is trying to disappear altogether, and Nishoni, who wears the warrior cuts and scars like the women before her.

"My name is Maddie and I was tortured physically and sexually by my stepbrother."

CHAPTER 7

Grace, Age 16

Albuquerque, New Mexico

Grace pulled herself out of bed. She felt like an old woman and she was only sixteen. She realized she was premenstrual and had no tampons for her impending period. She thought of Twyla, like she always did every thirty days or so. The memory of Twyla was about as good as it got, but remembering always brought fresh pain. Sometimes it was hard to believe that the people she missed were still out there living their lives. Except her mother, of course. Grace sometimes thought it was odd that she could miss someone so much and not remember anything about them. Karen must be tucked into some deep part of her, stored away like abandoned canned jars of summer peaches in a sealed-off root cellar.

If she were an old woman, she wouldn't have to worry about periods, or even Mitch, for that matter. The thought seemed unreal. Would she ever be free of him? He'd probably die without her saving his ass every five minutes, a job she'd had for as long as she could remember. Before landing in Albuquerque, they were last in Denver, where they almost froze to death. They were homeless for weeks at a time, in winter, of course. Somehow she still managed to go to school and get decent grades. She'd long ago stopped making friends, because she knew she wouldn't be around long enough to make it worthwhile. She always scoped out the nearest library and read a lot, but besides that, basic survival was all she had time for. School didn't start for another six weeks and five days, according to her homemade calendar, not that she was counting.

Did she even have any money for tampons? Did Mitch? She was working at a little pizza place in Nob Hill, the kind with the brick oven in the wall with a real wood fire, but she didn't get paid until Friday. Luckily they fed her there, her one meal a day, but it was good food and she had her choice of salads, soups, pizzas, calzones, and even three different pasta dishes. She tried to eat only half and take the rest home for Mitch.

The apartment was quiet. Mitch was either sleeping or out. He didn't talk about what he did for cash, but that was a no-brainer. He went out at odd hours and came back with jewelry and computers and televisions. He sold the stuff and bought mainly booze with the cash and hopefully kept enough for the rent on their shithole apartment in an area known as the War Zone. A college guy she worked with said it was also known as the International District, since there were Vietnamese and Cubans and Mexicans crowded together with nowhere else to go. But the crime rate, the knife and gun club, made it the War Zone.

Grace didn't really think about whether she was safe or not—she figured she wasn't, especially when she walked to Central Avenue to catch the bus for work and returned after dark. She didn't have the energy to be afraid; she just walked fast, kept her head down, and didn't carry a purse. Her blond hair had been attracting attention, so she dyed it black and cut it to chin length. It stuck out kind of funny, but what can you do? At least she blended in better. Even her white skin was starting to darken from the long walks under the ever-present Albuquerque sun. In the nearly two months they'd been there, she couldn't remember a single cloudy day, let alone any rain. She thought of San Francisco and Twyla wrapped in a misty fog.

"Mitch," she called as she walked out of the only bedroom. He was at least a gentleman about that; she always got the bedroom if there was one, and he crashed on the couch or floor if there wasn't one. His bedroll was on the couch, but he wasn't in it.

She made her rounds, collecting beer cans and liquor bottles to dump into the trash. It was already hot, so she flipped the switch for the swamp cooler but nothing happened. She tried the light switches. Shit. No power. They must have been cut off again. She opened the fridge and found half of a limp spinach salad from work and some cans of beer. She ate the salad before it went bad and figured Mitch could drink warm beer.

In the freezer she found only some shrunken ice cubes in a tray, left from the previous renter, she supposed. Nothing to lose there.

Grace checked her wallet. Two dollars and fifty-eight cents—her bus money and not enough for tampons. Maybe she could bum one off one of the girls at work to save until she needed it, which, judging from her sore boobs, could be any minute.

No televisions or electronic equipment in Mitch's stash in the closet, no signs of any loot anywhere. Maybe that's where he was, fencing his ill-gotten goods. When she got mad at him, she thought about calling crime stoppers to get him busted and collect the reward money, but she didn't want to end up in some foster home and she didn't want to try to survive on her own at sixteen.

Later, when Grace locked the front door to leave for work, she was startled by a man walking toward her with a determined stride. Men like that were usually after money.

"Where's your dad? He owes me rent," the man said, "or you'll be locked out and on the streets by tomorrow."

"He's at work and gets paid today, so don't worry. Come back tomorrow," Grace said in her well-practiced monotone. Shit, they were going to be homeless again. Being on the streets was the worst. Hungry she could handle. She thought of the shelter in Denver they had to crash in: smelly, noisy, and bedbugs for souvenirs.

The man looked unconvinced but then began to give her the eye. "How old are you, girlie?"

"Old enough." To kick your fat ass, she said in her head.

"If your dad can't come up with the cash, we might be able to work something else out to buy him some time," he said, smoothing his finger over his moustache.

"He'll have the cash," Grace said, and ran for the bus.

At work, the swamp cooler kept her comfortable while she chopped veggies for salads and pizza toppings. Her knife skills had improved, and she loved how she could zone out and create whole tubs full of diced peppers, onions, mushrooms, and thin ribbons of basil. She looked up to see the manager, Deb, watching her. "Nice work, Grace. Why don't you take a break?"

"I'm good," Grace said, and picked up a bell pepper.

"Come with me while I grab a smoke. I want to talk to you."

Grace followed her out of the back door. All the prep work, soup making, and lasagna assembly were done in the back kitchen. Out on the floor in front of customers, salads and pizzas were made to order, and the pizzas rode into the blazing heat of the wood-fired oven on long paddles. Jazz played while the college crowd and upscale neighbors drank microbrews and ate the little pieces of vegetables that Grace chopped for their salads and pizzas. She felt a strange sense of pride about that.

Grace stood nervously in the small slant of shade while Deb lit up, took a drag, and then exhaled, waving her smoke away from Grace. "You don't smoke, do you?" Deb said.

"Um, no," Grace said, wondering how you go about bumming a tampon.

Deb nodded. "You work hard and you do a good job. I'm going to bump your pay fifty cents an hour and start training you on lasagna, soups, and bread. More hours too. You'll have to start coming in earlier, by eight, okay? After school starts in the fall, we'll figure out your schedule. I want to keep you on."

"Wow, great, thanks," Grace said. That was the next rung on the ladder. If she did well, she had a shot at joining the line on the floor, where they made even more money.

"You earned it. Anything else I can do for you?" Deb was stomping out her half-smoked cigarette.

"Well, it's embarrassing, but I think I'm getting my period and I forgot—"

Deb began to laugh. "You are so cute. In the staff bathroom on the top shelf of the cabinet, I keep a box or two. Take as many as you need. And get some water or soda before you go back to work, it's hot as hell."

The rest of her shift went fast, and Grace felt dangerously happy. She had four tampons stuck in her socks under her jeans and a promotion. She packed up her allotted lunch and headed for the bus at nine p.m. She hoped Mitch was home so he could eat with her and they could celebrate.

When she got home, the house was dark and she remembered they had no electricity. The truck was out front, so he she knew he was there. "Mitch?" she called. She heard a groan from the couch.

Shit, was he that drunk so early? "Mitch, do we have a flashlight?"

Silence. She ran to the kitchen and put the food on the counter. In the drawer next to the old gas stove was a packet of wooden matches to light the burners. She grabbed them and returned to Mitch, striking a match. He wasn't drinking—he was covered in blood. "Jesus," she said. The match burned down to her fingers and she lit another one.

He looked unconscious, mouth gaping open, blood obscuring his face, down the front of his shirt. "Mitch! Wake up!" she yelled, and pulled at his shoulder.

Another moan. "I have to get you to the hospital!" Grace said. "Where are the keys?" Thank god she'd learned to drive when she was fourteen in San Diego.

"No," he said, coming around. "Can't."

"Don't worry about the money, they have to treat you. You could die or something." Grace felt panic like an icy hand around her heart, even as it had to be a hundred degrees in the cinder block building that radiated the heat it stored up all day.

"Cops," Mitch said.

"What happened?" Grace said sinking to the floor.

"Fucked up."

"Tell me," Grace said.

"Got interrupted at a house. Guy took a bat to me."

"So the cops are looking for you?"

"Don't think the guy got a good look at me." Mitch tried to shift and yelped in pain.

"Where did he hit you?" Grace asked, striking another match.

"Where didn't he hit me?" Mitch said. "Reach in my pocket."

Grace reached in his pocket and pulled out a big wad of cash with a rubber band around it. She held the match closer. Hundred-dollar bills.

"Don't burn it up."

"No wonder the guy was pissed," Grace said.

"Rich guy. Should have seen the house. No security system, asshole was asking for it."

Grace felt the weight of the cash in her hand. "I got promoted at work. Fifty cents an hour raise."

"Good girl," Mitch said, and either passed out or fell asleep.

Grace hoped he wouldn't die in the night from a blood clot to the brain or something. He must have been able to drive and walk, so if he had broken bones, they'd have to be ribs or maybe an arm. She'd just have to wait until sunrise to see what was what. She got her pillow and curled up on the ratty armchair next to the couch in case Mitch needed her in the night.

She woke with a start as the sun began to stream through the front window at six a.m. She had to be at work in two hours. It took her thirty minutes to get there on the bus including the walk to the bus stop. Plus thirty minutes to shower and get ready. That left her one hour to assess the Mitch situation.

Most of the blood seemed to have come from a gash on his scalp. She could only hope it knocked some sense into him. "Wake up, Mitch."

She went to the kitchen and filled the dishpan with soapy water and grabbed a clean dish cloth. His eyes were blackened and swollen, but he managed to open them a slit.

"I'm going to clean you up and see what the damage is." Grace began to sponge off the blood. His eyebrow was split, his ear was cut. His good looks would not be affected.

She felt along his upper and lower arms. The bones seemed to be in their right places. "Can you move your arms and fingers?"

He gingerly raised his arms but stopped. "Fuck! My shoulder—the left one ain't right."

She lifted his blood-crusted shirt. His ribs were purple. She began to feel them and he winced. "Shit, Grace!"

"Broken ribs. They can heal on their own, but it will take a while," Grace said. "The shoulder, who knows, but it doesn't look any different from your other one, so I don't think it's broken. Maybe you tore something. Have you peed yet?"

"Couldn't get up. My left ankle might be broke."

Grace pulled off his shoes and socks and rolled up his left pant leg. His ankle was massively swollen. "Can you move your foot?"

He tried. "Hurts like a son of a bitch."

Grace sat back to look at him. "You need a doctor. X-rays. Maybe a cast or surgery for your ankle."

"Can't risk it. The cops will be looking for a guy that got beat with a bat. I can heal up here. I broke my arm when I was a kid and it healed up on its own. Did it on my skateboard in the summer and my dad was so pissed he didn't take me to no doctor. He just tied it to a board, and by the time school rolled around, I was fine. What makes you such an expert anyway?"

"I read a lot. Your bones are different now than when you were a kid," Grace said. "And ankles are more complicated than arm bones. Let's just hope to god it's a bad sprain. Did he hit you on your ankle?"

"No, I just tripped and landed wrong trying to get away."

Grace about laughed.

"You think this is funny? Your old man near beat to death?" Mitch said, but his lip was twitching. "You probably would have liked to seen it."

"Probably," Grace said. "There's been plenty of times I'd have liked to take a bat to you myself."

"Karma kicked my ass. Hey, how much money did I score? I never got to count it."

"Two thousand six hundred dollars," Grace said. "Let me help you get to the bathroom, I want to see if you pee blood before I go to work, and I need to tie your hair to close that gash on your scalp." She'd read how to do it in a pioneer story.

He sat up and stood on his right leg and slung his left arm around her shoulder. That way, he could hop to the bathroom. He hung on to the sink. "I can take it from here."

"Don't flush."

Grace stood on the other side of the door listening to him whiz like a racehorse, as he always put it.

"No blood," he called.

She opened the door as he was zipping up. "Watch for it and tell me if you see any."

"You could buy me a cane at Walgreens. See if you can get someone to buy you some booze—just ask someone in the parking lot. Tell them it's for your old man who's laid up. Tell them you'll give them a twenty for a tip."

She helped him back to the couch and handed him some clean clothes. She made a series of tight, tiny knots using strands of his hair on either side of his three-inch scalp gash, closing it, and all the while, Mitch yammered about needing booze.

She quickly got cleaned up and ready for work and then stood over him. "Here's some food from last night. You won't be needing the truck, so I'll take it to work. The landlord will be coming for the rent later—it's on the table. I get off at three and I'm going downtown to the power company to get us hooked back up. Then I'm going to get some groceries and stuff I need. Then I'll go to Walgreens and get you a cane, bandages, a wrap for your ankle, and antibiotic ointment so you don't get infected. But no goddamned booze. Forget it. I'm in charge now, and you can't say anything or I'll call the cops on you myself. You're going to get sober, Mitch. Enough is enough. I don't care if you're thrashing on the floor in dt's when I get home, you get no booze. This money is going to pay our rent and buy us food and pay our bills until you heal up and find a legit job, and that's fucking it!"

"You wouldn't call the cops," Mitch said, but he looked doubtful.

"Try me. And don't bother trying to find the rest of the money either."

"That's my fucking money—" he yelled as she slammed the door.

"Everybody, circle up," Pat, the recreational therapist says, standing under the shade of a huge cottonwood tree. The rest of the Brazos group follows, along with the kids from Pecos Cottage. Maddie spots Desiree right away, who's pushing her way to the front to stand close to Pat.

"Today we're having experiential therapy, or ET as we call it. We're going to do some work on team building, communication, and trust. We'll be doing the ropes course," Pat says.

Maddie and Grace look at the tall, looming course. It was a crazy-looking high-wire circus act, with wooden platforms at the end of each challenge. "Holy crap," Maddie says under her breath.

"Let's review the Full Value Contract," Pat continues. "Who wants to start?" He eyes each of them until a hand shoots up. "Yes, Lucas."

"Safety, sir!" Lucas says, snapping to attention.

Pat arches his eyebrows. "What about it?"

Lucas's hand snaps straight up again, fingers together and rigid.

"Yes, Lucas."

"It is our duty to keep ourselves and each of our buddies safe at all times. We do that by strategic spotting and communicating what it is we need. Same as in Nam."

"Very good, Lucas. At ease," Pat walks among the group for emphasis. "If anyone exhibits unsafe behavior, he or she will be sent back to the cottage on room restriction with a writing assignment, am I clear?"

Everyone in the group nods. Pat leads them down the gradually sloping green hill to the ropes course behind the lower cottages. The grounds keeper rides a mower, sending up the sweet smell of freshly mown grass. Maddie thinks of Moonshine. Missing Moonshine is her constant state. She hates that Lesley is the one taking care of her now.

Pat and the other rec therapists, James and Todd, hand out scuffed orange helmets. Aaron stares into his as if it were a teeming bucket of bacteria. Maddie helps Grace with her chin strap. The guys start to bop each other on the head with their fists to test the safety helmets. Desiree's asking Pat to help her. She giggles when he pulls her chin strap tight under her second chin. Lucas is the first to have his helmet on and looks ready to charge into battle. All Maddie can see of Sam is the tiny tip of his yellow beak. Percy holds his helmet as if in suspended animation.

Pat hands out a fistful of waggling harnesses. "Everyone put one on." He steps into his harness to demonstrate, hitching it high and snug around his crotch, pulling the straps tight, his crotch protruding like a porpoise nose. Maddie instantly feels sick. She grabs Grace's arm to steady herself. They help each other with their harnesses. "Now pick a partner."

Maddie and Grace pick each other, of course. Cottage staff and the kids who are considered too unsafe to participate in the ropes course stand to watch in the shade of a tree. Maddie sees Kathy and Nishoni. They still haven't advanced enough in their level to be more than arm's reach from staff. Their job is to be supportive and cheer everyone on.

James and Todd demonstrate the climb up to the highest cable. "This is what I call the scooch wire." Pat says. "Your 'biners' will be hooked up to the safety cable above you as you scooch across the wire without any assistance except from your partner. If you fall, you'll just fly like Peter Pan."

Maddie likes that image and thinks of the days she wished she could fly out her bedroom window, past the second star to the right, straight on till morning.

"The first person scooches out on the cable, while the partner holds on behind. Then the first person's feet move, scooch, scooch, scooch." Pat demonstrates by shuffling his feet. "Then the second person's feet, scooch, scooch, scooch. Together you become a well-coordinated machine."

"Or not," says Aaron. Percy is his partner and Maddie doesn't blame Aaron for being skeptical. She doesn't have to be a genius like Aaron to gauge the chances of Percy and Aaron making it across the wire.

"Of course, the object is to get across the entire cable, which is twenty-five feet long." James and Todd demonstrate scooching on the wire. James pretends to fall and the group lets out a circus-crowd gasp as he dangles from the safety cable. Todd helps James back onto the wire and James scurries down the ladder like a squirrel. "Maddie and Grace, why don't you two go first? James will spot you going up the ladder; Todd will be waiting for you on the receiving platform."

"You go up first," Grace says to Maddie. "I'll be behind you."

Lucas and Abdias pull the rope ladder taut as Maddie and Grace ascend. Maddie pulls herself up each wiggly rung to the platform, where she holds on for dear life thirty feet above the ground. Grace climbs right behind her and then they and James perch on the small wooden platform. James connects each of them to the safety wire. The proximity of the male staff person in his obscene harness unnerves Maddie.

"Get your focus, Maddie," Pat yells from below.

Grace puts her hand on Maddie's arm. "You okay?"

"I'm a little freaked out."

"It's just you and me. Concentrate on the sound of my voice," Grace says.

Maddie nods. Even though she knows she can't fall to her bone-crushing death, the fear is there just the same.

"Start scooching out on the wire," James says to Maddie. She hates the sound of his male voice telling her what to do.

"Don't rush her," Grace tells him. "Whenever you're ready, Maddie, I got your back."

Maddie puts her sneaker on the cable and slides it forward, followed by her other foot. She feels the cable dip with Grace's added weight behind her as she scooches forward. Maddie's stomach drops to the earth below. She scooches forward a little farther, this time having to move her clipped rope above her along the safety wire. Kids are whooping and hollering their encouragement. From this height, their helmets look like a bunch of orange Tootsie Pops. Her view spans the entire eleven acres of the hospital grounds.

"You're a natural," Grace says, moving slowly along behind her. If Grace is scared, she doesn't show it. "A few more steps and we're halfway there."

"Keep going, girls," James says.

Maddie doesn't realize until this moment that James is following so close behind Grace on the cable. When he speaks, his sudden, deep male voice jolts through her. Her head swirls behind closed eyes, a flashback assaults her consciousness. "Get away from me!" she screams, clinging desperately to her safety line, a tidal wave of terror engulfing her.

"Maddie, listen to me. He's not here. You're safe. He doesn't control you anymore. You have taken back your power and your life." Grace's steady voice snaps Maddie out of her flashback. She opens her eyes. "Conquer this," Grace says, "and you've conquered that asshole. I'm right here. Trust me, you can do this. I've got you."

Maddie still feels frozen. Her brain has disconnected from the rest of her body. It's not about falling anymore. It's about moving beyond tough obstacles and making it to the other side. She takes a moment to find her center, her truth. "I'm going to start moving now, Grace," Maddie tells her, surprised at the strength in her voice.

"Just let me know what you need," Grace says. "You're doing great." In Grace's enthusiasm, she teeters and Maddie reaches back to steady her. "We're good," Grace says, reestablishing her balance. "Onward, dickless Christian."

"Don't make me laugh!"

"Sorry."

When Maddie's foot hits the platform on the other side, it feels like setting foot on the moon. Maddie and Grace laugh as they climb down the ladder. The rest of the kids cheer. When they get down to earth, Maddie hugs Grace like she's a mast in a storm. Their harnesses clink together like a champagne toast. "We did it, Grace!"

"You did it, Maddie," Grace says.

Maddie reaches for the cup of water Judy hands her and sees her hands have stopped shaking. She raises her cup to Grace. "Cheers!"

Maddie, Age 16

Corrales, New Mexico

Thank god Jeffrey decided to take a job in Boston for the summer. His best friend's father was a named partner in a prestigious law firm and he invited Jeffrey to work with him over the school break. Since Jeffrey had decided to go into law, Maddie knew he would not skip an opportunity to advance himself. Maddie also knew he had no interest in seeing his mother. He would sell her if he could get something out of it. If he came back at all, it would be to torture Maddie. She never spoke to him when he called, but Jeffrey ended his phone calls to Lesley by saying, "You make sure you tell

Maddie to behave herself." Even though Lesley thought it was cute brotherly advice, Maddie took it as the threat that it was.

The summer before eleventh grade, Maddie devoured the first four Harry Potter books and rode Moonshine every day. As long as her buttons and levers worked, so could she. Her dad was either at the gallery or at the spa with Lesley. He had invited her to go with him to the Old Town gallery several times, but she knew she would not be able to look her old friends in the eye. She was not the happy little girl skipping along the brick sidewalks they once knew. All they would see now was human garbage.

Maddie became morbidly fascinated by all the shark attack media that summer after the first report of the boy in Mississippi whose arm was bitten off. They took it out of the dead shark and reattached it. Then shark attacks became an epidemic, and all the news stations were airing stories about it. There were helicopter videos of shark migrations near the coasts. Maddie watched from the safety of her bed in the middle of the desert. She knew what it felt like getting the blood and life sucked out of you, and understood the phantom ache for what was torn away.

By the second week of September, Maddie was a few weeks into her junior year. Lesley, of course, bought her a new wardrobe. Everything was big on her, which she disguised with safety pins, belts, and layers. As much as Maddie tried, she still could not will herself to eat enough to keep her weight on. She felt full from stuffing down her all of her misery; there was no room for food.

One Tuesday morning as Maddie got ready for school, she glanced at her TV hoping to see more shark news. What she saw was a large tower spewing dark billows of smoke. Had she changed the channel? Some disaster movie? There was panic in the television voices. She sat at the foot of her bed and watched as a plane flew into the second tower standing parallel to the first. Now it, too, looked like a gigantic smokestack. People were screaming and running for their lives. Maddie's heart began to race with them. This couldn't be real.

She pulled the towel off of her wet hair as she watched the second tower collapse first in a cloud of dark smoke and debris. All those people buried under rubble. Surely most of them died instantly, others suffocating as she watched.

The voices from the TV faded as she fought for breath. She didn't know what was coming over her, but she started laughing hysterically. It was not funny-ha-ha laughing. It was a strange, unfamiliar sound erupting out of her. Crying would feel better. Was she going nuts?

Suddenly she was a little girl again, in her dad's arms back in Old Town whirling around the apartment. Everything was perfect in her world then. Her father's hugs were like the blankets firefighters wrapped around shocked survivors.

If they had stayed in Old Town, what would that Maddie have become? Would she still have been a virgin? So much had been stolen from her. That once wonderful child lay buried beneath rubble. She never had a chance in hell. But she was still alive, not like the thousands of people in this unfolding tragedy. Could she claw her way out? Was rescue even possible?

Maddie stayed in front of the television, school canceled. People were frantically searching for loved ones, not knowing if they were dead or alive. Some received final, helpless messages on their phones. Did victims cry for their mothers in their last moments? Real family never gave up hope. She saw that now. Was her mother dead or alive? If Maddie had found her years ago, would her life have taken such a devastating turn? She also knew she could not survive two more years at this place until she went off to college.

Suddenly Maddie could see a way out. Why hadn't she thought of this sooner? If she had to hunt all four corners of this round world, she would find her mother and leave this hell behind.

When Maddie gets to Dr. Swenson's office for family therapy, she sees that her dad brought donuts. Dr. Swenson is already in the middle of a Bavarian cream–filled donut, Maddie's favorite. Freshly brewed coffee is steaming from Dr. Swenson's and her father's cups. Her dad wears powdered sugar around his lips. She can't help but feel this is inappropriate. She isn't sure she condones her father getting chummy with Dr. Swenson over coffee and donuts, although it's common for the parents to meet with the therapist before family therapy. But does he have to be so cavalier about it? Like this is some garden party?

"Have one, sweetie." Her dad offers her the box to choose from. "I brought your favorite, Bavarian cream."

Okay, so he still remembers her favorite donut. "No, thanks," Maddie says in case it's some kind of bribe.

Dr. Swenson wipes off her hands and takes a long sip of her coffee. "So catch me up, Michael. How's it been with you since we last met?"

"Not good. I haven't been able to sleep. I'm worried about Maddie. Lesley's been distant and assuming the worst."

"What is 'the worst,' according to Lesley?" asks Dr. Swenson. Maddie knows what it is and so does Dr. Swenson: that he might believe his own daughter.

"You have to understand, I love my wife very much. She's a wonderful woman. We co-own the spa and business is booming—we have a great life together. I go over and over everything in my mind until it drives me nuts."

For the first time in Maddie's life, she sees her dad break down. Bending over his lap and raking his hair, he cries. "I love Maddie. But I can't lose Lesley. I'm scared as shit."

"I totally get your fear, Michael," says Dr. Swenson. "You suffered the pain of losing Renée, the first love of your life."

Maddie's dad cries harder. Maddie knows what it feels like to be validated for the first time. Maybe the stories he told of her mother were as much for him as for her.

"And now you find another love of your life and are afraid of losing her as well," continues Dr. Swenson.

Maddie is stunned. She has never thought about her dad having such deep feelings. He always wore a brave face in their Old Town apartment. What had he been thinking or feeling alone in the bed he had once shared with her mother? Did he cry at night for Renée when Maddie had been tucked in after one of his fairy tales? He must have kept his grief hidden to try to make Maddie happy.

"I know what Lesley must be saying, and I know you love her. But Dad, it's me, Maddie. You know me. I'm telling you the truth." She is near tears with frustration and anger. "You're all I've got." She bawls now at the thought of him abandoning her. She's mad enough to want to throw the filled donuts so they splat against the window, to turn over chairs. It feels as if she's being forced through yet another violation. She grips the chair, trying to slow down her crying. Her dad passes her the tissue box Dr. Swenson had passed to him.

Dr. Swenson said in individual therapy that people erect mental barriers to keep them from having to accept hard truths, truths that can threaten a person's entire world. If and when they're able to face it, is up to them. If only it was as easy as awakening with a kiss or reciting a magic spell like she and her dad pretended in the past.

"I know I'm all you've got. I will never leave you." He reaches for her hand.

"It wasn't so much that you left me, Dad. But your life went on without me. That's how what you don't want to believe happened *happened*." Her dad looks as if she just slapped him across his face. "You didn't want to see the signs. But they were there."

"You're saying I wasn't paying attention. That I've been too wrapped up in my own life," her father says.

Maddie can tell he's gritting his teeth so as not to defend himself, his usual reaction. This reminds her of when they would play cowboys and she'd make her dad be the bad guy and sit still while she tied him up, shot him full of lead, and fed him beans from a pie pan. She's in charge. "You only saw what you wanted to see."

"I'm not saying I don't believe you. Please don't see it so black and white right now, because it's not like that in my head."

"What I hear, Michael, is you asking Maddie for more time," says Dr. Swenson. "Is that something you can do, Maddie? Give him more time?"

When Maddie was little and her dad would put her on time-out, she'd give him her stinkiest of stink eyes. She tries not to do that now. Maybe she should go for the soulful eyes of Jesus in the bleeding heart statues and paintings in his gallery. All she wants is for him to gaze into her eyes and *know*, damn it. He used to be able to do that. At one time, his sense of her was as honed as any mother's could ever be.

Her father's eyes fill again. "Tu ressembles tellement à ta mère, ça me fait mal d'autant plus a te regarder," he says hoarsely, telling her she resembles her mother so much it makes it that much harder for him to look at her.

"Mais tu devez être capable de me regarder pour connaitre la vérité," she replies. She tells him he has to be able to look at her to know the truth. She doesn't know why he started speaking French, but it draws her closer to him.

Dr. Swenson wraps up the session, walks her dad to the door, and praises his honesty and bravery. After Dr. Swenson returns, she offers Maddie a donut. "You're going to tell me what all that French stuff was about, right?"

Maddie bites into her filled donut. It already started to dry on the outside, but she doesn't mind. It's the Bavarian cream she's after, the proof in the pudding. Not a bribe, just her dad starting to remember who she is.

CHAPTER 8

"SO, GRACE, HAVE YOU been practicing the relaxation and visualization exercises I gave you last time?" Janice asks.

"Yeah. I did breathing and relaxation when I did art in school. It's pretty much the same thing," Grace says. She sits in the art room enjoying the smell of it, lemons and pencil shavings.

"Did it help you then?"

"It practically stopped the panic attacks I was having, or at least turned them down a notch so I could still paint."

"I've been going over your portfolio—thanks for lending it to me—and I have an idea I thought we'd try today. I want you to paint a beach scene that includes your mom and you when you were kindergarten age."

"But I can't remember what she looks like." Grace tenses with frustration.

"I want you to use your imagination, not your memory. Imagine what a woman in her twenties would look like playing on the beach with her five-year-old. What have you been told about what she looked like—her build, her hair color?"

"Mitch said she was thin, like me, only taller, and she had long blond hair. That's about it, I've never even seen a picture of her."

"Long blond hair, tall, and thin—that's plenty of detail. You can paint the woman and the child from a distance, either from behind or in profile. That way, you don't need any specific facial features. Think of the woman and child as generic, not actually you and your mom. Let's remove as much emotional loading as possible. In fact, let's give them new names," Janice says.

"How about the woman is Hannah and her daughter is Emily?" Grace says, choosing names from a novel she's reading.

"Great. So, paint a scene with Hannah and Emily playing on the beach. Think you can do that?"

"I'll try."

"Give me an anxiety reading on your one-to-ten scale."

Grace checks her breathing and heart rate and looks at her hands. "About a four."

"Do your preparation exercises and then you can get started when you feel ready. I'll check in with you at the midpoint of our time and see how you're doing. If you need anything, I'll be loading the kiln in the court-yard—the door is propped open, so I'll hear you if you call my name."

Grace shuts her eyes to prepare. She does some slow, controlled breathing and visualizes the painting she wants to do. When she imagines painting the woman and the little girl, she feels her insides clench. She breathes through it and tries again. She repeats their names, Hannah and Emily, and soon she can visualize painting them without the accompanying anxiety.

She dips her brush into the jar of water and then into the sky-blue paint. Soon she's in the zone, removed from her surroundings, lost in her creative process.

After what seems like a few quick minutes, Grace becomes aware of Janice standing next to her. "We're at the halfway mark," Janice whispers. "You don't need to say anything—just keep going if you like."

Grace lets Janice slip away from her awareness without breaking her flow as she continues to paint. Her hand holds the brush as if it is an exten-sion of herself; the rhythm of brush to water to paint to paper is as natural as breathing. What her brain imagines appears on the page without effort.

And then she is done. She places her brush in the rinse water. As she blinks and yawns, it's like waking from a dream state, and her painting appears in front of her for the first time.

The sky is rife with streaming clouds that do not block the sun but rather seem to be moving with a strong breeze. The surf is high and rough, though the water is brilliant blue. Sudsy white foam gathers at its edge. Some seabirds stand facing the wind, their feathers blown back. The woman's long blond hair blows around her face as she kneels down to the sand-castle her daughter is building. The woman is tan, the child is pale with nearly white hair. Their colorful sundresses billow with the wind. The child holds a red bucket and shovel, her back to the observer.

Janice sits down next to her at the table. "Tell me about this."

"Hannah and Emily live on the beach. It's windy, but the wind doesn't bother them. They hardly notice it. It's windy a lot here. Like the seabirds, they just go about their business. The sun feels good. It keeps them warm even though the wind is from the north," Grace says, staring at the painting and not looking at Janice.

"How does Emily feel? What is she thinking about?" Janice asks.

"She wants to decorate her castle with shells. She wants it to be pretty for her mother, so that her mother will be happy," Grace says, suddenly crushed by overwhelming sadness.

"Emily feels her mother is sad?"

"She knows her mother is sad, and it makes her sad. She wants her mother to smile again." Grace begins to sob, as the sadness can no longer be contained. She leans forward into her paint-smeared hands to cover her face.

"Cry it out, Grace. You're strong enough to feel Emily's sadness." Janice put her arms around her and Grace leans into Janice and cries until she's spent. The sadness moves through her like a windstorm, and releasing it feels liberating.

Even as her ribs ache with each gasping breath, she feels a bizarre exhil-aration. She lifts her head to look at Janice. "What the hell was that?" she asks, afraid she might start to laugh with hysterical relief that she has just survived something she can't name.

"Catharsis, I believe," Janice says. "We'll talk it over with Dr. Swenson, but I feel safe in saying that you were able to feel Emily's grief because in our exercise, she is separate from you. But I think the grief you channeled is yours. We may have a clue here. Perhaps when you were Emily's age, you felt that your mother was sad. A child will pick up on her mother's feelings even if her mother tries to hide them. And the child doesn't just pick up on them—she will often experience those same feelings as intensely as if they originated from the child herself. Does that make sense?"

"So maybe my mom was sad and when I painted this, I felt it through Emily—like maybe I felt it when I was little, from my mom."

"How does that idea resonate with you?"

"I think my mom was sad when I was Emily's age—and I felt sad and afraid and like I had to try to make her happy, like it was my job. And I think I really had a red bucket and shovel," Grace says, feeling her words settle into her. She tries to question it, poke holes in it, but it's solid. It's memory.

Grace leaves art therapy feeling like she's been given a parting gift. Her mom was unhappy—she knows that now, she knows it from her own memory. She wishes Mitch were there so she could confront him about it. What was Karen so sad about? It had to have been Mitch's fault. His story about how everything was rainbows and lollipops and then one day she offed herself with an accidental drug overdose is crap. Grace knows it in her bones.

In therapy with Dr. Swenson, she gets in touch with how angry she is with her dad. Even as he dragged her all over the country from one bad situation into the next, he never abandoned her . . . until now. It hurts like hell. And it pisses her off that right when he could actually be of some help to her in family therapy, he's gone.

Grace, Age 16

Albuquerque, New Mexico

Mitch had been sober for almost four months. Grace thought about it every day. She didn't know if he thought about his "one day at a time" victory on a daily basis like she did, or if he just drifted along and the days were magically turning to weeks and weeks into months. He was working the day shift at an auto supply store for a boss named Dave, whom he seemed to like and wanted to do right by. Grace figured Dave was her guardian angel sent to earth to give her a chance at a normal life. Mitch said Dave was a recovered drunk, like him, and recognized that Mitch needed a leg up.

After Mitch's come-to-Jesus ass beating in late June, Grace had taken over the reins of their destiny. That meant employing a strict budget utilizing the stolen money, while Mitch lay crumpled and broken on the sofa, shivering in the heat and crying for alcohol.

She was glad he suffered, and told him so. She lectured him about how fucked up their lives had been due to alcohol and how she would never allow it again and how if he ever drank another drop he could backslide to hell for all she cared because she would be long gone. To her surprise, that threat seemed to matter to him.

By the end of July, Mitch was able to limp around without his cane. Grace drove him to see a neighborhood that was nothing fancy but a damn sight better than the one they were in. Humble but clean triplexes were interspersed between small houses. Yards were kept up, children played, and neighbors walked their dogs, smiling and waving to each other. Grace had scouted it out one day coming home from work, driving the truck so slowly she was afraid someone would think she was casing the neighborhood, and in a way she was—but her definition of breaking and entering had nothing to do with residential burglary and everything to do with upward mobility. The neighborhood was just off Lomas, so it was near the bus lines. A Catholic church stood guard on the corner and little children in uniforms played in the schoolyard.

By the next week, one of the triplexes had a For Rent sign so she pulled the truck over and wrote down the phone number. By the next day, she had paid the first month's rent and security deposit in cash and informed Mitch they were moving and it was time for him to find a job.

Guardian Angel Dave hired Mitch to clean and stock shelves at night, pointing out the security cameras in case Mitch had a mind to steal anything. Dave told Mitch if he did a good job, he could work his way onto the day shift, which he did after a month, finding himself in a navy-blue uniform with "Dave's Auto Supplies" emblazoned in red and yellow across his back, helping customers and installing batteries and windshield wipers.

Grace was working on the line now at the pizza place. On her days off, she obsessively scrounged through flea markets and junk shops, finding furniture and art for their small two-bedroom unit that had its own fenced-in patio. Two bedrooms! Her soul sang. She crammed in as many plants that would fit, and smiled when she realized she was decorating like Twyla. Funky art, bookshelves, throw rugs, actual bedspreads on each of their beds, and real curtains on the windows transformed the place into a comfortable home. Twyla would be proud.

Since school had started, Grace worked part time, mostly long hours on the weekends and occasional evenings after school if they really needed her. Grace went with Mitch to cash his paycheck and he handed every cent over to her without too much bitching. He never said it, but she thought he might be grateful.

"But you've traveled so much. You got to live in San Francisco, one of the world's most awesome cities," her friend Duc Trang was saying, dramatically rolling across her bed. "I've only ever been here. I haven't even seen Vietnam, since my overly acculturated parents have never taken me."

Grace removed his pink-sequined Doc Martens boot from her freshly washed lilac bedspread. "San Francisco was awesome until it all went bad," she acknowledged.

Robin sat on Grace's desk chair. "Make room, I want to be on the bed too." She swam between them, her head resting on Duc's shoulder. "Don't worry, honey, we'll be in New York City in exactly seven months."

"God, how will I ever make it?" Duc said.

Grace didn't like to be reminded that her two closest—well, only—friends in the world were seniors and would graduate in May and abandon her for the American Musical and Dramatic Academy in New York City. She loved them so much it scared her. And it scared her that they were going to New York City, where terrorists had attacked only one month ago. She had watched the devastation on television with Mitch, over and over again, hoping it would start to make some kind of sense. But it never did. It was chaos and loss and nonsense on a scale too immense to grasp. It was futility and grief and shock. Grace felt the fragility of her newfound stability and saw that she was lucky, which was no consolation. Luck was a fluke. It protected no one. She had suffered enough devastation and loss in her own life to know that much.

Robin turned her actress-pretty face to Grace. "Come with us and be our roomie. You can finish high school there and utilize your skills in one of a zillion pizza places."

"You'd have to adopt me," Grace said.

"I thought we already did," Duc said.

They had adopted her as she had stood awkwardly on the chorus riser, a new girl, an alto with a blend-in kind of voice, not the standout soloist kind of voice that both Robin and Duc displayed during warm-up exercises.

Robin approached her after class, commenting on the vintage paisley skirt Grace had found for two dollars at the Salvation Army Thrift Store. Grace's hair was back to blond since moving to the new neighborhood, and she wore a lime-green plastic headband that she hoped looked funky and artistic. She liked to try offbeat styles—she figured she was essentially invisible to her peers anyway.

"I don't know you. What are you, a freshman?" Robin asked.

"Junior. New here. Grace Willis."

"Robin Lamson. Senior."

Robin was a tall and shapely brunette who looked like a twenty-something ingenue portraying a high school girl. She moved like a dancer. Duc joined them. "This is my BFF, Duc Trang."

Duc performed a stage bow full of flourishes.

"Is that your new bow?" Robin asked, her green eyes narrowing.

"Too much?" he asked.

"It could work, but you'd have to fully commit to it, be all in. Duc, this is Grace. She's a new junior. I've sized her up as too cool for the other juniors, so she's with us."

Duc appraised her from beneath his asymmetrical bangs. He reached over and pulled off Grace's headband and jabbed his fingers into her chin-length bob and fluffed it. "You have great hair. Set it free, girlfriend."

"Isn't she cute? Tiny but with a real edge to her, like my grandma's Pomeranian," Robin said. "So what's your thing, Grace? What jazzes you?"

Duc put his index finger to his pursed lips. "No, don't answer that. I want to guess. You've lived abroad and are the ward of your rich uncle André. Your parents died of some insect-borne illness while volunteering in Somalia when you were three. You read Russian literature, sculpt in marble, and are a proficient student of the lute."

Grace nodded, swallowing her smile. "It's like you intercepted my complete dossier."

"Oh, Robin, we have to keep her." Duc had enveloped her into his embrace.

Mitch had made a friend too. Jane Shaw, in her late thirties like Mitch, worked as an administrative assistant at the university. She moved into the triplex shortly after they did and knocked on their door with a plate of chocolate chip cookies to introduce herself.

It worried Grace, at first, to have this woman come into their lives and potentially have influence over Mitch, when the key to their newfound stability was for Grace to keep him under her complete control. But then Jane explained to them over spaghetti dinner at her place one night that she was against all forms of alcohol and recreational drugs because of the damage they had done to her family.

"It takes good people and turns them into losers," she said.

"Grace here can agree with you on that."

"You'd better agree with her too," Grace said.

"I do. I'm sworn off that shit," Mitch said quickly, his lips stained red from the sauce.

Jane nodded her approval. "Why do you call your father Mitch?"

"I've never been much of a father," Mitch answered for her. "But I done the best I could after her mama died on us."

Grace clanked her fork onto her plate, her anger rising. "If that was the best you could do, I'd hate to see your worst. I've called him Mitch since I was old enough to know what fathers were supposed to be like and he wasn't it. Not even close."

"Well now, that was the alcohol . . ." Mitch trailed off, obviously confused about how to best play this.

Jane refilled Grace's glass of milk. "I'm sure you know that an important part of recovery is to take responsibility for your past behavior and make amends. Have you made amends to Grace?"

Grace folded her arms over her chest and glared at him.

Mitch looked even more confused; his fingers drummed the table edge. "I work hard and turn over my paycheck to her and I'm sober. I never did lay a hand on her, never."

Jane's plain face was almost pretty as she looked at Mitch with a combination of compassion and sternness. "It's simple, Mitch. Just apologize for the times you were a drunk and weren't a good father. That's all I ever wanted to hear from my own daddy."

Mitch squirmed in his hot seat. "Grace, I was a drunk and not a good father. I'm sorry. But I always loved you and tried to keep you safe—all that shit. We had some good times too, didn't we?"

"Oh yeah, real good times. Like the time when I was eleven and I woke up to some man pawing me in my bed," Grace said.

"As soon as you screamed, I threw that asshole out. I saved you!"

"You invited him to party with you in the first place. All those lowlifes!" Grace felt hot tears hammering the backs of her eyes.

"Grace, Mitch can't change what happened, he can only be sorry now and be different. He put you through a lot. You don't have to forgive him—yet or ever. But he's apologizing. It's a first step."

Grace felt the acidic tomato sauce crawl up her throat. "I've had almost seventeen years of bullshit, my whole life. I've had to grow up and be the parent. He's only been good because I made him be. If he can keep it up—like, forever—maybe I could grow to like him some."

Mitch broke into a wide grin, "I'll take it. I'll show you too. I got this in the bag."

Jane looked at Grace and she recognized the fatigue in Jane's eyes, the familiar sense of being the one who had to survive the behavior of others. Grace saw a kind of kinship there and it eased her fury.

Grace helped Jane with the dishes while Mitch watched television and nursed a can of soda pop. Jane's window overlooked her small patio, but beyond that, the mountains were illuminated by a fat moon. Lights from the tram and the restaurant on top of the crest twinkled erratically, as if transmitting a message. Halloween would be coming soon. She wondered if Robin and Duc would dress up and if she would join them, or if they were too old. She wondered what normal life was like, since she was so new to it. She thought about all the years she wished she could go back to, taking along this sober Mitch. Would he have taken her trick-or-treating, hand in hand, her in a princess dress, him keeping her safe from the monsters?

The scene evaporated as Jane pulled the plug on the sink and the foamy bubbles, red tinged from the tomato sauce, gurgled down the drain.

Jane dried her hands on a towel and handed it to Grace. "Mitch saying he's sorry doesn't begin to touch the hurt he caused you. But I never got to hear those words from my father and I never saw him get sober. He died a drunk. Mitch is trying, that's at least something."

Grace hung the towel over the side of the sink. She was suddenly bone tired and still had homework to do. "We'll see."

"It's weird that you're now seventeen while I'm still seventeen." Duc crammed the last of his green chile cheeseburger into his mouth and spoke while he was still chewing. "There's this disconcerting overlap. How am I supposed to be the boss of you when you're catching up to me?"

Grace swallowed her huge bite. "I'm not catching up. You're still a senior and I'm still a junior. But you aren't the boss of me to begin with, so I don't see your point."

"I'm eighteen, so I rule both of you," Robin said, daintily eating her naked burger with a knife and fork, the bun tossed aside. Bread had way too many carbs, she said, and she was shunning dairy at the moment. Duc ate her french fries after finishing his own.

They were at Grace's apartment, wearing pointed paper birthday hats. Duc wore two hats forming horns on top of his head. Robin wore hers as a unicorn horn on her forehead. Grace couldn't compete with that, so she wore hers in the usual manner, though the elastic chin strap was digging into her throat. The hats were made for small children—not that she'd ever worn one. Her last and only birthday celebration of any kind was five years earlier at Twyla's, right before Mitch pulled the plug on her life. Again.

Grace looked around as Duc and Robin's banter continued. Jane and Mitch had hung up black and orange balloons and crepe paper streamers—probably found on some Halloween clearance table—but she appreciated the gesture. Mitch and Jane were next door at Jane's, giving the teenagers some space, as Jane framed it. Grace's birthdays, when she actually noticed them, always unnerved her a bit. Her birthdays were almost always not happy, and birthdays also kind of made you look at your life and take stock, something she mostly tried to avoid. Then there was the whole topic of her mother, since a birthday is meant to celebrate the day she gives agonizing yet deliriously happy birth to you. And thinking of her mother was always accompanied by a punch to the gut.

"Grace!" Robin was saying, snapping her fingers in her face.

"Sorry," Grace said. "Yes?"

"God, you're spooky when you do that zone-out thing," Robin said. "I was asking you if you wanted to open your presents now or wait until after cake."

Duc groaned and held his skinny belly. "Presents before cake, please, if you have one ounce of humanity. I shouldn't have eaten all those fries."

"So don't have cake," Robin said, clearing the table.

"That's funny. I thought she said, 'Don't have cake,'" Duc said to Grace, and made the "She's crazy" finger-twirling gesture next to his head. "Just because you, Robin, aren't having any, why do you think I'd let painful gluttony get in the way of having birthday cake?"

"Presents!" Grace said, trying to end the discussion.

"Of course you wouldn't let painful gluttony stop you, I was being ironic. And I am having cake, so you're wrong on all counts," Robin said, yanking his plate away.

"If my memory serves from Home Economics, cake has dairy and a shitload of carbs in it," Duc said.

"It wasn't called Home Economics. It was called Family and Consumer Sciences," Robin shot back. "And what's a tiny amount of dairy and a shitload of carbs in the spirit of friendship? Besides, I didn't eat the bun and fries specifically so that I could have cake guilt free."

"What is this thing called 'guilt' you speak of?" Duc batted his eyelashes.

Grace smiled. They were her very own reality television show.

The table was cleared and two presents appeared, both so beautifully wrapped she hated to disturb them, so she just sat admiring them. "This is where you pick one up and tear off the wrapping to see what's inside," Duc coached.

"But they're so pretty, I just want to look at them a minute," Grace said. She could count the number of wrapped presents she'd received in her life on one hand. She had told them a little about her past, but not too much, so her friends didn't always understand everything.

Duc whipped out his phone and took a picture of the presents. "There. Saved for posterity. I'd send you the picture, but you have no phone and no email. Are you sure you aren't Amish or a pilgrim or something?"

"It's called poverty, look it up," Robin told him with a smack.

"This?" Grace waved her arms around the kitchen like a game show assistant. "This is not poverty. This is the best I've ever had. Poverty is nowhere to sleep and no food for days at a time. This is the fucking Ritz. Look it up."

"The Ritz?" Duc fiddled with his phone and then read from its screen. "The 1980s rock club in the East Village or the luxury hotel in London?"

"I'm sorry, Grace. Duc has had it so easy in his life I'm afraid it has stunted his character," Robin said. "Exhibit A, his expensive, state-of-the-art cell phone."

"Me? I'm second-generation American. At least I've heard of poverty. When have you seen poverty? On vacation in Mexico, or was it Puerto Rico?" Duc said. "And I'm Asian, so I'm required to have the very latest phone technology, duh."

As Robin began to answer him, Grace grabbed a gift, the smaller of the two, and began to rip the paper. "Oh, shut up, she's opening mine." Duc put away his phone.

Grace opened it slowly, just to watch Duc squirm. When she lifted the lid on the box, he covered his eyes. "I can't watch—tell me what she does when she sees it."

Grace pulled out a delicate necklace, a silver chain with a teardrop pendant of a sparkling yellow gemstone. "Wow. This is beautiful."

"You like it? I found it in this cute little gallery in Old Town. I bought it from the guy who made it. It's your birthstone. He wrote down the stone's properties—see his card?"

It was a business card. Michael Stuart. On the back he had written in tiny, neat letters: "Yellow Topaz strengthens faith and optimism. It assists in recognizing your own abilities, instills a drive toward recognition, and attracts helpful people. Bestows charisma and confidence, with pride in abilities."

"Thank you, Duc." She lifted the necklace up to put it on. Robin fastened the clasp for her. The yellow topaz lay just below the hollow place at the base of her throat, the place that was constricting as she tried not to cry. "I love it."

"Don't cry or I will." Duc hugged her.

"Good job, Duc. It looks great on you, Grace." Robin examined the back of the card. "This actually complements the gift I got you perfectly, it's like we planned it, and I swear we didn't know what the other was giving you."

Grace grabbed the large box and laughed as she ripped it open like a little kid. She flung tissue paper at Duc and Robin. It was an art kit: sketch pad, a carton of colored pencils, pastels, brushes, and watercolor tubes. Grace looked up at Robin.

"I've seen your doodles. I know you like to draw. Here's the deal. I have all my required credits to graduate, so I'm just taking fun classes second semester. Sign up for art with me, Grace, for your spring elective. We can take it together. Meanwhile, you can play around with these."

Grace gulped hard and tried to smile. "Cool," she managed. Her mom had been an artist. It was about the only thing she knew about her.

"How does my gift go with art supplies?" Duc asked.

"Yellow topaz bestows confidence and pride in abilities." Robin read from the card.

"They're both perfect. You guys are great," Grace said, prompting a three-way hug. She hoped they couldn't feel her trembling or hear the banging of her heart. "Cake?"

All of a sudden it's the Fourth of July. It surprises Grace that time is moving forward outside the walls of this separate world where time feels suspended.

Staff treat the kids to a center-wide barbecue, setting up a line of industrial grills to cook hot dogs and hamburgers. Some kids' families arrive. Gabe's mom and Aaron's parents are the only parents here from Brazos Cottage, so Maddie and Grace sit together under the shade of a cottonwood tree. Maddie seems bummed that Michael didn't come, but she won't admit it.

Gabe's mom is about his size, full figured with lots of makeup and jewelry, but she's affectionate with him and friendly to Grace and Maddie. Lucas, another motherless child, is drawn to her, especially after she pet Sam's head and cooed to him as if he were a real bird. Aaron's parents wear immaculate clothing too perfect for sitting on the grass like the rest of them are, so they stand, balancing their plates and appearing to regret sacrificing a more important social occasion for burnt Hebrew Nationals. Aaron worships them with his eyes and is on his best behavior. Grace figures there will be hell to pay later, when his parents are safely out of earshot.

After lunch, parents leave and the various cottages divide up for their own activities. Gabe leaves on a pass with his mother. Brazos kids assemble on the scorching heat of the basketball court, and Grace thinks she can feel the rubber soles of her shoes trying to melt into the cement.

Hippie staffer Paul appears, pulling a tall-sided red wagon that's piled high with water balloons, and stroking his beard with fiendish glee. Sharon arrives, as does Judy, who's wearing one of those vintage plastic-pleated rain hats tied beneath her chin.

Kids dive for the water balloons, lobbing them at staff, who run like trapped rats in front of the racquetball wall next to the court. Colorful balloons burst in the bright sunshine, water spraying like a sudden downpour over the screams and squeals of kids and staff. Aaron and Lucas throw them at each other while Percy pops one over his own head to feel the ecstasy of cold relief on such a hot day, steam rising from the cement before dissipating into the desert air.

Abdias hides two water balloons under his shirt, cradling them like breasts, sending Lucas and Aaron into giggles while Abdias struts his stuff. Maddie nails Paul relentlessly until he bends over and waves his hands in peace signs, pleading for mercy.

Sharon closes her eyes and twirls, releasing water balloons from each hand, letting them fly randomly, striking unsuspecting victims. Grace feels the water explode onto her like a baptism. For a moment she can almost believe she remembers splashing her mom in the surf.

Jackson appears and all balloons are turned on him. He scoops up Grace from behind, his strong arms folding around her waist to use her as a human shield, swinging her around and around while her peals of laughter ring in her ears, water exploding over both of them, Jackson's laughter booming like thunder to accompany the deluge.

When the balloons are spent, the boys shake their wet heads like dogs. Grace watches as Judy puts one arm around Percy and the other around Aaron, both boys leaning into her grandmotherly affection; Sharon, mascara running down her cheeks, links arms with Lucas and Abdias. Abdias pulls off Judy's rain hat, which had done little to preserve her upswept hairdo. Lucas waves Sam and chatters about how Sam's feathers are ruffled, before tucking him back into his damp shirt.

Jackson settles Grace gently back to earth. He puts an arm around Maddie, and Grace ducks under his other side, feeling the weight of his arm across her shoulder. "Ladies," he says, escorting them. As they all walk back to Brazos Cottage in a dripping-wet cluster, Grace looks around at this motley, makeshift family and claims it as her own.

At dusk, staff accompany the kids from each of the cottages who have earned the privilege to go out to one of the playgrounds and watch the fireworks display visible from the Albuquerque Dukes Stadium. A chorus of oohs and aahs goes up as vibrant, multicolored bursts of light explode in the darkness.

Grace and Maddie perch on top of the slide platform. Grace feels Maddie jump along with her when one of those unpredictable bomb-like fireworks goes off, the kind you feel inside your stomach but are nothing to look at.

"Do you ever wonder what's up there, past all the stars and planets?" Maddie asks.

"You mean like God or something?" Grace says.

"Or space aliens," Maddie says. "If there is a God, he is one perverse psychopath."

"Or powerless . . . and that sort of contradicts the whole definition." Grace watches a shower of white, twinkling fireworks that fall as silent as snow.

"What did you think would happen when you hung yourself?" Maddie asks. "Did you think you'd go to an afterlife and see your mom?"

"I didn't even think about it. I didn't want to go with Mitch and I didn't want to be homeless and alone. I just wanted out. I was on autopilot, stacking the chairs, tying the rope. I was weirdly calm and just kind of observing myself."

"I've done that, a lot. Reality was so bad that I would just completely detach from what was happening . . . and then, later, when I decided I was going to France to find my mother and I was buying a plane ticket, stealing money, and doing all these things, part of me was watching and couldn't believe what I was actually doing, but I had to do it. It's like my life depended on it."

"If I thought my mom was somewhere, I'd be the same way. I'd do whatever it takes to find her, to get to her," Grace says, and for the first time considers what that would be like, if her mother were alive like Maddie's. But Grace's search is limited to the confines of her own memory. Maddie has the entire world to contend with. "By the time you're seventeen, you're not even supposed to like your mother."

"Anybody who believes that hasn't been without one," Maddie says.

Fireworks burst in the sky in quick succession, one on top of the other, the grand finale. Grace listens to the cheers and clapping of kids spread out below them. Some with terrible mothers. Some with no mothers, like her and Maddie. And who gets to decide such things? God?

It's that moment after a fireworks display when no one moves, thinking it might not be over, that there might be an encore, and collective breaths are held. The long pause passes, and with a trail of smoke still hanging in the air, staff begin calling for their respective kids to line up for head counts so they can return to their cottages.

Grace slides down the slide. Maddie slides so close behind her that before Grace can dismount, Maddie slams into her and they both end up on the ground, laughing. Grace stands and puts out her hand. Maddie takes it and Grace pulls her up.

"Come on, dos amigas!" calls Lourdes, a young Brazos evening staffer. "Vámonos!"

"We're coming," Grace calls back. Dos amigas!

Maddie wakes from a dream. She wouldn't call it a bad dream, because she killed Jeffrey in it. The air conditioning seems messed up. She feels sweaty and kicks off the sheet, tossing in her bed before deciding to wake Grace.

"Psst, Grace. Are you awake?"

"Yeah, you rolling in your squeaky bed woke me."

"I just dreamed I stalked Jeffrey at college and murdered him. I stabbed him, over and over, his blood was everywhere."

"My god, are you okay?"

"It felt great. That's what scares me. Does that mean I could really do such a thing? In the dream, Jeffrey begged me to stop and I wouldn't. Doesn't that make me as bad as him?"

"It just makes you human. The dream was a way to turn the tables. You were the one with the power, and your rage came out as violence. It doesn't mean you'd actually do that."

"I used to have thoughts of killing Jeffrey, back when he was hurting me."

"Hell, I would have too."

They duck down in their beds when the night staffer shines a light through their door window on her routine thirty-minute checks, only to bounce up again as soon as she passes.

"Do you believe in karma?" asks Grace. "That he'll get his eventually?"

"I don't know. Why did I get mine? I never hurt anyone. Maybe karma is what people use to comfort each other when they can't take revenge."

"Sometimes it takes lifetimes for karma to come around."

"I don't have lifetimes. I'm going to see his ass in court. And when I do, I'm going to stare that motherfucker down. He'll go to prison and he'll know I put him there."

"With that detective on the case, it could happen. I hope you're the one to put him away, but even if that doesn't happen, he'll get his. Living well is the best revenge—that's the part you have control over."

"I don't think I can *live well* if my dad can't come through for me."

"You guys had a lot of good years together to draw from. He'll come around." Grace yawns.

"Thanks. Good night." When Grace doesn't answer, Maddie thanks karma for giving her this friend and slips back into sleep.

"Grace, your caseworker is coming to meet you," Jackson says from his usual post at the staff desk. "She's on her way from administration."

"I have a caseworker?" Grace knows about caseworkers. Kids who find themselves without a family are placed in state custody and assigned a caseworker. Lucas has one who visits him once or twice a month and is working to find him a foster or adoptive family to be placed with when he's discharged, since he has no appropriate family members to raise him. The state also supplies care and support money. She's seen staff take Lucas shopping for shoes and clothes with his check.

Jackson looks at her. "You know you do. When your dad left town, it was child abandonment because you aren't eighteen yet, so Dr. Swenson filed a report with the Children, Youth and Families Department—CYFD. She told you."

With so much else to focus on, she hasn't really thought about this. Besides, when she first got here, she had thought Mitch would be back eventually. It's a kick in the gut to know that he isn't coming back and she's officially an abandoned child. Meeting a caseworker makes it real.

A knock at their locked entrance prompts Jackson to fish his jangle of keys from his pocket and make his way to the door. Grace notices he rises with hesitation and walks stiffly. Old football injuries, she figures, though he never complains. But for a man in his midthirties, sometimes he moves as if he's someone's grandpa.

A young woman comes through the door smiling, dressed in big-girl clothes—a stylish black pencil skirt with a matching suit jacket—but she doesn't seem much older than Grace. She carries a briefcase and wears black-framed glasses.

"Grace, this is Cindy Dexter, your caseworker from CYFD. You ladies can go talk in your room, or you can go outside if you like," Jackson says. Just then, Aaron and Lucas tear down the hall in a race to tattle on each other about something. Abdias is blasting his jams (since he has earned his radio privileges). Percy's glued to the aquarium, engaged in a whispered conversation with the angelfish. Gabe and Maddie are playing cards, a rousing game of Speed.

Cindy waits for her to make the choice. "Let's go outside," Grace says, so Jackson unlocks the door.

Grace leads Cindy past the dolphin fountain, where a Pecos Cottage girl enjoying her level-three privileges sits astride the life-size dolphin that seems to float over the circular pool. To the right is a miniature cul-de-sac encircled with flowering shrubs and shaded by an overhanging tree. A smaller fountain burbles in the center of it. Grace sits on the bench.

"This is a lovely spot," chirps Cindy.

"You know I'll be eighteen in November," Grace says.

"Right," Cindy says. "I've met with Dr. Swenson and read her report, so I'm aware of your situation. Your father has been gone for eight weeks, two months, without any contact. My job is to try to locate him if possible, research any other possible family members who might want to be involved, and in lieu of that, help you transition into a group home that will assist you in becoming ready for an independent living situation. Also, you'll be getting a monthly care and support stipend for clothing and other necessities."

"I don't want him back. So you can save yourself the trouble. Besides, how are you going to find him? He might be in Orlando—or he could be anywhere. Maybe even dead."

"No one will force you to live with him again. But legally, he's responsible for you until you turn eighteen."

"Responsible for me? That's a laugh."

"I can understand your feelings, Grace, but wouldn't it be better to have some closure with him?"

"I think we're way past closure. And what you said about other family, good luck with that. Mitch doesn't have any and my mom is dead."

"Look, Grace, it's my job. It's what I do, and it's the law. If nothing viable comes out of it, well, like I said, you have other options."

"I won't hold my breath." Grace stares into the gentle tumble of water cascading down the tiers of the fountain. A robin perches on the rim, dipping its beak into the water to drink. It cocks its head at her.

"Is there anything else you can think of that might help me? Any family names your father might have mentioned, any towns or places, like where your parents met?"

"He said he was from rural Arkansas, I have no idea where, and he picked up my mom hitchhiking on Interstate 35 in Oklahoma—or it could all be bullshit. Mitch is a liar. I don't even know if Mitch Willis is his real name. And since I can't remember shit about my mom, I don't even know her name for sure. My birth certificate says my mother's name was Karen Rose, and he said her last name was Nelson, but that could all be made up too. I tried to find her family but couldn't get anywhere."

"I have access to databases that you wouldn't have had, so I wouldn't write this off as futile just yet. If you think of anything, give me a call." She opens her briefcase and hands Grace her card. "I have your first care and support check. I'll give it to Jackson and you can arrange to go shopping."

Grace sticks the card into the pocket of her faded and frayed jean shorts. Her sandals are about to fall apart. Her two bras and five pairs of panties force her to do laundry at least twice a week. What little she has was shabby and secondhand to begin with. It might be nice to get some new things. Yet, instead of gratitude, all she can feel is prickling shame.

"Don't give up hope." Cindy stands up, her high heels sinking into the soft sod. She lifts a foot to examine the small clump of soil adhering to the stiletto's tip.

Grace considers telling her that hope is a dangerous thing, that the hope she once naively nurtured led her to death's door. But someone like Cindy, whose life has obviously been so blessed that she's now out to save the less fortunate, would never understand.

CHAPTER 9

Grace, Age 17

Albuquerque, New Mexico

As the weeks went by and Mitch continued to stay sober and employed, Grace began to think ahead, which had always seemed nearly as dangerous as making plans. She'd catch herself thinking things like "Maybe in the summer I'll grow tomatoes in a pot on the patio." And instead of going into a panic attack about everything that could go wrong before then, she felt nearly hopeful. Or at least open to the possibility that the life she was living could actually continue without something disastrous happening, namely, Mitch screwing everything up.

The very real threat of that kept her on edge. It kept her vigilant. It kept her from trusting in a future that, at best, seemed like a crapshoot. But it didn't keep her from imagining tomatoes, red and juicy, flourishing in a pot on her patio.

But it was winter now, dry and cold. Her first day of winter break from school. Mitch teased that he was jealous and maybe he'd have to stay home with her. She'd made him a breakfast burrito and shoved him out the door, both of them laughing, Mitch spilling half of his coffee. She liked this Mitch. She wondered if this is how he had been when her mom was alive.

If Grace could live in the now and not remember everything Mitch had put her through, she'd like him even better. Ironically, during all the bad shit, she could only live in the now. Just basic survival, one moment to the next. Now that things were good, she wanted to embrace her life without worry. But worry stalked her. Worry lived under her bed and in the recesses of her closet. She knew it was just waiting for her to be weak. So she tried to be strong enough to keep worry at arm's length, outside herself, where it couldn't take her over with its destructive power.

With her index finger, she absently rubbed her topaz pendant, her talisman. The apartment was quiet, except for the rhythmic drip of the kitchen faucet. She wondered how Duc was doing on his family trip to visit relatives in California. She wondered if Robin had left for her ski trip in Aspen. She wondered how she would fill these days, aside from reading and working extra hours at the pizza café. Then her eyes drifted over to her desk where she kept the untouched box of art supplies Robin had given her. Before she could think about it, she grabbed the box and brought it out to the kitchen table.

Grace opened the sketch pad and looked at the blank page. She wasn't sure how to use the watercolors, so she opened the box of fifty colored pencils, every shade imaginable. She pulled out a light-blue pencil and began to sketch. Then a darker blue, then before she knew it, a pile of pencils she used and threw down and picked up again as she worked. She worked quickly, her hand connected to the image frozen in her mind's eye, and when there was nothing left to do, she stopped and looked at what she had created. It was a sunrise over the ocean, with a sandy beach full of gulls in the foreground. It was a scene that had been trapped in her memory and was now free to live on the page. It was the view from the trailer on South Padre Island where she had lived with both of her parents. Before her mother had died and life at the mercy of Mitch had begun. The time she couldn't remember, but there it was, spread out before her like proof.

Grace felt the trembling seize her, the sweaty palms, the ache in her throat that happened whenever she even thought about sketching. Damn it! She had to get control of this. Soon she would be in art class with Robin. She would just have to power through it—she had every right to do art and she would not let her dead mother ruin this for her. Grace turned the page, wiped her palms on her jeans, and began again.

Jane loved the holidays and was their personal Christmas-spirit elf. When

Grace said they couldn't afford a tree, Jane directed them to her favorite lot, where she knew the family. After Grace picked out a modest five-foot tree, hugging the soft fragrant bows to her face, Jane bought it for them. Mitch threw it into the back of the truck and Jane had them singing "Jingle Bells" all the way home. Jane shared some of her copious decorations, and they made ornaments from cookie dough and strung cranberries and popped corn. As Grace watched Mitch, his face boyish and clean shaven now, his long hair still in a braid down his back, happily stringing popcorn, she realized he probably hadn't had many Christmas celebrations either. From what she knew of his childhood, a backwoods, hardscrabble life in Arkansas, she didn't picture Christmas carols or visits from Santa. He never wanted to talk about his family and maintained they were all gone now anyway.

Funny, but Grace thought Jane was getting prettier as she and Mitch got cozier. He seemed to like her and Grace realized this was the first woman Mitch had been with that he wasn't using in some way. Jane had started dyeing her mousy hair a rich chocolate brown and it had grown to her shoulders. When she smiled, which seemed to be all the time lately, her eyes came to life and her laugh was contagious. She wore dangling silver earrings and more colorful clothing. But it was her goodness, Grace realized, that made her so attractive.

On Christmas Eve, they filled lunch sacks with a shallow layer of sand and then placed votive candles in them to make luminarias, a New Mexico tradition. Grace carefully cuffed the top of each sack so it would stand properly as Mitch and Jane lined them up in the driveway and along the sidewalk. The tenant in the third unit, a retired firefighter named Rudy, emerged to help and invited them in for some posole, a stew made with pork and hominy and red chile.

After dinner, the spicy stew warming her belly and tingling her mouth, Grace went with Mitch and Jane to Old Town Plaza to see the elaborate luminaria displays the merchants and residents put out every year. She had never been to Old Town but remembered that Duc had found her necklace there. After they lucked into a parking space by the Albuquerque Museum, she followed behind Mitch and Jane. Mitch had his arm around Jane's shoulders and they were laughing and talking.

Grace was bundled up in gloves and the scarf Jane had knitted for her and a thick wool coat, with hardly any moth holes, she'd found at a thrift store. From a narrow brick walkway between shops, they emerged onto the plaza, and Grace was dazzled by row upon row of glowing sacks that were transformed into something magical in the dark, lining sidewalks and curbs, sitting on walls and rooftops.

Throngs of people moved around them, taking pictures, and kids chased each other with puffs of white breath exploding from cherry lips.

"Isn't this great? Didn't I tell you?" Jane was saying.

"Like a fairy tale," Mitch said.

At first Grace thought she imagined it, one fat flake and then another, and then as if someone had shaken a snow globe, snow swirled around them, coming down in thick clouds.

The crowd responded with cheers and dancing, so rare was a white Christmas in Albuquerque. A brass quartet played carols under the cover of the gazebo and people began to sing along. Mitch leaned into a kiss with Jane. Grace tilted her face up to catch snowflakes on her tongue.

So this is joy, she thought, feeling her chest expand to hold it, feeling it leak from her eyes as tears. This is joy.

Grace walked into art class with Robin, who was feigning nonchalance in a way that made Grace seriously question Robin's acting skills. Robin had witnessed Grace's anxiety attacks that accompanied her artistic endeavors and was now apparently in the throes of secondhand anxiety. In fact, the whole class had been there when Grace's anxiety had erupted, when she couldn't seem to catch her breath and the school nurse had been summoned.

Luckily the school nurse had been around long enough to recognize an anxiety attack when she saw one, and had calmly told Grace to breathe into Peter Garrison's lunch bag for a few minutes. Kids had gathered around her in their unabashed teenage gawking mode until the nurse had barked them off. They turned their attention to dividing up Peter's dumped lunch components, which sat upon his desk like a junk food tableau, while Grace felt her fingertips tingle with oxygen and her heart beat slow to that of a hummingbird's.

Cass, the art teacher, was a rebel in several ways. Along with being openly gay, she was rumored to have nearly lost her job because of giving students rides on her Harley in the long expanse of adjoining school parking lots. Cass was also unique in her approach to teaching art. Materials were laid out on a long countertop at the rear of the classroom. It was up to the students to pick out what they wanted and to get to work. Cass circulated, giving some individual help with technique, but mostly telling kids their art was up to them. As long as they shut up and worked, she was fine. Cass tolerated no shenanigans, no sleeping, no off-task behavior. You came and you worked, or you were sent to the office. Production was her emphasis. They were told to do art and nothing else. It was, after all, art class.

At first, Grace thought this was rather lazy of Cass. But after a few weeks of kids seeming lost or bored or blank like sheep waiting for a dog to herd them in one direction or other, she noticed that they actually got down to the business of making something. Granted, for some, it was distorted drawings of celebrities copied from *People* magazine, or gang graffiti, or wish lists of tattoo art they vowed to make permanent on their bodies as soon as their asshole parents let them. But because Cass refused to spoon-feed them, they were becoming self-directed. Most moved away from rote repetition and started to experiment with more materials, becoming so absorbed with their own creations that they would mutter in frustration when Cass announced it was time to clean up.

Despite her accompanying anxiety, Grace was driven to paint, and her medium was watercolor once Cass had taught her some basic tips. Which is why, when Cass met with her about her problem, Grace told her quitting was not an option. Cass had leaned forward in her chair, her elbows resting on the table between them. "Art isn't supposed to kill you."

"You can't die from an anxiety attack," Grace said.

"What do you think it's about?" Cass shoved her black-framed glasses up onto the crown of her bleached-blond tufted head. Her gaze was penetrating.

Grace shrugged.

"I have to ask—are you being hurt in some way?" Cass managed a gentle tone then, somehow conveying she herself may have been hurt in some way.

"No. Like sexually or getting beat up? No," Grace said. She realized Cass wasn't stopping until she had some kind of answer. "My mom died when I was little and she did art. I paint the place where we lived when she was still alive."

Cass nodded. "Does it happen when you paint something else?"

"I don't paint anything else. I'm not going to paint anything else, so I just have to get over it." Then, seeing doubt in Cass's expression, she spoke more forcefully. "I have to do this, all right? And if it means facing my grief for my mother, then so be it." That had been Duc's theory plucked from the pages of his older brother's Psychology 101 textbook.

"Keep it short of needing the nurse and I'm fine with it. Authentic art brings up shit. I won't stand in the way of authentic art," Cass said. "Look, I'm not great at this verbalization stuff, but we have like a team of school counselors wishing they had something more interesting to deal with than kids slugging their teachers. Maybe you should talk to one of them. It would make their day."

Grace's instinct was to lie and promise Cass she would seek counseling and thereby be let off the hook, but she appreciated Cass's honesty and wanted to return it in kind. "Thanks, but I can do this on my own."

Cass shoved back her chair. "Unless you want to help clean brushes, you can go."

Grace had done some reading about anxiety attacks since then and had learned some coping strategies. Robin was her self-appointed research assistant, printing out articles from the internet and letting Grace use her computer for her own searches on the topic. So today she sat at her table and closed her eyes and did her measured breathing: five seconds to inhale, two seconds of holding the breath, and five seconds to fully exhale, concentrating on relaxing her body and her mind. She placed her hand over her abdomen to feel her breathing expand and deflate her center, to confirm she was doing it properly. Then she began to paint.

"Clean up and put away." Cass's voice slit the silence. Grace stirred as if from a dream and looked at her work. Rolling sand dunes with detailed plants vining over them, plants she could not name, yet she had captured specific leaf shapes and varying shades of green. A solitary herring gull flew over, heading for the unseen ocean behind the dunes. She hadn't finished the sky, which was going to be gray and moody with the ghost of a sun visible behind a thin cloud. She hated to stop before she was done.

"Clean up and put away," Cass repeated. "Do it now and do it right. I'm not your lackey."

Chairs shoved in unison, breaking the spell. Grace's classmates, looking like toddlers disturbed from their naps, carried proof of their labor to the drying shelves or to shove into portfolios.

Robin showed off her drawing of a dancer, always a performer in search of applause. "Nice," said Grace, "really nice." Robin sketched from black-and-white photographs of dancers in a vintage book she had found on one of their thrift store forays, but transformed their stark realism into something more impressionistic.

"You think?" Robin beamed, soaking it in. "How did you do today?"

Like a mother would ask, Grace guessed. "Not bad. About halfway through, I had to stop and breathe again for a minute or so."

"That's really good! See, it's working. I'm curing you."

"Whatever." Glad she could serve as another one of Robin's accomplishments.

Since Duc and Robin had rehearsals after school for the spring musical, Grace spent more time alone. While walking home from school that day, she stopped in front of the Catholic grade school near her triplex. Parents, mostly moms, had parked their cars up and down the block and were standing vigil for their children. Kids were streaming out, the smallest ones first. What were they—five, six? Grace watched as they threw themselves into open arms, their faces joyous with relief. The mothers' faces mirroring the same. She could feel the heat of their bonds from where she stood. It struck her with a dizzying force that she had suffered a terrible loss at that age. Her mother had been there one day and gone the next. And yet she could not remember it. And not remembering meant not feeling—and this compounded the loss. Her mother was lost to her in every way. Only now did this occur to her.

It was like the time she cut herself prepping vegetables at work. She saw the blood spreading faster than she thought possible, but there was no pain. The wound was obvious, yet she felt removed from it. Eventually it hurt like hell, but in those first moments it seemed to be happening to someone else. The scar across her left index finger verified it. She looked up from her scar to watch a little girl with long brown braids clutching her mother's hand, babbling about her day. She imagined this little girl suddenly losing her mother: the confusion, the searing pain tearing through such a narrow chest, the inconsolable rage and grief. The trauma would play out for years, perhaps forever. Raw and fresh every birthday, every motherless mother's day, each and every bedtime.

Grace had been vaguely sad to not have a mother, mainly when she needed rescuing from Mitch's ongoing stupidity. But it was more the idea of a mother, nothing specific, that she pined for. Yet for over five years, she'd had a mother, who was—at least according to Mitch—a loving and kind mother who cared about her very much. Whom she had loved. Whom she had spent all her time with while Mitch worked on shrimp boats. No extended family. Just the two of them playing on the beach, doing art together in their own little universe, Mitch had said. Karen had even homeschooled her for kindergarten, not being able to bear sending her on the long bus ride across the bridge to the mainland school in Port Isabel at such a tender age. She heard these accounts from Mitch, as if they were from a distant galaxy and not from her own life.

Grace turned her back on the scene. She passed cars where moms were carefully strapping their kids into booster seats, and averted her eyes. She was damaged. She was some kind of freak who could go through such devastation and not even remember it. She remembered every fucking thing about Mitch, which was no consolation. Her face burned with the humiliation that it had never occurred to her that this gigantic lapse was abnormal. She had just accepted it like she had accepted every other Mitch-inflicted atrocity.

Was this his fault too? Or did blame for anything just naturally flow in his direction, into the well-worn trough of his culpability? Or was it her? Maybe she didn't want to remember. Maybe she was too weak to feel the pain her mother's death warranted. Guilt rose as bile in her throat. Maybe Grace had lost her mother because she hadn't loved her enough.

Valentine's Day only rubbed her nose in it. Watching kids giggle over stupid cards, chomping down those gross, chalky heart candies. Duc and Robin brought her a potted azalea and Godiva chocolates and goofy cartoon cards. Numbness enveloped her. She smiled and gave them homemade cards she had painted herself and tried desperately to feel something when they hugged. It was exhausting, the smiling and laughing, the pretense. She remembered loving them. She remembered feeling stuff. It was as if the previous apathy she had maintained about her mother was now infiltrating all aspects of her life.

At least she could paint in peace. All that tremulous anxiety—the shaking hands, the feeling of suffocation—had abandoned her. No more sweaty palms, only the steady, slow beating of a heart that refused to feel.

If her heart had failed her, her mind was sharper than ever. Grace viewed her absent memories of the life and death of her mother as a conundrum to solve. Mitch knew everything. But she couldn't just ask him, he'd make up some bullshit. She knew now that all these years, he'd hidden the truth deliberately, which meant he was protecting himself. Whatever had happened, he was grateful for her bovine, cud-chewing ignorance. As far as Mitch knew, Grace was still comfortable not knowing, not asking, not being remotely curious how the woman who had given birth to her and raised her for over five years could simply vanish and take Grace's memory with her. She had to keep it that way.

Jane made chicken piccata for Valentine's dinner at their place. At first, Grace tried to stay in her room and let the lovebirds have their romantic dinner, but Jane came to her. "If we'd wanted to be alone, we'd be at my place."

"You just feel sorry for the dateless teenager. Truth is I turned down Robin and Duc's invitation to go out as a threesome to dinner. They like to make people wonder."

"Why didn't you go?" Jane sat on the one patch of her bed that wasn't covered in books and papers.

"Homework, cramps, take your pick," Grace said. Neither was true.

Jane reached for her hand. "Come on. You have to eat and then you can go back to being a reclusive, moody teenager."

Mitch was grinning in his chair when they emerged. He had placed a gift-wrapped box on Jane's plate. Grace resisted the urge to wrap both hands around his neck and squeeze the truth out of him.

Jane's eyes filled with tears even before she opened the present. Grace wanted to blurt out the long list of Mitch's transgressions and dispossess Jane of her belief that this loving, responsible, seven-month-sober Mitch facsimile was the real deal. But Jane would blame his prior behavior on the booze, and while that was a part of it, Grace could name many disasters when alcohol or drugs were not heavily on the scene. It saddened Grace that only recently she, too, had believed in this glossy new Mitch, that even as she worried he might fall off the wagon and destroy her now stable life, she, too, had celebrated his one-day-at-time success.

Now she just saw he was more than likely performing some long con for which sobriety was required. Her hatred of him bloomed fresh now that she believed he was benefiting from her not remembering the circumstances of her mother's death and the prior precious years of her mothering.

Jane opened the gift and pulled out a heart-shaped locket with one miniscule diamond chip in its center, probably from Walmart. "Oh, it's beautiful! Mitch, I love it!"

He beamed like a good dog and received her hug and kiss. "You deserve it, babe. I owe my whole new life to you. I'd be in some gutter without you. I'm a lucky guy."

Grace felt her eyes roll. Where was Jane when Grace had kept Mitch on house arrest through the dt's? Cleaning up his puke and listening to his scorching rants about what he was going to do to her for making him suffer. He'd gotten past that only because he'd been too broken to crawl a few miles to get booze. But Grace didn't blame Jane for Mitch giving her all the credit. Jane was a victim too; she just didn't know it yet.

Jane was reading the accompanying card, one hand pressed to her heart. Mitch was watching her, his own eyes glistening, and then leaned in for a kiss.

"Well." Jane wiped her eyes and cleared her throat. "Sorry about all that, Grace. I have a card for you too. Mitch, didn't you get your daughter something?"

"She knows she's my number one gal, next to you, of course. You think I should of?" Mitch looked momentarily worried he would lose points with Jane.

"It's fine. We don't really do this holiday," Grace said, unable to stop herself from rescuing him.

Jane handed a red envelope to Grace. "Consider this from both of us."

Grace opened and read the very nice card and smiled appropriately. "Thanks, Jane."

Mitch opened his wallet and pulled out a five-dollar bill. "Here, Grace. I'd give you more, but my daughter has me on a tight allowance."

"Are you sure you won't need this for gas or lunch money?" Grace said.

"Gas dropped again, and Dave bought me a burrito for lunch a few times, so I'm money ahead."

She took the five and shoved it into her jeans pocket.

Jane served up the food, delicious as always. Grace watched Jane touch the locket on her chest while she ate, as if to make sure it was real.

While Grace ate, she tried to figure out how to work her mother into the conversation. The truly tricky part was how to get information without revealing she didn't remember anything.

When Jane was up getting Mitch a second helping, he caught her eye. "Sorry I screwed up about getting you a card—I was all wrapped up in what to get Jane."

"I didn't get you one either," Grace said. "It's not like we have family traditions about it. Did you and Mom do Valentine's Day?"

"Karen and me? Where'd that come from?" Mitch said as Jane rejoined them with his steaming plate.

"It's okay," Jane said. "She was your wife. You must have."

Mitch chewed, buying himself some time. "Well, sure. Grace, remember that last Valentine's Day? We had a picnic and we made big hearts out of shells on the beach and wrote our names inside them with a stick."

Grace froze. Should she pretend to remember something that was possibly bullshit? Or should she admit to not remembering something that might have actually happened? She decided it was safer to roll with it. "Was I still writing my name with the backward *r*?" It was a habit she had dragged into first grade in Tucson. That, she could remember.

"Hell, you were only five. Karen was doing good teaching you and you were smart. She was always bragging on you when I got home from work, telling me stuff you learned, showing me your papers."

Grace examined Mitch's lit-up face. It seemed real. His eyebrow wasn't twitching, his handy-dandy lie-o-meter. She seized the opportunity. "I like hearing you tell about that time. Since I was so young, it's a little fuzzy in places."

"You were a happy kid. We were all happy—you and Karen and me. Great times," Mitch said, nodding in emphasis. Then his eyebrow twitched.

Grace started a secret notebook to document everything she found out about her mother. She had the idea that if she would just stumble upon the right fact or anecdote from Mitch, it would all come flooding back. Then she could feel close to her again and be able to properly grieve. She had to admit that some of her motivation had to do with getting the goods on Mitch.

Grace was convinced that this mental block was what caused her prior anxiety attacks with art. The anxiety attacks stopped precisely when she realized how wrong it was that she had no memory of anything before living with Mitch in Tucson, as if she had first come to consciousness seven years into her life. The absurdity of that was her number one clue that she must learn the truth. The door was shut tight—she had to know what was on the other side.

So far in her notebook, she'd written that on November 14, 1984, she was born in Harlingen, Texas, to Karen and Mitch Willis. She studied her birth certificate—obtained for her job so that she could get a Social Security number—as if it were a code she needed to crack. She noticed that under "Mother's Maiden Name" someone had written "Rose" in the space between middle and last name, as if it could be either. But if it was the middle name, the last name was missing.

Grace approached Mitch about it one night while he and Jane were watching an old black-and-white movie on television. "I need to know my mother's maiden name. On my birth certificate it says 'Rose' but it's written in between the middle name space and the last name space."

Mitch tore his eyes from the cowboy action on the screen. "Let me see that. Where'd you get this?"

"The State of Texas. I had to send off for it to get a Social Security number for work."

"Rose was her middle name. That's Karen's handwriting—she must have filled out this thing. She didn't want her maiden name on there."

"But why not? What was it? I need to know," Grace said.

"Why?" Mitch narrowed his already beady eyes at her.

"For a school thing."

"You don't know your mother's maiden name?" Jane asked.

"It never came up until now," Grace said, feeling even more stupid.

Mitch muted the movie. "It's kind of nosy for a school thing, ain't it? Tell them it's none of their GD business. Make something up."

Jane patted his jiggling thigh. "But Grace has a right to know, it's her family history."

"I already told her, Karen and I were the only family each other had. She left it off on purpose, they just didn't catch it."

"Well, you weren't hatched out of eggs. Your folks are dead, but she knows your family name. Just tell Grace her mother's family name. What are you afraid of, babe?" Jane said in that hypnotically soothing voice of hers.

"It's private, that's all. We both left home for a reason and I don't think Karen would want me telling—it'd be like breaking a promise."

"I'm her daughter." Grace tried to keep calm. "I don't even know where her home was."

"Her home was with me. That's all you need to know." Mitch stood up and stomped off to the bathroom.

Jane patted the spot he had vacated, but Grace was too worked up to sit. "Let me work on him, Grace. It's obviously a sensitive subject. But I agree you have a right to know. He might be afraid you'll go looking for relatives and he'll lose you."

"There were plenty of times I would have wanted to find family who would take me to get away from him. But not now. That's not what this is about." Why hadn't she ever thought of that before? But if her mother was fleeing them, there was a good chance they wouldn't be people she'd want to live with anyway, or that they'd even want anything to do with the child of their runaway daughter.

Mitch came back into the room and sat next to Jane. Grace noticed how their hands found each other and clasped. "Here's the thing, Grace. Your mom died all of a sudden, so there was all kinds of shit we never had a chance to talk out. But she made it real clear, from the first minute I laid eyes on her hitchhiking on the side of the road, she never wanted anything more to do with her family ever again. She never changed her mind about that in the years I knew her, so I got to believe she was including you in that deal. She never went into details, but it musta been bad, it gave her nightmares. And she loved you more than anything, so why in hell would she want me putting you on the path to those same people? Give it up, Grace. Respect your mother's wishes."

"I don't want to meet them or anything. I just want the name," Grace said quietly. "That's how you met? She was hitchhiking?"

"She was on the southbound side of Interstate 35 in Oklahoma. Just a little backpack, wearing flip-flops and it weren't forty degrees out. I pulled over and said, 'Where you headed?' and she said, 'Any place warm.' So we drove south all the way near to the tip of Texas and crossed the bridge to South Padre Island. Grace, she had a cut lip and a black eye. Her people did that to her. You still want their name?"

"Yes," she said, feeling tears overspill her eyes.

"Nelson," Mitch said.

Karen Rose Nelson. Searches on Robin's computer using that name brought up all kinds of useless garbage, including sites that, for a fee, promised to locate anyone. Without a credit card, she was stymied. On

Saturday, Grace sat at Robin's desk, staring at the list of Karen Nelsons who were not her mother.

Robin lounged on her queen-size bed while Duc gave her a manicure. "What are you looking for, Gracie May?"

Grace shut the laptop. "Just playing around." She had not and would not tell them about her pitiful memory problem and her quest to find out more about her mother. It was not a decision born from careful thought and consideration—her gut just told her not to share this with them or anyone. Not even Jane, who would probably be helpful but might say something to Mitch. To get the focus off of her, she said, "How do you know how to do nails, Duc?"

"Are you kidding? I'm Vietnamese. Half of us own nail salons and the other half are divided into Vietnamese restaurants and car repair shops. But all of them are raising their kids to be doctors or engineers. You can imagine how pleased they are with me."

"I'm pleased with you," Robin said. "That's all that matters."

"You are pleased I'm doing something about your hideous attempts to do your own nails," Duc said. "Doctor who treats himself has a fool for a patient."

"Fortune cookie?" Robin said.

"We should totally go to my uncle's place for lunch. A big bowl of pho sate. Yum."

"Maybe. I have to go to work in three hours and twenty-seven minutes," Grace said. She was actually looking forward to it, a slamming Saturday night and she got to man the wood-burning pizza oven. The seven-hundred-degree heat made her feel alive.

"I just remembered I had one of those cool dreams last night—from when you are like really little—and you remember shit you never do when you're awake," Robin said. "Like I dreamed about this dog we had that died when I was three, but in the dream, I could remember how his fur felt, the red speckles on his white coat. And how young my mom looked—before she cut her hair. She wore those stretchy headbands."

"I love those dreams. I have this recurring dream that I'm playing in my tree house at the old house that we moved away from when I was four. So

I have all these toys I loved, little action figures and transformers, and my first friend, Tommy, was there," Duc said.

"What's your earliest memory?" Grace said.

Robin blew on her red-lacquered fingernails to dry the first coat. "I have this little fragment of memory where I'm flat on my back under the Christmas tree looking up through the branches under the glow of the lights. I remember I have on this top I don't like because you can see my undershirt underneath. It was the Christmas just after my third birthday."

"I can remember being in my crib and thinking I was too big for it since I could easily climb out of it. I wanted a big-boy bed like my brother. We shared a room. I remember scowling at him through the bars of my crib while he jumped on his cool race-car bed. He had what I wanted. My first taste of extreme envy and I was probably still two," Duc said.

"You still resent your brother," Robin said.

"Mr. Perfect? I don't know what you mean," Duc said. "What about you, Grace?"

"The beach on South Padre—with my mother," Grace said, though she didn't really count it as a normal memory since it had only surfaced in her artwork and she couldn't attach any particular moments with her mother to it. The beach was a setting without characters. Its emptiness mocked her. The gulls laughed at her.

"You've never really said what happened to your mother," Robin said.

As Grace tried to figure out how to answer that, she felt a sudden surge of nausea. She had to swallow hard to keep herself from gagging.

"You don't look so good, girlfriend," Duc said.

Grace clamped both hands over her mouth and staggered to Robin's en suite bathroom, slamming the door behind her. As she gagged over the toilet, she heard them on the other side of the door.

Duc said, "The nail polish fumes can do that to you. We should have opened a window."

"Grace, are you okay?" Robin called.

Grace quelled her gagging with slow, deep breaths. At least she didn't fully vomit—she despised vomiting. Her face felt hot. She pulled herself up from the floor and looked at her face in the mirror. "I'm okay." Her skin was flushed red and her eyes blinked away the tears that had gathered from all the gagging. She smoothed her frantic hair and drank some water from her cupped hand under the tap. She hated how weird she was becoming. Becoming? Maybe she had always been weird but her life had been too wrecked to notice.

She dried her face and stood still, listening to Duc and Robin breathing on the other side of the door. Whatever had hit her seemed to be passing.

Grace approached the door and opened it. She almost smiled as Robin and Duc dove away to try to hide they had been lurking. She solemnly faced them. "Duc, I think I'm pregnant, and the baby is yours."

"Honey, if you're pregnant, we're starting a whole new religion. Can you imagine a Vietnamese savior?" Duc said, laughing with what sounded like relief. "Seriously, though—are you all right? Was it the fumes from the banned nail products I got from my auntie?"

Robin scrutinized her. "Have you traded panic attacks for nausea attacks?"

Grace walked past them to sit on the desk chair. "I think the fumes got to me. You were asking me what happened to my mother. She died of some kind of drug overdose. Mitch won't really talk about it. I was only five, so my recollection of the events is sketchy. All I know for sure is that's when my life went to hell. Any more questions?" She stared them down.

Robin gave her the sad look but shook her head no.

Duc gathered up his nail supplies and threw them into his bag. "I'm treating us to lunch at my uncle's place. A big bowl of pho with cilantro will cure what ails you. And then you can go off to bake pizzas and we'll go to play rehearsal."

"Gotta love a man who can take charge," Robin said. "And do great manicures!"

Grace thought about Duc's and Robin's dreams and early memories. Her dreams seemed to parallel her memory in that they only reached back to age seven. She began to go to the nearby library to use one of their computers, with the privacy she needed. She read articles about dreams and early memory. She read about the practice of lucid dreaming and self-hypnosis to access the secrets in her brain. One commonality in the vast array of articles was that the inability to remember usually served to protect the individual from some horrendous trauma. Her panic attacks, and now the bouts of nausea she was experiencing when she consciously tried to recall her fifth year, told Grace that events she must have witnessed around her mother's death, and not just the death itself, were at the root of it.

Grace began to practice deep relaxation with self-hypnosis, repeating the suggestion that it was safe to remember. She recorded her dreams in her notebook. Before going to sleep at night, she invited her subconscious to take her to the memories of her mother. She tried to draw her mother and but only got as far as long blond hair and a generically shaped head. When she tried to sketch in some eyes, a nose, a mouth, her hand remained poised over the paper, the pencil hovering helplessly over the stubborn white, blank space.

Whatever she did, the door remained slammed shut and tightly locked.

Robin and Duc interpreted her quietness, her preoccupation, with her anticipating their graduation and departure. It was true enough that it provided her with a great cover story to hide behind. Suddenly it was April and they were graduating on May 15. Seven weeks. The airline tickets were already purchased for their May 17 move to New York City, where they would be greeted at the airport by Robin's aunt who was a Broadway costume designer in constant demand. They couldn't shut up about it, giving Grace the space to turn to her internal dialogue. When she did think about them leaving, she knew she was sad, but she didn't really feel it. Maybe it was still too soon for it to seem real.

One day after spending a couple of hours at the library, Grace got home as Mitch was pulling into the driveway after work. The sun was only starting its descent in the western sky, since they had sprung forward into daylight saving time the previous Sunday. Grace had tied around her waist the hoodie she'd needed in the morning. She felt hot after the walk from the library, even though the temperature was only in the upper sixties.

"Hey, girl, how was your day?" Mitch greeted her.

"Fine," Grace said, squinting up at him as they walked to their courtyard together. Where were her damn sunglasses? A person could be blinded by this sun. "How was yours?"

"Same old, same old," Mitch said, unlocking the door.

As Grace entered their home, she realized it really was a home. In the quiet that greeted them, she let her gaze wander over the secondhand furniture that now felt like it had always belonged to them. An open magazine here, an empty glass there, but not messy. Lived in. It had the particular smell of home, and the walls with the art she had chosen seemed to be welcoming them. It was a place of peace. Uncontaminated by drama. Bordering on boring, but theirs. At seventeen, she felt like she finally understood how a place can become a home. She felt drawn into its embrace. "I like this place, Mitch," she said.

A grin spread over his quizzical expression. "It's a good place. I'm glad you found it for us. I wouldn't have met Jane otherwise."

She threw her backpack onto the table. "You really like her. Like, a lot."

"She's my rock," he said. "Not my usual type, that's for sure."

Grace thought back over the years, the disposable women he partied with, slept with, until he uprooted for some new city, never looking back. The other exception was Twyla, who, despite her partying, was a person of substance, like Jane.

"That says something about you, Mitch," Grace said.

Mitch sat down in his place on the sofa and leaned back in a stretch with a yawn. "Yeah, I'm just this working stiff now. Bringing home the bacon," he said.

She sat down next to him, her spot. "We had a lot of times with no bacon. I like bacon."

Mitch looked at her. "You ain't talking about bacon, are you?"

"I just like how things are now. That's all."

"I am sorry, Grace. For all I put you through."

Grace nodded. "The important thing is what we have now. We can't go back." Even as she said it, she realized that was exactly what she was doing. Trying to go back. But only so she could find the missing pieces, fill in the blanks, know her own history. Wasn't that important too?

Mitch seemed to read her mind. "Jane says it's natural for you to have questions about your mama, since you're growing up and all."

"I do have questions. But you always get so mad."

"It's just the hardest thing for me to do—to go back to that time when we lost her. Why do you think I was so fucked up for so long? Karen was everything to me."

"I was only five. She was my whole world, aside from you, and you were working a lot," Grace said, not from memory, just from the bits and pieces he had given her. As far as his laying his fucked-up-ness all on losing her mother, she was highly skeptical.

"Jane says I should talk to you more about her."

"So talk about her."

"You're like her, Grace. When I came home all bashed up and you took care of me but also took charge—that's what she would have done. She was strong like that. Like you are."

"Do I look like her?"

"Hell, you don't look like me, so who else? Especially now that you're getting older, I see her in your face. She was only a tad bit older than you when we met up. Long blond hair, brown eyes. Skinny legs. She was five foot eight, though, I don't think you'll get there. What are you, five three or so?"

"And a half," Grace said. "If things were so good, why did she take drugs? Why did she overdose?"

She could feel him tense as he changed positions. He looked to the dark television screen. "We smoked pot once in a while, but not that much. She didn't like to drink, made her sick. She had nightmares, you know, about her past. Bothered her in the daytime too. She came upon some heroin from a friend of ours, and she tried it. Just that one time, only she had no idea what she was doing and took too much. They couldn't save her." He squeezed his eyes shut with his fingers and she heard him sniffling.

"Where was I? When my mother died, where was I?"

He looked at her then, with his red, puffy eyes. He looked at her a long time. "You don't remember, do you? You were playing with your little friend Sage at her family's trailer, just up the beach a ways. I came and got you after they took Karen away—still trying to save her. We followed them to the hospital over in Harlingen, where you were born, but she was gone. She wanted to be cremated, so that was done, and later I borrowed a friend's boat and we sprinkled her out on the ocean there in the gulf. A pod of dolphins came. We threw red carnations. She liked red."

Grace looked away. She couldn't let him see the blankness in her eyes. None of what he said jarred anything loose. The tears she shed were out of sheer frustration that her mind could betray her so, that it could lock away all the time she'd shared with her mother, right down to the frantic drive to the mainland hospital an hour away, following helplessly behind her ambulance. Learning her mother was dead. Saying good-bye to her on a boat with red carnations and dolphins. Hearing it gave Grace nothing. How desperately she wanted to know it, feel it, remember what it was like to lose her so that she could remember ever having her. It was all gone. All trace of her life with her mother and her mother's traumatic departure was gone. She was robbed. She'd hoped that hearing what had happened would restore what she had lost. She had counted on it. Now she cried for having no more hope. Because how could she trick her unwilling mind into revealing anything when hearing the bald truth didn't budge it an inch?

Mitch put his arm around her as she sobbed. She replayed his words, wishing for an aha moment. She tried watching his story as a little movie in her brain. Nothing. And then she was hit with a terrible smell. The smell pulled her breath away, suffocating her. She stopped crying, put her hands over her mouth and nose, and looked wildly at Mitch. "Don't you smell that?"

"What, Grace? I sweat a lot today and need a shower—is that what you smell?" He sniffed at himself.

She leapt from the sofa and ran to the bathroom, where she heaved over the toilet. She threw up mucous and kept on gagging, no relief to it, no stopping it.

Mitch stood in the doorway with a look of horror on his face. "Grace— what's happening? Do you need a doctor?"

"No!" she said in between gagging. And then she slumped to the floor, breathing raggedly. The smell was gone but it had left a taste in her mouth. "Water."

Mitch grabbed the cup that held her toothbrush and filled it with water, handing it to her. She drank from it, the freed bits of dried toothpaste in the bottom catching in her throat. Mitch sat on the floor next to her. "Maybe Jane was wrong about telling you stuff."

Grace grabbed the tip of a towel within reach and wiped her face with it. "I needed to hear it. I had blanked it out."

Mitch wiped his tearstained face with a fist. "Would if I could."

The way he sounded, so sad, so tortured, made her wonder if she hadn't given him enough credit for his own suffering. Maybe all the moving, the fuckups, his inability to live a normal life until now had more to do with his reaction to Karen's death than Grace had been willing to admit.

She never would have believed he was capable of such deep emotion until now. Watching sober Mitch grow so attached to Jane made Grace wonder if losing Karen, the love of his life, could be responsible for the chaos that unfolded for so long.

Maybe, though, if they had had this talk a long time ago, things never would have gotten as fucked up as they had. Maybe if he'd been able to share this with her right from the start, her mother's memory wouldn't be sealed up inside of her in some living tomb.

They sat together on the bathroom floor listening to the drip of water from the tap. Grace had to consider the possibility that his not sharing the details of Karen's life and death all these years was not to hide some terrible fault of his but was a pathetic attempt to protect Grace and himself from reliving it. She could see the flawed logic of it. He wouldn't have known any better.

She let out a long sigh. Mitch tried to get up, but his smashed ankle had never healed properly, so he fumbled around a moment. She stood and gave him a hand.

Grace was determined to go back to normal after her talk with Mitch. She now knew what had happened to her mother, even if she couldn't remember it. She had been only five; she had to accept that the loss she experienced had wiped her memory clean.

Time to get over it and get on with things. She wrote a final entry in her notebook about what Mitch had told her and put it away. Grace took stock of her life. She was seventeen and nearly one-half. She would turn eighteen in the fall. She had one more year of high school. Two semesters. Then what?

Her life at the mercy of Mitch was coming to a close. One year from now she would be graduating. If he could maintain the status quo, if he could manage to keep the job he'd had for the last eight months, if they could stay in this apartment, she could apply for a lottery scholarship to the University of New Mexico, live at home, and be a full-time student. She could still work at the pizza café around classes and studying, just like she did now, to cover things the scholarship didn't, like certain fees and books. A lot of ifs stood between her and her goal.

It made her nervous that her plans hinged on Mitch's maintaining his sobriety and job. This was a long good stretch and he showed no signs of crapping out on her, but she felt as if they were in a wobbly boat and if she could just make it to land and get one foot on shore, she could start her own life. So she hunkered down in their little boat and kept her eyes on the shimmering strip of approaching land, still so far in the distance.

CHAPTER 10

SATURDAY MORNINGS ARE COTTAGE cleanup time, meaning whatever chores are assigned for the week get an extra hour or two of attention before the kids can go outside. Bedrooms have to be tidied to perfection, including beds made with fresh sheets and used towels exchanged for new ones. Grace has laundry room duty, so she mops the floor, wipes down the machines, and folds and stacks towels, washcloths, and sheets. Then there's the array of abandoned unpaired socks, which she takes door to door trying to find their rightful homes.

Poor Maddie's stuck with bathrooms, the ghetto of chores. But she attacks the nastiness with admirable fervor. She's scrubbing the shower in the bathroom across the hall from Grace, so Grace can hear Maddie's voice rise in unintelligible, grossed-out exclamations. Aaron stands in the hallway lecturing about the eons of enslavement his people suffered and relating that to his plight on cottage cleanup day. He recites some variation of this sermon every Saturday, which is, of course, the Sabbath, a further affront to his religious expression.

But after having his say and receiving no reaction from his fellow slaves, he plugs in the vacuum cleaner and begins to roar down the hallway.

Percy has the dayroom, so he straightens the game shelves, waters plants, and assists Paul in cleaning the aquarium.

Abdias and Gabe have the kitchen, second only to the bathrooms on the yuck scale. Gabe is tossing expired leftovers from the fridge into the trash while Abdias scrapes dried food from chairs and tables. Lucas, who has doors and windows, is spraying glass cleaner on the three huge windows that separate the kitchen from the dayroom and wiping them down with a rag, his skinny body wriggling with exaggerated effort.

Lourdes, who seems tired and grumpy after doubling back from an evening shift the night before, is circulating to chide the kids into greater productivity. Her strident voice can be heard over the vacuum cleaner, barking in Spanish that crosses the language barrier.

Kellie, a college student who only works weekends, sits behind the desk with a textbook open in front of her. Kellie is pretty and nice, usually too nice, meaning easily manipulated by the boys. She often looks as if cheerleader camp just hasn't prepared her for the likes of Brazos Cottage, especially that time when Abdias sauntered up to her to say, "What's up, home slice? Looking good, muchacha."

After passing inspection, the kids circle up on the sofa with staff.

Paul takes the lead. "Good job on cottage cleanup. Everyone earned full points, so we can all go outside. Capitan Cottage invited us to play capture the flag. Kellie has the sunscreen, so you can line up at the desk to get some. Be sure to drink some water—it's a hot one out there."

Abdias is playing with his shoe where the sole is tearing away at the toes, a good third of the way down his foot. He pulls at the loose flap. "I can't run in these—look!"

Percy begins to laugh and point at Abdias's shoe.

"What's so funny, freak? I only need me some shoe glue," Abdias says.

"You have a hungry shoe." Percy continues laughing.

Abdias makes his shoe's mouth flap talk. "I'm hungry! I'm going to eat me an Indian kid."

"It does look like a mouth," Paul says. "Percy, where'd you get that expression? Did you make it up?"

"That's what we call it in Zuni. It's like a joke. So many of us have hungry shoes," Percy says.

"So many of us *are* hungry shoes," Gabe says. "Think about it. We have these ripped and starving souls. We hunger to be whole."

"In Zuni," Percy says, "it's funny to have a hungry shoe. Or even to have a hungry stomach is not so bad. But wounds of the spirit are serious. A torn soul is the worst of all."

Percy's soft voice, the cadence of his accent, droned a hypnotic song that lulled the group into some spellbound trance. He had never spoken for so long or made so much sense.

"A shoe gets hungry when the bond that's supposed to hold it together gets weak and breaks down," Percy goes on. "In Zuni, it is our families, our clans, who nourish us and hold our bodies and souls together. When that breaks down, our souls become lost, confused . . . hungry."

"It ain't just in Zuni," Lucas says, petting Sam, who has escaped his shirt to sit on his lap.

Grace looks around the group, each of their faces already etched with the evidence of painful pasts. Even Aaron appears thoughtful. The silence surrounds them, unifies them. Grace's past hurts flash in her memory, a little girl just wanting some love, some attention, some stability, someone she could depend on, and instead getting chaos and upheaval and never-ending loss. And while that was happening to her, Maddie and Gabe and Abdias and Percy and Lucas and Aaron were all going through their own special hells. And here they are now, sitting together in a psychiatric facility with some adults who are trying their best to repair the damage. It will take more than shoe glue.

But it's a start. Kellie brings the tube of shoe glue from behind the desk to Abdias and helps him mend his shoe while the others look on in silent witness.

Once outside, they learn Capitan Cottage will not be joining them for the game—the entire cottage is on shutdown after some sort of riot broke out. Grace feels lucky she wasn't admitted to that cottage. Capitan staff are always calling for backup on the walkie-talkies to help deal with out-of-control kids, though Sharon told her all the cottages take turns having a rough group. Still, whether it's the way the staff handle things or just pure luck of the draw, Grace appreciates the relative peace of Brazos.

Paul starts a basketball game with the boys and Gabe talks Maddie into giving it a try. Grace watches as Maddie holds her own on the court, small like Grace, but with a feisty, competitive side emerging. Anything that helps Maddie feel strong is a good thing.

"Grace, I'm talking to you," Lucas says.

"Sorry." She tries to focus on his pale, lightly freckled face, his blue eyes with their heavy fringe of light-brown lashes. Lucas might be thirteen, but the puberty stick has missed him so far.

Satisfied that he now has her full attention, he takes a deep breath and continues. "Listen," he commands. "Close your eyes and listen."

They are perched on a piece of playground equipment they call The Cheese, a cluster of hollow yellow columns with swiss cheese holes dotting their sides, which the little kids like to climb through and peek out of like baby mice. Bigger kids sit on the top rims and dangle their legs into the cylinders while having private conversations out of earshot of staff.

Grace closes her eyes and hears little kids squealing a ways down the grassy hill, where Cibola Cottage is playing with a Frisbee. Ahead of her, she hears the thump of the basketball hitting hot cement and the squeak of tennis shoes as they pivot and skid to a stop. Abdias's music throbs. Paul pleads with Aaron to pass the ball for once. "I don't hear anything unusual," she says after a long-enough interval to prove she tried.

"It's what you ain't hearing that has me worried," Lucas says, squinting into the sun, a sprig of clover between his teeth.

"Lucas, you have to narrow it down some. There are about a gazillion different sounds I'm not hearing right now, which one has you worried?" Grace notices how Lucas has begun to trust her, how he turns to her in crisis, which in his way of thinking is a constant state of affairs. Not that she minds. She never had a little brother, not that she would have wished that fate on any innocent child. Bad enough her dad had one kid.

"I first noticed this morning that it was strangely quiet on the southern perimeter, especially as heavy as casualties have been with the Tet Offensive. But I thought, 'Hold on, soldier, it's just combat jitters.' So I started to monitor it hourly, and look here." He produces a tightly folded square of notebook paper that he had hidden under Sam's wing. As usual, Sam is tucked into Lucas's shirtfront, his watchful eyes staring Grace down.

Lucas pulls a pencil stub from behind his ear and points out his smudged notations. Grace scans the meticulous hour-by-hour account of their day. "I don't see anything missing."

Lucas rolls his eyes and mutters something to Sam about women in combat. "Do you see anything here about Lifeguard missions?"

Grace is aware of Lucas's obsession with the comings and goings of the Lifeguard helicopter that is easily heard from its rooftop helipad at the university hospital down the hill, the same hospital that brought Grace back from the dead. "So you missed it. It probably took off in the opposite direction or something."

"You're either saying I am incompetent as a soldier or deliberately not fulfilling my duties. Grace, Lifeguard must be down! I tell you, something is wrong!"

"Maybe it just hasn't been needed today," Grace says.

"Not needed? Girl, where is your head? Lifeguard is the only thing saving our boys. Their only chance is a quick medevac to the MASH over at Phu Hiep. I keep picturing them laying there, bleeding, their eyes searching the heavens for their one chance and it ain't coming."

Grace sees how this runty boy is in the grips of panic. She knows how it makes your blood go from hot to cold with every frantic beat of your heart. How it takes your breath and will not give it back.

"There's only one thing to do then," Grace says, spotting Jackson on the basketball court.

"You want me to do what?" Jackson asks, dripping with sweat. He came in on a Saturday to get caught up on paperwork but first joined Paul's basketball game.

"I want you to help Lucas call Lifeguard headquarters at the hospital so he can quit worrying about it."

Jackson takes them inside. Stepping into the small back office behind the desk, he strips off his drenched T-shirt and mops off with it. Grace tries not to stare through the slats of the blinds in the window.

Lucas stands next to her, rapidly fraying at the edges. Jackson eyes him through the doorway as he buys time, puts on a clean T-shirt from his gym bag, and reaches underneath it with his Old Spice deodorant for a quick swipe under each pit. He steps back out to face them. "How will it help Lucas to bother those poor people who have enough to contend with?"

"It'll take less time to call them than for me to explain. Trust me, Jackson," she says.

He sighs. "What do I say to them?"

"Ask if it's been shot down and what was its last radio coordinates!" Lucas says, an octave higher than his normal high voice.

"Just ask them if everything is okay with Lifeguard," Grace says. "Maybe they'll reassure him."

Jackson limps over to the phone behind the staff desk. Grace knows his right knee is bothering him and she'll get him an ice bag after he makes the call. He pulls out the tattered university directory and looks up the number as Lucas tries to calm Sam, who's apparently as distraught as he is.

"Yeah, hi, we were just wondering about Lifeguard . . . oh, is that a fact? Would you mind telling a friend of mine about it?" Jackson hands the phone to Lucas.

"I see, sir," Lucas says, standing at attention as he listens. "Well, sir, I just keep track, like any good soldier. It ain't nothing. Proud to serve."

Lucas hands the phone back to Jackson. "Not a crash, praise the lord, just a mechanical that has it grounded for twenty-four hours while they wait for a part. Don't worry, he says the ground buggies have us covered." Lucas sniffs and swaggers off to his room.

Grace looks at Jackson in amazement. "How did he know?"

"Hypervigilance, Grace. Whatever he's been through has left him with the need to be in constant surveillance of his environment, scanning for any perceived threats. This time it wasn't the addition of some stimuli he noticed, it was the absence of one he's grown to depend on to feel safe. He's not playing at being at war, he's trapped in one. Most of us have experienced some hypervigilance one time or another."

Grace thinks of how she monitored Mitch. How she knew his relapse was coming way before Jane could see the signs. Even when she was little, she learned to watch for Mitch to become jumpy and irritable. It meant he was about to flee whatever bad situation he had gotten himself into, and she was about to lose everything, again. "I get it."

Maddie, Age 16

Corrales, New Mexico

Maddie dug out the old postcards her mother had sent, scant as they were. Maybe she had missed something, a vital clue that would lead Maddie to her. The first postcard had come within a month of her mother leaving. Had she felt guilty? "Kiss the baby for me" was just a postscript. Is that all Maddie had been to her? An afterthought? This card had come from France. Had she gone home to visit family? Maddie's family? Suddenly Maddie knew it was not just about finding her mother but about finding herself. Half of her was composed from a genetic pool that resided across the ocean. One that she resembled so much they could never deny her. She would finally be able to close the gap and be whole. Maybe it took surviving her torture to finally have this urgency to find her mother. To start over. To be reborn.

She took a magnifying glass and studied each postmark as if they were fingerprints. Every time she discerned a location, she put a tack on the map she had stapled onto her wall, creating the trail that would lead her to her mother. A very cold trail after all of these years. But seeing tacks on the map somehow made her mother more real than ever. Red dots of pure intention.

Maddie decided to use the long-neglected laptop her dad and Lesley had gotten for her last birthday, suddenly grateful for the extravagant gift. At the time, it had felt like some kind of payoff, so she had rejected it. Now it was more precious than anything because it would help find her mother. When it finally chimed its welcome, she Googled "Renée Duval."

Duval had to be one of the most common French names, and Maddie was overwhelmed by the number of results. She narrowed her search down to the region of Alsace, where the first postcard came from. Still, with a population of over one million, there was an enormous amount of Duvals. A few named Renée. She would call them all.

It was Thanksgiving weekend, and her dad and Lesley were home, the spa closed. Lesley had made a big turkey dinner on Thanksgiving, but it was more about the friends she had invited than being a thankful family. At least Jeffrey hadn't come home. Just as Maddie had predicted, his maternal bond was not sufficient to compete with his new life. Lesley had trouble even mentioning his name anymore without looking like she would cry.

Maddie figured she had to get her dad involved with her search and try to grill him for any details he might have withheld from her about her mother. She caught him alone in his studio making something out of chalcedony; the stone was nearly the same color as the New Mexico sky outside his window. "Dad, I need to talk to you."

She could see in his eyes that she had shocked him. It had been a long time since she'd had a talk with her dad. "Sure, honey," he said as he pulled a chair up next to him, nearly stumbling in his eagerness. Except for the emerging gray around his temples, he looked the same to her. It was hard looking into his eyes. So much was waiting and wanting to leap out of her, so much she couldn't say. Hiding everything had come at a huge price, but it had spared her father his life. Of that she was certain. And he would never know.

"I have to find Mom," she said. She let out the rest of the air held tight in her lungs. His eyes studied her for an uncomfortable length of time.

"It's amazing how much you look like her, now more than ever," he said, eyes beaming with what she remembered as love. Luckily she now wore a protective shield against that sort of thing. If Jeffrey had taught her anything, it was how to manipulate people into getting what you wanted.

"Peux-tu m'aider?" She asked for his help. She hoped the French would put him back in touch with his unrequited love. Instead, he looked concerned.

"What's this about, Maddie?"

"I have to find my mother. I told you. Listen to me for once," she said, beginning to get irritated.

Her dad jerked his head back with a quizzical look. "Maddie, honey, it's been a long time and I—"

"Don't even go there," she warned. She had served as the sacrificial lamb for his happiness. "You owe me," she said. "You have to remember something."

She could see the concern in her father's eyes as she stared him down. She felt cold inside, suddenly seeing him only as a vessel of information. He could not deny her this. He could not withhold anything that would help her. Not after everything she had done for him.

He managed a tense smile. "She was pretty vague and my French was not great. Renée was all about living in the now, so our pasts didn't come up much. She knew her wines. But what French person doesn't?" He paused for a moment. "Are you sure you're okay?

Maddie jumped up and started pacing in order to contain herself. "Alsace is vineyard country. That's where she went after she left us. Something keeps telling me vineyards, vineyards, vineyards . . ."

"But it doesn't prove that's where she was from. And it certainly doesn't tell you where she is now, all these years later."

"It doesn't prove that she wasn't from there. And it's a place to start. She could have family there who know where she is!" Her dad could be so thick. She was stupid to think she could count on him. "Why won't you help me? I never ask you for anything!"

"Calm down, Maddie. I just don't want you to get your hopes up. She moved around so much. It's hard to accept, but the truth is she would have shown up by now if she wanted to have contact. That's the way we left things. It would be up to her."

Maddie fled his words and his betrayal, slamming the door behind her.

From the map on her bedroom wall, Maddie knew Alsace was the easternmost region in France, right on the border of Germany. As she searched images of Alsace, she was taken back to the little girl who wanted to live in fairy-tale lands: castles, high-steepled churches, timber-framed buildings, narrow cobblestone streets, rolling green hills, and valleys full of vineyards. And here it all was in Alsace. What a perfect new life to step into. She'd even be happy living in a small stone cottage with dirt floors. Maybe squish grapes under her feet.

There were hundreds of Duvals out there to call. It was like playing a genetic lottery—all it took was the right number. And she couldn't wait to call each one. She would buy long-distance calling cards with her allowance so their home phone bill wouldn't list the charges.

By Christmas break, Maddie had called fifty-three Duvals searching for her mother's family, with no luck. She had stayed up all night most nights and napped during the day. But she seldom felt tired. The next phone call could be the one.

Jeffrey had come home for Christmas with his girlfriend, and Lesley couldn't have been more joyous. Presents were perfectly wrapped under a tree that could have donned the front of a magazine. The house smelled like mulled wine and roast beef. But nothing could ever cover up the stench of what Jeffrey had done to her under that roof. He and his girlfriend brazenly shared his bedroom, so thank god there had been no nighttime visits from Jeffrey. But even now, as Maddie sat across from him and his girlfriend at Christmas dinner, flashes of his torture kept penetrating her thoughts. She kept a can of Raid under her pillow just in case he appeared. Sleep was difficult, so she lay in the dark and imagined spraying his face, eyes, and lungs with the toxic poison while he writhed, curled up, and died like some disgusting bug.

Maddie realized her dad's eyes were on her as she sat to his left at dinner, folding her napkin and unfolding it, folding, unfolding, again and again. It somehow soothed her frantic hamster-wheel mind. A voice inside her never rested, and being in front of people heightened her anxiety. She released the napkin and pushed her food around instead, pretending to eat.

She noticed her dad still keeping a watchful eye on her as he shoveled in mashed potatoes. Too little, too late, Daddy dear. You should have been watching years ago. Just ask Jeffrey here. She felt the irony of that and giggled into her napkin.

"What are you doing over break?" Jeffrey's girlfriend asked. Maddie couldn't remember her name, but she was stupid and blond and suited Jeffrey. Maddie couldn't help but wonder if Jeffrey ever tied her up or did horrific things to her. Maddie could still feel the rope burns on her wrists. She stared into the safety of her lap, where one of her mother's postcards was hidden in her pocket, and rubbed at her wrists.

"So, Maddie, what plans do you have for your Christmas break?" Jeffrey's nameless girlfriend tried again.

"I plan to find my real mother. Lesley's not my real mom. I don't know if you knew that. I've discovered, with a little help from my dad—hey, isn't that a song? 'I get by with a little help from my'—oh, it's 'friends'—my dad used to be my best friend, so that's ironic. My mom is from Alsace, France. I buy phone cards with my allowance and call everyone with her last name. Sometimes they're a little hard for me to understand because their French has such a German influence. Anyway, Alsace is a beautiful fairyland, just like the ones I always dreamed about when I lived in Old Town. I can't wait to find her. I bet my dad can't wait too. It's such a romantic story because he's never stopped loving her and—"

"Maddie, that's enough," said her dad.

"Holy crap, squirt. You haven't put that many words together since you've lived here," Jeffrey said. Lesley looked frozen, still holding her fork up to her lips, as if Maddie had plunged the carving knife into her back.

"Shut up, Jeffrey! Just shut the fuck up," Maddie yelled, pushing away from the table. "What are you all looking at? I don't belong here. I've never belonged here." She ran from the room in tears. She stood around the corner listening, her hand pressed against her lips to keep from sobbing out loud. She heard her father apologize to Jeffrey's girlfriend.

"See, what have I been telling you, Michael? You've fed into her fantasies for so long it's come to this," Lesley said, sounding concerned. She should be concerned. Who knew what would happen if Renée were back in the picture?

"The kid's trippin'," Jeffrey said. "She attacked me for no reason."

"We'll give her some time to calm down and then we'll talk to her after dinner," her father said.

Maddie was on her computer checking whether she could apply for French citizenship after finding her mother. Her insides chugged like the Little Engine That Could on speed.

A rap came at the door, followed by her dad and Lesley. Maddie didn't look up from her reading about France's nationality laws. They hadn't been in her room for ages, and when they walked in, they stopped cold.

"My god, Michael," said Lesley, looking around Maddie's room. Maddie stood up and stiffened like a trapped animal. She watched as her dad took it all in: the walls haphazardly collaged with hundreds of pictures of Alsace, and surrounding regions; the frenzied, Jackson Pollack–style French flag painted across the wall above her bed; piles and piles of paper, dirty dishes, and clothes everywhere. Rotting food overflowing from her trash can. Maddie didn't smell anything, but Lesley fanned her nose and said, "I agreed to not allow the housekeeper to come in here to preserve your privacy, but no more."

"Jesus Christ, Maddie. What's happening to you?" her dad said.

"See what you've done to her? Catering to her fantasies? This has to stop," Lesley said.

"Maddie, listen to me. Renée never wanted to be a mother. She would have stayed if she did. You have to believe me. But you have a stepmother who loves you and a father who loves you. You need to face the truth, honey, your mother doesn't want to be found."

"Maddie, you had such a beautiful room," Lesley said. "Here, I'll help you clean it up."

Maddie stopped her pacing when Lesley started on her walls. Her dad joined in to help. Up until that moment, Maddie had sent their words flying with her imaginary force field. "Don't touch my stuff! You have no right!" She felt her insides collapsing like the twin towers, her heart dying three thousand deaths. "Stop it!"

"Maddie, your grades have gone down, and just look at all of this," her dad said. "We're your parents. We're worried sick about you."

"You can't make me stop. I have a right to know who I am!"

"Yes, but until your grades come up and your room is clean, we can restrict you from Moonshine, if that's what it will take," said her dad. "It's up to you."

"Honey, we're only trying to help. We don't know what else to do," Lesley added.

How dare they threaten her with Moonshine? Maddie's horse was still the only friend she had, the only one whose love was unconditional. She would not survive the time she had left without Moonshine. She looked at her father with her meanest death stare as he held a fistful of Alsace he had taken down off the wall. They could do whatever they liked. She knew when to lie down and take it—but she wouldn't be stopped.

Maddie lost all respect for her dad after that. She donned her cloak of invisibility, ready to go it alone. They had taken everything off her walls, but not out of her heart. Only recently had she felt it revived to beat again.

The following week, Jeffrey and no-name flew to her family estate for New Year's, and Lesley and Dad went back to work, but Maddie was still on winter break. One morning she waited in her room until she heard them leave, and then took the keys hanging behind the kitchen door to Jeffrey's vintage Camaro that he drove in high school, still parked in the four-car garage.

She slid into the cream leather bucket seat. The car was cold and didn't want to start, so she stomped on the pedal a few times. Finally, after sputtering, it roared to life. She lay on the gas. There were a couple of holes in the muffler and it went *potato-potato-potato*, but not as loud as a Harley. She hoped she wouldn't get stopped by a cop; she only had a learner's permit.

It was an easy drive down Rio Grande Boulevard to Old Town. The day was overcast, and the dark winter bareness looked like something out of *Edward Scissorhands*. Christmas decorations were still up in Old Town, hanging around like guests who overstayed the party. Where had the magic gone?

She couldn't find a parking place anywhere near the plaza. The streets were swamped with people shopping the after-Christmas sales, and families swarmed the museums.

Maddie kept her head down walking to Le Crepe Michel—not that anyone would have recognized her in a pulled-down stocking cap, sunglasses, scarf, and long sweater, especially after over four years. Except for Toes, the thumbed cat from Ye Olde Town Cat Shop, who came up to her and wove himself between her ankles. She almost lost it. That was why she was afraid to recognize things, like her old balcony, the gallery door, a glimpse of Hector selling his jewelry. It had all been dead to her for so long; she was not prepared for resurrection.

Le Crepe Michel wasn't open yet, but Maddie knew Mimi was in there. She knocked on the door and when no one answered, she pounded. Finally, obviously disturbed, Mimi answered. "We don't open until eleven."

"Mimi, c'est moi, Maddie." Maddie pulled off her stocking cap and sunglasses.

Mimi's eyes were wide now. "Mon dieu! C'est pas possible!"

"Oui, madame, très possible," Maddie replied, now ashamed of her long absence. But she was determined to get through this. "Peut-on parler?"

"We can talk all you want." Mimi opened her arms and Maddie walked into them.

Maddie suffered through the usual questions Mimi had over café au lait. She had to dig deep to pull off the act and present herself as a normal teenage girl with a normal life. But revealing the truth was not an option. From what she'd been able to gather, Dad hadn't visited Mimi for a very long time, and Maddie suspected it had something to do with Lesley not tolerating any remnant of Renée left in her dad's life. Especially Maddie at this point.

"I need to find my mother," Maddie finally told her when there was a lull in Mimi's barrage of questions. Maddie laid out her map of France. "She went here after she left us," said Maddie, pointing to the map and showing Mimi the postcard. "But I can't make out the town on the stamp. Guess I handled it too much when I was little."

"Oui, she was from Alsace. I have never been. I came from all the way on the other side of France." Mimi bit into a croissant.

"Dad remembers her saying something about vineyards. Does that ring a bell?"

Maddie could smell the fish from the small kitchen, where Mimi's sous-chef was prepping for lunch. Mimi's eyes searched the ceiling. Maddie knew her mother had not talked much about where she came from to her dad, but maybe she was more forthcoming with Mimi. Still, more than sixteen years had passed since then. Maddie held her breath. "Oui, now that you mention vineyards, I remember her talking about Obernai. Such a beautiful place, she would say. Like a fairy tale. But, mon cherie, I do not know if that was where she was from." A pencil still stuck out of Mimi's makeshift bun, as if it had never moved in all these years. Her eyes were warm and loving, and Maddie wondered if that was what she would see in her mother's eyes.

"You've helped me a lot," Maddie said as she stood to go. She couldn't take any sentimental good-byes with a kiss on each cheek without dissolving into Mimi's arms, so she hurried to the door.

Mimi held a white linen napkin to her nose. "Come back soon! A bientôt!" she repeated in French as Maddie opened the door and ran out.

She got home to put some half-assed effort into her chores and whisper her news to Moonshine before her dad and Lesley returned. She worked on her room, emptying the garbage and clearing some of the piles, but she secretly kept her pictures and papers in a folder under her bed. At least she was able to see her bedroom rug again. She did some of her homework while hanging with Moonshine. Maddie hated the thought of having to leave her horse behind when the time came. So, like all the other undesirable thoughts, she put it in a vacuum-sealed compartment in her brain, locking it away.

By sunset, she was sequestered in her bedroom, hunkered over her laptop. She examined everything she could about Obernai, magnifying pictures bigger and bigger, searching every millimeter, compulsively reading each word of text about the town and its history. Even the website called it a fairy-tale town. Dad and Lesley could think what they wanted. This was a sign. Maybe this was why she always had a fascination with living in a fairy-tale land; something in her blood and bones drew her there.

She also noticed that all the wine villages in the region lay outside Obernai, not more than eight or nine miles away. They were not as densely populated as Obernai, but there were several. Still, things were narrowing down, and she could breathe again.

The pictures were awesome, and she enlarged them so much that she felt she might walk right into them. A moment of euphoria swept her upward—this was how she imagined going to heaven felt like. The pictures beckoned her. If only she could dance down the cobblestone streets like the people in the traditional green garb. The slideshow on the screen mesmerized her, taking her to her mother's homeland until she could smell the air and taste the grapes.

Maddie touched the screen tenderly. "I'm coming," she said.

Maddie dragged the wooden Mexican chest from the foot of her dad and Lesley's bed over to the walk-in closet so she could reach the top shelf where he kept their passports in a strongbox.

When she was young, he took her on an outing to get her passport, "just in case." It was all part of his act to feed her fantasy back then. The "just in case" kept her waiting for a phone call or a letter inviting her to join her mother. That never happened of course, but luckily last year they had updated her passport for a trip to Costa Rica, where Lesley promptly got food poisoning. It had been a terrible trip, but Maddie saw now that its true purpose was to ensure her passport was up to date—another clue that the universe supported her mission.

Planning her escape for the last few months, she pretended she was with the French underground, carefully hiding any evidence since she knew she was being watched. Each passing day excited her more. It was a new, exhilarating danger. Maddie spoke only French to herself and Moonshine. Or around Lesley, who didn't understand a word. She made sure she deleted all history from her laptop after each use. She kept all her research on a thumb drive she wore on a leather cord around her neck, tucked under her shirt. In a way, it was all so easy. She felt she was drifting among the clouds, up there with the charmed. She channeled the persistence and might of Joan of Arc. With Joan's shield and her own powerful gems and stones, Maddie was invincible.

Armed with a screwdriver and ball-peen hammer in her leather belt, she set the old metal box on the floor. First she tried to pick it with a straightened metal paper clip. When it wouldn't budge, she attacked it with the screwdriver and hammer until it broke. She was sweating and out of breath as she removed the lock, which now looked like shrapnel. Right on top was her dad and Lesley's marriage license, probably the last thing he put in there. She dumped out the contents. The blue booklets slid out, along with her birth certificate. She grabbed her birth certificate and passports—including Lesley's and her dad's, just in case they'd try to come looking for her. She quickly put them to the side as she thumbed through the rest of its contents.

At the bottom was a lock of dark hair wound with silver jewelry wire. Maddie knew instantly whose it was. She had never seen it before. She caressed it, smelled it, and rubber-lipped it as if she were Moonshine. She put it in her pocket to place with the rest of the magical items in her buckskin pouch.

She put the remaining papers back in the box and returned it to the closet shelf, turned backward so the shattered lock wasn't visible.

More and more, it was hard to turn her mind off long enough for sleep, but she discovered she didn't need any. She imagined herself channeling some divine spirit who kept her going. She had to hide under her covers at night so her parents would not see the light from her laptop under her door.

Her father kept his credit card on him at all times, so she would have to sneak into his room while he and Lesley slept, take it from his wallet on the dresser, copy the numbers, and sneak in again to put it back. This called for her cloak of invisibility.

Maddie figured their deepest sleep would be at about three in the morning. So she waited patiently in her room, humming a song to herself, shopping for plane tickets. For once in her life, she felt heady with power.

Dressed in black, she stealthily entered their bedroom. It was pitch dark, but she knew where the dresser stood. Such a rush came over her that she had to stifle a fit of giggles. She felt her way along the dresser until she found the wallet. She couldn't see well enough to just take the credit card, so she would take the wallet to her room and then return it before morning. Lesley was much easier to pinch some money from since she left her purse lying around—a twenty here, a ten there. It had been adding up. Plenty for the cab ride to the airport. Lesley had a credit card, but Lesley wasn't the one Maddie wanted to stick it to. It had to be part of the divine plan, which had to be executed exactly. Despite her shatterproof bravado, she was well aware of the fine silken thread that held her plan together.

At the beginning of May, she bought her one-way ticket set to depart the day after school let out, May 27, eventually flying into Strasbourg-Entzheim Airport, fifteen miles outside Obernai. Dad shouldn't get his credit card statement until the middle of the following month. By the time he could get a new passport, she would be hidden deep within Alsace. Maybe even in the arms of her mother. Maddie knew for certain she needed to be immersed in her mother's embrace to be reborn.

She wore her buckskin talisman with her mother's hair in it at all times. At night, she lined up her gems and stones and her mother's hair, lit a candle, and chanted her mother's name. She would leave her body and travel to all the places she had memorized down to the last cobblestone. More than a mother now, Renée Duval was Maddie's religion, and the search for her a holy pilgrimage.

During the last couple of weeks of school, Maddie forced herself to act as normal as she could so as not to alert any teachers, who might call her parents. Her excitement caused her to be gabby at times, especially in French class, which was not her norm, but if she chewed big wads of gum, it helped keep her mouth shut.

She also kept a low profile around her dad and Lesley. According to them, she was doing much better. According to her, they were evildoers. Her detachment from them had been swift and mighty. They had no value to her anymore—they were as much her captors as Jeffrey had been. Trusting no one, she checked her room daily for hidden cameras or microphones. She knew she must be unstoppable because the alternative was to perish in this senseless, tortured life.

On the last day of school, Maddie felt as if she were on speed. She had barely eaten or slept for days, flying high on adrenaline. She had upgraded her talisman to a bigger pouch she wore on her belt, which slapped against her as she hopped, skipped, and jumped down the halls drenched in crystals and saying au revoir to her soon-to-be ex-classmates. Some did the twirling-finger cuckoo gesture when they thought she wasn't looking. But she was cuckoo. Cuckoo with hope and possibility and freedom. When the school bus dropped her off, she walked down the middle of Corrales Road to prove her indestructibility. Cars swerved and honked around her as she laughed and cried with joy.

"I'm sorry you're not enough," Maddie told Moonshine as she cried against her horse's white belly. She took a pair of scissors and cut some of Moonshine's mane and wound silver jewelry wire taken from her dad's studio around the bundled hair like a Navajo chongo. Moonshine nickered. "I love you too," Maddie said, hugging Moonshine's long head. "But the day I leave, it'll just be a bientôt. Comprend tu? We die inside, but no big scenes." Besides, Maddie believed that once she found Renée, the two of them might travel back to New Mexico and arrive unannounced at her dad and Lesley's doorstep. She laughed, hugging Moonshine, her tears still streaming down her face and onto her horse's sleek damp neck, imagining the look on their faces. *Victoire!*

She packed what she could fit in the carry-on duffel bag she found at a yard sale. She locked herself in her bathroom the night before, folding and unfolding, packing and unpacking her bag. Mostly sweaters and jeans; it never got hot in Obernai. A pair of sneakers for city walking and boots for terrain. Because of 9/11, she had to keep in mind a list of dos and don'ts for what she could bring on the plane. She put her laptop in between her folded clothes.

She tucked her mother's postcards in her passport. The girl in the passport picture looked back at Maddie in gratitude. Maddie counted and recounted her cash, putting the bills in order of large to small, no, small to large, and sticking them in her wallet. No loose change was taken for granted. Her jeans pockets bulged, so she changed into her cargo pants with many pockets. Why didn't she think of that before?

Maddie might have dozed for a minute or two, but she was wide awake again when the sun began to rise. She kept quiet and listened as her keepers got ready for their workday, pretending to sleep in on her first day of summer vacation. Her plane would take off at 1:30 p.m. She would get to the airport about two hours early since security was so tight. She giggled maniacally into her pillow. Home free. And no one suspected a thing.

Dad and Lesley were out the door by eight. Maddie went downstairs and helped herself to a cup of strongly brewed coffee, then finished the pot. She brought down her bags and set them by the door. She looked around this house of hell to bid a relieved farewell. As flashbacks of Jeffrey intruded, she climbed back up the stairs two at a time to Jeffrey's room and began trashing it, tearing things off the walls, breaking his dresser mirror, pulling books out of the case and ripping them to shreds. Then she hopped on his bed, pulled down her cargo pants, and peed.

The taxi picked her up right on time. She knew as soon as they merged onto I-25 southbound from Alameda, it would be only a matter of minutes to the airport. Elated, she zipped and unzipped her bag until the driver glared at her in the rearview mirror.

Her heart fluttered when the cab drove up to the international departure drop-off. The driver handed her the duffel bag, and she tipped him ten bucks.

KLM Royal Dutch Airlines. Her eyes searched frantically for the desk. The ticket agent seemed to scrutinize Maddie as she handed her a boarding pass. Maddie babbled in French, which seemed to reassure the agent.

She scanned the long line at security. People were taking off their shoes, and some passengers were put off to the side to be swiped with a wand. Maddie took off every piece of metal she had on and stuck it all in her bag, then dumped handfuls of coins into the little dish provided.

Throwing her bag on the conveyor belt, she walked through the sensors. Good-bye, New Mexico. Maddie bent to put her shoes back on when she heard someone yell, "That's her!"

Maddie grabbed her bag and bolted down the corridor, weaving in and out of passengers, pushing those who got in her way. Her duffel bag smacked a little boy and sent him and his burrito flying.

She didn't look behind her, as that would have slowed her down. She finally saw her gate, her boarding pass fluttering in her outstretched hand. People in line to board were watching her approach, mouths agape. Suddenly she felt herself lurch forward, the floor coming at her face, her boarding pass flying out of her hand.

Someone held her like a pinned chicken before the fall of the ax.

"Let me go!" she shouted, whipping her head from side to side. "Mommy! I want my mommy!" Confused, she thought it was Jeffrey who straddled her. She clenched her butt cheeks, rage and humiliation churning a hard knot in her bowels. As she kicked and screamed, she could taste blood from where she hit her mouth on the floor. She would kill Jeffrey before she'd let him touch her again.

"Be careful with her," she heard a voice say. What was Jeffrey going to do now? Not the hot candle wax. She winced in anticipation.

She heard another voice say, "She's strong for such a little thing. You need to calm yourself down, missy. I'm not trying to hurt you."

Maddie huffed and puffed her images away, cussing at the airport security agents who had her cuffed and on the floor. Then, in one quick motion, they stood her up to face her father and Lesley. The scene circled before her eyes as if she were riding a merry-go-round.

Her father looked horrified. "Maddie, what are you trying to do? I—I got a call from my credit card company asking me to verify the charges for the plane ticket—so I came home, and you were gone."

Lesley was crying. "Michael, she's having some kind of breakdown."

Maddie tried to gather herself. She just needed to explain and then she wouldn't look crazy. "I'm going to France. It's all worked out. I'll call you when I get there. But let me go, or I'll miss my flight."

"Maddie, honey, you aren't going to France, not today. You're coming home with us and we'll get you some help," her father said, motioning to the security agents to uncuff her.

She stood stunned while her dad and Lesley picked up her bag. The agent still had her by the arm. "You going to be a good girl now and cooperate, or do we take you into the interview room and call the police?" he said. "Your choice."

Maddie nodded, but only to buy time. Her brain had suddenly slowed, and it was hard to think. She had to think. She smacked her head a few times to try to jar things loose.

"Maddie, it's time to go home with us, understand?" Her dad's eyes searched hers.

Maddie heard them announce the last boarding call for her flight. A searing pain ripped through her center, and she began to sob. She sobbed so hard she couldn't hold herself up and she sunk to the floor. A wheelchair appeared and she was helped into it. She leaned forward, her hair covering her face, her palms pressed to her eyes and sobbed.

"Thank you, Officer, I think we can take it from here," her father said.

Her sadness gushed through and out of her uncontrollably. It seized her—all she could do was be its conduit.

Then they were in the parking garage and she saw their car in the half light. She wanted to bolt, she commanded herself to leap from the wheelchair and run, but her body refused to respond. Lesley and Dad helped her into the back seat. Dad sat next to her and buckled her in while she heard Lesley stowing her bag in the trunk.

Lesley drove. Her dad reached for her hand. The sobbing had stopped, and it was replaced by a thick wad of wool that filled her and wrapped itself around her. She thought of her laptop when it froze and she would have to shut it down and restart it. So she shut down. And in a minute, she would restart.

When they turned onto their private drive, Maddie could feel her circuits reviving. Restart. Flashes of light and a surge of electricity flooded through her. When she saw the house, she began to scream. She unbuckled her belt and tried to open the car door but her dad had her by the arms. She fought against his grip and he wasn't her dad anymore. Maddie ripped into his skin with her nails, connected to bone with her kicking feet. Still, she was held by this malevolent force, holding her, suffocating her, killing her. Maddie struggled for her life. "Just fuck me and get it over with!"

"Maddie, for god's sake, settle down!" her father pleaded. "What's the matter with you? It's just home—your home." Lesley parked the car. Michael pulled Maddie from the car and onto her feet.

"Do you think she's taken something?" asked Lesley, helping to drag her to the house.

Maddie swung around and faced her, her mind suddenly clear. "I've taken something, all right. I've taken your shit, and his shit, but most of all, I've taken Jeffrey's shit! I could put that motherfucker in jail for the rest of his life!"

"She's got to be on something, Michael," Lesley said. "What did you take, Maddie? Acid? Meth?"

Maddie summoned her superhuman strength and broke free of their grasp. She sprinted to the kitchen, her dad and Lesley running after her.

Maddie opened the fridge and took out a beer, opened it, and guzzled its fizzy amber liquid, draining the can. Dad and Lesley stood in the doorway gaping at her. Maddie looked at Lesley, and everything was so clear it was like a door had flung open in her brain and illuminated all the hidden recesses. "I should be on drugs after what your son did to me. He fucked me over and over and over again since I was twelve—torturing me, threatening me every day for years not to tell. He was going to kill Moonshine and kill me and kill you, Dad. So I had to shut up and take it. There's your precious Jeffrey!"

"Maddie, you don't know what you're saying," her father said. The look on his face said he didn't believe her. She finally told and he wasn't even going to believe her.

"She's totally out of her mind," said Lesley, tears streaming down her face again, an expression that confirmed Lesley would never believe her. "Jeffrey loves you."

Out of her mind? Maddie would show them what out of her mind looked like. She grabbed the large chef's knife and held it out. "Raping, torturing, and threatening are love?"

"Maddie, you're confused. Just put down the knife, baby," her dad said, coming closer. Maddie lunged toward him with the knife and he put his hands up and stopped.

"You fucking son of a bitch!" She seethed, saliva foaming from the sides of her mouth. "Say you believe me!" She put the knife to her throat and felt its sharpness and then a warm trickle of blood. "Say you believe me! Say you believe me! Say it!"

"Lesley—call 911!" he yelled.

Sexual Issues Group is beginning to delve into the worthlessness Maddie has felt for years. Dr. Kaye asks the girls to diagram their feelings on an iceberg worksheet. She explains that an iceberg sticks out of the water, but the portion you can see is only a very small part of it. The rest is hidden beneath the surface of the ocean. Dr. Kaye asks them to name and describe their submerged feelings. Desiree has a hard time snapping to the metaphor, and a harder time naming her feelings. Kathy doesn't make this group session because she's in the main hospital with a feeding tube, due to her weight dropping again. Nishoni writes so much she has to continue it on the back of her worksheet. Maddie stares at her completed diagram and understands it's massive enough to take down the *Titanic*, not to mention a defenseless girl such as herself.

Even though Maddie's thin, she wears baggy clothes to hide her body and won't go swimming in PE unless she wears a man's T-shirt over her suit. She can remember a time she didn't have these bad feelings about her body. She used to love to stand in front of the mirror and try on costumes and party dresses when she was little, feeling like a princess. Jeffrey's abuse started right when her body started changing with puberty. He left her a total wreck, not worth salvaging. But Dr. Kaye says she must confront these feelings and actively work to change them. She has no idea how to do this. Her body is the scene of a crime, Jeffrey's crimes, and it disgusts her. She has begun to talk to Gabe about it, since he had the most extreme case of body issues she can imagine and yet he's taking charge and transforming himself. Gabe suggested she start an exercise program to feel more in tune and positive about her body. But there's only so much she can do in her room by herself or outside during structured activities with staff and her peers. She envies Grace's and Gabe's freedom to go outside freely with their level-three privileges, but it spurs her to earn her points and impress the staff.

Then, in the following week, Maddie finally earns her level three. She's proud to see Jackson write it on the board next to her name in front of her peers and other staff and therapists, enjoying their applause. Not only does it validate her hard work, but now she can use her checkouts for exercise. She talks Grace into joining her, so they use their fifteen minutes of freedom to jog around the track before checking in with staff. Due to the unrelenting Albuquerque late-July heat, they alternate their jogging with fifteen minutes of collapsing in the shade to drink ice water. As her conditioning improves, she begins to sprint past Grace with the image of Moonshine's full-out gallop in her mind.

It's now the last Saturday in July, and a lot of the kids across campus are on passes. Therapists and docs rarely come in on weekends unless called for an emergency or an admission. Once cottage cleanup is done, cottages combine to play games on the field. Staff take level twos and threes on outings like bowling, roller-skating, or seeing a movie at the dollar theater to practice their social skills in public.

After a lunch of Indian tacos made by Lourdes and the kids as a cooking project, Maddie can still feel the burn of the roasted green chile on her tongue and lips as she and Grace jog around the track. The open expanse of the green field always reminds her of Moonshine and how she misses her, the sound of the horse's nickering, her musky scent, the feel of her slick coat under Maddie's hand.

Maddie stops at the sight of Dr. Swenson and Sharon standing on the hill waving for their attention. Sharon starts to descend the hill, trying to keep herself balanced over her green sneakers.

"They want one of us," Grace says. "Must be important."

"Can't be good." They hurry to intercept Sharon.

"Dr. Swenson wants to talk to Maddie," says Sharon. Maddie can see Dr. Swenson standing on the basketball court under the shade of the gigantic cottonwood tree. She does a little side step back and forth until Maddie and Grace get there. Grace wishes Maddie luck and goes back to the cottage.

Dr. Swenson puts her hand on Maddie's shoulder. Maddie winces and expects the worst. "Your father called Sharon to say he needed to have an emergency family therapy session, so she paged me. He'll be here soon. I'll meet you back at my office."

Maddie hurries to change out of her sweaty clothes and to tell Grace what's happening. She wipes her face with a wet washcloth in front of the shiny metal rectangle riveted to the wall that serves as their bathroom mirror. Will Lesley be there? Was this the big kiss-off she has been dreading? Will she exit Dr. Swenson's office an orphan?

Maddie does push-ups against the porcelain sink, sucking in deep breaths and blowing them out like G.I. Jane, summoning the warrior in herself.

She thinks of every horrible possibility as she walks to Dr. Swenson's office. Her heart is in her mouth, but the taste of blood is from her chewed lip.

"What's taking her . . ." she hears her dad start to ask through the open door of Dr. Swenson's office.

When she stands before them, her dad sweeps her in his arms and off her feet in a tight embrace. Maddie can hardly breathe, and she can feel his tears against her face.

"I couldn't wait until next week—I believe you, Maddie." He sets her back down. He looks bedraggled and sleep deprived. "I kept thinking about things you said, and stuff started hitting me. Like the looks I use to catch Jeffrey giving you, or finding him in the hallway next to your room one night when I got up to use the bathroom—I didn't let myself imagine what that could mean. And you became so sad and so quiet—and I never asked why. I never asked what had become of my bubbly, happy little girl. All these pieces started to come together, and it hit me like a ton of bricks. Oh god, Maddie, I am so sorry. Please forgive me." He holds her hands and cries into them. "I should have seen it. I'll never forgive myself." His tears feel like diamonds in her hands.

Her father is suddenly transforming back into the man she used to call Daddy. She clings to him, crying the tears of so much suffering. "He hurt me so bad and I was so afraid he'd kill you—he said he'd poison you if I told—I had to let him do whatever he wanted to me and never tell."

He holds her as she cries. "I'll kill that son of a bitch."

Her dad wants to kill Jeffrey.

"How is Lesley taking this?" Dr. Swenson asks.

He looks up, his eyes red and swollen. "I haven't talked to her. I called and came here as soon as I knew."

Dr. Swenson says, "I could meet with just the two of you, help her to accept this."

"I need to talk to her first. I haven't thought that far ahead. She's going to have to listen. It's going to kill her, though." Will Lesley be able to shake her dad's certainty?

Instead of blurting her worst fear, Maddie puts her arms around him. "I love you, Dad."

Maddie's dad does not mention Lesley in his phone calls that come like clockwork for the next few days. She can tell in his voice he is stressed and exhausted. They make small talk; he always asks if she needs anything, and with loving words and apologies promises he'll see her soon in family therapy. She tries to remain positive.

Tonight they have to say good-bye to Abdias. Everyone knew all along he would be discharged to the juvenile prison, where he will be locked away until he's twenty-one, so the usual discharge celebration isn't appropriate. Lourdes decides he can still choose his favorite cake and ice cream like in all the other discharges. Maddie would never have guessed his favorite badass cake would be carrot. Lourdes doesn't believe in box cakes, and making carrot cake from scratch, as Maddie learns when she and Grace help her make it, is a labor of love that they hope Abdias will feel and carry with him.

"Eee ho la!" he says when he serves himself a humongous piece after dinner. Maddie's sad to see him stuff in as much cake as he can, knowing it will be his last for a long time.

After a quick transition time in their rooms, they're called back out for Abdias's good-bye group. He jiggles nervously as he sits before them.

Jackson stands behind Abdias, his big hands on Abdias's shoulders. Sharon, Lourdes, and Paul sit with the kids.

"We're gathered here to say our good-byes to Abdias," Jackson begins, "but first I'd like to ask Abdias if he wants to say anything to the group."

"Yeah, I want you guys to know that, um, well, I appreciate everyone being so nice to me, knowing what I did." He swipes at his nose. "I never thought I'd get tight with anyone here." He shakes his head in disbelief. "Aaron and Lucas, man, you guys drove me nuts, but I love you like brothers, man. You guys made me laugh."

Jackson squeezes his shoulders, encouraging him to go on. "I told you what I did, but not how it went down. When you're initiated in a gang, sometimes they make you shoot someone to prove your loyalty. So this one night they took me cruisin' and drove down this neighborhood street and pointed out a house. They told me some vato lived there who'd done them wrong and I'd be the triggerman in the drive-by. I was scared shitless, but when they yelled 'Now,' I closed my eyes, pointed, and shot up the house.

It turned out I killed the little kid. Once I found out, I felt like shit and was so sorry—I would have given my life if it would bring back that little kid who didn't do nothing to nobody." Abdias stops, fighting tears, his hand to his brow like a visor. "Now I have to live with it and pay the price for what I did. You guys helped me take responsibility. I just want to say thanks."

Abdias has softened during his time here and Maddie wonders how that's going to serve him in juvenile prison with older, hardened criminals. He let his guard down here, surrounded by a bunch of kids who love him for who he is in this time and space. She's very fond of him, even though he's a murderer. People are not entirely their behaviors—Maddie knows Abdias well enough to know that he's not a sociopath. He has a conscience, and it will demand he do better.

"So now we do the magic box," Jackson says, taking an invisible box from Sharon. "We go around the group and each of us puts something in the box for Abdias to take with him. Who wants to start?"

Lucas raises his hand and Jackson hands him the invisible box. "Abdias, I'd like to give you all my medals from the war so that you can be a good soldier and stay out of trouble." His shaking, bony hands pass the box to Gabe. Even Sam looks sad.

"You turned into a real person here. I'm putting a whole bunch of patience in your box," Gabe says. "I'm gonna miss you, bro." Gabe hands the invisible box to Aaron, who pretends to set it heavily in his lap. He drums on his chin as he thinks. "Abdias, we are the perfect example of two very different cultures living in harmony. In your box I put a telescope so you will never lose sight of your hope for the future. Now who am I going to bug?" Aaron says, inciting some laughter.

"I'm going to miss your funny little hat," Abdias says.

"Yeah, you finally stopped knocking it off of me."

More laughter but smiles quickly flatline. Aaron stands and brings the invisible magic box to Percy, who says, "Good-bye doesn't exist in my language, but I wish you safe journeys."

Grace puts in an abundant supply of strength and perseverance. "You can do this," she tells him. Abdias nods. He begins to chew his nails and focus on the clock. They all look at the clock. Maddie can see tears on his lashes. It wrings her heart.

Grace gives Maddie the box, which she holds as if it were as delicate as blown glass. She knows Abdias has a little crush on her; it shows in his big brown eyes.

"I'm going to miss you, Abdias. You helped me learn to laugh again. Inside the box is my promise to never forget you." Abdias covers his eyes with his hand again. Maddie brings the box over and hands it to Abdias.

"Thanks," he says, taking the invisible box. Then the outside buzzer rings.

Jackson says, "It's time." Abdias collapses the box in his hands instead of completing the ritual of pressing the full magic box into his heart for safe-keeping.

It's customary to walk the discharged kid to the parking lot for final hugs and to wave good-bye as they are driven away. So when Abdias stands to be led by Jackson to the officers who are waiting out of view in the hall-way, the kids stand too. "No," Abdias says, finally breaking down. "I don't want you to walk me out. I don't want you guys to see me like that. Please, stay here."

They sit back down and watch as Jackson takes Abdias, head hanging down, to the hallway, where they can no longer see him. The group waits in silence. They hear the click of handcuffs, a soft moan from Abdias, and then the sound of the door being unlocked as they take him away, the door slamming shut behind him.

CHAPTER 11

Grace, Age 17

Albuquerque, New Mexico

Despite letting go of her quest to recover her memory, Grace still experienced bouts of nausea. Her sleep was troubled. She would wake in the middle of the night and lie panting in the dark, in total fight-or-flight mode, and have no idea why. Whatever nightmares had brought her to that state evaporated as soon as her eyes were open. Sometimes it was the terrible smell that woke her, prompting her to turn on the light and perform a futile search of their apartment to try to find its source. Fortunately Mitch slept soundly, his snores uninterrupted as she crept ghostlike through their rooms until she was convinced it was all in her mind.

In school, Grace walked through her schedule in a daze, sleep deprived and cotton brained. She studied for hours and felt like the material just wasn't sticking. Her straight As slipped to Bs. In art class, she began to paint New Mexico landscapes instead of beach scenes. Cass looked at her technically proficient mountains and deserts, stunning sunsets, and jagged mesas, and said, "Where is your soul? It's missing from these."

Where was her soul? Instead of Mitch's truth setting her free, it had snatched her soul and left her a dried husk of a girl. But it also took her curiosity, her giving a damn. She barely noticed what was happening to her and when she did, it was with a sense of complete detachment. April slid away, May arrived. Duc and Robin were leaving in two weeks.

"Our poor little lamb has to go to school until Memorial Day," Duc said as they sat at a table at Flying Star, a local café and student hangout, drinking coffee and sharing some delectable desserts, ostensibly studying for final exams.

"And then there is all of next year," Grace said with a yawn.

Robin looked at her. "You are in serious need of concealer. It looks like you smeared purple paint under your eyes."

Duc nodded. "I might have some in my bag." He began to dig through his bag of tricks. It was amazing what he could pull out of there. One time he pulled out a hot glue gun and repaired Grace's shoe.

"Duc, you'll never get half that shit through airport security, the way they are now. And how are we ever going to get our packing down to two suitcases?" Robin said, pulling off a chunk of his lemon curd muffin and popping it into her mouth.

"Our parents will just have to ship boxes to us after we get there," Duc said, using his pinkie finger to pat some concealer onto Grace's under-eye areas.

"Aunt Sybil said we could stay with her as long as we need to, but her place is way small, so we'll have to start looking right away. It could take a while to find something we can actually afford," Robin said.

"You mean something our parents can actually afford. God, we're so spoiled! I love it," Duc said, appraising his efforts on Grace's face. "Better. But there is no substitute for actual shut-eye. Why do you think they call it getting your beauty sleep? Quit studying so late."

"Yes, Mother." Grace took a sip of her coffee, loaded with cream and sugar. Maybe all the caffeine she was consuming was screwing with her, but she needed it to function. A vicious circle.

"We still haven't decided which graduation parties to go to. I mean, we both have the obligatory family receptions with the relatives, but after that there's like twenty parties to choose from," Robin said.

"I say we hit them all. Or we could skip them all and stay home to finish packing—we only have one day to get ready after that. I don't know, I'm torn, you decide, surprise me," Duc said, covering his eyes.

Grace rested her arms on her open American history book. She watched Robin and Duc, their banter slipping into something unintelligible, like a foreign movie with no subtitles. She absorbed their company, their expressions, the music of their voices and laughter into a part of her brain she hoped would reliably store it. She wanted to remember this.

Grace was ready for school to be over and her friends to be gone. The anticipation was excruciating. Seeing them, knowing she soon wouldn't be seeing them, the whole countdown was way too depressing. Once they were gone, she would get through her final two weeks of junior year and then throw herself into working her summer schedule at the pizza café, and in general, survive their loss.

Robin told her to adopt a friend the way they had adopted her. Make a project out of it, she instructed. Observe candidates, test the waters, obtain first impressions, take the plunge. Grace looked around but did not get beyond observing candidates. None appealed to her. She decided it was too soon. Duc and Robin were still there for a few more days.

Graduation was a strange mix of boredom and sadness. Grace sat alone, embedded among families who cheered and clapped and wept as their children walked the stage to receive their diplomas. Robin's mother had invited her to sit with them, but Grace couldn't find them in the crowd and besides, she didn't really know Robin's family well enough to take the invitation as more than a polite gesture.

Robin's name was called about halfway through the four hundred graduating seniors. With her statuesque height, her perfect hair and makeup, Grace imagined she was collecting a Tony or an Oscar as she glided across the stage, instead of her high school diploma. Her family revealed themselves with flash photography and cheering across the university basketball arena, where the event was held. Grace thought ahead one year. When they finally got to her name, under the Ws for *Willis*, would her dad and Jane be in the stands? Would her adopted underclassmen friends clutch tissues and tremble when her name was called?

Duc, of course, danced across the stage, eliciting his last eruption of high school laughter. Everyone loved Duc. He disarmed even the most homophobic people with his infectious humor and style. Like a court jester, he got away with stunts for which others in the kingdom would be banished or beheaded. Underneath it all, Grace decided, it was Duc's bravery that endeared people to him. The guy had balls.

She decided to skip their family receptions; Duc and Robin would be distracted and pulled in eight different directions anyway. Tomorrow, the day before their 6:00 a.m. flight, they had promised to come over for good-byes.

Grace paced in her room. It was Sunday. The dreaded day had come. She looked at her clock: noon. She had to go to work in four hours. Were Robin and Duc even up yet? Were they too busy packing to come over before she had to go to work? They would come, of course they would, they promised. She sat on her bed a full five seconds before jumping up to pace again.

Grace realized she was nearly a virgin when it came to saying good-bye. Could you be nearly a virgin? Mitch had deprived her of good-byes. They always fled in darkness. They disappeared. People were left to wonder about them. Twyla was the only one she had the chance to say good-bye to, both of them sobbing, holding each other tight, as if that could somehow help. Then the release, the last of their molecules parting forever. Maybe Mitch was right about good-byes after all.

She looked down at her hands, which were already shaking. She felt her pulse racing like it did after gym drills. How did people do this? How did people say good-bye to those they loved without falling apart?

Then Mitch called from outside her closed door, "Your friends are here."

Grace took one more big breath and opened the door.

Robin and Duc entered her room, Robin in a tangerine sundress and sandals, Duc wearing baggy khaki shorts with a vintage sage-green bowling shirt advertising Pepe's Lounge. Both carried packages. Shit. She didn't even think about presents.

"Do you want to go somewhere? Carb out at Flying Star?" Robin asked.

"It's science. Carbs help you numb out, especially refined sugar," Duc said.

"Or we could stay here like it's any other day," Robin said.

Grace began to cry. "It's going to suck no matter what we do."

They stood in a three-way hug, crying, smoothing each other's hair, then laughing.

Grace passed out tissues for careful eye dabbing on Robin's part and an exaggerated bout of nose blowing on Duc's.

Grace said, "You should never have come up to me that day in chorus. We wouldn't be going through this now."

"That's a terrible thing to say! Think of everything we would have missed out on," Robin said. "We're not dying, you know. Our parents live here. We'll be back for visits, and you have to move to New York."

"I'm going to get a lottery scholarship and study art at UNM after I graduate," Grace said. "But after that, if you still want me."

Duc pulled them down to the bed and they lay on it with Grace in the middle, holding their hands. "Of course we will. We'll stay in touch, have lots of visits, the years will fly by. In five years, Robin and I will be regulars on Broadway. Maybe even with a Tony or two on the mantel. I'll have this handsome boyfriend who worships me and is making his name in the fashion industry," he said.

"I'm engaged to his brother, an architect who is renovating our apartment that overlooks Central Park," Robin said.

"Does he have another brother?" Grace asked.

"Yes," Duc said. "There are three of them. All handsome and loving and funny and talented and smart. We marry into the same family and become officially related. We spend all of our holidays together. Our kids are cousins. Every summer, we rent a big beach house on Cape Cod."

"Grace paints. Her husband, the famous chef brother, cooks us elaborate feasts that we consume outdoors on a long table draped in white, decorated with candles, and Christmas lights in the trees overhead," Robin said.

"I love my chef husband," Grace said.

"We all do," Robin said. "We're family."

They lay there, living that life together in their minds until Grace began to think about how she didn't want the spell to be broken, which of course, broke the spell.

"Flying Star," Duc said. "Mass quantities of caffeine and sugar."

"Yes." Robin and Grace agreed.

They got up and began to adjust their mashed hair and clothing. Leaning up against the wall was Grace's bulging art portfolio, which Cass had sent home with her after she graded it. Grace flung it up on the bed and opened it, paintings spilling out. "Pick a few to take with you, if you want," she said, finding the perfect gifts for them. She smiled as she watched them go through the stack, oohing and aahing and finally settling on two each. Robin selected two from the South Padre series: one of a serene sunrise reflected over calm waters and another of a stormy day, big surf and dramatic clouds.

Duc chose a close-up of a trio of petite sanderlings chasing a receding wave on the beach, their little legs nearly a blur. His other choice was of the Sandia Mountains at the edge of town, blushing vivid magenta at sunset. "To remember home," he said. "We'll hang them in our new place. Our very own Grace gallery."

"Easy to pack," Grace said, "since they're not framed. And who knows, maybe someday they'll be worth something."

"They're already worth something. They're priceless," Robin said. "Open ours!"

Grace opened Duc's present first. A photo album filled with pictures of the three of them that he'd taken with his phone. "I uploaded them onto my computer and printed them myself. For you old-school types."

Grace began to page through, seeing pictures she had only previously seen in quick glances at his phone screen. She stopped at one of them. Duc had held out the phone and snapped it of all three of them making goofy faces. She laughed.

"He made me one too. Isn't it perfect?" Robin said. "But quit looking or we'll be crying again, and I just got my makeup fixed."

Grace set the album aside and reached for Robin's gift. Inside the box was a book, *The Naturalist's Guide to Coastal Texas*. Along with the book was a velvet-lined carved wooden box containing a handful of seashells. "I got ones native to the South Padre area. This is called a sundial and this one is an olive shell, oh, and this one is a shark's eye. You can look them up in the book. The book has all the shorebirds and sea turtles and fish—everything."

Grace picked up one of the shells, a sundial, and ran her finger along its textured shape, which was like the swirl of frosting atop a cupcake. In the barest wisp of memory, she could see her own little hand holding such a shell. Instead of freaking her out, the memory filled her with a sense of having something returned to her that she had lost. "These are great, Robin. And the book—I can't wait to look at it."

"But wait you must," Duc said, pulling her up from the bed. "It's time to self-medicate, remember? There's a chocolate éclair with my name on it."

With just enough time to change and go to work, Robin and Duc dropped her at home. They stood leaning against Robin's car. The intense May sun tried to dry their tears.

"I can't believe you still don't have a phone, even a frickin' landline, so we could call and hear your voice," Duc said.

"I have an email account I can use at the library," Grace said. "And I plan to send you actual letters and artsy postcards." She worried her lack of accessibility would make it more likely that Robin and Duc would drift away from her like untethered helium balloons.

"We're coming home at Christmas, I think, so that's only like seven months. Time will go fast," Robin said. "Just be strong, Gracie May. Whatever happens, be strong."

Grace nodded, wondering what doom Robin might be predicting. She felt herself want to crumple into a little ball onto the hot cement. "I just want to thank you guys. You'll never know how much—" Her voice broke into sobs.

They gathered her into their arms and told her they loved her. Then they let her go and got into Robin's car. Grace made herself watch the car get smaller and smaller as it traveled up the street, until it turned and there was nothing left to see.

School without Duc and Robin was tasteless and colorless. Grace tuned out the frenzied din of the last days of the school year, so it was nearly silent as well. As if her five senses decided it wasn't worth the effort, Grace felt wrapped in some kind of impenetrable fog. She turned in assignments, took final exams, watched as teachers, who seemed to have aged years instead of months, took down faded posters from their walls. Classrooms became as empty as she felt. Her junior year was sputtering to a stop. In only one more week, she could escape this living monument to her past life with Duc and Robin. She could only hope that next year, as a senior, enough time would have elapsed that living without them would not be so debilitating. She would be counting off the months until her own graduation and the start of her independent life. Maybe by then she would give a damn.

There was a familiarity in this muffled existence. She had spent most of her life that way, until awakened by Duc and Robin's spell. Settling back under the eiderdown quilt of loneliness provided her only comfort.

After class on Friday, Grace went to the library to read emails from Duc and Robin and send her replies before walking home. The sun scorched her scalp and reflected off the cement in visible waves of heat. By the time she reached home, the back of her shirt was wet beneath her backpack.

Mitch stood at the door. "Where you been?"

"The library. I go every day to check in with Robin and Duc. It's the only way we can communicate since I can't afford a phone, remember?" Grace walked past him to the kitchen, where she stood with the refrigerator door open, sighing as the cold air wafted over her. She took out the pitcher of water, poured a large glass, and drank it down.

"Jane's making us dinner. She's got some kind of news for us."

Grace poured herself another glass of water and set it down. She took off her backpack and lifted her soaked shirt in the back to peel it away from her skin. She walked to where the swamp cooler blasted from the ceiling in the hallway between their bedrooms and let the cold breeze pour down on her. Mitch followed and handed her the glass of water.

"I could just dump this on you," he offered.

"I need it more on the inside," she said, taking another gulp. "So what's Jane's news?"

"I don't know. She's been real secretive about it. I can tell she's been dealing with something lately." He leaned against the wall, his head nodding in agreement with himself.

Grace led him back to the living room and they sat on the sofa. "You look nervous."

"I don't like surprises. Things are just right, you know? So I'm hinky about whatever this is."

Grace felt his nerves ignite her own. Jane was Mitch's self-proclaimed rock. Anything that affected Jane would affect him. She looked at Mitch and saw him as a helpless little duckling when it came to his sobriety, and her entire life and future depended on this fragile creature. "She's announcing this at dinner?"

"That's the plan."

"Then it must be something good. Nobody makes a special dinner to deliver bad news," Grace said even as her insides twisted.

Mitch smiled. "You're a smart girl, Grace. Thanks for saying that. I just need to calm down and stop jumping to the wrong conclusions." He sunk back into the sofa.

"Yes," Grace said, hoping to take her own advice.

"How are your friends doing in the big city?"

"They went with Robin's aunt to see Ground Zero, so that was hard. Robin said next week there's a ceremony they're going to attend, to take down the last support beam. I guess that ends the clearing of the debris stage. Her aunt lost a close friend in the towers."

"Makes me know how lucky we are, Grace. It was just a normal day for those folks—going off to work—shows you how life can turn on a dime, man." Mitch looked nervous again.

"When are we supposed to go to Jane's?"

Mitch looked at his wristwatch, whose strap was held together with a blue rubber band. "Shit. Right now."

Grace felt her waterlogged stomach lurch.

Jane met them at the door. "It was too hot to cook, so I made chicken salad and got these croissants from the bakery, and here's a fruit and cheese platter to go with it. Ice tea?"

"What's this big announcement you have?" Mitch blurted.

Jane was pouring tea. "Sit down and we'll eat first."

Grace watched Jane's birdlike movements and began to worry. Mitch was right, whatever this was, Jane was jumpy. Grace kept an eye on her while she split a croissant and spooned chicken salad into it. Grace took some grapes and cheese but didn't start to eat. She should be starving—school lunch had been something gray and inedible.

Jane sat and then looked at her and Mitch's untouched food. "Eat," she said, a little too forcefully. She filled her plate and began to take bites, as if demonstrating how it was done.

"Not until you tell us what the hell is going on." Mitch folded his arms over his chest.

Jane pointed to her full, chewing mouth and then swallowed with a drink of tea. Mitch and Grace sat completely still and watched her.

"Good lord, you guys," Jane said. "I thought we could do this after we eat, but obviously you two aren't capable—"

"You said you have important news—don't string us along. Spit it out already—I ain't good with all this kind of buildup," Mitch said.

"Me neither," Grace said, trying not to believe that all surprises were bad.

"Okay. So here it is. I have a younger sister, Jill. She's twenty-five, so ten years younger than me. She had to be around all the drinking and bad stuff in our family from a younger age and was only eight when I got out of there. I felt bad leaving her behind, but I was only eighteen and could barely take care of myself. So she started drinking at a young age, plus drugs and all the rest of it. She's had a hard life. We lost track of each other until a month ago, when she contacted me. She was in some trouble and I helped her get into rehab. She's getting out tomorrow and I've agreed to let her come live with me. I know it's a lot, but I'm hoping we can all help her together, you know, to stay sober and get a job and get back on her feet."

"Is that all?" Mitch said. "Shit, I thought you had cancer or were moving away or something. Shit. Any sister of yours is like family to us, right, Grace?"

Grace tried to nod, but her head was stuck. "What about your craft room? Your sewing and stuff? You love that room."

"I found a twin bed at a garage sale and I've moved stuff around and boxed up some of it. I was hoping you could help me set up the bed frame, Mitch," Jane said. "This is only temporary, Grace. I can't be stingy with my spare room. Jill needs my help, and I owe her."

Mitch bit into his sandwich with sudden gusto. He was obviously relieved. Grace wondered how he could be so stupid.

Grace was at work when Jane brought Jill home. When Grace got home after ten o'clock that night, she found a note from Mitch saying he was at Jane's and to come over. She was tired from a long shift and only wanted to soak in the tub and go to bed with one of her library books. After all, she had a double shift starting in the morning covering for a coworker. But her curiosity about Jill made her change her clothes and walk over to Jane's. Rudy sat in a lawn chair in front of his enclosed courtyard, listening to a traditional Mexican music channel on his portable radio.

"Hola, Grace. How was work?" he said after turning off his music and picking up his chair for the night. He groaned as he stretched out his back and tried to get his legs to work.

"Busy. Did you meet Jane's sister yet?"

"I saw them get here," Rudy said. "But I stayed out of the way. Your dad helped them bring in her one bag. She looks like a puta, but who am I to judge? Good night, mi'ja."

"Good night, Rudy," Grace said. She wondered if he had been waiting for her to get home safely before turning in for the night. The thought made her smile.

She went on to Jane's and peered through the glass part of the door before knocking. Mitch and Jane were next to each other on the couch. Jill sat in the chair, her back to Grace.

Jane looked up and waved her in. Even though all of Jane's lamps were on, it seemed kind of dim. Mitch jumped up and pulled over a kitchen chair for Grace to sit on.

"Grace here has been on her feet like, what, nine hours?" Mitch said, patting the chair as if he'd made it himself.

She sat, taking her first real look at Jill. "Yeah. I cook pizzas in a wood-burning oven." Jill was pale with long black hair. Her cutoff jeans were cut so short the pocket liners were sticking out from under the fringe. Her tank top barely covered her large breasts, and the tattooed head of snake emerged from her cleavage. This puta, as Rudy had so aptly described, was identical to any number of bimbo skanks that Mitch had brought home from countless bars over the years.

"Jill, this is Mitch's daughter, Grace. Grace, this is Jill, my sister," Jane said.

This earned her an eye roll from Jill. "Duh. I think we had that figured out."

"Nice to meet you," Grace said in support for Jane, and leaned forward to put out her hand to shake. Jill looked at it and then offered Grace her fingertips for one of those creepy handshakes. Her fingertips were cool, her nails long and painted. Did they give manicures in rehab?

Jill played with her long hair, raking through it with her nails, pulling it up from her neck only to let it fall again. "I'm dying for a beer," she said.

"The want for it never goes away, but you don't have to give in to it. Gets easier after a while," Mitch said. Jane was holding his hand.

"I don't think beer should even count. I could draw the line at hard booze, wine, pills, that kind of shit—but beer is like Kool-Aid for grown-ups," Jill said.

"That's not how addiction works," Jane said.

Jill began to laugh. "Addiction doesn't work, does it? I'm talking about responsible drinking—that's what rehab should focus on—not this all-or-nothing bullshit."

Grace watched as Mitch looked from Jane to Jill. His brow was furrowed, his eyes darting between them, not knowing where to land. She could feel his anxiety from where she sat.

"So, what are your plans, Jill?" Mitch said.

Jill took a long moment to look at him. "Get through the next five minutes." She rubbed at her skin as if it were crawling. She rubbed her nose with a slender finger. The snake between her breasts seemed to stretch as she moved. "I need a smoke."

"Maybe you should quit those nasty things while you're at it. They're expensive and you aren't even working yet," Jane said in her mother tone.

Jill pulled a cigarette pack from her purse, knocked out one, and inserted it between her full lips. "Until then, I'll just go outside." When she stood, Grace could see she was taller than she had thought, with long legs. She glanced over at Mitch.

"I could go out with you, since it's getting late," Mitch said. He followed her out of the door. They stood in the courtyard in the dark, the glowing tip of Jill's lit cigarette dancing between them.

Jane's face looked pinched. Her eyes were glassy in the dim light.

Grace didn't hold back. "This is trouble. She is trouble."

"She's all talk," Jane said. "She'll settle down. She doesn't have any choice."

"I know her type and you are wrong, Jane. She's going down and she's going to take my dad with her," Grace said, feeling panic rise in her like a fever.

"I won't let that happen," Jane said. "You have to trust me. Mitch is stronger than you think. He told me he loves me. We're talking about a future together."

"Get rid of her, I mean it." Grace shivered in the warm room and sat on her shaking hands.

"I have to give her a chance, Grace. If she backslides even once, she's out. She knows that. You don't have to worry."

Grace had to get out of there, away from stupid Jane and her blindness. She stood up and started to go, then turned back around to face Jane. "I trusted you to keep us safe."

Jane started to say something, but Grace got up and bolted out the door. "Mitch," she called to him in the semidarkness, her eyes teary and unable to adjust in the moonless night. Jill's smoke hung in the stillness of the air, a veil around her and Mitch. "Come with me."

He walked over to her, assuming the form of her father as he drew near. "What's up?"

"I need you to come home with me," Grace said, trying to keep the desperation from her voice. "I'm not feeling well."

Jill emerged to stand next to him. "Duty calls."

"Yeah, well, yeah," Mitch said. "You know how it is."

Grace knew Jill had no fucking clue how it was.

Jill reached out to give his shoulder a squeeze. "Check you later."

"What's wrong? You sick to your stomach again?" Mitch asked as they went through their gate. "That's been happening a lot lately—is it girl trouble?"

Grace let out a quick hysterical laugh. "Girl trouble? Yeah, I'm having girl trouble."

Mitch looked like a confused dog.

Grace paced around him. "Sit."

He sat on the sofa.

"I see what's happening, Mitch. That skank is playing you and you are going to fall for it and we're going to lose everything," Grace said.

Mitch shook his head. "That ain't happening. I'm just being nice to her because she's Jane's sister. I'm with Jane."

"I know you, Mitch. That big-boobed skank is just what you go for—please, Mitch—don't do this. I finally have a life here. I want to finish high school and go to UNM. I need you to stay sober—please—just don't crap out on me now!"

Mitch stood up and put his hands on her shoulders to stop her frantic pacing. "Grace. Stop it. You're going off for no reason. I ain't done nothing and I ain't going to do nothing, so calm yourself. It's late. Go to bed and you'll feel better tomorrow. Now I need to go back and say good night to Jane."

Grace got into bed. She was too hot with the sheet on and too cold without it. She tried to read, but the words swam before her eyes in no particular order while her mutinous brain spit out flashes from her past like passing billboards. She saw herself as a little girl, playing with María and getting yanked away. Time after time, finding a tender moment at a new school, a kind teacher, a friend at recess, only to have it all yanked away from her helpless grasp, until she knew for sure that life was predictable only in its unpredictability. Every loss battered her heart until she imagined it spongy and sluggish, quivering and nearly unable to pump her blood. When she was nine, she had learned in school that her heart was about the size of her fist. She made a fist and looked at it and then when the pain in her chest was more than she could stand, she struck herself on her breastbone over and over as hard as she could until it hurt more on the outside than on the inside. She woke the next day with a sore hand and a magnificent deep-purple bruise blooming over her heart. She had stood in front of the bathroom mirror, naked, her dull eyes taking in what she had accomplished and feeling satisfied.

At the center of the shitstorm, Mitch.

He did this to her. If only her mother hadn't died—but she had died from drugs, so maybe if she had lived, she would have had two fucked-up parents to deal with. No. Her heart told her no. Her mother was nurturance and home and protection and stability—if only she could remember. But she could know it in her bones without remembering.

She lay there, shaking and shivering and sweating and crying and praying to the God she didn't believe in because he would have to be cruel if he existed, and she prayed to her mother, who left her to this hell. She prayed please please please, just give me one more year before it all falls apart again. One more year.

If she could just reach her own life, graduate from high school, get the lottery scholarship, take out student loans if she had to and live on campus if Mitch was long gone, and finally, finally get hold of something that no one could take away from her.

Grace saw the signs. Mitch was irritable, jumpy, sucking down their cheap Walmart sodas one after the other. She watched him. She could hear the tickticking of the bomb about to go off, and her helplessness manifested as stomach cramping, panic attacks, and insomnia. The last five days of school mocked her with their uselessness. But she would go and sit through the hours that the teachers seemed to have no idea how to fill.

Meanwhile, Jane's false cheer and obliviousness was yet another betrayal. She took her sister to buy new clothes for some pie-in-the-sky new job fantasy, except the clothes were two sizes too small and the only job Jill looked ready for was streetwalking on east Central Avenue. Without a high school diploma or any kind of résumé, that seemed like her most promising option, until Mitch talked Dave into trying her out on the cash register three days a week. Grace's head swam as Jane thanked him and Jill purred like a satisfied cat.

On Tuesday, Grace came home from the library, where she had lied through omission to her best friends, assuring them she was fine, to find Mitch and Jill hanging out at Grace and Mitch's apartment.

"I'm just helping her get orientated to her new job so she does good," Mitch explained, trying to put a little daylight between him and Jill's position in the exact center of the couch.

"Where's Jane?" Grace pulled off her backpack and got some water.

"She's at the store, getting hamburger meat for dinner," Mitch said.

Grace glared at them and went into her room. She heard Jill say with obvious pride, "Oooh, that girl doesn't like me one bit."

In her room, Grace racked her brain with the same obsessive thoughts. What was she going to do? How could she stop this when Jane was practically setting the whole thing up? She heard Mitch and Jill laughing. Grace opened her door and crept into the hall, where the noise of the swamp cooler masked the sound of the creaking wood floor under her feet.

"Let's go out on the patio," Mitch was saying.

Grace heard the front door slam as the swamp cooler wind caught it. Grace crouched and made her way to the door, staying below its window. She peeked over the edge to see Jill lighting a tiny pipe and taking a big drag from it before passing it to Mitch, who did the same.

Grace stood up and flung open the door. "Busted, you assholes!"

Jill burst out laughing, a puff of blue smoke escaping her lips. "Shit— you made me lose it!"

Mitch looked guilty for about a millisecond and then launched his defense. "Jesus, Grace. For your information, pot ain't no problem. It ain't even addictive. It can help us to stay away from the booze by smoothing out the rough edges when we get tempted, see?"

"What's this 'we' bullshit? I could give a rat's ass about this skank—she can go to hell. Mitch, you can't do this and stay sober!"

Jill laughed again and took another toke from her pipe.

Mitch had on his stoned face Grace remembered so well: red, puffy eyes and slack jawed. "Go on inside. This ain't none of your business."

"The hell I will." Grace shoved passed them to the gate and strode out to the parking lot. Jane's car had returned. She rounded the corner of the triplex to Jane's place and found her carrying two big sacks of groceries inside.

"Hi!" Jane greeted her. "Taco night!" Her smile was so big Grace felt bad having to be the one to rip it off of her.

"While you're launching taco night, your sister and my dad are smoking pot on my patio. I told you this would happen—you have to get rid of her."

Jane's smile dissolved as she took in the news. She put the bags on the counter and looked at Grace. "Well. At least it isn't alcohol. It's not okay—it's a setback, but it can be fixed."

"Yeah, it can be fixed, as soon as you get rid of the problem. Mitch will listen to you if she isn't around. Get rid of her—you promised." Grace felt her voice getting shrill as her brain kept exploding in mini fireworks displays.

"I understand your worry, Grace. But this is a grown-up issue and I will take care of it." Jane brushed past her, her groceries still on the counter. "Would you please put those away while I go talk to them?"

Instead, Grace followed her out the door and stayed on her heels as she walked to Mitch and Grace's courtyard. Jane swung open the gate to find Mitch and Jane sitting innocently on two plastic lawn chairs next to Grace's potted flowers and tomato plants. She had planted them in a lame gesture of hope.

Jane turned to her. "Please, Grace. Let the adults talk privately."

"This affects me more than you. I'm staying," Grace said.

"Let her stay," Mitch said amicably. "There's two more chairs there. Take a load off."

"They won't sit, Mitch. They want to yell down at us," Jill said.

Jane pulled over a chair for Grace and one for herself. "Jill, we have an agreement that for you to stay with me, you must be sober. Pot may not be addictive, but it lowers your ability to resist alcohol. It weakens you. You need to hand it over to me and promise not to do this again. Where did you get it anyway?"

"A friend," Jill said.

Here it comes, Grace thought. The showdown. The fight that will end with Jill leaving and their lives getting back to normal.

Jill seemed to read her mind and reached into her cleavage and pulled out the tiny pipe with its screw-on lid. She handed it to Jane. Then she reached into her shorts pocket and pulled out a two-inch ziplock bag with a quarter-size wad of marijuana inside of it. "It's all I have."

"Sorry, Jane," Mitch said. "But I ain't never had a problem with pot. I don't even think of it like booze. I didn't think of it as cheating."

"Well, let's get clear about this. Any mind-altering substance, any drugs, any pills, any pot, ecstasy, acid, spice, Special K, anything remotely related to getting high, stoned, or drunk is not part of the deal," Jane said. "Do we understand each other?"

Jill nodded. "Sorry. I slipped up. I won't do it again."

"Me neither. Sorry, Jane," Mitch said.

"What—and now we go eat tacos?" Grace said, jumping out of her chair. "They don't mean it! How can you be so dumb?"

"Grace, say you're sorry to Jane. That's just rude," Mitch said.

"It's okay, Mitch. She's very worried about you," Jane said.

Grace looked at them and couldn't take another minute. She went into their apartment and slammed the door. She looked down at her trembling hands and they didn't seem to belong to her. As she stared at them, the trembling stopped. All feeling left her, as if she were the one who had gotten high. A bewildering calmness settled over her like freshly fallen snow. She went into her room, lay down on her bed, and immediately fell asleep.

On Wednesday, Grace went to the pizza café after school. Her manager, Deb, stared at her. "Grace, you look like shit. What's going on?"

Grace startled from the salad-making trance she was in. "Nothing. Just haven't been sleeping well."

Deb leaned over the bar separating her from Grace's salad station. "I've known you, like, almost a year now and you haven't looked like this since we first met. All spacey and withdrawn."

"Sorry," Grace said, and continued to throw spinach leaves into the stainless bowl with roasted red peppers, slivered red onion, piñon nuts, and a sprinkle of gorgonzola to toss with the house-made dressing.

"It's not about sorry. It's about me caring about you. Are you still bumming hard about Duc and Robin leaving?"

"It's only been two weeks, so yeah, I'm still bumming hard," Grace said, turning the salad out onto two plates and shoving them onto the bar next to Deb's elbows.

Deb left her alone after that. The bus took her home at about ten o'clock, and she walked down the block from Lomas, past the church, in the sweet, cooling night air. Even under the streetlights, the stars were visible. She stopped to look at them a moment. It was where Mitch had said her mother was. Even when she was seven, she knew it was too far for her to reach, even from the rooftops or from the highest branch of the tallest tree.

Rudy sat in his lawn chair, his radio in his lap. He turned it off when she came near.

"How was work?" he said, as usual.

"All right. How are things here?" Grace asked, meaning, Have there been any drug busts or drunken brawls of note?

"All quiet on the western front, mi'ja," Rudy said, and began to stand. Grace took the radio for him as he folded his chair. "Time for all good, God-fearing people to go to bed."

"Good night, Rudy."

"Buenas noches, mi'ja."

Grace entered her place to find Mitch watching the news. She sat down next to him on the couch. "Are you talking to me yet?" Mitch asked.

She shrugged. "Are you behaving?"

"Yeah. No worries, Grace," he said. She stared him down until he looked away. "What? Jesus. I worked, I ate a sandwich with Jane and Jill, and I came home."

"How are things between you and Jane?" Grace asked.

"Fine. She gets it, Grace. She's cool. Everything is cool," Mitch said, but his knee was bouncing. He noticed her looking and stopped.

Grace's body was exhausted. If only her brain would cooperate. Two more days and at least she wouldn't have school to deal with. Ironic—school was usually her escape. Now she felt like she needed to be at home to monitor the situation, as she seemed to be the only one to truly "get it." "I'm going to bed."

"'Night, babe," Mitch said, and began to channel-surf. Grace left him to it.

A few hours later, Grace jerked awake to the sound of yelling. She jumped out of bed and lunged, blinking, to the bright hallway, where the ceiling light was on.

Jane stood in the hall just outside Mitch's bedroom, crying and screaming something unintelligible. Grace realized she had never seen Jane cry. Then Grace started to make out Jane's words. "You used my key to sneak over here! You slut! You fucking slut! And is that a vodka bottle? You're both drunk! That's it! I'm done with both of you! Fuck you, Mitch! Fuck you! I loved you—you asshole!"

"Jane, she crawled into my bed while I was asleep and started messing with me. I wasn't even awake! Shit, Jane, I didn't want this!" Mitch was up now, his jeans half on, his long hair loose and flying.

"Did she pour the vodka down your throat too? You deserve each other. I'm moving out—don't bother trying to find me, either one of you! I'll call campus police if you show up at my work—I'll take out restraining orders!" Jane turned around and ran straight into Grace.

"I'm sorry, Grace," Jane cried, and then pushed past her.

Grace grabbed her arm. "Take me with you!"

"I can't!" Jane said. "I'm through with Mitch and I'm sorry—but that includes you."

"What did I do?" Grace heard herself wail. "Jane, don't leave me here!" She began to run after her, but Mitch had her by the shoulders. "Let go of me—I hate you!"

Mitch's hand struck her cheek with such force she flew backward and landed hard on the wood floor. She sat stunned, her cheek hot as if pressed by an iron.

"I'm sorry, baby, I'm sorry. Grace, I never meant to do that," Mitch said.

She got herself up from the floor. Behind Mitch she could see Jill, wrapped in the bedsheet, leaning against the wall. Jill lit a cigarette and took a swig from the nearly empty vodka bottle.

"You're sorry? Prove it," she said, her hand against her stinging cheek, the sound of the slap still reverberating in her ears.

"Name it, 'cause I'll do anything to make it up to you."

"Kick her ass out. Now."

Mitch looked over at Jill. "She's got nowhere to go. You want I should kick her to the streets? In the middle of the night?"

"It's where she belongs. And if you don't kick her out, *we'll* be on the streets. I won't do it, Mitch. I won't go back to that—I told you I wouldn't!" Grace began to cry, the sobs hitting her like a seizure.

"I'll figure something out, Grace. In the morning, I'll figure it out. Just be cool so I can figure something out, okay? Just stop crying. It'll be okay," Mitch said, reaching for the vodka bottle that Jill held out for him.

"Dave will fire you if you go in to work like this! And then how do we pay the rent?" Grace said through her sobs.

"If I lose this job, I'll get another one. I always do. I always take care of you, Grace."

Hysterical laughter broke through her tears. "You've never fucking taken care of me!"

"Shush now, Grace, you want Rudy calling the cops on us?"

"Yeah!" she screamed. "They can arrest her and take her away!"

"She ain't doing anything wrong, Grace. We're two adults having a drink in the privacy of our own home. You don't have to like it. Just go on to bed, you got school in a few hours," Mitch said, and turned back to Jill and his room.

Grace stood under the glare of the light, watching as Mitch disappeared into the darkness of his room. Jill lingered in the doorway long enough to reach her slender arm back in Grace's direction with her middle finger extended. Then she shut the door behind them.

Grace didn't get back to sleep. She writhed and cried until she was spent and then she just lay there watching the light seep into her room. She got up and got ready for school, which was hard given that her brain seemed unable to function. She was behind on laundry since life lately had left little time or energy to go to the laundromat. She didn't work on Thursdays, so she'd have to get laundry done tonight after school. Two more days of being a junior. It seemed unreal, but everything did.

Before leaving, she stood outside Mitch's closed door. He should be up and getting ready for work. She knocked on the door. "Mitch—get up!"

Nothing. She opened the door. Mitch and Jill lay in a tangled knot, half-covered by the sheet. Two empty booze bottles nestled against them. "Mitch! Get up and go to work!"

He stirred then, looking up at her with bleary eyes. "What the fuck?"

"Go to work!" Grace yelled. Jill still didn't move a muscle. The phrase was probably not in her vocabulary.

"I'm not going," Mitch said. "I never missed a day yet, so don't worry about it."

"Go to the convenience store and use the pay phone to call Dave and tell him you're sick. I have to go to school now. You have to call him, or he might fire you," Grace said.

"Yeah, just let me wake up. Go on to school. I'll take care of it," Mitch said. The breath that came off him was a mixture of booze and dead animal.

"Please get her out of here, Mitch. We can't live like this. Please. Take her back to rehab or to a shelter or something. She's taking you down, Mitch. Can't you see it?"

He rubbed his dark stubble and looked at Jill, still sleeping or unconscious. "I'll figure something out. Don't worry. Go on now, or you'll be late."

As she rushed to school, she wished she had left early and called Dave for Mitch instead of trying to get him to make the call. Odds were slim he would actually do it.

In art class, Cass took her aside while the other kids were watching a film about van Gogh. "Grace, I'm worried about you. I can tell something's wrong. Should I send you to the school counselor?"

"I'll be okay. I'm getting the problem fixed," Grace said.

Cass eyed her a long moment. "Maybe you need some help with it."

"I have help. The worst is over. It'll be fine now." Grace tried to smile and was afraid it looked as fake as it felt.

Cass nodded. "I hope so."

Somehow she made it through the rest of the day. In American history, she must have slept with her eyes open, because it seemed that as soon as she sat down, the bell rang and she remembered nothing that had transpired.

Grace skipped going to the library. Not only did she feel panicked to get home, but she also didn't have it in her to make up some bullshit to fool her friends. All the way home, her brain chanted, Please let Mitch be okay and Jill be gone, over and over, until the words sounded like gibberish.

When she got home, Rudy was in his lawn chair in the narrow strip of shade in front of his courtyard fence. "Jane left. A truck pulled in and two guys loaded it up for her. She said good-bye to me."

"Oh." It was shocking to hear it, even though she knew Jane would be gone.

"I knew that puta would be trouble," Rudy called as Grace ran to Jane's door. She peeked in the window and saw that it was empty except for a large, bulging garbage bag in the center of the floor. She turned and walked back to her place, dreading what she might find. Please let Mitch be okay and Jill be gone.

Once through her courtyard gate she could hear music. Mitch never listened to music; they didn't own anything to play music on. Her flowers and tomato plants were limp in the sun. She should water them. She came up to the door and looked in through the glass. Mitch and Jill were bent over the kitchen table doing lines of coke. A cluster of booze bottles covered the rest of the surface. A boom box blared some kind of heavy metal. Jill was in her bra and panties, Mitch was shirtless in jeans that sagged low around his hips. Each with their long dark hair flowing down their backs, they looked like twin demons, otherworldly and evil.

Grace knew then she had lost him. She opened the door and walked in.

Beer bottles littered the floor. Open bags of chips leaked out onto the couch. When neither Mitch nor Jill looked her direction, she stepped around the bottles and hit the off button on the boom box, slamming the air with silence.

Jill began to laugh. Mitch broke into a grin. "Grace! Come in! We're celebrating!" He lifted his shot glass and dumped it down his throat.

The scene became a movie. She watched from outside herself as her backpack slid off her sweating shoulders onto the floor.

"Have a drink with us, Grace. You're old enough. Shit, I drank beer when I was eleven," Mitch said to Jill's laughter.

"What are you celebrating?" she watched herself ask, somehow knowing her lines.

"We're free!" Jill said. "To freedom!"

"Was this your last day of school? You're free too!" Mitch poured himself another shot and raised his glass.

"I still have tomorrow." It seemed important to get the facts straight.

"That's the thing, Grace. We're leaving tomorrow. It's great—we have it all planned out," Mitch said.

"I have to go on my last day," Grace said. "And what about your jobs? What about Dave?" Her voice sounded distant, as if there was a problem with the soundtrack.

"Fuck Dave. We went over there to get our last paychecks on account we won't be there tomorrow or ever again, and he gets all bent, saying shit. So I said, 'Give us our fucking money,' and he did and said to never come back and we said, 'Don't you worry about that, man, we're going to Florida.'"

Grace sat down on a kitchen chair. The coke trail looked like powdered sugar, and she had to stop herself from tasting it. Her brain kept trying to shut down, she shook her head to try to clear it—she had to see what happened next.

"Disneyland, Grace! We're going to Disneyland!" Mitch said, lifting both arms in a ta-da gesture.

"Disney World, babe. Disneyland is in California. We're going to Orlando," Jill corrected, lighting a cigarette.

"See, Grace, Jill here has a friend who works at Disney World, and she said they need workers. Tons of jobs for the summer. And we can stay with her until we get paid. We can all work there—won't that be fucking amazing? You could be a princess or something."

"Is the rent money gone?" Grace asked, mildly curious.

"We ain't staying here, I told you. The money that's left is for traveling—shit, I can't wait to hit the open road, man. We spent some of it on our party and I bought Jill this nice boom box because she needs her jams, and to thank her for helping us get the fuck out of here," Mitch said, all smiles.

"I want to go to school tomorrow," Grace said. She hated missing school, even the last day. "What if I don't want to go to Florida?"

"You're going," Mitch said.

"No, I'm not." She was thirsty, so thirsty from her walk home in ninety-degree heat. She got up and went to the refrigerator and poured a glass of water into the last clean glass and drank. It made her smile that she got the last clean glass. It was there when she needed it.

"You can't stay. What would you do? Your little pizza job won't cover the rent and give you anything for food and shit. You got to come with us. Come on, we'll get a place with a swimming pool—you've always wanted a swimming pool."

Did she? She'd like to plunge into one that minute, maybe it would clear her head and help her think straight. Did she know how to swim? The water was like heaven going down her throat. She poured another glass.

"If she don't want to come, don't make her. She's old enough to be on her own. I was taking care of myself at her age," Jill said.

"But Grace and me—we're a team. Ain't we, Grace?" Mitch said. "We can wait to leave until you get off school tomorrow—how's that?"

"You and me are the new team," Jill said. "This girl wants to live her own life. You need to face it, babe. Your little girl is all grown up."

Grace looked at Mitch, who had big tears pooling in his eyes. "Is that how it is, Grace? You ditching me?"

Grace watched herself put the last clean glass into the refrigerator to keep it safe, hidden behind the water pitcher. "I don't know," she said. She didn't know much of anything, especially what would happen next. She'd never seen this before.

"Maybe you just need some time to get used to the idea. Think about it, Grace, we'd be by the ocean again. You can go out in your own yard and pick an orange—it's Florida, man! You could get paid to be at Disney World, where everyone else pays to go. You pack some things, just in case, and we'll wait on you to come home from school tomorrow and then we'll all go together. Doesn't that sound good?"

Grace looked at him and yawned. And said the only thing she knew for sure: "I don't know." She walked past them to go to her room. She stood a moment under the swamp cooler downdraft, letting it ruffle her hair and cool her baking skin. The rumble of the motor was like the purr of some magnificent beast.

She walked to her room and fell into her unmade bed. Sleep seized her like Dorothy in the poppy fields. *Poppies will make them slee-eep.*

When Grace woke, she had to scramble to get to school on time. After a shower, she opened her drawer to find the last pair of clean panties and remembered she was supposed to do laundry last night. The last pair of clean panties seemed to glow in heavenly light. Like the last clean glass, it held special meaning for her. A little gift, precious and miraculous.

The last day of school. So many lasts. So many endings. She found a top and shorts that were mostly clean and brushed out her hair. When she looked in the mirror, she saw someone she used to be. Grace Willis, ah, yes, I remember that girl . . .

Mitch's door was half-open but she didn't look in. She walked carefully through the living room, strewn with bottles and old food, to find her backpack where she had dropped it. It came back to her then, the whole Florida insanity, and the choice she had to make. Go or stay.

Grace left the apartment and stood on their patio, the rising sun already warm on her face. She fished her sunglasses from the front pocket of her backpack to shield her eyes from the bright morning light. Her pots of flowers and tomato plants hung limply, still in desperate need of water. She remembered the feel of the potting soil—a real splurge to buy—and its smell, so rich and fertile with possibilities. Her heart had pounded with the thrill of daring to believe she and Mitch would be there to see tomatoes form and redden. She had been so brave—or foolish. She didn't have time to water them now and couldn't stand to see them suffer. And what was the point anyway? Whether she went to Florida or not, she wouldn't be there to give them their next drink or the one after that.

She suddenly grabbed the plants and yanked them from their pots, throwing them to the cement. They gave way easily, tender young roots shriveled and helpless, some still clinging to dark clumps of soil. She scattered the flowers, snapdragons and pansies, over the patio and thought of Mitch's story that they had scattered her mother's ashes and red carnations over the gulf waters. She had a brief sensation of the cement beneath her feet transforming into the slosh of a wave. The plants seemed to swirl in the water as it receded. She looked once more before leaving, feeling nothing except the relief of surrender.

At school, she made her way through her first several classes as if still acting in a film. Her character, Grace, smiled at kids and teachers, recited her lines, and generally seemed to embrace the role given to her. She watched, a little impressed at how well she played her part.

In art class, Cass played another short film, this one about the life and work of Picasso. It became difficult to stay in the moment when the question about what would happen at the end of the day began to intrude. Would she go with her drunken, fucked-up father and his skank girlfriend on some hairbrained quest to Florida and theme park nirvana? Or would she face being homeless and alone here? She rejected both choices as out of the question. She would not go with Mitch one more time; that decision had been made nearly a year ago. And yet she had no illusions about what it meant to be homeless. She knew hunger and cold and heat and cruelty. So going back and forth between these two options was an exercise in futility. But her mind kept slamming against one and then back to the other in an obsessive loop. She felt trapped—panic began to engulf her, adrenalin coursed through her veins, the horrendous smell filled the art room and she swallowed hard against her rising nausea.

Grace left her backpack hanging on her chair and walked over to Cass, who was organizing her supplies and stowing them away for summer break. "I need the restroom."

Cass walked over to her desk and pulled a hall pass form the top drawer, filled it out, and handed it to Grace. "Don't take all day." She said this every time to every kid claiming to need a restroom break, and now most students recited it with her. Grace smiled at the little dollop of normalcy atop the huge mound of disaster that was her life. "Thanks." She remembered in San Francisco when Madam Claudia told her she had angels to help her. Cass was one of them.

She walked out of the classroom. The linoleum floors were waxed to a high sheen and glimmered in the light flowing from the tall windows at the end of the hallway. She walked toward the light, passing the restrooms, to the double exit doors. The panic eased, the smell subsided. Replacing it was a kind of detached wonder. She walked outside, noticing how blue the sky was, how fresh the air seemed. Little tufts of clouds floated overhead. She looked back at the main building, the first school in her life where she had completed an entire year and felt proud that she had made that happen. Where she met and came to love Robin and Duc. Where life was finally normal, at least for a little while. She appreciated how wonderful normal was and wished all those kids inside its walls could realize how lucky they were.

Behind the main building, a major renovation on the old gym would soon start. She walked through its unlocked doors into the high-ceilinged basketball court. A trapped bird beat against the high windows. It must have thought that was its only option, to beat with futility against closed windows, anything to escape its confinement and reach the light and freedom beyond, when far below it, a door was propped open.

And then it hit her. She was also trapped by illusion. She didn't have to choose between chaos with Mitch or suffering on the streets. There was a third option. Escape.

She looked over her head to see the basketball backboard. She looked to the wall where folding chairs were stacked. She looked to the storage area, which held bins of gym equipment. She walked over to them and found coils of jump ropes entwined like sleeping snakes. It was like finding the last clean glass and the last pair of clean panties. Perfection. It was meant to be. Just what she needed, right when she needed it. She knew how the film would end—and was filled with relief that it *would* end. No more decisions to make, no more heartache, no more good-byes, no more hope, no more loss.

She grabbed six folding chairs and stacked them in a pyramid underneath the basketball backboard. She knew from gym class that the rim was ten feet off the ground. She grabbed a handful of jump ropes and began to knot them together. As she did this, she watched from outside herself. She seemed to hover high above the scene, next to the frantic bird. Was she really doing this? It was so unreal all she could do was watch in amazement. Grace was knotting ropes. Grace was standing on a rickety pile of chairs, throwing her new long rope up over the basketball hoop, where it looped agreeably over the back of the basket. Grace had both ends now and she was tying them around her neck, wrapping each end around and then knotting them together. The chairs teetered beneath her feet and then she kicked them away. It would be over soon, just some pain—but she knew all about pain—and the physical kind was the least of it. A sharp jolt as the rope held her body by the neck, her lungs cried for air, her mind watched as the windows exploded and the little bird escaped just before the mother of all waves knocked down the walls, flooding the space with cascading water and brilliant light—and then, sudden darkness.

CHAPTER 12

GRACE FEELS HERSELF WAKING and tries desperately to hang on to the images of her dream. But the elusive pictures fade into the darkness as her eyes open. She was with her mother. The feeling of her small hand enveloped by her mother's stays with her. The tactile sensation, of warm, smooth skin holding her hand and the nurturance it conveyed felt so real. She struggles to picture her mother's face and sees only the long swath of blond hair, the recurring tease her memory provides. But this time there is more: the sound of her mother's voice singing to her and her happiness hearing it. But that, too, is a fragment, a snippet, incomplete, and fading fast.

She tries not to feel frustrated. Dr. Swenson says she should feel thankful for these moments of recollection without putting negativity around it. Getting aggravated will only tighten the seal around the memory. Dr. Swenson suggests feeling appreciative when anything at all breaks through without demanding more.

In art therapy, she paints more scenes of Hannah and Emily, her surrogate characters. Since the grief unleashed by her first painting of them, all her paintings elicit only positive feelings. She paints Hannah with Emily on her lap, reading her a story, Hannah's head bent down, hair hiding her facial features. She paints one of Emily standing in the small kitchen of the trailer, her mother with her back to her, cooking something on the stove. That time, she can smell the fish frying and hear its sizzle in the pan.

Grace examines these paintings for clues. They feel real. Janice discourages her from trying to distinguish imagination from memory. "Don't try to define it," she'd said, "that will only inhibit your subconscious. Just go with it as far as it takes you."

Dr. Swenson had nixed Grace's request to be hypnotized, even though Grace practically begged her to do it. Dr. Swenson empathized with her wish that hypnosis could unlock all the mysteries her mind refused to yield but informed her that memory is a tricky thing. Undergoing hypnosis puts a person in a highly suggestible state, making whatever comes out of the process highly unreliable. "You want to make sure whatever you remember is real, don't you, and not some fabrication your mind is trying to appease you with." Grace couldn't argue with that.

Instead, Dr. Swenson offers something known as EMDR, a technique that is accepted in standard psychotherapy guidelines. Its goal isn't to recover memories but to decrease the intensity of the disturbing thoughts and feelings associated with them. EMDR is showing promise in treating people with post-traumatic stress disorder, which Dr. Swenson says is part of Grace's diagnosis.

Dr. Swenson explains that she believes the trauma of Grace losing her mother is at the root of her panic attacks and her other dissociative symptoms, like when she felt as if she were outside herself watching her suicide attempt or when she had sudden bouts of nausea and smelled foul odors that no one else could smell. To Dr. Swenson, the emotional issues that arise from trauma are more important to address than trying to find out the details of the trauma itself. The fact that her mother is gone is enough. This is not a fact-finding mission—this is therapy.

Grace read an article about EMDR that Dr. Swenson gave her. EMDR stood for *eye movement desensitization and reprocessing*, and came from the research of Dr. Francine Shapiro. Dr. Shapiro found that when she experienced a disturbing thought, her eyes involuntarily moved rapidly. She then noticed that when she brought her eye movements under voluntary control while thinking about something traumatic, her anxiety was reduced. Out of that experience, Dr. Shapiro developed EMDR therapy for people with post-traumatic stress disorder.

It's funny to Grace, to sit while Dr. Swenson snaps her fingers and moves her hand back and forth, asking Grace to follow with her eyes. It's like Dr. Swenson is performing some bizarre dance to music only she can hear. But once Grace stops snickering and follows with her eyes while thinking about losing her mother, she realizes there's something to it. With her eyes moving laterally, following Dr. Swenson's snapping fingers, the clenching anxiety begins to reduce its grip.

And after a few weeks of these sessions, Grace notices her dreams begin to include her mother with increasing detail. Sometimes even when fully awake but doing something mundane, like setting the table for dinner, a little memory will flash into her mind of standing in line at the grocery store with her mother, or getting her hair washed, her mother's sudsy fingers scrubbing her scalp. One time, she remembers being hugged by her mother, the tightness of her arms around her, the feel of her soft throat against Grace's cheek, the throb of her pulse when Grace placed her fingers in the groove of her mother's neck.

These memories are not the big answers she's seeking. They are of every-day life, little moments, common moments in the life of a child, yet miraculous in that they are returning her mother to her, bit by bit.

In her bed, Grace feels drowsiness return. She yawns and turns over. The gratitude she once needed to practice like an unfamiliar language is as natural and effortless as her next breath.

"Is that another letter from Duc and Robin?" Maddie asks, sitting down on Grace's bed next to her.

"One from each of them." She hands the letters to Maddie. Grace always shares them with her since Maddie never gets mail. When Rudy comes for his weekly visits, Grace invites Maddie to sit outside with them. Sometimes Maddie joins them and shares in the candy Rudy always brings and listens to his stories about when he was a firefighter. Maddie's dad is calling more reg-ularly now that he finally believes her, but he hasn't visited. Maddie says he's dealing with Lesley and so she's trying to be patient. But Grace can tell Mad-die's on edge. She's astonished that she, the officially abandoned girl, has more support from the outside world than Maddie has.

"Wow. They got to see Robin Williams at the Broadway Theatre," Mad-die says as she reads. "Wouldn't that be cool?"

"Sometimes it's hard to wrap my head around how life can be so good for some people. They have their stress with school, but they're living their dreams. Life is going on outside these walls," Grace says.

"Yeah. And here we are." Maddie folds both letters and stuffs them back into their shared envelope.

Grace puts the envelope onto the stack on her desk that has accumulated. After Duc and Robin's initial shock about what happened to her and their pledging undying friendship and support, their letters are now like getting to hang out with them—light and funny and full of their New York adventures. "I don't even want to think about leaving here. Gabe got discharged and I'm not at all jealous. I don't even want to imagine what's after this," Grace says.

"What does it say about us that we're fine with being shut away? I guess too much hasn't been figured out yet for us. Like, where would we even go?" Maddie stands to pace around. "If my dad stays with Lesley, I can't live with him, and then what?"

Grace watches Maddie, her face hard, her body wound up with anger. She feels so bad for her. At least Grace doesn't want to live with her dad anymore, not that he's here to turn down. "I really believe your dad is going to be there for you. I know he will. He believes you."

Maddie stops, her face frozen with an emotion Grace knows all too well: The temptation to hope weighing against all the countering possibilities. The leap of faith against uncertain odds. It's terrifying.

A knock at their door startles them both. Quiet time still has another half hour to go. The door swings open and in strides Dr. Swenson. "Grace, your father showed up here about an hour ago. I've been meeting with him, and I'd like you to come back to my office with me to see him."

"Mitch?" Grace is too stunned to move.

"I know it's sudden and you've had no time to prepare, but the opportunity is here, so I think we should take it. We need to get to the bottom of some things," Dr. Swenson says.

Grace wondered how she would feel if he came back, and now she's too shocked to feel anything.

"Let's go, we don't want him to get any ideas about taking off while I'm gone. We can talk on the way," Dr. Swenson says.

She's surprised at how fast Dr. Swenson can walk when she wants to, her scuffed flats a blur against the cement walkways on the way to her office in the administration building. "What does he have to say for himself?" Grace jogs to keep up.

"I think he's finally hit rock bottom, which can be a therapeutic opportunity. Look, I just want you to be yourself, express whatever you feel, be as confrontational as you like. Hold his feet to the fire." Dr. Swenson opens the door to the administrative building and punches the button on the elevator instead of running up the stairs.

Grace and Dr. Swenson stand breathing hard as the elevator doors open. On the quick assent to the second floor, Grace tries to calm herself but it's no use. The trembling in her stomach seems to be infecting her limbs.

When the doors open, Dr. Swenson stands back, allowing Grace to enter her office first.

Mitch stands from his chair, a smile breaking out on his craggy, unshaven face. Even from where Grace stands, she can tell he stinks. "Grace. You look good."

"You don't." She sits before her legs give out.

"I came straight here from being on the road. I called the hospital after I left and they said you were moved over here, so I knew you were safe," Mitch says. "It's been hell without you."

Grace stares at him. His long dark hair is greasy and disheveled, though he has tied it back with what looks like a piece of string. His clothes are streaked with dirt. He appears ten pounds lighter, and his skin is sunburned and leathery. He looks like a homeless man.

"I hope it's been hell," Grace says.

"Mitch, I'd like you to fill Grace in on where you've been and what you've been doing these last months that she's been here," Dr. Swenson says.

"I'm sorry, Grace, I'm just so sorry," Mitch says, and to Grace's horror, he begins to cry. Not a little trickle of tears but heaving, snot-producing sobs. Dr. Swenson hands him the tissue box. "I'm a worthless drunk. I'm an addict, I know that. I fucked everything up. But I been clean two weeks now and your doctor here is going to help me get into a rehab place. I'm going today. But I had to see you and tell you I know how wrong I've been and that I'm the cause of all your problems."

"Tell me something I don't know," Grace says.

"Jill dumped me and took off with all my money and my truck right after we got down to Orlando. That friend of hers that said there was jobs was full of shit. Anyway, nothing went right and Jill wasn't who I thought she was. She's just some hustler who didn't give a shit about me—she just used me to get down there. And I thought I might could love her." Mitch cries some more and blows his nose into another tissue. "I just gave up after she left, and hit the bottle hard, got my hands on whatever drugs I could find. I was on the streets, went to soup kitchens, about drowned in all the rain. And then one day a few weeks ago, I woke up. It was like God or somebody hit me over the head with a two-by-four and I seen the light. I knew I had to get sober and get back to you, Grace."

"I tried to stop you, Mitch. I told you Jill was no good." Grace says, feeling more disgust than pity. "Do you get that I tried to die instead of going with you?"

"It's all my fault. I been walking for days on end. I hitched when I could get a ride. I panhandled for bus money. But I'm here now and I'm going to get straight and we can start over. I'll get a job and we'll get us another little place and fix it up nice, like before." His sunken eyes are hopeful.

Grace takes a minute to try to figure out how to say what she knows to be true. "I'm glad you're back and that you're going to get help. But I want you to do it for you, not for me. I can't see ever living with you again, Mitch, not ever."

"I know I got to prove myself and all, but I'll show you I can do it. I did it before, right?" Mitch's pleading tone makes her heart twinge.

Dr. Swenson speaks before Grace can think of what to say. "I hear you saying, Mitch, that you have every intention of turning this mess around, and good for you. I hear Grace saying she wants you to but that it will not necessarily mean she will ever live with you again. So let's take living together off the table for now and instead focus on what it will take for Grace to have any relationship with you at all."

"We got a relationship. I'm her daddy and she's my daughter," Mitch says.

"I'm almost eighteen. I can make my own life without depending on you. I have no trust in you, Mitch. However much you want to do better, I just can't put my eggs in that basket anymore. If you want to even have contact with me, you have to earn some trust back."

"I told you I'm getting sober—I'm going to that rehab place. What more do you want from me?" Mitch says.

"I want the truth. I want to hear about your family, your growing up, and the truth about my mother. With none of your lies and bullshit—I mean it! This is your last chance with me, Mitch, or you'll never see or hear from me again, I swear it." She leans forward to drill her gaze into his.

Mitch leans back in his chair but maintains eye contact. "I don't know what you mean, Grace, I told you everything important."

"Liar!" Grace gets up to leave.

"Wait now, hold on," Mitch says. "Give me a minute."

"The truth should take no time at all," Grace says, still standing. "This is it, Mitch. If I walk out that door, you will never lay eyes on me again. I swear it on my mother's soul."

Dr. Swenson rolls her chair closer to Mitch. "She means it, Mitch. So if you want Grace in your life at all, you better start talking, and believe you me, I have the most well-developed bullshit detector known to man, so don't even try it or I'll kick you out of here myself. Are we clear?"

"Yes, ma'am." Mitch looks down to his jiggling feet. His mud-caked boots have a hole worn through by the right big toe; dried mud is flaking off onto Dr. Swenson's blue carpet.

Grace sits back down.

"Grace, with your permission I'd like to interview your father, but you feel free to chime in whenever you like," Dr. Swenson says.

Grace nods. Her heart races in anticipation of what Dr. Swenson might actually get out of him.

"What name is on your birth certificate, Mitch? I have reason to believe it isn't Willis."

"Mitchell Wallace Ribideaux," Mitch says. "From near Hot Springs, Arkansas. My daddy was a drunk who beat my mother to death when I was seven, so long story short, I ended up in foster homes and the like. I was tough to handle, so I was moved around a lot and some of those homes was bad news. Real bad news. Willis had been my mama's name—I took that once I was on my own. I didn't want nothing from my daddy."

Dr. Swenson was writing down some notes. "Do you have any outstanding criminal warrants under that or any other name?"

"No, ma'am. I ain't never been arrested for anything. I ran out on a few shady deals, but I swear I ain't got no record anywhere. Take my prints and check if you want," Mitch says.

"So you met Grace's mother when and where?"

"Karen was hitchhiking, like I told Grace. I picked her up along Interstate 35 in Oklahoma. Her face had been beat up some, but I fell for her right away, the love of my life, man," Mitch says, his voice catching, fresh tears filling his eyes.

"Tell me everything you know about Karen's family, her upbringing, where she came from, her real name."

Mitch fidgets more, shifting in his seat, biting his thumbnail. "Karen was eighteen when I picked her up, not even graduated from high school yet, a runaway. Like I said, her lip was cut, her eye was black. I didn't ask questions, I just got her out of there. Later she told me she was from Cushing, Oklahoma, some small oil town. Her last name was Fox. She had a mama, but her daddy had died in some work accident. Her mom was a school principal and the choir director at their church, kind of a leader in her town."

"Why was she running away?"

"She'd hooked up with the wrong guy. He was married and his old lady found out and he beat Karen up and told her to get the hell out of there. Karen thought the guy would leave his wife for her, but he wouldn't and it was a small town and her heart was broke and she was afraid of shaming her mama, so she ran off."

"Where did you two go?"

"South Padre Island, Texas. I worked the shrimp boats, Karen waitressed. We bought us a sweet little trailer off a snowbird whose wife had just died and he had to move into a nursing home. Got it cheap. We lived right on the beach way on the north end of the island, nice and isolated. Grace came along and we were happy. She won't believe me, but we were. Karen loved her and took good care of her, she was a great mama."

"I know she was really sad before she died, so don't lie about it," Grace says. "I'm remembering stuff."

Mitch looks at her and Grace can see he's afraid. "What do you remember?"

"Mitch, tell us what led up to Karen's death," Dr. Swenson says.

Mitch rubs his chin stubble. "I'd lost my shrimp boat job and Karen had to pick up more shifts waitressing than she wanted—on account she didn't like being away from Grace. She knew some people who worked at the restaurant who were running drugs from Mexico. We'd hang out with them sometimes. This woman, Misty, was involved, and Karen didn't like her since Misty was hung up on me, I guess, but Karen liked the big wad of cash Misty always had. We smoked a little pot back then, but Misty and Fernando were getting into harder stuff, heroin, sampling the merchandise. So I started running drugs with them and the money was great. Karen was happy at first because she could quit working and just be with Grace, homeschooling her. But she started getting all paranoid that I was carrying on with Misty, picking fights with me, accusing me of shit. She just wouldn't get it out of her head. Even Fernando tried to tell her it was bullshit. But then Fernando had to skip a run, his dad had a heart attack over in Harlingen, so Misty and I went on our own. That time, Misty spiked my drink and we had sex, and Misty bragged to Karen about it and the shit hit the fan. Man, I was in deep trouble with Karen. I felt terrible and told her it wouldn't happen again, I didn't even like Misty, she wasn't my type at all. I only wanted Karen. But I had to keep working with Misty, see, because Fernando had to help his mama and family, what with his daddy laid up. Karen and I were fighting a lot then, she wanted me out of drug running, even though she was the one who got me started in it—all on account of Misty. But she didn't want to work, except for selling her paintings in a local shop, but that wasn't steady money. I promised her this was the last run and then I'd find a job. Sometimes Misty and I would be away for a few days at a time making the run, getting the merchandise to our distributor. The last time, it dragged on over a week . . ." Mitch trails off, covering his face with his hands, hunching forward.

"Keep going, Mitch. You were gone over a week, and when you got home, what happened?" Dr. Swenson says.

Mitch lowers his hands and looks at Grace. "You don't remember and it's a blessing you don't. Don't make me tell you! Please, I can't do that to you."

As Grace looks into his terrified eyes, she sees it in flashes. Her mother lying so still. The syringe with the needle still stuck in her arm. Grace sees herself as a five-year-old, taking the needle out of her mother's arm and trying to wake her up, but she won't wake up, and she's so cold. She covers her with blankets and waits for her mother to wake up. She brushes her hair and tries to feed her bread and peanut butter and give her water, but she won't chew or swallow. And then the smell comes. The sickening, powerful stench that makes Grace throw up on the bathroom floor. And her mama's face that was so beautiful is turning ugly, like a monster, and her tongue sticks out and her face gets fat and turns colors. Five-year-old Grace tries to get the trailer door open, but the door's locked and it's bolted up high where she can't reach. She tries standing on a kitchen chair, but she still can't reach it. She piles pillows onto the chair and falls off and cuts her knee. She claws at the door like an animal. She breaks the window but is too scared to try to climb out with all the pointed shards of glass, and it's too far of a drop anyway, so she screams and screams, but no one can hear her.

Grace begins to scream. "She died and I was trapped with her body! For days and days! Oh my god! Oh my god!"

"See what you done! Making her remember! Poor little thing!" Mitch is standing over Dr. Swenson. "This ain't helping her—this is fucked up! This is mean!"

Grace sinks back in her chair, rubbing her eyes as if she can erase what she's seen. She's shaking and shivering uncontrollably. She emits anguished cries because this is beyond the realm of tears. She pulls at her hair and gasps for breath.

Dr. Swenson is next to her. "Grace, slow down your breathing. You're okay. What you remember is not happening right now, it's over. It's horrible, but you survived it. You're strong. You can survive remembering. Stay with me in the here and now. Look at me, Grace."

Grace tries to control her breathing, but the gruesome images keep intruding and with them, the noxious odor, causing her to gag.

"Do you need some medication, or can you do this on your own?" Dr. Swenson asks. Her right arm is tight around Grace's shoulders, her left hand smoothing back Grace's hair.

Grace swallows hard and focuses on Dr. Swenson. "I can do it. I'm okay." She stops cold. The shuddering ceases. The smell vanishes. Something bizarre starts to happen. She begins to remember her mother before her death. She can see her blue eyes and wide smile and entire face in detail. She can hear her voice and her laughter clearly. She remembers her mother dancing with her, reading to her, teaching her to paint. The memories are swirling through her—a blizzard of moments—fresh and new, with vivid colors, exploding with life. She begins to cry tears of joy.

"I'm remembering everything about her now," Grace says. She looks at Dr. Swenson in amazement. "There's so much!"

"Until you faced the horror, everything was blocked," Dr. Swenson says.

Grace glances at Mitch. "You came home and got me out and there was a fire."

"I was crazy with grief," Mitch resumes. "I loved Karen more than my own life. I didn't know she had any heroin. She must have gotten it from Misty. There weren't cell phones back then and we didn't have a landline. I couldn't call Karen and tell her we were held up in Matamoros waiting for the shipment a few extra days—that's all it was. I blame myself, I do, but if she just could have hung on . . . I got you out, Grace, and packed up the truck and then I blew up that trailer. I used the propane tank under the stove and made it look like an accident. It was all I could think of to do. I stopped by and told Misty what happened and told her to keep her big mouth shut. I knew she wouldn't tell anyone, I had too much on her. And then we got out of there."

"You told me Mom would want me to forget what I saw. That she wouldn't want me to remember her like that."

"Not remembering protected you. But it came at a high price," Dr. Swenson says. "How are you doing now?"

"I'd rather know the horrible part than not remember everything else. I had to remember all of it to finally get out of that trailer. I've been trapped in there all this time."

Dr. Swenson turned to Mitch. "Why didn't you call the police when you found Karen? You left it like a crime scene. We'll have to call the authorities and report what happened twelve years ago, and contact Karen's mother to let her know what happened to her runaway daughter. Are you ready to finally face the consequences of your actions?"

"I didn't call the cops that night because I was afraid they'd take Grace away from me, and I'd just lost Karen—I couldn't lose Grace too."

"Why did you think you would lose Grace?" Dr. Swenson asks.

"Karen made me promise to always take care of Grace, and I vowed I would. Karen never wanted her mama or anyone back home to know about Grace." Mitch stops and looks at Grace with wincing pain. "You want the whole truth—I'm about to give it to you, even though I could lose everything."

"My god, what could possibly be worse?" Grace asks.

"Just hear me out. Karen was three months pregnant that day I picked her up. The father, the married man, was one of her teachers at school, her mother was his principal. Karen never told me his name. It was a small town. Karen had gone to him to tell him she was pregnant, and she thought for sure he'd leave his wife and marry her, but instead she got a beating and was told they'd ruin her and her mama's lives if she stayed around and had the baby. They told her to get an abortion and they'd pay for it, but Karen loved her baby already, so she did the only thing she could: ran away and never looked back. She figured that was the best she could do for her mama, who she loved and didn't want to make trouble for."

"You aren't even my father?"

"I tried to be. I did the best I could, Grace. I know I fucked everything up. But I loved you like my own and Karen wanted me to be your daddy, so I never would have quit on you, no matter what, I made a promise to her. I'm sorry I ran off with Jill—I was fucked up on the booze and it hurt like hell when you wouldn't come with me, so I guess I went on ahead out of spite or something, and Jill was egging me on. Plus I thought you'd come down, I could send you bus money after I started to work. But that's why I had to get back here. I was wrong to leave you, and it broke my vow to Karen. I'll never forgive myself for that."

Grace is too stunned to speak. She thinks of all she's been through with Mitch. It replays in her mind, the upheaval, the moves, the uncertainty. And all along, he was just some guy who had made a promise to her mother.

Mitch turns to Dr. Swenson. "I loved her when she was still in Karen's tummy. I helped her be born and I cut the cord. After Karen died, I didn't want her to be put in the system, you know, foster homes and whatnot. I'd lived that hell, and I loved her too much to send her down that road. And I didn't want to go against Karen's wishes and take her back to Oklahoma. Maybe that married asshole would have taken her away since she was his—I just couldn't take the chance. Besides, from the minute I met Karen and heard her story, I was Grace's daddy. It was a done deal. For better or worse."

Grace looks at Dr. Swenson, who despite her decades of experience in dealing with crazy people, appears completely flabbergasted.

"I think you did the right thing," Grace hears herself say. "My biological father wanted me gone. My mother picked you to be my father. I'm glad I wasn't put in foster homes, even though I know they aren't all bad. For better or worse—some of it was better, and a lot of it was worse— you're my father. You told me the truth and I'm grateful. You have to get sober and turn your life around, once and for all. But if you do, I'll still be your daughter."

Mitch hugs her then, crying and stinking all over her, but she hugs him back. Grace releases Mitch and peers into his wet eyes. "Do good, I mean it."

Mitch tries a smile. "I promise—and you know how stubborn I am to keep a promise."

"Mitch, that facility I'm taking you to is expecting you in an hour—and you and I have some phone calls to make. Grace, I'm coming back to check on you after we're done with all of that. Are you sure you're okay for now?" Dr. Swenson says.

Grace faces Dr. Swenson and takes a deep breath. "I'm okay. I can get back to the cottage by myself. Just don't go looking for my sperm donor; I don't want anything to do with him." She starts toward the door and then turns around. "But if you can find my grandmother, I'd like to meet her, if she wants."

"I'll get on it first thing tomorrow."

When Grace returns to the cottage, she finds major turmoil. Paul and Sharon have just brought the group inside after some outdoor time. Lourdes has her arm around Lucas, who's leaning into her. Percy is chanting something about eagle medicine, his arms outstretched, stomping in a rhythmic circle. Aaron is yelling that he's going to kill Conner in Capitan Cottage.

Maddie came up to her. "How did it go with your dad?"

"You won't believe it—I'll talk about it in task group. What's going on?"

Maddie shakes her head, her bangs spilling into her eyes. "We were hanging outside with Capitan Cottage kids, and you know that new kid they got in, Conner? Well, he was teasing Lucas about Sam and then he grabbed Sam and tore him up. Aaron had to be pulled off Conner. Talk about a suicide mission—Conner is twice Aaron's size, so Aaron was lucky staff were right there. Then Conner went berserk and they had to do a backup call on the walkie-talkie. He punched a staff member and tried to run but they caught him, so now he's in seclusion."

"Oh no! How's Lucas?"

"Circle up for task group," Paul says. "Pronto."

"You can give me whatever consequences you want. My only regret is I didn't get the chance to inflict great bodily harm," Aaron says, but takes his seat.

Lucas sits between Grace and Lourdes, cradling what is left of Sam in his hands. He's strangely quiet. He breathes hard and his dilated pupils turn his usually pale eyes into black disks. His finger prods Sam. One wing is hanging by a thread, his head is turned backward, his chest is ripped open, white stuffing billows grotesquely from his wound.

"On the battlefield, you know this can happen. You even try to prepare for it, but how can you?" Lucas says as the group sits in rapt attention. "He wakes you up at night. You're so tired from all the chores you did during the day. He works you around the clock, calls you his prisoner of war."

Lucas gulps hard but continues. "Two hundred acres on that ranch. Ain't nobody to hear you scream for help. 'Get up, you little piece of shit! Time for the cage, G.I. Joe.' He's crazy from the booze, crazy from Vietnam, never been the same. Stuck with his long-gone daughter's bastard. He used to be a good man. He fought for his country. He was a POW. He got them once, now he gives them—the beatings, starvation, no water until you can feel the inside of your mouth peeling off, and the taste of your own blood . . . is sweet."

Lucas strokes the top of Sam's head with one finger. "He put me down in that tiger cage for days sometimes. Piss on me, shit on me. 'You little slanty-eyed gook! Take that, Charlie. How you like them apples?'"

Lucas is crying now. "I'd pray for rain. It'd come sometimes, down through the bamboo-cage roof. One summer monsoon, water came in a wave and I thought I'd drown before he remembered to come let me out. Then there was the pole. He'd strap me to this pole up on a hilltop. Interrogate me for hours and then wander off. At night it was cool, and Lord, the stars were something beautiful. The sun would come back up and I'd start to bake . . . go near blind from the heat. I'd hang there, feel the blisters open up and drain down my face. I looked up this once and I could hear his piercing cry before I could see him, soaring in circles over me. His white head—whiter than snow. His black wings—spread wider than I am tall. Dipping and turning . . . if that ain't freedom . . . I'd weep for joy watching him. I'd call to him, 'Come down here, Uncle Sam, tear through this old rope with your beak and take me with you.'"

Lucas shakes his head. "Grandpa died before I came in here—over at the veterans' hospital. They asked me, 'Did he sometimes act peculiar?' I never told on him. Hell, he was a patriot and he couldn't help what he'd become. That's when I got my caseworker and she put me with some nice people, a temporary placement, she called it. 'What do you want for your birthday?' they asked me. 'An eagle,' I told them. So they got me Sam."

Lucas pushes Sam's stuffing back into his chest. "Sharon? You got any of that suture string we could use to sew him back up?"

"We have the sewing kit. I'm sure we can get him mended," Sharon says.

"I don't think he's feeling much pain," Grace says.

"Of course not, Grace. He's just a little old toy, that's all," Lucas says, managing a smile.

Grace puts her arms around him and holds him tight. She feels his heart thumping through his skinny, Sam-less chest, and it fills her eyes with tears. When she lets go, Maddie, Aaron, and Percy take turns. Lourdes, Paul, and Sharon follow, wiping tears from their eyes.

They all gather around Lucas and shake his hand, as if it's a funeral. In a way, it is, Grace decides. She gazes over her shoulder at Sam, who is laid out on the sofa, momentarily forgotten.

CHAPTER 13

WHILE GRACE SLEEPS THAT night, her dreams are nothing special. But when she wakes, the memories she recovered about her mother are still fresh, as if she's just lived those years with her. She doesn't dwell on the final nightmare in the trailer. Her mother was despondent, afraid Mitch was never coming home. She tried to numb the pain and made a terrible mistake in a moment no one could take back.

But now Grace possesses her in a way she hasn't since she was five years old. The memory of her now is as constant as the sun rising in her window.

At first, it was tempting to try to imagine how her life would have been if Mitch had taken her back to Oklahoma after Karen's death. But that would have been a betrayal to Karen, and besides, it was ultimately futile to try to reconstruct her life in such a drastic way. Maybe she will have a clearer idea of what she missed out on once she meets her grandmother—*if* she meets her grandmother, who lost her husband and then her daughter. Would a woman who has lost so much even want to know Grace? Maybe Grace would just be a painful reminder of a loss she has finally put to rest. Or she could be dead by now, or long gone and untraceable.

Grace views her years with Mitch differently now. Here was a guy who had no business trying to raise a kid, and on top of that, the kid wasn't even his. The love and loyalty he had for Karen had somehow extended to Grace, and it was impossible not to feel good about that despite the rough times that had come from it. His inability to give her a stable life, taking flight when things got hard, always believing his luck would change in a new place, unwilling or unable to live life by the rules, combined to make him completely unsuitable for fatherhood, and yet he loved her and tried to protect her. His love was always palpable, despite his extensive flaws.

And even though she almost hadn't made it out alive, how could she think about trading her life with Mitch for a complete set of unknowns? It happened the way it happened, and she can live with that.

Waiting for Dr. Swenson is excruciating. Every time someone comes to their classroom, Grace's head swivels to see who it is and then sighs with exasperation when it's Janice picking Lucas up for art therapy or the speech and language therapist picking up Percy for his session.

When she dawdles over her half-finished geometry assignment, Mr. Z looks at her with concern but doesn't redirect her. He's cool that way; he doesn't push when kids need some time to just be with their thoughts.

Lucas had appeared at breakfast that morning wearing his stiff new jeans and plaid shirt bought with his care and support money, unused until now, and no sign of any camo gear or Sam. Grace knows it's a sign that he's reached a major turning point and no longer believes he's a soldier or that Sam is his war buddy. She's happy for him but selfishly misses her wacky little brother with his military lingo and the stuffed eagle who lived in his shirt. When Percy asked him where Sam was, Lucas said Sam would be staying on his pillow from now on.

They'd run out of time in task group before Grace could tell everyone what she had remembered and what Mitch had revealed, so only Maddie knew, though Grace is sure Dr. Swenson briefed the staff during her short return to the cottage at bedtime. She had looked in on Grace and told her Mitch checked into his treatment center. Grace wanted to talk, but Dr. Swenson looked exhausted. Grace only told her she was fine and thanked her, and let her go talk to Lucas, who no doubt needed her more than Grace did.

Finally in the afternoon, the classroom door swings open and Dr. Swenson appears. Grace notices she isn't the only one looking hopefully in Dr. Swenson's direction; in fact, everyone but Percy seems to have a pressing need for her.

"Grace," she says. "I'll be back for Maddie and then Lucas after that. Aaron and Percy, I'll see you tomorrow."

When Grace joins her in the large, sunny library that connects to each of the six classrooms, Dr. Swenson leads her out of the school building but does not proceed to the administration building. Instead, she takes her to an out-of-the-way shaded bench. "I can't stand the sight of my office right now," Dr. Swenson says. "I've seen too much of it the last twenty-four hours."

Grace looks at her expectantly. Dr. Swenson says, "I know, I know, you want me to get down to business. I called the authorities in South Padre Island. They pulled up the trailer incident, and it looks like their investigation concluded that the trailer exploded from a faulty propane tank and a spark from bad electrical wiring. The one victim's remains were never identified, just listed as a Jane Doe and buried in the Port Isabel Cemetery. I told them Karen's name and said I would be trying to locate any survivors but assured them I had no reason to suspect foul play. When they asked me how I knew this, I told them I was a psychiatrist and that my source was confidential. That seems to be the end of it. I didn't get the impression they were all that interested after twelve years."

Grace nods, relieved Dr. Swenson couldn't see the point of dragging Mitch into it.

"I found your grandmother. I called the high school and they gave me her contact information. By the way, her name is Ruth. Ruth Fox. She moved to Tulsa a few years ago to live with her widowed sister, Ruby Atkins. They were listed in the directory and I was able to reach them, so I spoke at length with Ruth this morning." Dr. Swenson pauses.

"Well, what did she say? What's she like?"

Dr. Swenson grins. "I think you may have hit the jackpot, Grace. She sounds great and she can't wait to meet you. She's making flight arrangements, and you'll meet her sometime in the next few days."

Grace glances down to see a ladybug on her thigh. She puts her finger down to it, and it climbs aboard before opening its wings and taking off.

"Ladybugs bring good luck," Dr. Swenson says.

"What did you tell her . . . about everything?" Grace asks.

"I told her the truth. That her daughter had died of an accidental drug overdose but that she was not a junkie, that she was a responsible mother to her child and had become a successful local artist. And that you had been raised by Karen's partner, Mitch Willis, and though you'd had a sometimes difficult time of it, you were doing great now and hoped to meet her. She sounded like she'd been told she won the lottery. She said she had long ago accepted that Karen must be dead since she never heard from her again, and when she finally let go of any hope of having her back, she moved to Tulsa to be with her sister. Ruth also said she'd be contacting the authorities to have Karen's remains transported to Tulsa for a proper burial in the family plot."

"What did you tell her about my father?"

"I told her I didn't know his name but that he had been a teacher from Cushing and had basically run Karen out of town with his threats. She stopped me and said she knew who it was. The guy had been busted the following school year after getting caught with a fourteen-year-old student. He was convicted of statutory rape and sent off to prison. She always thought there was a connection to Karen's disappearance and had even gone to authorities with her suspicions, but nothing came of it."

"I'd rather have to worry about what I've inherited from Mitch than from that guy. He sounds like a total creep," Grace says.

"Grace, look at me," Dr. Swenson says. Grace turns to face her, meeting her eyes. "Whatever genetic roulette created you was a lucky spin of the wheel. You're wise. You're kind. You're talented, and you're one of the strongest and most resilient people I've ever met. Don't you question where you came from—all you have to do is appreciate who you are. The rest doesn't matter one whit."

"You think my grandmother Ruth will like me then." Grace smiles.

"Oh yeah. But remember, this is a two-way street. So here's the plan. Ruth says she's retired and can stay for several weeks, as long as it takes for you two to get to know each other. She's interested in having you come live with her and Ruby if you decide to, but she understands that it is up to you and she hopes to be in your life in whatever capacity you are comfortable with. How does this sound?"

"It's happening so fast. I guess it scares me some."

"We're going to take all the time you want, Grace. Maybe you'll decide to go to the group living situation we discussed, which would prepare you to live on your own when you turn eighteen or after you graduate high school in the spring. You have options, and I will be there for you every step of the way. But whatever you decide, I think you'll be ready to leave this place in about a month. That gives us plenty of time for you to transition to your new situation."

Grace feels tears flood her eyes, and her throat aches. It's so overwhelming—the thought of leaving hurts. But Abdias left and now Gabe is gone too. Maddie and Lucas seem to be heading that way. It was never going to last forever. Nothing does.

"The fact that you're a little scared shows how intelligent you are and that you're strong enough to tackle it."

Grace lets the tears flow freely as she thinks about saying good-bye to Dr. Swenson and the staff, especially Jackson and Sharon, and the kids—Lucas and Percy, and even Aaron. But most of all, Maddie. How will she ever say good-bye to Maddie?

"You've had a lot of hard good-byes in your life. This will be another tough one, but we're here to help you through it—and this time, you'll be moving toward something better," Dr. Swenson says, her arm around Grace's back.

Grace rests her head on Dr. Swenson's soft shoulder. Her thoughts drift toward Ruth Fox. Is she packing her suitcase at this very moment? Is she excited to meet her granddaughter?

She has family. A grandmother and a great-aunt. A little thrill runs through her as she lets herself imagine the scent of home-baked cookies.

Another few days pass with only superficial phone calls from Maddie's dad. When she finally asks him outright how things are going with Lesley, he tells her not to worry, that he's working on it. But this morning he calls to tell her he's coming for a visit that evening during visiting hours—six to eight. And that he loves her. That's it. When she complains to Dr. Swenson that she wants her dad to give her the details, her doctor tells her Michael is dealing with grown-up issues and to have a boundary, be patient, and try to trust him.

In her room, Maddie flops down on her bed. "My dad's coming to visit tonight. Why is this scaring the hell out of me?" she asks Grace, who's folding her laundry and putting it in her wardrobe. How Grace can fold her clothes so nonchalantly after she found out her dad wasn't even her dad is beyond her. That would have been the end of Maddie.

"Because you're thinking the worst again. It's okay to be hopeful. Look how far he's come," Grace tells her. She holds up a tattered T-shirt. "I think I'll put this in the trash. I'll be getting new clothes soon."

"No, I want it," says Maddie. "For when we're discharged." She grabs it out of Grace's hand and clutches it to her heart.

Grace smiles. "Okay, you sentimental slob. Trust and believe the best possible solution is unfolding for you."

"Sounds like a fortune cookie," says Maddie.

"I really believe that, which is something coming from a kid who tried to hang her hopeless ass." She snaps her jeans straight and lines up the legs before folding them. "At least things can never go back to the way they were." She seems to speak more to herself than Maddie.

"My dad loves this ancient Beatles song that goes, 'It's getting better all the time.'" Maddie sings the line.

"It can't get no worse," Grace sings back. "Duc was into the Beatles and was compelled to educate me."

Maddie collapses backward onto her mattress. "It's easier for me to believe things can always get worse."

Grace throws another balled-up ratty shirt, hitting Maddie in the face. "Snap out of it!"

At the stroke of six o'clock, the cottage phone starts ringing with calls from nursing to send a staff member to escort visitors to the cottage after they have signed in. The expectant group of kids waits on the couch.

Percy is waiting for his grandmother to come from Zuni Pueblo for a two-day visit. Jackson has reserved the guest room for her, which is like a little motel room connected to Pecos Cottage. Percy doesn't see his grandmother very often; their truck hardly ever works well enough for her to make the three-hour drive. No telling when she'll arrive, if at all. But Percy sits ready, never one to complain. His lashes flutter on his cheeks as he looks down in his lap. Maddie wonders where he goes on these silent voyages of his. He doesn't even look up when the phone rings. Nor does he look up when Sharon brings his grandmother through the door and stands at the desk talking with her.

Maddie strolls by to throw her apple core in the trash and then hovers within earshot. Sharon is trying to describe Percy's conversations with electrical appliances while holding out a paper, a consent form for a new medication to stop the voices his grandmother believes guide him.

His grandmother's eyes are watery, peering out from her cracked skin. "Sometimes the spirits talk to him. It is the way. They are his ancestors," she says, her worn hands begging for understanding, an intricate silver-and-inlay bracelet on her branch-like arm, a round needlepoint turquoise pin on her collar.

Percy sits motionless, his hands in his lap as if holding something delicate. His lanky legs end in new huge, white athletic shoes, no hungry shoes for Percy. He seems to pay no attention to what's going on between Sharon and his grandmother, who now beckons to him in their native language. He rises, and Sharon escorts them out of the cottage.

Lucas doesn't have family to come visit him, but his caseworker is working on that. Aaron hustles his professor parents into his room for their visit. They're dressed up as usual, as if they have plans for later. Grace's grandmother hasn't arrived in Albuquerque yet, so she's in their room writing letters to her friends in New York.

Sharon finally comes through the door with Maddie's dad, who looks pounds lighter and years older. "Maddie, do you and your dad want to visit outside?" Sharon offers.

As Maddie and her dad walk out the door, Maddie looks at his drawn appearance with concern. "You're not sick, are you?" she asks. Great, now he'll die on her.

"No, honey. Well, sick at heart." He leads her over to the iron Victorian fountain in a lush corner with hovering trees.

"It's not Moonshine, is it?" she asks, feeling the weight of dread in her gut.

"No, no, honey. It's not going to work out with Lesley and me. She refuses to believe what Jeffrey did, and she's furious that he's being investigated and blames both of us. She's going to stand by her kid, and I'm going to stand by mine."

As relieved as Maddie is, she loves her dad enough to not show it. "I'm sorry."

"Maddie—none of this is your fault. I'm going to be fine. I've started to move our things back to the old apartment. That's where we'll be living, okay?"

"Of course, but what about Moonshine?"

"I'll come up with something. I'm going to make this right."

"Promise me you'll eat more—you're getting too thin." She knows how emotional pain kills your appetite. He nods and smiles. "I'll try." He's being brave. He'd rather Maddie have her happy ending than trouble her with his loss. Sacrifices are choices, and he makes it clear he will survive his.

Maddie knocks on the door to her and Grace's room before entering. "Grace?" Maddie says. "I want you to meet my dad, Michael." She pulls her dad in. "Dad, this is Grace. My best friend in the world and personal savior."

"Wow, that's some title, Grace," her dad says, shaking Grace's hand. He notices her necklace. "Hey, that's one of mine."

"I know!" Maddie says. "Her friend gave it to her. Isn't it freaky?"

"I hope it's brought clarity and courage into your life," her dad says.

"It's good to meet you," Grace says. "Both as Maddie's dad and as the person who made my necklace. It means a lot to me."

After a few awkward moments of standing together in the small space, her dad hugs Maddie and says he needs to get going. Maddie walks him to the door and gives him another hug. She wants to thank him and tell him how relieved she is, and ecstatic that it would just be the two of them again in Old Town. She holds back. Seeing her dad as a person who needs time to heal just as she has makes Maddie love him all the more.

She returns to her room. "He's leaving Lesley."

"Tell me," Grace says.

"You were right. Once he believed me, and she didn't, there was no turning back. We're going home to Old Town, can you believe it?" Maddie allows herself to feel some selfish joy.

Grace hugs her. "That's awesome."

"I feel bad that I'm so happy when it's costing my dad so much."

"Jeffrey caused this, not you. If Lesley could face that, she wouldn't be losing your dad."

"Almost six long hell years later . . . but now we can start over." Maddie cries with relief. She looks at the pendant sparkling near Grace's heart, multiplying through her tears.

Grace follows her gaze. "This necklace connects me to the people I care about. The ones who gave it to me. The one it led me to. And now, full circle to the one who created it. I think it means we're all going to be just fine."

Grace returns to Brazos Cottage after her art therapy session with Janice. She wants to corner Jackson before the rest of the group comes back from the classroom for the day.

Jackson peers up from the staff schedule he's working on, his black-framed reading glasses perched on his nose. "Why did you not walk yourself back to school, Miss Grace?"

"Because there's like ten minutes left of the school day and they'll all be coming back here anyway. And I need to ask you a favor," Grace says.

"Go on then," he says, sticking his pencil behind his ear.

"You know how my care and support money has been sitting around because there's never anyone who can take me shopping?"

"You know how I have to maintain a one-to-three ratio of staff to kids."

"You know how my clothes are gross and embarrassing? Do you really want to have to explain why I look this way to my grandmother, who will be here to meet me the day after tomorrow?" Grace raises her eyebrows.

"She's coming that quick?" Jackson breaks into a grin. "She can't wait to meet her little darling granddaughter."

"Who looks like Little Orphan Annie."

"Maybe if you look all tattered and pathetic, it will tug at her heart-strings," Jackson says.

Grace shoots him a dirty look.

"Here's what I can do. Kellie comes on shift soon. She can take you shopping while I cover through quiet time and rounds. Be back by dinner-time so I can get out of here."

"That's only two hours. I'm a girl, Jackson, not some boy who can get by with a couple of pairs of jeans and some T-shirts from Kmart. This involves a trip to the mall, style consultation, mix-and-match strategizing, shoes-and-accessories coordination, and a hair appointment. Stay until seven and we'll try to be back before then," Grace said.

"Do you remember me waking you up this morning? If I stay until seven, that's a twelve-hour day. What's in it for me?" Jackson has a grumpy face and tone, but Grace can see the twinkle in his eyes.

"My grandmother won't have to wonder what kind of shoddy opera-tion you run here that would allow her granddaughter to—"

"Okay, okay, I see how it is!" Jackson breaks into his belly laugh. "I give up. Shop till you drop. Shop till *I* drop, more like it."

Grace leans over the desk to hug his big neck. "Thank you!"

"Seriously, Grace, I'm happy to do it for you. This is a big deal and you deserve to have new clothes and get all spiffed up. I just hope your grand-mother knows how lucky she is to find you in her life."

Grace looks into his gentle face and knows how lucky she is to find Jackson in her life.

On Friday morning, Maddie helps Grace choose which of her new outfits to wear to meet her grandmother.

"I like this flowered peasant blouse with the jean skirt and your new sandals," Maddie says after Grace models various combinations. "And don't brush out your hair—just scrunch it with your fingers to let the nat-ural wave do its thing."

Grace's hair is now cut into an angled, chin-length bob, the same way she wore it when she caught Robin's eye the previous fall. Now early

August, it has almost been a full year since Grace started her junior year of high school and met Robin and Duc. How could so much happen in only eleven months? She feels completely different, yet more like herself than she ever has. It's as if she had been functioning with only partial consciousness. The girl she used to be had operated within such a narrow scope that it made Grace think of a pie chart. Where before she inhabited only a sliver, she now occupies the full 360 degrees, whole and restored. She puts on her topaz pendant and the new matching earrings Maddie's dad brought for her. "Well?"

Maddie smiles. "Excellent."

As Grace walks to the administration building, she looks up to Dr. Swenson's office windows, wondering if she is being watched. If her grandmother is sizing her up. But all she can see is the reflection of the trees and sky. Her solid, unshakable good feeling about this meeting is giving way to sudden and serious doubts. What if her grandmother expects her to be like Karen, whatever that is? What if she only wants her as some replacement for her lost daughter? After all those years with Mitch, maybe Grace is too damaged for normal people.

She climbs the staircase, light headed and queasy. Who does she think she is, anyway, to expect a happy ending? Hasn't life taught her otherwise? Something must be wrong with a woman who claims her granddaughter sight unseen, as if taking delivery of a package. She must have some hidden agenda. Grace should just say "Thanks but no thanks" and get emancipated and not rely on anyone else ever again. Family just lets you down. Look at her mother. Look at Mitch. She is stupid to set herself up for yet another crushing disappointment.

She stops a few feet away from Dr. Swenson's open doorway. She can hear their voices, their laughter. It isn't too late; she will just have to set them straight. It's her life. She doesn't owe anyone anything.

Grace strides into the room and stands as if ready to make an announcement. Dr. Swenson beams at her. "Here she is."

The other woman stands and walks right up to Grace. Grace looks down, unable to look into the woman's smiling face, her searching eyes.

The woman cups her hand under Grace's chin and gently lifts until she holds Grace's gaze. "Oh. You look so much like her."

"I'm not her." Grace backs away.

"No, of course not. You're Grace, and I look forward to getting to know you."

Grace can feel Dr. Swenson's eyes on her, those eyes that can see straight into her. Grace feels naked and on display. She sits down and hugs her knees. The woman takes her seat.

"What's happening, Grace?" Dr. Swenson asks.

She shrugs and averts her gaze to the yellowing art hanging on the walls. Grace wonders what became of the kids who created them, if they grew up to be happy, if they grew up at all. She has to wonder what kind of toxic waste has seeped into these walls from all the hours and years of witnessing messed-up kids pouring their guts out. Unspeakable words, obscene rages, raw pain . . . it all came from somewhere, it must have gone somewhere. She feels like a human Geiger counter, picking up on it, clicking faster and faster, louder and louder.

"Grace, can you help us understand what you're feeling right now?" Dr. Swenson says.

Grace turns to look at the other woman and sees that she's tall and lean with graying blond, shoulder-length hair. Her tanned skin contrasts with her pale-pink knit shirt and white capris. Her toes look fresh from a pedicure. Her silver earrings catch the light. There's an elegance about her. Her face . . . Grace nearly gasps. It's her mother's face, only older, her mother's face she has only recently seen again. The straight nose, the delicate mouth, the wide blue eyes under lightly arched brows. Even her relaxed expression, one of open acceptance, is eerily familiar.

"I don't know." Grace's voice is shaking, tears welling in her eyes.

"It's overwhelming," Dr. Swenson says.

"On the way over here . . . I just started freaking out. We're complete strangers."

Dr. Swenson folds her arms over her ample stomach. "You're right. Neither one of you has a clue about the other. And there's all this built-in pressure in the situation. I think what we need to do is take any conclusions off the table. We're starting a process here and none of us knows the outcome. I admire both of you for being willing to find out. But at the start, I think we need to table the whole living-together idea. It's just not time yet to be making any decisions about that. Do you agree?"

"Yes." Grace and her grandmother answered simultaneously.

"I think the way to look at this is that it's about getting to know each other. People generally do that by talking to each other, you know, having a conversation. You are simply Ruth and Grace, two people who have just met."

"Grace, I guess the first thing you're going to find out about me is that I don't hold back. I have something I need to get off my chest," Ruth says. "May I?"

Grace looks to Dr. Swenson. "She asked you, Grace, not me."

"I guess," she says, becoming curious.

"The biggest regret of my life is that I failed my daughter. And that set into motion the life you've had to lead that brought you here. I need to confess. I need to have you know the worst about me before we go any further." Ruth's voice is strong at first and then cracks by the end. She speaks in a soft, refined accent.

Grace looks at her face and can see the anguish Ruth feels. "Okay."

"Karen was a happy girl as a child. Bright and enthusiastic about everything. A real daddy's girl too. My husband, Henry—he went by Hank—was a great father. Those two were so close I'd feel a little left out sometimes. But I was also happy for them. They loved to fish and camp. Hank loved birds, and he and Karen would make birdhouses and feeders and collect bird books. Meanwhile, I was a busy schoolteacher and I went on to get my master's degree, so I was relieved those two could stay busy while I was studying and taking classes over in Tulsa, about an hour away. Then Hank was killed in a work accident when Karen was thirteen." Ruth stops to swallow hard. "I can't tell you how terrible it was. He was our rock, the center of our lives, and then he was gone. We both took it hard. It's a blur now, but somehow we got through the immediate aftermath. Karen went back to school and I went back to work and classes. I cut off my feelings. This is when I failed her. I couldn't share my grief with Karen, and instead

I threw myself into my studies—I didn't even realize it at the time, but I checked out on her. Here she was, only thirteen and she'd just lost the most important person in her life. I was hardly home and when I was, it was just 'How was your day?' and not really waiting for an answer. We drifted apart, like two roommates sharing a house but little else. The years managed to slip on by. Karen continued to do well in school and have friends, so I didn't worry about her. Then in her junior year of high school, a new teacher came to Cushing. He taught art and photography. Karen loved art. All the girls were crazy about him, he was young—his first teaching job— and handsome. I was the high school principal by then and I didn't pick up on anything. He seemed like a good guy who could deflect the inevitable schoolgirl crushes that came his way. He had a new wife, who worked in the school office as a secretary, and they seemed like a couple of newlywed lovebirds. Then Karen became a senior and turned eighteen. I didn't notice anything different with her, but then, how would I? I was working on my doctorate by then and putting in long hours. Then one day she was gone. I found a note saying not to look for her, that she had to do this for both of us." Ruth stops and pulls a tissue from her purse to dab at the tears collecting in her eyes.

"I had no idea what she meant in that note. I went to the police, but they wouldn't do anything since she was eighteen and free to do what she wanted. I drilled her friends for information and got nothing. I don't think she told a soul. I hired a private detective and he couldn't even find the beginning of a trail to follow. It was as if she'd disappeared from the face of the earth. I was devastated. I knew I'd let her down. I knew I'd let Hank down. It was all I could do to keep going. My sister helped me a lot. She begged me to leave Cushing, move to Tulsa, where she and her husband lived. But I stayed in case Karen came back, you know? Then the next year a fourteen-year-old freshman girl told her parents that she and the art teacher had been having sex. They charged him with statutory rape and the girl testified, and he was sent to prison. I had this horrible feeling in the pit of my stomach that he was the reason Karen left. I tried to talk to the police—they asked him about it, but he denied everything of course. Now I know she was pregnant with you, Grace, and she couldn't come to me, her own mother. Right when she needed me the most. I would have helped her and I didn't get the chance. It was my own fault. And now she's dead. I have to live with that." Ruth finally breaks down crying.

Grace watches as Dr. Swenson reaches over to comfort Ruth, who clutches Dr. Swenson's hand, her knuckles turning white as she sobs.

Grace feels tears prick behind her eyes, thinking about how alone her mother felt, a pregnant teenager, beat up and threatened by the man she thought loved her. Karen left home to spare her mother, the school principal, the scandal of her daughter getting knocked up by a teacher. No wonder, when hitchhiking and alone in the world, Mitch looked like her savior.

Ruth composes herself, blowing her nose and heaving big sighs. "I'm sorry, Grace. If I'd been a better mother to my daughter, we would have met a lot sooner."

Grace isn't sure what to say. "I guess people do the best they can. I can't blame my rough life on you. And Karen was a good mother. I remember her painting and singing. She was happy. I remember her and Mitch holding hands when we walked on the beach. I know they loved each other and me. I believe we had a good life right up until the end."

"I just wish that man had brought you home to me when Karen died," Ruth says, the anger vibrating in her voice.

"Mitch isn't all bad. He stuck by me and did his best. He thought he was following what my mother wanted. I can't fault him," Grace says, surprised to be defending him.

"Ruth," Dr. Swenson says. "My heart goes out to you for all you've lost. You seem like a strong and caring person who is maybe a little hard on herself. Reminds me of someone." She catches Grace's eye. "Can you tell us what your life is like now?"

"Well, I'm sixty and my parents passed away a few years ago, in their late eighties, one right after the other. My older sister, Ruby, moved into our family home in Tulsa since she was widowed too by then. Soon after that, she finally convinced me to move in with her into that big old house. She told me if Karen wanted to find me, she would think to try her grandparents' phone and address, which hadn't changed, because it was a place she had visited often. I retired when I left Cushing." Ruth pauses and smiles. "I putter in the garden while Ruby collects and restores furniture to sell at her antique co-op. I teach voice and piano to a few students there at the house. I'm in a book club and garden club, so I have some friends that way. I managed to shake off being so driven. I even dug out Hank's old bird books and put up some feeders in the garden. I like to just sit with a book on my lap and listen to them sing."

"It sounds as if you've found some peace," Dr. Swenson says.

"Oh, Ruby and I bicker at times, but mainly we get along. It's a big, three-story Victorian house with plenty of places to hide. My father was successful in the real estate business and left us well situated, so we don't have to work. Plus we both have retirement and Hank's death benefits. We're comfortable enough."

"How are you doing, Grace?" Dr. Swenson asks.

Grace glances at Ruth. "Better than when I first got here."

"I didn't scare you off? At least not yet?" Ruth says.

"Not yet," Grace says.

"The plan was a weekend pass with your grandmother. How do you feel about that now?" Dr. Swenson asks.

Ruth studies Grace with hope in her eyes.

Grace wonders how in one short hour this woman has transformed from a stranger into her grandmother. She smiles. "My bag is packed."

By Sunday after dinner, when she's packing her bag to return to Brazos Cottage, Grace knows she is meant to be with Ruth Fox. Her certainty was built moment by moment over the weekend. Ruth brought photograph albums of Karen growing up, playing with garden toads, grinning—with missing teeth—on her father's lap, reading books in her mother's arms. Hank looked like a Hank, lanky with a blond buzz cut and kind eyes. Grace felt cheated to miss out on knowing her grandfather. She saw relatives, dead and living, on both sides of the family, with names that don't stick but with faces that all seem uncannily familiar.

Her great-grandparents' house, where she will live, has big trees and a wraparound veranda with an actual porch swing. In one photo, her great-aunt Ruby poses in her overalls, proudly displaying an antique bedroom set she had restored. In another, Midge, the black Lab, naps on the veranda with two yellow cats, Goldie and Sunshine. It calls to her, this place, as if she has known it once and is finally coming home.

Despite plans to sight-see, Ruth and Grace hole up in the hotel suite. They take their meals in the hotel restaurant or order room service. They watch vintage comedies on television, propped up on Ruth's bed, eating microwave popcorn and laughing themselves silly. They compare feet and discover they both have crooked second toes, just like Karen had. They talk late and sleep in. They sit in silence on the balcony and watch the sun set over the mesa.

What isn't said is how much time they've lost or how different everything would have been if Grace had been raised by her grandmother. Grace thinks about it, though, and ping-pongs between the life she has lived and the one she might have had, until she realizes the two paths have finally converged and all she can do is move forward.

CHAPTER 14

MADDIE'S NEXT FAMILY THERAPY session is about planning a pass for her to go home to Old Town. Her dad says he hired someone to clean the apartment from top to bottom, and he bought some new furniture. She can't wait to see it—especially her room. He says she can pick out what she wants in there, but he had the walls painted a soft, serene purple and replaced her twin bed with a queen-size one. She's dizzy with new hope and it's now easier to keep her moods on a more even keel. Everything that was upside down is righting itself. She detects a twinkle in her father's eyes when he signs the paperwork for her pass.

She promises to keep her eyes closed while he fumbles with the door key. She peeks at the familiar stairs beneath her feet as she climbs them, seeing her shoes transform into the small rubber-toed tennis shoes that ran up and down these stairs years ago, pretending the stairs were the scales on a dragon's back. She hopes her imagination will return to her after it left her, like when people get their sense of taste or smell back after they've been sick.

"Okay, you can open your eyes," Dad says, opening the door. The old wood floors have been buffed to a sheen. There's a new leather couch that Hector's sitting on, watching TV. Mimi, Otilia, and their friend Marsha, are hip to hip in the kitchen cooking. "Surprise!" Dad says.

Maddie runs to each for hugs. "Ah, mi'ja, you're so grown," Otilia says, pressing Maddie to her breast, her scent as familiar as home.

Mimi's hug smells of cinnamon and crepe batter. "Welcome home, cherie. I'm making your favorite apple crepe for dessert. I'm so thrilled you and your dad have come home." Mimi kisses Maddie on each cheek.

"Welcome home, Maddie," says Marsha. Her red hair is tied on top of her head like a big bow of curling ribbon. "I've been helping your dad move in and get situated. I helped him pick out the furniture, freshen up the place."

"It's good to see you, thanks for helping Dad," Maddie says, giving Marsha a hug. Marsha squeezes her tightly, as if taking Maddie deep into her heart.

Maddie sits on the new leather couch next to Hector. "Hey, Hector," she says, giving him a fist bump.

"Nice to see you again. Glad you're back," he says. Hector isn't one for emotional displays, but his smile is warm.

"I can't tell you how good it is to be back."

He reaches into his pocket and hands her a carved-stone bison fetish. "For spiritual protection and fulfillment of power," he says. It feels warm and powerful in her hand.

Her dad appears to be thriving with all the mother hens around him. They throw him out of the kitchen when he gets in their way.

"Who's ready for Otilia's enchiladas and chiles rellenos?" says Otilia, bringing casserole dishes to the table. The kitchen and dining area are decorated with shabby-chic touches, Marsha's doing, Maddie guesses.

Maddie listens as the rest of them talk around the table. It becomes a din of perfection. Marsha hangs on her dad's every word and waitresses in between, refreshing everyone's water. It feels every bit like a real family dinner.

By the time Maddie finishes her apple crepe topped with homemade whipped cream, she can't keep her eyes open. She kisses her father good night before she shuffles off to her new favorite-color-of-purple room and crawls into her new bed. Countless times she desperately hungered to be back in this room, safe and secure. Nothing holds her back from sleep.

When Maddie's dad wakes her, for a minute she thinks everything has been a dream. It's morning and Dad hurries her to get dressed. "I have a surprise," he tells her. There's that twinkle again. They drive up Rio Grande

Boulevard into the North Valley and turn down a little gravel road to a property Maddie remembers as Marsha's. She still has alpacas for her weaving that scatter like pool balls when the car approaches. Marsha comes out of her house to meet them wearing a white tank top and faded jeans tucked into mucking boots. Her fiery hair, beneath her cowboy hat, frames her tanned, freckled face. Her green eyes sparkle with excitement.

"Follow me," she says, leading them to her barn and pasture.

"Moonshine!" Maddie yells. Moonshine pricks up her ears, whinnies, and trots to the fence, where Maddie reaches for her, petting her velvet nose. "I've missed you, girl. I'm back now," she says. Marsha hands her a carrot to give to Moonshine, who chews without taking her eyes off Maddie.

"Marsha offered to board Moonshine for you," says her dad.

"Thank you, Marsha." Moonshine nudges her for more attention. "I'll be here as much as I can to help take care of her."

"She's ready to be tacked up. Everything's in the barn," Marsha says. "Take your horse for a ride. You've got six acres to explore and access to the bosque trail."

Moonshine lumbers after Maddie. She supposes she'll have that nervous, hypervigilant feeling for a while when she tacks up Moonshine inside the barn. But she's safe now. She mounts Moonshine and they trot out into the pasture under the vast, blue New Mexico sky. She waves to her dad and Marsha, who stand so close together they appear as one. Dad snatches Marsha's cowboy hat and puts it on his head. Laughing, they begin to scuffle for it.

Maddie nudges Moonshine into a gallop, the sound of her own laughter filling her ears.

Maddie isn't sure if it's all the excitement on her pass or her dread about having to leave Grace, but she wakes up feeling sick after her pass weekend. She stays behind in the cottage on sick bay, as it's called, with Sharon. A plastic gray wastebasket sits next to Maddie's bed in case she can't make it to the bathroom to puke. On top of that, she writhes with menstrual cramps. It's good to be around other understanding women during her bad periods—she'll miss that.

"I brought you some Midol and a hot water bottle," Sharon says. She wears denim overalls with a Janis Joplin T-shirt peeking from beneath the bib. The hot water bottle is wrapped in a thin hospital towel, and when Sharon places it on Maddie's tummy, it feels like heaven. Is that because of its warmth or the warmth of Sharon's mothering? Who knew leaving a psychiatric hospital could be so sad? She tries to memorize the feel of Sharon's fingers taking her pulse, and the cute way she ticktocks her head side to side, counting under her breath, her beaded earrings swinging beneath her dark wavy hair, her lime-green sneakers tapping the beat.

Maddie moans with a twinge, even though it isn't that bad.

"Oh, poor baby," Sharon says with an empathetic frown.

"I think I should be on a morphine drip," Maddie says.

"You're going to be on chicken noodle soup," Sharon says. "Not through a drip, though, noodles clog up the tube."

Having Sharon with her makes her feel better, and yet her chest aches at the thought of never seeing her again.

Sharon perches on the edge of Maddie's bed. "I'm glad we have this time together. I won't be able to come to your discharge party, so we'll have to say our good-byes today." Sharon's brow furrows as she seems to hold back tears.

"I hope my dad finds a woman like you someday," Maddie says. She can share him now. He deserves a new beginning too.

"That's so sweet, thank you. I've really enjoyed being here with you on this journey, Maddie. I care about you and I hope you'll let me know how you're doing. You're one of those special kids I'll never forget." Sharon's lips try to smile, but the corners quiver down.

Maddie hugs Sharon tightly. "For me and Grace, not having mothers, you've been like a mom to us."

"Any woman worth her salt would be proud to have you as a daughter. I know I would," says Sharon. "Hang in there. Be strong."

Maddie nods, knowing Sharon is referring to the legal battle ahead, trying to bring Jeffrey to justice. Maddie cries against Sharon's solid shoulder as Sharon holds her. As much as Maddie loves her dad, she wants this;

a woman she can trust and whose shoulder she can cry on. A woman who knows her every scar and still loves her.

Maddie and Grace allow Paul and Lourdes to choose the music for their discharge party. The furniture in the dayroom has been pushed back to make space for a dance floor. Maddie overheard that the staff took up a collection and special-ordered their cake from the best local bakery. Maddie's dad is treating everyone to enchiladas and tamales, some vegetarian instead of pork for Aaron, upon Maddie's request. The cafeteria sent over a couple of gallons of ice cream. Grace's grandmother decided not to attend the party, staying in her hotel room to pack and rest before their early flight the next day.

"Maybe we can hide in here and never come out," Maddie says to Grace right before their discharge party. She looks around the dingy walls of their room. "Hard to believe it's only been three months, with everything that's happened."

"We made it happen, and we're going to keep making it happen. I never thought I'd be walking out of here with a grandma and a great-aunt. And Mitch in treatment? Blows my mind." Grace shakes her head. "Don't quote me, but there might be a God or Goddess after all."

"Yeah, and her name is Dr. Swenson. In a couple of hours, I'll be out of here, waking up in my own bed in the morning. Breakfast and coffee on the balcony. Riding Moonshine in the afternoon."

"For all that great stuff to happen, we have to leave this room," Grace says.

"And each other." Maddie follows Grace, glancing back to see her bag waiting to go.

Maddie's dad is in the kitchen setting up the food he brought. He's wearing a goofy apron with a quilted chicken on it and a UNM baseball cap.

Jackson's getting the beverages set up, throwing plastic glasses behind his back and catching them like a bartender.

"Here they are," Dad says, gathering Maddie and Grace under each arm. "I hope you come visit us soon," he says to Grace with a fatherly hug. "I want you to think of us as family."

After they all eat dinner together, the cake is cut and passed around on paper plates. Paul plays disc jockey and the music begins.

Aaron and Lucas dance to "Day Tripper" by the Beatles, a song that dares you to sit still. Aaron plays air guitar and head bangs until his yarmulke flies off his head like a small velvet Frisbee. Lucas stomps in his cowboy boots, hands on his hips like a Spanish dancer, showing off for his prospective adoptive mom, who is visiting. They seem to be a perfect match, as she sings along, watching him with adoring eyes. She lives alone in the country on a small ranch with a couple of horses. Thank god Lucas seems to have found a good mom.

Percy seems to like the cake, picking up another piece with his hands to eat it, white butter cream frosting oozing through his slender fingers. His innocence brings a knot in Maddie's throat. What will become of him? How will she walk out the door and never know?

"Percy, I'm really going to miss you," Maddie tells him. He smiles, frosting on his lips. She wants to hug him, but you just don't do things like that to Percy. "You'll be in my thoughts."

Percy gently gives Maddie a side hug, which shocks her. "Send your thoughts on the wind and I will hear them," he tells her.

"I will, I promise."

By now, Aaron has fastened his yarmulke to his head with masking tape that comes down and around his face like a chin strap. She knows she won't get a decent good-bye from him. With his Asperger's diagnosis, Aaron is socially awkward and emotionally distant, especially under stress. She knows he dances wildly, not for joy that she and Grace are leaving but as a coping strategy. He isn't so hard to take once you understand the code. She'll actually miss the little guy.

Vanessa, the new girl in Brazos Cottage taking Gabe's place, was dragged in by four male staff when she planted her feet against the door like a resistant cat. She now sits in a corner looking pissed as hell next to her one-to-one staff person, Kellie. With Grace and Maddie leaving, Vanessa will be the only girl for now. Aaron has already homed in on her weak spots for his masterful button pushing. Maddie and Grace tried to tell her that if she lets this place help her, it will. Jackson called it "passing the torch" when he encouraged them to give her a pep talk about the benefits of inpatient psychiatric care. When Vanessa kept blowing out their torch with a huffy "whatever," they gave up.

Maddie looks around and tries to memorize every detail of the cottage and the faces around her. As fast as her time here has gone, if she measures it in how far she has come from the day she arrived on a stretcher, wounded and lost, she has completed an epic journey.

"Can I have everyone's attention?" her dad says, coming out of the kitchen after cleaning it with Jackson and boxing up the leftovers. Paul turns off the music. Maddie looks over at Grace and rolls her eyes. Even though he's probably going to embarrass her, Maddie is proud of him. A lot of kids' parents aren't there for them, and she very well could have been one of them. "I'd like to thank the staff, therapists, and you kids who've supported Maddie, helping her through this tough time. I couldn't be more grateful that my little girl landed here that terrible day." He begins to clear his throat and blink back tears. "From the bottom of my heart, I thank you. And, uh, there's plenty of food left, so uh, staff, take some home." Jackson gives her dad a man hug, clapping him on his back. Her dad wipes his eyes with his chicken apron.

The party is winding down. She has basically already said good-bye to everyone except for Grace. How will Maddie find the words? They can stay in touch, but that isn't the same as whispered conversations as roommates dodging the night-check flashlight, getting each other through a bad night. Maddie can't imagine healing and growing as much as she has, if not for Grace. Maddie hopes one day she'll be able to repay her.

Jackson unlocks the door for everyone, except Vanessa, to make their pilgrimage to Michael's car. Aaron and Lucas squabble over who gets to carry Maddie's belongings, until Jackson divides them equally between them.

Grace hangs back, watching Jackson say his final good-byes and give Maddie a hug. Michael stows her stuff in his trunk, looking as proud as a new father preparing to take his baby girl home from the hospital.

Lucas sheds some tears and clings to Maddie until his prospective adoptive mom puts a hand on his shoulder and tucks him back to her side.

Percy pulls a folded piece of paper from his shirt pocket. It's a drawing he made of an eagle carrying a pair of hungry shoes by their laces in its beak, soaring over a mountaintop. Maddie holds it up to show everyone and then thanks him with a quick hug, which he allows.

Aaron steps toward her, scowling. "I didn't like it when you got here, and now I don't like it that you're going away."

"I just can't do anything right, can I," Maddie says. "Do I get a hug or not?"

Aaron puts out his hand and as she shakes it, his other hand pats her on top of her head as if she were a good dog.

"Grace?" Maddie looks past the crowd of boys.

Grace steps forward, the boys parting for her. She stands in front of Maddie. "This feels unreal."

Maddie nods, tears streaming from her eyes. "Thank you, Grace."

Unreal starts to feel all too real. "I'll call you from my new cell phone once I get it. But I want letters too. Big, long, fat letters," Grace says.

Maddie grabs her then and they stand in a lingering, tight hug and cry. Grace closes her eyes so she won't see Jackson or the boys, or Michael standing next to Maddie. It's just her and Maddie in this last moment, and there's nothing left to say.

They let go and Maddie turns to her father, who opens the car door for her. She gets in and rolls down her window to look at them all.

Grace feels Jackson next to her, his hand landing on her back as if he's infusing her with the strength to remain upright. She leans into him as Michael carefully backs out the car and pauses before pulling away. Maddie waves out her window, with a big grin now on her face.

"She's going to be just fine," Grace hears Jackson whisper to himself.

Grace finishes her packing and gets ready for bed. She and her grandmother have packaged her art portfolio and mailed it ahead since it would be difficult to manage on the plane. Tucked inside her suitcase, though, is the last painting she completed with Janice, a portrait of her mother, her face in precise detail, a gift for her grandmother.

The cottage seems unnaturally quiet. Grace leaves her room and walks down the hall. All of the kids' doors are shut, their lights out. Paul is moving the dayroom furniture back into place. Jackson has finally gone home. Kellie is charting at the desk. The night staff will be here soon.

Kellie looks up. "Need anything, Grace?"

"Just to say good-bye. I know you and Paul won't be here in the morning," she says.

"Oh, it's later than I thought. I was going to come to your room." Kellie closes the chart she was working on and comes out from behind the staff desk to give Grace a hug. "We had fun on that shopping trip, didn't we?"

"Yeah, thanks for everything."

Paul comes up to them. "It was a pleasure having you here, Grace, and believe me, I don't say that very often. Go out there and have yourself a good life."

Grace gives him a hug, inhaling the soft scent of patchouli oil that seems to emanate from his pores, his beard tickling her cheek. "Thanks," she says. "Good night."

She walks back to her room and looks at Maddie's empty, already stripped bed. Her wardrobe door stands open, attached hangers empty. The chair is perched on top of the desk like a flood victim seeking higher ground, in preparation for the mopping the janitor will do in the morning. He will scrub down and sanitize the room for the new admits that Jackson said were already scheduled.

Grace switches off the light and climbs into bed. Tomorrow she'll fly on a jet for the first time and land in her new life. She will meet her great-aunt Ruby, who she has already talked to on the phone. Ruby, according to Ruth, is the comedian of the family and acts more like her shoe size than her age.

Grace thinks of her honorary brothers down the hall: Percy sleeping in his bed, perhaps on an out-of-body journey visiting his ancestors. Does Lucas still let Sam sleep with him as he dreams about getting adopted and riding horses with his new mom? He only wears cowboy clothes now, since he left the military with an honorable discharge. Aaron's a heavy sleeper; staff complain about how hard it is to get him started in the morning.

Aaron's complicated mind needs as much downtime as possible before rebooting for a new day of living among his inferiors.

She hopes that Abdias is safe in his cell and Gabe is contented under his mother's roof.

She tries to picture Jackson in his bed and realizes she doesn't know if he sleeps alone or if he has someone he loves next to him. She hopes he has someone. With all the love he gives, he deserves to get some in return. But she pegs him for a snorer, so his partner would have to put up with that—a small price to pay to have Jackson.

Dr. Swenson probably sleeps under a pile of dogs and cats, uncomplicated beings who give unconditional love and comfort to a woman who arrives home in need of replenishment before another consuming day.

Grace figures Maddie is still awake in her bed in Old Town, or maybe she's out on her balcony gazing at the stars and breathing the cool, late-August night air. Will she wish upon a star or does she now have everything she ever wanted?

And Mitch. Is he lying in his rehab bed craving a drink? Or maybe he's thinking of the girl he raised and smiling, remembering one of their happy times.

Rudy has folded his lawn chair and gone in for the night by now. She said good-bye to him on a pass with her grandmother, when Grace showed her where she used to live. She promised to write to him and send pictures that she knows he will place on his refrigerator next to those of his grandson.

It's two hours later in New York City, but that doesn't mean Duc and Robin are home for the night, unless they have that killer dance class first thing in the morning.

Grace pictures her grandmother in her hotel suite, her bags packed, her clothes laid out for the next day. She knows Ruth is a night owl and is either reading or thinking about how different life will be sharing her home with a teenager.

But Grace doesn't feel like a teenager. She feels like a very old soul who's already lived multiple lifetimes in less than eighteen years: the one with her mother, the one with Mitch, and the one in a psychiatric hospital.

Those lives are in the past. But her story endures for her to carry forward, not as a burden but as an essential part of who she is.

Her next life beckons, unknown but tantalizing, filled with infinite possibilities. A life she will create. Grace closes her eyes to sleep. When she opens them in the new day, she will begin.

Acknowledgments

This story has been gestating within us for over forty years, since as a young nurse, I (Sue) first stepped into Brazos Cottage and a young boy from Zuni Pueblo used the term *hungry shoes* in reference to his tennis shoe that had split open at the toe, creating a mouth. I asked my coworker (and future husband—but that's another story), who had spent his formative years growing up in Zuni, if he had ever heard the expression. He had, so I filed it away for the title of a novel I hoped to write someday set in the incredible world of milieu therapy inside a children's and adolescents' psychiatric hospital.

After Mare moved to New Mexico, she began her long career at the same facility and discovered, like me, that this unique place held her soul's work. We had the privilege of learning from a gifted team of multidisciplinary colleagues (too many to name here, but you know who you are!) dedicated to supporting kids in their healing journeys. We learned from the kids themselves that no matter how horrendous their past abuse and neglect was (and how it spawned their own desperate, out-of-control behavior), there was hope.

Our decades of this work generated the underlying theme in all of our novels: although it is the human condition to be wounded in relationships, it is only through the alchemy of nurturing relationships that one can fully evolve as a human being.

We thank our literary agent, Liz Trupin-Pulli, for her continued expertise, wisdom, guidance, and love. More than our agent, she is our dear friend. We thank our longtime first reader (and former coworker from the same psychiatric facility), Corinne Armijo, for her invaluable feedback. We turned to our former colleague, Dr. Molly Faulkner, to review our manuscript to ensure the competency of the therapy scenes. Thank you, Molly! Any errors are ours alone.

Although the setting is based on a real place as we experienced it in the 1980s and 1990s, we set the book's time period in 2002 for reasons that support the story. We each moved on from there many years ago, so our milieu may differ from what the facility currently provides. It is our mission to show what milieu therapy can accomplish without the present-day constraints of funding and the sad reality of a more litigious society.

Our fictional patient characters are entirely invented or composites of the hundreds of kids we worked with and remember fondly. Our goal is to represent truthfully the connection between their trauma and their behavior and symptoms. Names and all other identifiers were changed.

Our special education teacher character was created as our homage to an actual teacher colleague who approved his appearance in our story. Thanks, Mr. Z! You're the best!

Our RN character, Sharon, was inspired by our late dear friend and nurse colleague, Sharon Smoker, who was taken from us far too soon after a brave seventeen-year battle with the cruel disease scleroderma. All who knew her loved her. Her kindness, patience, and expertise with challenging kids set examples we all tried to emulate. We hope you're still dancing in those lime-green sneakers in the great beyond. We love and miss you!

Thanks to copyeditor Marie Landau (Raised Type LLC), whom we highly recommend for her keen eye and proficiency!

Immense gratitude to Lynda Miller and Lynn C. Miller, who selected *Hungry Shoes* as one of the first four releases to launch their esteemed Lynn and Lynda Miller Southwest Fiction Series. What an honor! Huge thanks goes to all the talented professionals at the University of New Mexico Press, especially Elise McHugh (senior acquisitions editor), Stephen Hull (director), and James Ayers (manager of editorial, design, and production), along with his entire team. You all helped us birth a book we can be proud of and launch into the world with our message of empathy, respect, and hope for young people with behavioral and mental health challenges and to honor the staff who tirelessly assist their healing and recovery from unspeakable trauma.

We remain eternally grateful to our spouses, families, and friends for their endless love and support. We could not do this without you!

Questions for Book Club Discussions

1. As roommates in the psychiatric hospital, what impact does Maddie and Grace's friendship have on each of their healing journeys? What does each offer the other?

2. What do you see as the most detrimental aspect of Grace's years with Mitch? Was there anything positive about their time together? Who were her "angels" along the way?

3. Maddie's early years with her father seem idyllic on the surface. What seeds were planted that might have eventually contributed to Maddie's mental health crisis?

4. The kind of therapy shown in Brazos cottage is called *milieu therapy*. *Milieu* is a French word that refers to the social environment of the individual. The goal is to create a safe and caring place where change can happen, utilizing group dynamics and feedback. What effect does the Brazos peer group have on Maddie and Grace? How do Jackson and the other Brazos staff impact their recovery?

5. We see snippets of therapy sessions with Dr. Swenson. How did you respond to her approaches with each girl and their family members? How did the adjunct therapies of art therapy for Grace and Sexual Issues Group for Maddie contribute to their recovery?

6. Maddie and Grace both suffer in silence for years leading up to their hospitalizations. Why is it so hard to ask for help? Did Michael's reluctance to face the truth of Maddie's abuse confirm her fears? What did Michael stand to lose by believing her? Did you understand Lesley's refusal to believe her?

7. We see the downward spirals of both Maddie and Grace, leading to their desperate acts that trigger their hospitalizations. What do you think their lives would be like now had they not received help? At the book's conclusion, how do you imagine their lives will unfold? What do Maddie's and Grace's futures look like? Will they stay connected?